OBSIDIANUS

OBSIDIANUS

LUKE DEAL

Obsidianus

Editing by The Pro Book Editor
Interior Design by The Book Designers
Cover Design by R.T. Lovatto and Rachel Ross

Citations:

The Gladiator: The Secret History Of Rome's Warrior Slaves by Alan Baker (Da Capo Press, October 2002)

https://www.ancient.eu/article/1028/roman-shipbuilding--navigation/

https://www.britannica.com/topic/Islam

https://www.romae-vitam.com/roman-ships.html

https://www.wavesboatclub.com/blog/51/15-Basic-Boat-Terms

https://en.wikipedia.org/wiki/List_of_Roman_gladiator_types

ISBN: 978-1-7360189-1-0

Main category—Fiction>War & Military
Other category—Fiction>Military Thrillers

First Edition

To the unworthy,
The sick and the dead,
Christ is your worth, your health,
and your life.

A special thank you to my family for loving me and being the steppingstones to reach my dreams. And to Jacquie, who has been there every step of the way, helping me fulfill it.

CONTENTS

1

THE BEGINNING

The door was jammed, but Ethan Miller knew all too well how to deal with this particular problem. He leaned in with all his weight and turned the knob while hitting the bottom of the wooden structure with his knee. The door immediately swung open, and he stumbled into his darkened apartment, sweat still dripping from his forehead, and his shirt leeching onto his saturated skin. He had been meaning to talk to his landlord about the old door, but being lazy had taken top priority.

Ethan threw his keys on the coffee table that had been set close to the door for just such clutter. The keys slid across the surface, dove over the edge, and plummeted to the floor. He stood watching the keys fall as if they were purposely instigating a cruel joke about his luck, then leaned toward the light switch to awaken his apartment. As the switch was flipped on, the bulb in the center of the room exploded. He shuffled his feet back automatically as his hands rushed to cover his head, and he bent over in a defensive stance while scanning the room for any possible movement or sound.

After taking a second to recover, Ethan stood back up and

regained his composure. Shaking his head with disappointment, he thought about the little things that set him off, like waiting in line for a bus ride, or even grabbing a cup of coffee only to find out on his first sip that it had too much sugar. These were surely small complications that would rarely cause someone to yell and throw a fit but would spark a small fire within Ethan's mood. His thoughts of these headaches made his blood boil, and he was suddenly furious with everything around him.

Having just returned from the gym, which was the only place where he could ever release his anger and stress over all the problems that crossed his mind, Ethan was able to press it down quickly. He made sure going to the gym was a daily routine and knew never to skip it. He made it such a common goal that if he were to skip a day, he would be grumpy for the rest of the evening.

Part of the bad mood was of course because of his apartment. Still standing in the same dark room near the door, he took a gander at the little place he called home. The walls were plaster that had been turned tobacco yellow by the previous occupants. To his right, a pile of dirty dishes that had been stacked in the sink for what could possibly have been over a week taunted him. Microwave pizza sauce was cemented to plates, and glasses were half-filled with sour milk. Cardboard and paper plates seeped over the top of the garbage can, and a noxious smell mustered over the entire small apartment. It lingered in the air, but only for a few more minutes until Ethan's sense of smell bowed in defeat and ignored it all. Between the cabinets stood the half-sized refrigerator, which was only keeping some juice and a few packets of cheese and meat from expiring too quickly. Walking over to the kitchen sink, he dipped his hand into the pile of dishes and pulled out a glass. He sniffed it to determine if it was clean enough to reuse. His nose disagreed, but he didn't care. He filled his glass with tap water and began drinking as he scanned over the mess.

Moving past the kitchen, he chuckled at his old couch along the wall nearest the window in the living room. The soft brown couch, set out for the garbage men, had been found on the side of the road while he'd been jogging through a suburban neighborhood. There were a few cuts and stains, but it had suited Ethan just right. He'd made a few calls and was able to get it in his apartment for free. He didn't really care for a TV, so the living room sat empty except for the lonely couch.

Finally, Ethan made his way into the bedroom. Toward the back was his bed and across from it only one shelf with pictures. Beside the bed were two doors leading to a bathroom and walk-in closet. Ethan didn't have a ceiling light, but he did have a standing corner lamp in the corner between the entry and the bathroom door. Pulling the lamp's string, he half expected the light to explode in flames, given his luck so far today. But to his amazement, the light brightened the room with no restraint.

Ethan crossed his arms, grabbed the bottom of his sports shirt, and lifted it above his head. Throwing the shirt on a pile of dirty clothes in the corner, he thought about whether he should take a shower or lie in bed for a minute first. He never liked lying on his bed dirty because it was the only thing he ever kept clean. He debated for another second, then plopped down on his back. His arm hit something hard, drawing his gaze to his laptop. Ethan pulled the laptop onto his quadriceps, opened it, and clicked a few times to get into his Facebook page.

Since being discharged from the Marine Corps, Ethan had kept to himself and barely ever left his apartment except for work. However, he would use social media to keep track of his family and friends. There was a comfort that came from being able to overlook everyone else's lives. Though he didn't like when people entered into his own or even checked up to see how he was doing, for that matter. He had made sure to cut everyone from his life. It was simple and easy to ignore all the texts, emails, and calls that came his way from family and friends, asking if he was " hanging in there," or if he "needed someone to talk to." All emotional support and anything related to feelings were purposely cast out of his life.

The laptop's light reflected off his glazed, sweaty body as he tapped lightly on the keys, careful not to put too much pressure on them, and he used his other hand to scroll through his feed. He paused scouting the recent posts to open his playlist and chose to put on jazz music to help him relax a bit.

After some time scrolling through his Facebook feed, a notification popped up. It was a friend request from a girl named Jessica Marshall. The name wasn't recognizable, but he decided to scout out her page and see if there might be any mutual friends or if a few pictures would recall a previous friendship. To his surprise, Jessica seemed to be friends with a few of his military buddies. He didn't really care to add anyone new to his media account. The girl was probably a hookup of all of his mutual friends. He was swaying his mouse over to decline the request but took a closer look at the default picture Jessica had placed, lingering over the thought of scrutinizing her. He clicked on the box to enlarge the photo.

Ethan was stunned at how attractive this girl really was. Lying down on a towel surrounded by sand, she had her arms behind her to keep her top half lifted and chest firmly pressed proudly outward, making a slight arch in her back. She was a beautiful girl who was very fit and tan, and a dirty blonde with long hair dangling down by her elbows. Her smile was big and bright, and she looked like she was really enjoying herself. She had on a white bikini that perfectly fit her athletic build. Ethan was more intrigued by her beauty every second he looked at her. Her skin glimmered and contrasted against the bikini well. He clicked off the picture, and his desire still didn't outweigh his previous decision. As he was about to hit decline, a slight creak coming from the walk-in closet immediately drew his attention.

The apartment he rented always had weird sounds, which

never bothered him, so he retreated back to the laptop only to be met with a louder thud from the same area. This time, Ethan's heart beat faster. He shut off his music to listen for anything else. He waited for a minute or so, but nothing. Then he threw his laptop off his legs and reached for the drawer in his nightstand, quickly retrieving the 9mm Sig Sauer pistol he kept there. Ethan grabbed it and released the clip to confirm the ammo he knew would be loaded. There on top was a round followed by many others underneath. Popping it back in, he grasped the slide and pulled it back to make sure there was already a round in the chamber. Confident he was ready to search out the mysterious noise, he began creeping toward the closed door in an offensive stance. He pressed himself against the wall closest to the doorknob so he could open the door forcefully and take the intruder by surprise. Certain there was something or someone in that closet, he wanted to be the first one to make a move. Once against the wall, Ethan took his left hand and grasped the knob, then took his shooting hand and crossed it over the top of his left arm and slightly back toward his body to gain more leverage when he opened the door. His heart beating as hard as a drum, he needed a second to take a deep breath. He told himself on the count of three.

One...two...THREE!

Ethan turned the knob and threw open the door, placing himself in the center of the opening to take aim at the threat.

A dark human figure raised its arms above its head. "Don't shoot! Don't shoot! It's just me, Tyler!"

Ethan held his aim on the dark figure, his finger slowly applying pressure on the trigger. His entire face squinted with laser focus, his eyes sharp and not daring to move from his target. No one from either side budged an inch.

"Look, I was going to jump out at you and scare you. But it was a horrible joke, and I can see that now as I look down the barrel of your gun. Will you please just turn on the light and see for yourself?"

Ethan noticed his breathing, and his tunnel vision on the figure expanded. The light from his lamp showed a somewhat familiar face in the dim closet. His body began to relax, and his finger slowly yielded from the trigger; then he dropped the pistol to his side, feeling relieved and pissed. Reaching around the wall on the inside of the closet, he flipped the switch to expose the stupid intruder.

There on his knees, hands still raised, was the person he'd said he was. The light showed a broad-shouldered male with short black hair; he looked in his late twenties. Tyler Hawkins had a long narrow head with a sharp jawline. He'd had some acne from high school that had left craters around his cheek area. From where he was kneeling, his fear-filled brown eyes pleaded from under his bushy eyebrows. What struck Ethan more was Tyler's long neck that connected to his square chest, part of his short torso. In a way, Tyler's body always seemed to look alienated to him. They had been friends since high school. They'd met on the football team and gotten along ever since. Of course, they hadn't talked much after Ethan joined the Marines. Tyler had stayed local to pursue exercise science and become a personal trainer.

"Are you partially dumb to come in here and try pulling that kind of shit?" Ethan let out a sigh of relief and walked back over to his drawer to put his gun to rest. After closing the drawer, he turned back to Tyler.

Tyler hesitated before dropping his hands and working up a smile as he walked out of the closet. He threw a sock that had been resting on his shoulder back into the small, enclosed space behind him. "Well, you know, I wasn't trained to be a tactical killer, so cut me some slack."

"Yeah, well—wait. How in the hell did you get in here?" Ethan asked in an aggravated tone.

"Your mother had a spare key and told me to bring you over some lasagna, which, by the way, was great!" replied Tyler.

Now more annoyed, Ethan went about putting on a semi-clean T-shirt from the dirty pile of clothes so he didn't feel so naked in front of his friend.

Tyler walked over to the only shelf and looked over the few pictures there. "Ethan, you know your closet is atrocious! How do you find anything in there?" He lifted each frame and looked at the pictures more closely.

"I hate small spaces, and I honestly couldn't care less to spend any time in there organizing clothes. It's not on the top of my priority list."

Ethan sat on the edge of his bed and slouched, looking straight ahead at the wall and regretting his rash behavior. "Sorry if I might have gone too far with the gun in the face and all. Sometimes I can't help it."

Tyler turned his head and gave Ethan a reassuring nod. "It's no problem, man. I'll make sure to knock at the front door. That way I can be greeted with a less threatening weapon, perhaps a butter knife next time."

Both men laughed at the exhausted joke.

With a puzzled look on his face, Tyler scrutinized the picture he held. He seemed to ponder for a moment before asking Ethan a personal question. "You know, it's been five months since being back from deployment and out of the military. She had to have moved on. Shouldn't you?" He placed the picture of Ethan with his arm wrapped tightly around a girl back on the shelf and turned to Ethan, waiting for a reply.

Ethan still sat on the edge of the bed studying the wall hard. He'd heard what Tyler had asked, but keeping that picture of Eileen and himself certainly showed he hadn't moved on, and he didn't care to admit that to Tyler. Showing some sort of emotion for someone, especially a girl, was something Ethan planned to keep hidden out of the way of his life.

Tyler broke the silence. "Your mom says you've been distant from the family. Says you work a lot at Bob's Construction and always move from site to site wherever they need you. Not a bad gig, but you know, they would love to see you when you get the chance."

Ethan broke his hypnotic stare at the wall and grabbed his laptop, moving it from his bed to his nightstand. "Yeah, I've been kind of busy lately. I'll get around to seeing them." He knew what he was saying was bullshit but hoped Tyler would see it as a conversation he didn't wish to open.

Ethan swiped his face with both hands in the hope of wiping his tiredness away. "Look, man, it's getting late, and I need to take a shower. How about we catch up later?" He stood up and raised his hand for an upper handshake.

Tyler looked down at his feet with a slight smirk, then completed the handshake and gave Ethan a half hug. "Sure thing, man." He turned and walked out of the room.

Ethan leaned against his bedroom wall and watched Tyler open the front door to exit.

Tyler made it halfway out and then yelled in a high-pitched voice, "Oh, by the way, I told your family you and I are going to have dinner with them tomorrow at seven. Okay. Bye. Lots of kisses!" He slammed the door and was gone.

Ethan was left gazing after him in total astonishment at how he was able to work his way into the cracks of a chicken coop and not get shot.

Retreating to his bathroom, Ethan started undressing again so he could finish the night with a hot shower. As he undressed, he noticed the picture frame Tyler had picked up was facing the opposite direction, toward the wall. He rolled his eyes at Tyler's ignorance and grabbed the frame to turn it around. As he did, he couldn't help but freeze and look at the picture in his hand.

He saw two happy people holding each other. Eileen was wearing that short green dress he had bought her that stopped at the edge of her knees. Her eyes were bright in the picture. Because of the dress, her green eyes stood out more than any of her other features. However, that didn't stop her smile from competing. Her teeth were slightly bucktoothed, yet each tooth stood white as snow. Her face was round, and she had chubby cheeks for being a lean girl and on the shorter side. He'd always noticed the smaller details in Eileen, such as her soft freckles around the nose and under the eyes. She was everything he had hoped for in a girl. He studied the picture and as he did, he welcomed back all those feelings of the past. It built from his stomach until it reached his throat. A low grunt could be heard leaving his lips. Reaching farther into his heart, he knew why he still held on to this picture and stared at it every day.

Shaking off the reverie, Ethan set the frame back on the shelf facing the correct direction. After taking one last glance, he lethargically moved to the bathroom and tried to muster enough energy to take a quick shower.

Ethan finished removing all his clothing and reached into the tub to turn on the water. It usually took a minute or two before the temperature reached lukewarm, so he turned to the mirror. His face registered shock at what he saw in the mirror. He always kept his brown hair at a medium fade and the top short. Ever since the birth of his time in the Marine Corps, it was the only style he had known, and he didn't wish to change it. But now his hair was messy, knotted and dirty, and the tips of each strand were frayed. He hadn't bothered to condition it since he couldn't remember when. Scanning lower, he noticed bags under his blue eyes, and the skin around his squared face was rugged and worn. His job required workers to have a basic, clean cut, but Ethan viewed that rule as more of a guideline than a firm order. His jaw and chin were scruffy, though not as bad as his hair.

If it weren't for having such a physically demanding job, he wouldn't have kept in shape. His chest was barrel-sized, tapering to a V at the bottom. But he took no notice of the shape. He placed his finger on a circular scar over his right shoulder. He slowly looked at himself and turned around to see a few shorter white lines that settled a little below his neck. He turned to face the mirror once more and leaned over, placing steadying hands on the bathroom sink. What he saw was not a man whose health was at its prime. Nor did he see himself as a warrior, survivor, or a story. He simply saw a man who was dying. He cringed, and his neck strained as he stared at his reflection. He was suffocating on his guilt and shame, wallowing in what some would call self-pity, but to Ethan, this was the main course that devoured him every day. He deserved it. He greeted it with open arms nightly, lying in the dark, deteriorating until his soul completely withered away. His teeth ground together, and the muscles flexed until he could no longer stare at himself. He whipped away from his self-examination and got into the shower.

After drying off, Ethan threw on a pair of briefs and jumped into bed. He reached over and pulled down on the lamp's metal chain, surrendering to complete darkness. He lay there as his body accumulated goosebumps from not having any source of warmth. His covers sat in a bundle at the top of the bed, but he never grabbed them. Lying on his back, he stared up at the ceiling until he drifted off to sleep.

Eighteen-year-old Ethan awoke to a sound projecting from his phone, announcing that someone was calling him. Still adjusting to the light from the morning sun shining through the window, he kept his eyes closed and reached over to his nightstand, feeling for his phone.

Once he had it in his grasp, he quickly opened one eye to search for the answer button before shutting it again. "Hello?" Ethan whispered in a raspy voice.

"Good morning, Mr. Miller. I'm calling you concerning your

recruit training," a male voice said deep and strong, keeping every word sharp. "This is Sergeant Thomas, and it seems that someone popped on a certain drug and will be discontinuing his path into the Marine Corps. That leaves an opening for you to jump in and take his spot. You are next on the list. You leave at 1900 tonight from the recruiting office, and I'll be escorting you to the airport. Congratulations again, Mr. Miller. I will see you soon." The man hung up the phone, leaving Ethan in shock.

Ethan sat bolt upright on his bed, quickly trying to recover everything that had just been said. A smile swept across his face, and a sensation of joy filled him. Leaping off the bed, he pulled out a drawer looking for something to put on.

"Mom, Dad! Anyone who is sleeping, *wake up*!" Ethan trumpeted from his bedroom. He had found some blue basketball shorts and, in his excitement, started putting them on backward as he headed out of his room. "Can anyone hear me! This is really important!" He managed to hop down the hallway, putting one leg through the shorts and then struggling to put the other leg in.

"Oh, gosh! Please stop hopping around and just put your shorts on for everything that is good and holy!" Ethan's sister stood in her PJs behind him, a hand out in front of her to block out the indecent exposure of her brother.

"I'm sorry, sis, but I have some important news. Get downstairs, and I'll tell you in just a second."

She gave a quick huff and rolled her eyes before retreating back into her room and shutting the door.

Ethan could barely hold his joy any longer, and his excited whoops echoed throughout the entire house.

His parents ran out of their room, both still wrapping their robes around their bodies and tying them shut. "What's the matter, Ethan? Why are you yelling? Is everything okay?" Ethan's mom said while looking him over from head to toe for any sign of a problem, or worse, evidence that the the house was on fire.

"No! I just got a call from the recruiter, and he says there is an opening and I get to go to recruit training!"

"That's great, son! We're very happy for you. When do you leave?" Ethan's father asked.

"Tonight, at seven. I have to call a few friends and tell them so I can see them one last time before…"

Ethan rambled on, but his parents' facial expressions had almost instantly changed from excitement to disappointment.

"Honey, isn't that a little unexpected and a short amount of time to get prepared?" his mother said.

"Mom, I'm ready to go. There is nothing to prepare for. I've been waiting months to get out of here and start a new chapter in my life. I finally get to do something extraordinary!"

His mother's face went ashen, and she dropped her hands to her side. His father put his arm around her shoulders.

Ethan realized the damage his exciting news was causing his parents, then sighed and took a step closer to his parents. "Dad, Mom, you have nothing to worry about. I'll be fine, and I will take really good care of myself, and I'll be back soon. It's only three months of training."

His mother wept.

Ethan's sister appeared in the hallway again. "What's going on?" She wrapped her arms around him like a pretzel.

"Your brother is leaving tonight to go to boot camp," their dad said while still comforting his wife.

Ethan's sister unwrapped her arms, dropping them to her side, and looked up at him. Her face drooped into a whimpering expression as she considered her impending loneliness.

"Ahh, it seems like my sister actually might miss me for once." He laughed as he folded one arm around his sister's neck.

She quickly reached both arms around her older brother and squeezed a hard hug before breaking free and running downstairs.

Ethan made his way back to his room to call a few of his friends. It was early April, and he wasn't supposed to be leaving until August. This change was sudden but did not give him a feeling of unease. In fact, he was more than ready to leave and face the challenges ahead. Most of the day consisted of constant pacing and mentally preparing himself to leave behind the only world he knew.

It was moving closer to Ethan's time of departure, and Tyler was the first of his friends to arrive. Ethan and Tyler exchanged handshakes and discussed what the three months might be like and how much different it would be without Ethan at home. They'd both graduated high school last year and were going in two opposite directions. But both were very happy for each other. During their talk, Ethan laughed at a smart remark Tyler had made and looked over his shoulder to see Eileen walking up the driveway. Tyler noticed the line between the two and slapped Ethan on the back, giving him a confirmed nod as he walked away.

Ethan composed himself before walking down the driveway toward his girlfriend. As the two met, Eileen looked up into Ethan's eyes, and they both just stood there, neither saying a word.

"Hi," Eileen struggled to get the one word out before she broke down in his arms.

"Hey...hey...come on," Ethan said with genuine warmth. "I know things are going to be different for a while, but I have to do this, or I will regret it for the rest of my life. We can still keep in contact, given it will be snail mail."

He laughed at his joke, then noticed Eileen was still buried deep in his chest. He wished he could feel a little melancholy rather than just the excitement of leaving. He hoped that this didn't mean he was broken or didn't love his family or friends, especially Eileen. He knew he must show some sort of sorrow for leaving her behind.

Ethan softened his voice and said, "No matter. I love you and promise when I come home, I'll take you out to a nice steak dinner." He grabbed Eileen by the shoulders and pushed her out so he could stare deeply into her eyes. Once he saw clarity, he gave a slight smirk and kissed her on the forehead before hugging her.

Eileen gave a nod of acceptance while in his embrace before the two made their way back up the driveway to join the rest of his family.

His parents decided it would be best if Tyler drove Ethan to the office so his family could see him off from their home environment. He was leaving without any personal items or extra belongings, with only the clothes on his back, as instructed. His parents met with him one last time before he embarked upon his adventure.

"Ethan, I want you to do something for me." His mom was still crying but had found the strength to keep a smile also. Her voice was tender and delicate. "I want you to take your phone."

"But, Mom, I *can't* take my phone. I told you the recruiter sa—"

"I know, honey. I want you to take your phone and call me," she said with confidence.

"Why, you're standing right here?" Still confused, Ethan chuckled at the instructions his mother was asking of him.

"No, I want you to call me and leave me a voicemail. That way when I start to miss you, I can always go back to it and hear your voice." She handed him his phone, wiping tears from her eyes.

Ethan was shocked at his mother's unusual request, at the idea of talking on a phone to someone standing right in front of him, but he didn't hesitate to perform what was asked of him. He took the phone and dialed his mother's number. It rang, and his mom stared at the phone until the ringing stopped and the call went to voicemail. Ethan really had no idea what he wanted to say. This was something he had not prepared for. He was startled by the beep on the phone giving him the cue to start his message.

"Uh, hi, Mom. I'm standing right here in front of you, surrounded by family and friends. Pretty much all my loved ones."

Ethan felt silly at having blatantly stated the obvious, then took a moment to think of what he wanted to say next. "I guess I should be thanking you and Dad for raising me to be the man I am today. I remember you taught me something really important that I will never forget. When I step outside that door, I represent three things. God is the first of what I represent. The second, my name. And the third, my family name. I carry those names with honor and pride and will make sure to keep them in dignity. I love you and the family and will see you in three months. Also, I didn't really clean my room. I just shoved everything under the bed. Love you, bye!" Ethan hung up the phone and hugged his mom.

With a firm handshake to his father and a kiss for Eileen one last time, he hopped into the passenger seat of Tyler's maroon Chevy Silverado. Turning around, he waved at the group of people he'd been so happy being a part of. He thought to himself that when he returned, he would be a brighter and wiser Marine who could conquer the world and stand at the top of the pedestal.

A sound emerged from Ethan's nightstand. His phone was sounding off with a crazy and obnoxious noise. He reached over and snatched it off the table. He looked at the screen. The alarm on his phone read 0300. Ethan sat up and wiped his face. He looked around apathetically and saw the pile of dirty clothes in the corner of the room. He lethargically scanned the picture frames on the shelf and shifted his eyes to the bundled-up blankets he never touched, still sitting at the bottom of the bed. He was awake and living again in his nightmare.

2

MANIFESTATION

Ethan walked out of his apartment and headed straight for his car at around 0330, while the sky was still covered in darkness. It was early March and he could feel the sting of the cold wind reddening his cheeks.

Despite growing up in Wisconsin before moving to North Carolina, Ethan had never cared much for the cold. He always made sure to wear a sweatshirt in the morning, knowing it would soon warm up, but it was better to bring something than nothing at all. He remembered a friend had once told him while they were hiking during a snowy day, "You can always take an article of clothing off, but you can't put one on if you don't have it."

Ethan smirked as he remembered that short conversation and the long, grueling hike. He had chosen not to bring extra warming layers because he'd figured he wouldn't need them. Then he'd suffered through an entire hike that left him chilled to the bone.

As he crossed the parking lot, his dark green two-door Honda with slashes of paint that had been scraped off, leaving white streaks, came into view. Rust had claimed some of the body, from the front to the back and on the edges along the bottom. Ethan had found the car online dirt cheap. After coming back from deployment, he had saved more than forty grand but rarely ever touched it. He knew he had money for a brand-new car, but he didn't deserve it. He'd told himself this was the car for him. He grabbed the handle of the driver's side door and pulled. The slim black handle released from the door entirely, the momentum throwing him back with the object still in his hand. His shocked eyes just stared at it for a moment and then looked back at his car. He gave a weak kick to the vehicle, afraid that a harder kick might break another body part. Stepping closer, he placed the handle on top of the hood and slid his fingers along the broken handle's home in the door, searching for some kind of leverage. Two teeth from each side still clung to the mechanism in the door, and he used both hands to lift enough of the broken handle outward that the door opened.

He hopped in and sat in his car for a moment to regain his composure. Not only did his car look terrible, with the body of the car in bad condition, but the internal structure of the car was no better. The fabric lining was torn and shredded, leaving strains of material dangling from the top and sides. Sometimes as he drove, the lining would remarkably appear near his head from above, swaying in front of his face. He would blow at it for a time, trying not to realize he was driving in a broken-down junk of a car. The armrest and plastic material were also worn and scratched with indented places where too much weight had been placed.

He put his key in the ignition and started the car. He backed out of his parking spot with enough speed to sling his broken handle flying off the hood. He knew where he was headed and wasted no time getting there.

Bob's Construction was owned by a man named Bob, but Ethan only dealt with Pete, the co-owner of the business. They handled highways, local roads, and building sites, so what Pete required of Ethan from one day to the next determined where he would report for the day. Pete used Ethan as a mobile man who could move from site to site if one man called in sick or wasn't able to show up. Sometimes, Ethan would be on a different site each day or, at other times, he could end up working an entire contract until it was finished. He didn't have a lot of experience with the trade, but he picked things up quickly.

Tyler's father was the company's accountant and had put in a good word for Ethan when he was discharged from the Corps. Since then, Ethan had been working full time. It was a great job and paid good money, but Ethan only worked the job because of the long hours and the tasks that required little social interactions. Today, he would be working on part of highway 96 near Apex, which was quite a drive from where he lived, but driving had never bothered him.

When he finally arrived at the site, the time read 0500 and, since it was still dark, the AC tripod lights were still being used as well as lights from generators. The lights exposed the line of trees about ten feet from the road. Near the site stood a bridge that led to the city of Apex and, beyond the bridge, the exit ramp. Cones had been placed far out from the site to attract cars toward the left side of the highway, allowing the workers to be in a safer area. To make drivers more aware, there was a digital warning sign attached to an orange trailer placed at the front of the cones a mile out. Ethan trailed off through one of the orange-and-white striped cones and parked his little green Honda next to a few full-size trucks. As he worked to get out of his car, he was greeted by a large man.

"Ethan, my man! I was wonderin' when Pete would git ya a job with us. I figured since Larry called off that you'd be sent to us." The man had an orange-and-white reflector vest over a gray T-shirt. A big, round stomach protruded through the shirt such that a little bit of skin peeked out from the edge. He was a very dark man, but Ethan could still see black hairs that straddled his arms all the way up past his triceps.

Ethan was then lifted off the ground by the large man.

"Jonas, I can't breathe." He whimpered a demand to have Jonas release him from his strong grasp.

"Oh, come on now. I know you're happy ta see me too!"

Ethan fought to make a smile, to show some happiness, so Jonas wouldn't feel obligated to take another stab at hugging him again.

Once Jonas was tired of the awkward silence, he broke it with a slap on Ethan's shoulder.

Ethan took a step forward from the solid slap.

Jonas flailed his hands about, matching his excitement as he said, "Pete asked me to keep an eye on ya and give ya a job fer t'rday. I got here not too long ago and released the night crew ta go home. We got a couple slabs gone bad, had ta cut 'em out. We already put some of them dowel bars in. We just need ta set in the rebar and later on we're goin' ta have the cement truck come in and we'll start compressin'."

Ethan stood like a statue, attempting to control the shivering. He kept his hands in his pockets while staring blankly at Jonas, doing his best to pay attention. But really, he was wondering if Jonas was cold or if the extra weight was keeping him warm.

"Then what I'll have ya do is take some flat scraper and…"

Ethan zoned off again, consciously nodding at Jonas while waiting for him to finish the instructions. He had worked on repairing roads before, and the instructions weren't anything new, but he knew Jonas was always a bit high-strung and just wanted a reason to talk to someone. For some reason, the jovial man always took it as a challenge to make Ethan laugh or smile or get some kind of emotional reaction out of him. Ethan just didn't care to interact with anyone.

As Ethan and Jonas set about getting a few things set up so they could get straight to work, the rest of the crew showed up.

Jonas exclaimed, "Woo, my boys. I'm glad y'all could make it. I sure am excited to git this day started!" He opened his hands wide as if he were going to hug every one of the men. "Hey,

Carlos. Ben, nice ta see ya. Looks like I'm gonna have to tag all us on my Facebook 'cause people are gonna to be jealous of this party!" He pulled out his phone and started tapping on his screen and chuckling.

The others rolled their eyes and smiled. Jonas never meant any harm, and the men knew it and greeted it openly.

Ethan went to work drilling holes in the nearest slab and inserting dowel bars that were around 1.5 inches in length. Next, he would coat each bar with a green epoxy spray that prevented corrosion. Around six in the morning, he noticed traffic driving past the site had gotten busier with the usual morning commute. Fridays usually being the last day of work before the weekend, the crew typically watched how much more careless the drivers would become.

The men had stumbled into comfortable conversation about their families and how old their children were and how one had had a birthday just the other day. The talk was lighthearted and continued to flow as the workers progressed with installing the reinforced steel bars.

Ethan listened a little more intently when someone spoke about how their kid's face lit up as they were presented with a new bike, or a dad's pride over their son scoring a touchdown at their last football game. He thought back to his own life and how much his parents had taken care of him, and how much they wanted to take care of him now. His parents had always presented kindness and sensitivity toward Ethan. For any child, that's all one could ask for. But he hadn't asked for it, and he didn't need it. *Do they not think I can take care of myself or make it in the world on my own?* His blood beginning to boil, he drilled the holes for the rebar with greater force and aggression.

One of the workers nearby noticed and made a sly remark under his breath. The workers knew never to talk to Ethan because it only ended up in an argument or awkward silence. Even if they only worked with him on rare occasions, they knew to avoid him.

Ethan paid no attention to the worker who had whispered the comment, his mind wandering back into deep thought. He limited his time with his family because, ever since coming home from deployment, being around them felt strange, abnormal. At first, he had not signed up for an apartment and had to stay at home for a while. The entire time he'd tried to avoid each family member at all costs. He knew he was the way he was because of his own deeds and his own choices.

His distant and isolating behavior had caused the family to act very differently as well. Their confidence in him dwindled as they expected less and less from him. His dad told him, "You can live here as long as you want, free of charge," and excused Ethan from chores or anything work-related. They pitied him.

Even with all the love and attention that was given to Ethan, he couldn't accept it. A house full of affection meant he would be treated well. His sister would come in when he was out of the house and clean his room. A small act of doing something such as cleaning his sheets and clothes meant she felt sympathy. A word that could harbor two possible outcomes, something evil or something positive. It's human nature to be sympathetic toward someone you love, yet it was something that made Ethan feel weak inside. For him to disregard an act of kindness would make his sister angry and sad. As the days wore on with the family performing these good deeds, Ethan became torn between acknowledging them for the kindness and support or hating them for the weakness their deeds had fostered within him.

Arguments broke out between him and them over simple matters, such as cleaning the dishes. Ethan thought back to a time when he'd yelled at his mother after dinner.

"There is no point in not placing dishes in the freakin' sink. It's what it's there for!" Ethan yelled ferociously at his mom in the kitchen.

"Honey, keeping the plates out of the sink prevents the sink and the dishes from getting scra—"

Ethan interrupted, "I don't care what the point of it is. Why don't we just take the sink out!" After a while, Ethan just avoided the family altogether. He didn't show up for church service or even dinner and spent most of his time in his room. He had become the destruction of the family, which drove him finally to move out.

The worker who had made a comment earlier interrupted Ethan's thoughts, saying, "Hey, you missed spraying one of the bars with epoxy."

Ethan looked down and then back at his coworker.

The man said, "Look, man, I don't give a shit about you, and I have no idea why Pete still calls you for work. You're just some dumb kid who apparently never learned how to work a day in his life and apparently doesn't have an eye for detail." The angered man knelt down and swiped his finger across the unsprayed bar and inspected it.

Some of the men stopped what they were doing to witness the heated display.

Ethan resumed drilling a hole in which to place another bar.

The man bent down on one knee and leaned in closer. "Are you deaf? Can you hear me, you freakin' moron? You just might be one of those lazy guys who expect others to do everything for him. Don't worry, I'll take care of the bar you forgot to spray."

Sweat dripped from Ethan's forehead as he moved faster and concentrated more.

"That's what we're here for! To babysit!" The man continued to torment Ethan by flicking his ear and looking back at the others for praise.

Ethan refused to give in and satisfy the instigation.

"You're only here because you couldn't make it in the military. You're basically helpless if you couldn't even make it as a soldier." His laugh became devilish as he poked Ethan, looking for something to pop like a corn kernel.

Ethan stopped what he was doing and set the drill down. His

mind raced through previous encounters when self-control had been needed. He wanted to keep his job and knew if he didn't, then he would suffer to find another one that could end up having him deal with the public. That would be horrific for him.

"Your breath is a waste to America. Did you hear me, you lazy piece of shi—"

Ethan grabbed a short rebar lying nearby and quickly turned around to face his antagonist. He shoved the bar underneath the man's right armpit, then reached over with his right hand and grabbed the other end, twisting the pole clockwise and creating an armbar that wrenched the man's elbow behind him at a painful angle. Ethan moved behind him and stood up, pushing down even harder. Any more pressure applied, the elbow would dislocate, and the shoulder tendons would snap. The worker went straight down to the ground, his face smacking against the side of the cement.

Ethan felt the tenuous hold on his patience snap. "You wanted a reaction, you got one. But don't think for the slightest second that you weren't going to feel anything. You can talk shit about me all you want. But you will never tell me that I am a waste to America."

The man's upper lip bled from where his face hit the road, and he moaned in pain.

Ethan brought his face closer to the man. "You know nothing of work and nothing of sacrifice. I know you wouldn't last one day in the grunt life. Want to know why? Because you don't deserve to. You have no honor. You have no brothers. And I'm not a soldier. I'm a Marine."

Ethan was pulled away and found himself staring into Jonas's face. "What in tarnation is goin' on right now? What is this? Ethan, explain y'self!"

Ethan remained silent, diverting his eyes from the man who had taunted him.

Jonas sighed. It was now 0630 and the temperature was

already fifty-four degrees. He looked around at the other workers, who stared back blankly as they waited for his reaction. After noticing the generator and tripod lights still on underneath the bridge, he gave a nod and said, "Ethan, brother. Why don't ya go ova there and shut them lights off? I'll take care of him."

Walking away from the group, Ethan immediately felt himself calm. He ran a hand through his hair. He knew he should have left the situation, possibly going to Jonas to move him somewhere else on the site. The higher-ups would probably find out about the whole ordeal, and he knew Pete and Bob would definitely hear of it. He mentally kicked himself, wishing he had never reacted. He'd wanted to defend himself and the military. Ethan moved closer to the light fixtures. He knew that if he turned around, he would see the stares he felt behind him. He instead focused on the sounds of the cars driving past and the crunch of the gravel waiting to be paved.

About a half mile away from where the incident had occurred, Ethan weaved in and out of all the crates and boxes filled with rebar, shutting off the lights one by one as the sun was quickly rising. It was a simple task, but he felt at ease, which convinced him he was a complete introvert. Traffic had become heavier with the onset of morning rush hour, and Ethan remained inside the construction cones blocking the far right lane of the highway.

"Ethan!" Jonas screamed.

Ethan heard him but paid no attention. He just wanted to be left alone.

A loud thump sounded behind him, followed by a screech of tires. Ethan turned around to find a white van racing toward him. It ran over the cones lining the edge of the road, rocking back and forth as it reached the unpaved lower level. The van was not stopping or turning away, and Ethan scouted for possible ways to escape being hit. A five-foot water trench ran parallel to the road, and beyond it was a tree line.

If I can just make it over the trench, he thought.

The vehicle swerved back and forth, increasing its speed and ramming by a crate full of steel rebar. Ethan stared into the tinted window as he tried to make out the driver. The van came closer, and there was no time to lose. He heard a loud pop and the sound of released pressure as the van ran over equipment that pierced a tire. Material flew into the air as the vehicle plowed through without slowing down.

Ethan ran along the side of the road toward the tree line. He took three strides before leaping in the air over the trench. The van swerved to avoid making a nosedive into the gully. The hood of the car missed Ethan by a few feet, sweeping a cloud of dust into the air. He hit the ground and rolled forward, landing on his side before turning to see if it still gave chase. He watched as the van veered toward the exit ramp, not losing any speed despite the blown-out tire. A few men raced toward Ethan to check on him, clearly startled by the event.

"Ethan, ya all right? That driver was a madman!" Jonas bent down to help him up.

Ethan raised onto his knees, keeping an eye on the deserted ramp. At first, he suspected the worker he'd fought with earlier, but he knew better. It seemed as though the driver had intentionally aimed for him. Determining the threat was gone, Ethan got up, brushed off his pants, and scanned the leftover scene.

Scattered throughout the site and on the road were small bars. Cars were at a halt, and drivers beeped their horns and left their vehicles to inspect the scene. The van had knocked out a few lights and hit the end of a generator, which would set the workers back by a few hours.

Jonas was already on his phone with the cement company to call off the appointment. Another worker called the police to come down and write a report. They would want to speak with Ethan as well and get a statement.

"Ethan, afta the police make their investigation and git ya

statement. I think it's best that ya head on home, yeah?" Jonas put a hand on Ethan's shoulder.

Ethan nodded and walked away to sit in his car, waiting for the police to arrive.

After giving his statement, he remembered he was expected at his parents' house for dinner that night. It was the last thing he wanted to do, especially after the events of the day. As he drove away from work, he was in no mood to socialize on a personal level, particularly with friends or family. Tyler, who had originally invited him, was good at persuading him into anything. He knew his friend did it out of kindness, but it never ended well.

With almost the entire day to waste before dinner, he decided to head to the gym and work out some of his frustration. He made sure to keep a slow, smooth pace on every exercise he did. It was the only thing he felt he could control in his life without messing it up. Although, he continued to lift until his muscles would shake with exhaustion and he would drop the weights from failure as if he needed a reminder about how his life had been consumed by a formula that would play out the same way every time.

After a good three hours in the gym, which was normal for him, Ethan needed to relax his muscles and sweat out some of his tension, so he made his way over to the steam room the gym provided. It was empty except for the generator tubes placed sporadically in the wooden walls that produced a thick steam, making it difficult to see. But Ethan knew the room was massive, probably eight-foot by twelve-foot and able to hold quite a few people. He swiped away almost playfully at the lifeless steam as he walked toward the back of the room to sit on the wooden bench. He plopped down, placing his back up against the wall and letting out a sigh of relief as he closed his eyes.

Ethan sat there like a stone, letting the steam cover him completely as he replayed the morning's incident in his head over and over, trying to figure out if there something he could have done differently. His anger got a hold of him once again. He knew Jonah was going to have a fire under him from his boss, Pete, meaning he'd now put Jonah's job in jeopardy. He let out another sigh, but this time it was a sigh of guilt. He gently banged his head against the back of the wall a few times, wishing he could have a do over.

When Ethan opened his eyes, he was startled to see a shadow in the shape of a human in the corner opposite him. He straightened himself up with his hands clenching the bench while contemplating whether he should say something or just let the man be.

"Hey, man, how long you been in here?" Ethan said finally.

No response.

"Buddy, you hear me? You alright?"

Still nothing.

Becoming concerned for the mystery gentleman, Ethan slowly stood up and moved closer, pushing through the steam. As he shuffled, the shadow formed a more defined figure that resembled someone in Ethan's past. Ethan's chest expanded and retracted faster as his breathing became more aggressive, then he stopped once the shape of the face became more defined.

"'Scuse me, bro!" Ethan said louder, trying to get the guy to wake up.

Again, there was no movement.

Ethan could feel his fist tighten as he kept staring at the ghost. His nose flared while his eyes dared not blink. He made the conscience decision to push through. With three calming puffs in and out, he then pushed through the fog and came upon what he had not expected. It was a pile of dirty towels the previous users had stacked in the corner, but somehow still shaped like someone Ethan used to know. His face drooped as he imagined the bundle of towels to be alive. He continued to stand there in a daze, waiting for the towels to talk to him—to tell him everything is going to be okay.

The room was silent as Ethan's mind began to paint a realistic picture of skin on the towels, adding tone, then a face with exact eye color and hair color. He was building a replica in his head of the person he wished was really in front of him. He could feel his blood pulse and flow through his veins as the human became clear as day.

When the door pushed open as a man came in to use the steam room, Ethan's trance was broken and he looked to the door, then back to the bundle of towels. The human Ethan had formed in his head was now gone. Startled, he veered past the confused man and escaped through the open door, skipping his shower and rushing to his car.

He sat there looking forward through the window while internally screaming as he worked to remain calm and try not to think about what had just happened in the steam room.

Horrible images from his past flashed through his mind, and he began to physically feel pain as well as a massive headache that hammered his temples. A feeling of being trapped in these thoughts made his eyes squinch and he grinded his teeth together to distract him from the imaginary sounds of gunfire and screams. He attempted to control his breathing by inhaling a big breath and exhaling all of it in a big explosive blow, but his panic attack only grew more violent.

He hit the steering wheel a few times before separating his mouth as wide as he could to open his ear drums, hoping it would stop the gruesome sounds.

Ethan remained in this state for a few more minutes before his body fell asleep due to mental and physical exhaustion.

He awoke sometime later to a phone a call from Tyler telling him he better be at dinner tonight. Ethan looked at the time and saw that he had slept in his car for almost the entire rest of the day but had enough time to get there just as dinner would start. He sat up and looked around, remembering what had happened before his slumber. He took a few moments to regain his composure before starting the car and heading to his parents' house.

Ethan had made sure to bring an extra set of clothing, but he had planned to take a shower at the gym rather then come dirty and change there. Upon arriving at the house, he grabbed his extra clothes, got out of the car, and stripped down to change.

"Woah now there, killer. We have places called rooms to walk in and close the door, giving privacy to yourself and, in this case, others." Tyler laughed as he walked up the driveway.

Ethan stood and finished putting on his shorts before grabbing the shirt on top of the hood to toss it over his head. "Yeah, well… It's just easier and quicker if I do it now."

The two of them headed up to the front door and rang the doorbell. Ethan's sister arrived to greet them. "Don't you two look cute." She left the door half opened as she returned to the living room, screaming to her mom that the two lovebirds had arrived.

Ethan's mom appeared at the front door, wearing an apron. She smiled and gave each guest a hug and kiss. "You boys arrived just in time, the plates are set, and dinner is ready. Fried chicken…mashed potatoes with gravy…and some delicious honey buns." Tyler looked at Ethan with wide eyes. He licked his chops and moved from the front door to the dining table.

The family sat down, including Ethan's father, who had been upstairs attending to some last-minute business. As they sat down, Ethan heard the TV behind him. It sounded like they had left it on a news channel, but he couldn't tell for sure. Each member at the table reached to their left and right, grabbing each other's hands and creating a link. They all bowed their heads as Ethan's father said a prayer to bless the food. Ethan too bowed his head but kept his eyes open.

"Dear gracious Lord…we thank You this day…for the blessing of the food to nourish our bodies."

Ethan thought to himself, why do we pray over something as simple as food? Of course, we eat food to survive, and food gives us strength. However, does God sometimes not grant food to nourish us in a positive way? He felt guilty at not paying attention or concentrating on the prayer. But he also felt ridiculous, maybe because his human nature made him feel that way. He found himself becoming annoyed, but he kept his head bowed and waited to say Amen.

As the family dove into their plates, the conversation dwindled. Ethan did enjoy the meal, and he thought it was delicious. He generally ordered takeout or ate a microwavable dinner. The surrounding atmosphere was warm and bright. It was much like a winter evening spent indoors with candles or the scent of fire from a firepit as wood crackled. Ethan couldn't ignore the feeling even if he tried.

"So, Ethan, I wanted to ask you what you would like to do with a few things that we had found in the attic?" his mother said softly while she sipped her wine.

Ethan sat back and placed both his forearms on the table while looking directly at his mother. "I don't care, just get rid of whatever it is. If I didn't take it with me, it must not be important." He took a gulp of the cheap beer he had found in his parents' garage.

"How about we just take the items we find and place them online to sell, and then we can give you the profit?" His father scooped some mashed potatoes onto his spoon and took a bite.

"No, thank you, I'm not some charity. I have enough money and can certainly take care of myself." Ethan became irritated because the act of sympathy could be seen clearly across the table.

As he glanced around, he noticed Tyler taking an uncomfortable gulp of water and switching his eyes back and forth between the family members.

The table was quiet for a few moments, and Ethan could finally hear a little bit from the TV.

"Breaking News Update: Hello, everyone, and welcome back to Fox News. I'm Jennifer Randall. We bring you fast and updated news. Currently, we are covering all we can with the recent reports of missing veterans from multiple states. We go live from the Capitol where our reporter Johnathan Mendalle is currently awaiting FBI Director Gabriel Andrews to speak to the public. Johnathan..."

"Thank you, Jennifer. Yes, right now we're standing outside of the Capitol waiting for the director of the FBI to give us current news about the situation. All we know is that after a few reports of missing veterans from west Texas to California, the Federal Bureau of Investigation has taken over and is treating the incidents as a major concern. We do not have any information on whether this is indeed a terrorist threat, although there is speculation. I was able to talk to— Hold a minute, it looks like Director Andrews is about to address the reporters."

Director Andrews said, "Good evening, and thank you all for coming on such short notice. I understand that there are many questions concerning...and in this case right now we are doing everything we can to get down to the bottom of this. We have top men and women...each case individually and have reached out to Central Intelligence to see what...be happening in other countries. We will not expose this as a...and we are not shadowing the idea that it could be...right now, we are sta...and we sincerely send our deepest care for...are affected by this. We will keep you all in the loop and once we hear more, a detailed..."

Ethan couldn't hear much of the news over all the clanking sounds of silverware scratching against plates and plastic cups being set down. Even the sounds of dinner had made him uneasy and edgy. He felt awkward as the conversation about his belongings in the attic had taken a tiring turn. His mood had changed, and he was now in a hurry to retreat back to his lonely apartment.

"Mom, if you want me to just take the stuff, I will. I'll get it out of your hair, and that will be the end of the discussion," Ethan said with frustration as he furrowed his brow. He pushed his plate forward toward the middle of the table and leaned back on the chair.

"Don't talk to your mother like she is one of your friends. She is your mother, and all she is trying to do is help." Ethan's father brought his hands together, folding them, and rested his chin on top of his fingers.

"I don't need your help, and if I'm bothering you, then maybe I should just leave. Will someone shut that TV off?!" Ethan got up and moved the chair back with his legs. "Let's go, Tyler. I've had enough." He was outraged and knew he had been set off by nothing, so had no idea why he was so angry. All he knew was that he didn't want to be there any longer.

Tyler looked at Ethan's parents and then longingly at his food. He looked back at Ethan, who had already moved toward the door. He gave the parents an apologetic expression and got up. As he passed by Ethan's sister, he took the bun from her plate and raised it up as though toasting the family.

Ethan stormed out of the house and turned around to confront Tyler. He knew his friend wanted to say a few things that he didn't want to hear.

Tyler spoke first. "Bro, your family is just trying to help and support you. There is no need to get all bent out of shape over it." His words were broken and muffled from the bun he was eating.

Ethan paced back and forth. Tyler was right, but he wasn't going to admit it.

Tyler finished his bun and walked past Ethan. "You have two choices at this point. We can go to a bar and get hammered. Or we can go to the gym and release some of that energy, man!"

Ethan had actually asked Tyler to be his personal trainer since his friend had gone to school for it. Tyler also worked for the gym Ethan used to train at before he had gone into the military.

Ethan looked down at his feet and silently debated the choices. He gave a sigh of defeat and raised his hand as he followed Tyler. "I choose wasted!"

3

QUERY

PENTAGON

The heavy door swung open, and in walked a very sturdy man carrying a briefcase. Government defense officials filled the room, and they gathered around a cluttered conference table. Some of those officials included FBI Director Gabriel Andrews, Director of the CIA Jonathan Pompus, and even the Commandant of the Marine Corps, David Fernando. The men and women sat at attention, keeping their eyes forward as the man strode past them.

The large office had dark blue walls and hanging on them were previous presidents of the United States. Some flags stood in the back corners, including the American flag, POW/MIA, and the secretary of defense flag. All but one seat had been filled.

The man reached the seat in front of the entire group. He set the briefcase gently down on the table and moved the chair back. Settling into the chair, he moved the briefcase back and forth until he felt comfortable. The entire table leaned their heads forward, their eyes shifting to one another, waiting nervously and knowing they had nothing to report.

Fat, loose cheeks were framed by a rugged and weary face, making him appear like a droopy dog from the cartoon shows. Although he still had a full head of hair, the layers were thin and white.

No one was fooled by his aged appearance. His eyes were blue and toxic. Even a glance into them showed a history of adventure and loss, experience and life. He wore a plain black suit with a blue tie. As he stretched his arms out, the sleeves retracted back and allowed him to move his hands freely. He held the sides of the briefcase with his hands, placing his thumbs on the combination locks on both sides of the handle. They heard a click, and the briefcase opened.

Secretary of Defense Michael Harrison grabbed a bundle of papers from his briefcase and patted them against the top of the table to straighten them. He set them in front of him before taking a sip from a glass of water. He slid the glass away and folded his hands over the table as he scanned the attendees.

"Good morning, ladies and gentlemen. I sure hope you had your coffee. We will not be leaving until we figure this out. And if I don't have an answer to give the president, then we will sit here until we do. Do I make myself clear?" Harrison's voice was well defined, and his deep, hard tone spoke with authority.

"Yes, sir," could be heard many times around the room.

"Mr. Andrews, would you be so kind and give me an update on what your team has found since the last time we spoke?" The sturdy voice resonated throughout the room and grabbed the attention of the FBI Director.

"Well, sir," Mr. Andrews responded, "we know that whoever is in charge of these kidnappings is targeting veterans from any branch of service. There have been no reports of civilians. We've sent teams to investigate more into each individual's personal life. We are interviewing their family members and friends; however, not one person has given us valuable data. We've seemed to hit a wall, sir. We are thinking that we have to move further up the scale with enemies. We were thinking along the lines of terrorism, sir." The director spoke with confidence as he addressed the secretary of defense.

Mr. Harrison nodded. He reviewed a paper on top of the stack he had pulled from his briefcase. "I see that we are not the only ones in this predicament, are we?" Mr. Harrison lifted his eyes to the table, awaiting an answer.

"Yes, sir, we've been receiving calls from France, Germany, Australia. Sir, the list of countries keeps growing. And again, it seems that specifically it's just veterans of military forces," CIA Director Pompus said, giving his best answer to the current problem.

Mr. Harrison leaned back in his chair and folded his hands, allowing both his index fingers to rest on his lips. The table waited for some direction. They were all stumped. No one had any valuable insight as to what could be behind the missing veterans.

"Could it possibly be the ISIS terrorist group? No one has made an assumption apart from the media regarding the group we've been at war with for over ten years. Those members have every reason to manage an act like this. They want to gain control over our morale and crush it just like they did with 9/11," one of the women from the front of the table said passionately.

Another man, who sat across from her, waved his hand and reacted to her statement. "If it had been them, they would have already bragged about it. They wouldn't keep that a secret. If it doesn't have anything to do with using propaganda to gain control, then they can be checked off the list. No, this could possibly be North Korea or Eastern Europe. Someone with anticolonial sentiments creating a motivation to target veterans." The man ended his counter and waited for affirmation from the rest of the table.

Everyone averted their eyes toward the wall or on their papers. One even hid behind her glass of water, sipping it during the awkward silence.

Mr. Harrison stood and looked at everyone. He took a moment to collect his thoughts. He knew his entire team had worked hard, but not hard enough. He needed more information. The more intel he could gather, the faster he would reach those veterans.

The people around the table were tired. He saw it in their faces. He also saw defeat in the distance. If he didn't set them back on track, the trail would be completely lost, and they would lose their chance of finding the veterans. He walked around the table, his hands behind his back, and prepared to motivate his lackluster team.

"We have the entire nation on our backs. They are looking for us to find their brothers, sisters, husbands, and wives. Americans are in need of their government to protect and serve. This is why we are here. If our nation breaks from being united, then we fail, and they win. And we will not fail. We will work harder. We will go more in depth than we ever have. I want our top men and women working on this around the clock. And I want our people to know that they have nothing to fear. I want to take every precaution. We know that it's our veterans they're after. We will publicly announce that until further notice, every veteran is highly recommended to have a guardian or someone with them at all times. Until then, united we stand. And stand we will."

4
THE CALLING

E than's head pounded when he woke the next morning. It was so severe that he felt veins on both sides of his temple pulsating.

How much did I drink last night?, he thought.

He looked at his alarm clock and it read 0500. He was going to be late to work. No one had contacted him about the situation with the worker who had instigated the fight. Thinking about the outcome of the situation, he chuckled, but it was followed by a gasp as pain shot through his head.

He pressed down on the veins to ease the pain. He was trying to think about the night before, but he couldn't remember where they had gone. He also didn't remember coming home. Ethan had his phone plugged in and on the nightstand. He reached over and grabbed it, holding it above his head.

He had a couple texts from Tyler. Probably wondering if he'd made it either home or to jail. But he also had one from Pete.

"Good evening, Mr. Miller. I am very sorry to write to you after what happened to you yesterday. I do hope you are all right from that crazy incident. However, concerning the incident before that, in this company, we cannot have such violence. This will be your letter of termin—"

Ethan threw his phone, which hit the wall and knocked down one of the picture frames.

The coworker was a bully and deserved what Ethan had given him. He'd started the whole thing anyway.

His head pulsed with pain as frustration coursed through him. He could feel the blood rushing through him, but he also knew that he was still intoxicated from the night before. Anger swept through his stomach and surged to his throat.

He held his hands over his face. He didn't want to deal with any of this anymore. Nothing was helping him cope with his guilt, his loss. Nothing was going right. "Nothing going right is what I deserve," he told himself.

His heart pounded faster, and heat swept through him. Memories flashed through his mind, seeming like they wanted to jump out of his skin. Simmering in his anger, Ethan looked toward his nightstand and reached for the drawer concealing his handgun. He pulled it out, and there sat the gun as if it were lying on a pedestal for everyone to see. He looked at the glorious display, trying to contemplate his time of living a double life. He was tired of maintaining this dual existence. It could be over in just a blink of an eye.

He sat up and grabbed the pistol, its coldness sending a shock throughout his body. He rested the medicine on his lap and felt a bizarre numbness. His eyes wandered around the room, although he didn't look at the walls. He just stared into oblivion. There was a feeling of floating outside of his body, but he still sensed his headache and the pounding of his heart. Sweat formed over his forehead, and droplets fell down his face. His hands shook, and the walls compressed around him. His time of drowning had never felt so real.

Adrenaline raced through Ethan, and he noticed his hands swelling. He reached for the handle and cradled the weapon as if it were his only child. His breathing became inconsistent and harder to control as every second went by. He couldn't tell for sure but thought tears were falling down his cheeks, though it could have just as easily been sweat. He knew it was the right choice.

He raised the gun to his right temple, the open end of the barrel kissing his skin. His whole body viscously vibrated back and forth.

Where is my strength?, he wondered.

His own body fought against him, and his pose was still and silent.

"Screw you, self-preservation!" he screamed.

He gasped for air three more times and held it like he was going to dive under water for an eternity. He clenched his eyes shut, his body froze, and time seemed to stop. He pulled the trigger.

A dead click echoed through the room. He opened his eyes and let out a sigh of relief. He coughed, and time started up again. He'd forgotten he had put the safety on, preventing the gun from firing.

He threw the pistol back in the nightstand as though his hand had touched lava, then wiped his sweat-covered face. The adrenaline that had been pumping throughout his body slowed, and he began to breathe normally. Ethan looked around, not believing what had just happened. His stomach turned, and nausea threatened to overwhelm him.

He turned toward the wall where the picture frame had fallen. His heart ached, and he bowed his head in defeat. Trying to take in the last few minutes, the confused boy lifted his body off the bed and got dressed. He knew he had to get out of the house before he reacted to the situation.

Ethan grabbed his gym clothes that he determined by a whiff were clean. He dressed himself and quickly put on his shoes before leaving the haunting apartment. He jumped into his car, spinning out of the parking spot, and headed to the gym where he knew Tyler would be. He needed to be next to someone he knew, even if he didn't want to talk, which he didn't. He understood that if he were alone any longer, his thoughts would overtake him once more. The next time, they might be successful. He drove without following any of the traffic laws. After swerving in and out of lanes for five minutes, he finally pulled into the gym lot. He found a spot to park and quickly jumped out of the car without bothering to lock it.

Ethan headed for the door, his nerves on edge. He reflected on what had happened in his apartment. It played over in his head a dozen times and scared him.

He barged through the door, scurrying past machines and weights. He noticed Tyler with one of his clients, and Tyler hadn't noticed Ethan's arrival.

Ethan wanted to go straight to either the bench or a squat rack where he could lift and feel pain. He couldn't decide right away.

Tyler looked up from training and said, "Hey, bro. Wha—"

With a determined look on his face, Ethan moved briskly past his friend. "I need a spotter right now!" He didn't make eye contact with Tyler and soon heard him speaking apologetically to his current client.

Tyler smiled, putting one finger up toward the client, and said, "Could you give me just one second, sir? Thanks." He then bolted toward Ethan, finding his friend putting weights on one of the bench-pressing bars. He stepped behind it, preparing to spot Ethan. "Want to tell me what's up?" he asked.

Ethan said nothing and focused on his plan to do as many repetitions as he could until his entire body burned. He lay down and grabbed the bar.

As Tyler stood behind Ethan, he pulled out his phone and opened Facebook. He typed in, "Hanging out with my good friends, Mr. Weights and Mrs. Machines...and, of course, Ethan Miller!" He tagged the location of the gym and Ethan as well, then sent it out for all to read and placed the phone back into his pocket. Propping his elbow onto one of the legs of the bench, he said, "So, do you want to talk about it yet, or do I have to wait a little longer until you can't lift the bar anymore?" Tyler nodded and smiled as he looked up at his client, who was now very agitated. He quickly bowed his head toward his friend to ignore the stare.

Despite starting to cave from exhaustion, Ethan still pushed the bar up and down. He had lost count after twenty reps. He heard Tyler ask him a question, but he just wasn't ready to talk yet. He honestly didn't even know how or what he was going to say to Tyler. What was there to tell him? *Hey, attempted suicide today and went through with it but forgot that the safety was on,* he thought. Ethan struggled more and more, and Tyler reached toward the bar.

At that point, Ethan couldn't think, as he'd used all his energy to push the weight. He could see now that his friend was helping him lift the bar and slowly set it back down to his chest. "One more!" he yelled to Tyler. He gave one more grunt and placed the bar back on the pegs with Tyler's help.

Ethan sat back up and looked toward the ground. In a sorrowful voice, he said, "I'm going to do another set."

Tyler nodded and ran back to his client before they either became mad enough to leave or write a negative email to Tyler's boss.

Ethan got up from the bench, taking the weight off of one end of the bar and throwing it to the side. It slammed against one of the pillars.

A man who had been using one of the machines nearby noticed Ethan and how he had thrown the weight. He left his machine and walked to Ethan. "Hey there, buddy. We don't like it when people slam weights down on the ground here. It's not good for them. How about you walk over to that weight and set it down properly?"

Ethan didn't acknowledge the man and continued to place the weight that he wanted for his next set.

"Are you deaf? Can you not understand basic English?" The man yelled, grabbing Ethan's shoulder and pulling it around so Ethan faced him.

After Ethan was forcefully turned around he looked up, his eyes widening when he found a large man. The other man's height had to be around 6'3 to 6'5, but he couldn't directly tell. The man's bald head glared under the gym lights. He wore a white tank top that exposed his enormous biceps and gigantic forearms. Ethan looked down and noticed that the man's calves were shaped like tear drops.

He apparently never skips leg day, thought Ethan.

"You better say something, you frikin' pip-squeak, before I make you talk!"

By this time, the commotion had alerted Tyler, who ran over, placing himself between the two agitated adults. "What seems to be the problem, Tim?" He looked at Tim as he asked the question, but he didn't receive a response because Ethan interrupted with a laugh.

Tyler gave Ethan a sharp look as if to tell him this was not the right time to laugh.

Ethan walked slowly to the weight but picked up a much lighter one that he could grab with just one hand. He walked back toward them, but he didn't return to his original spot. Instead, he stood next to the man towering over him. Both Tim and Tyler seemed shocked at Ethan's overexaggerated laughter and awaited an explanation.

"I'm sorry, it's just funny to me that your name is Tim.... I mean who would have guessed this large mammoth would be named Tim?!" Ethan had yelled so loud that almost everyone in the building heard him and turned their attention toward the commotion.

Tyler had a shocked expression on his face, probably because no one would be able to stop Tim if Ethan said something he would regret.

Ethan stepped close enough to smell the sweat and after-shave from Tim's body. He set himself into position and formed a plan. The burning sensation built inside, and Ethan couldn't control it. He needed this like an addict needed a drug. Ethan had directly challenged Tim, and the giant was ready to pounce like a ferocious beast.

"What's the matter with Tim, little man?" Tim leaned over Ethan and waited for his answer.

Tyler just bowed his head and placed his hand over his face, knowing what would come next.

Ethan stared at Tim and said, "Because of Tiny Tim!" At that very same moment, he took the weight that was in his hand and swung it into Tim's crotch.

The goliath went straight to his knees, cupping his now swollen genitals. He screamed in agony and looked up at Ethan just as the same weight smacked into his face and knocked him unconscious.

Ethan dropped the weight and turned around, walking toward the exit. Tyler and a couple others went to Tim's aid. Ethan heard a large commotion behind him over what had just happened as people cleared the path, afraid to be caught in the line of fire. He reached the door and shoved it open, heading toward the street instead of his car. He needed to calm himself down and take a walk. He thought if he were to drive, it would end up resulting in a car accident and hurting more people.

Ethan walked at a fast pace down the street, passing through the neighborhood until he eventually reached an open field. He had always been close to the countryside of North Carolina and the solace it provided.

After around five minutes of quietly walking, Ethan had finally calmed down and could think again. He couldn't believe how far he had let his anger go. Who was he becoming? Protect and serve was his sworn duty, but he was failing miserably at it. Where was his life leading him? If there was a God, then surely He had abandoned him. Overlooking the harvested field, Ethan noticed a breeze ripple through the broken stalks toward him, cooling the sweat on his skin. A hush fell over him as he let his guard down, feeling defeated. A white van stopped behind Ethan, disturbing the gravel and making a quick drifting noise.

Figuring it was Tyler catching up to him, Ethan kept walking, knowing his friend would be pretty mad at him. After this, there was no chance that he would be allowed back into the gym, given what he had just done. Hearing no response though from Tyler, Ethan felt that he owed him at least an explanation for his actions.

"Look, Tyler, I'm sorr—" He turned around and was met with darkness.

"All right, recruits, your next exercise involves a combat search and rescue. This will be a full team effort, and I do not expect to see any of you sitting on your ass in the back. Do I make myself clear?!"

SSgt Hill received a huge reply of "Yes, sir!" from the entire platoon.

Ethan was in front of the platoon, taking a knee and listening to their objective for the exercise. He couldn't ignore the raggedy voice that his drill instructor had. His voice box seemed to be very small and dry. SSgt Hill must be really trying to spit out his every word without losing the rest of his voice. Not only was his voice weakening, but Ethan noticed it in his face as well.

His drill instructor had pale white skin, and his entire body was very slim. So slim that his uniform was a size small, yet it made SSgt Hill look as if he were wearing an extra-large. Ethan took more notice of his baggy eyes and how thin and weak his skin actually was. It was as if he were looking at the beginning of a decaying person. Although, in his eyes, he noticed how young the drill instructor really was. He couldn't be more than thirty to forty years old.

"Recruit Miller! Is there something that is more important than what I am saying right now? Is staring into space going to give you the answers to the questions that I am asking?!" SSgt Hill's raspy voice strained to finish his last words.

Ethan was caught off guard and embarrassed to be called out in front of everyone. "No, sir, this recruit understands how important the assignment is." He awaited more of a reprimand from his instructor, but SSgt Hill continued to carry on with the mission briefing.

During the beginning of recruit training, it was top priority to always refer to yourself as 'this recruit.' It was part of the breaking down of whoever you were before you walked into boot camp. This process was designed to strip everything away and build an entirely new killing machine. To Ethan, it was an easy process, and he'd learned very quickly.

It was almost the end of June, and the day was coming to a close. The air was humid, and the temperature was at least in the mid-eighties. Ethan saw the drooping faces of the other recruits. Some had been sipping water the entire time they had been listening to the directions of their next assignment. If you run out of water, then you have to wait until you hit your next supply point to refill. Ethan was disciplined and would only take sips from his own canteen when his body was really begging for it. It was crucial not to be careless with your food and water during the Crucible.

'The Crucible' was what the Marines called it. It was the final rite of passage the recruit must endure to earn his Eagle, Globe, and Anchor. The last obstacle before becoming a Marine.

It encompassed three days and entailed more than fifty-four hours of hiking, exercises, and navigation with only eight hours of sleep allowed in its entirety.

SSgt Hill noticed the recruit's sleepiness, and he stopped speaking to look down. He put his hands on his hips and took off his cover. The sun was beginning to set, but the light still reached his eyes from over the trees.

He squinted and spoke in a normal tone. "It's been three months of continuous training, I understand. You all are tired and sore. You have been busting your asses, and I'm pretty proud of all of you. But we still have work to do, and even though you might be able to see the light at the end of the tunnel, you must continue to push forward or else that light could be the front of a train. Do I make myself clear?"

The mouth of every man in the unit dropped. It was the first time hearing the instructor's human voice. Ethan couldn't tell if it was because of the SSgt's struggle to keep his instructor's voice or because he needed to find a new motivation for the platoon. However, this time the reply that SSgt Hill received was a motivated one. The recruits all stood up and packed their belongings.

Ethan was one of the first to finish. As he waited, he looked around as the sun filtered through the trees. He enjoyed a few moments of rest while the others finished packing. The scent of the pines from the Carolina woods filled his lungs with delight, reminding him of home.

They were still on Parris Island but had hiked a couple miles away from base. They'd reached a deserted airstrip that had been used as an airport but was abandoned later. The cement of the strip had been broken up by weeds that had grown in different patches, which streaked across from one end to the other. Acres of trees surrounded them in every direction, extending into the distance as far as the eye could see. Ethan could easily have gotten lost if there were no instructors to guide them.

"Now remember, you are on a search and rescue to find two

pilots. Their helo had an engine malfunction and crashed a few clicks away. You have exactly nineteen hours to reach the coordinates that were given to you and return with both pilots. This will be a hostile environment. If you do not make it within the time period given, the medical evacuation helicopter will leave you, and you will have failed your mission. If you understand me say, 'Aye, sir!' "

"Permission to speak, sir?" Ethan stood at attention next to his instructor.

He never liked to ask questions or even speak for that matter, as he risked being taken to a sand pit to do jumping jacks or some sort of horrible workout. It wasn't the workout that he minded so much as the reason why he was there. Any time there was a one-on-one workout, it was because of a disciplinary action.

"What is it, recruit?" SSgt Hill managed to spit enough of his saliva on Ethan that he could not only feel it spray onto his face but could see foam hanging from the instructor's bottom lip.

"These recruits were not given any coordinates for the crash site."

Ethan seemed to have sparked a smile across the instructor's face. "Exactly what I was waiting for. Good job, Miller. You'll be taking point. Here are the coordinates, and your time starts now!"

Ethan did not intentionally ask for the position of taking point. Point was always the first to go, regarding being shot and leading the patrols. It was also the job of point to take down the coordinates and calculate the correct path. It was not as simple as plotting it down on paper and subtracting a few numbers. It involved having tools such as a map with a grid, a protractor that had a scale, and a compass. It was very tedious, and if someone was off by a little, it could make a big difference and take you somewhere you didn't plan to go.

Half of the platoon stood behind Ethan as he worked out the numbers. Placing his protractor on the map, he traced a line to figure out the actual distance from the starting point to the crash site. Even though this was an exercise, it still was a serious matter, and he did not want to be the one to screw it up. He'd never let pressure become a hinderance to him when it came to problem-solving or bad situations. In fact, he hoped he might work better under harder circumstances.

Ethan worked at a consistent pace, being careful not to rush and wary of making a slight mistake. Time was of the essence, and the sooner they had the plot point, the faster they could begin their patrol to the site.

"What the hell, man? We don't have all day!"

Ethan could tell that the recruit behind him was Douglas Woods, an overweight recruit with orange hair and about as many freckles on his face as he had hair strands. Which was quite a few, Ethan thought to himself, smiling. His voice was very high-pitched and could be confused with the voice of a very masculine female if you closed your eyes.

"I would have been done already. All you have to do…"

Ethan ignored Woods. Since day one, he had been the obnoxious kid who could be put under the title of 'the one-upper.' The kid who could outfight you or outdrink you and knew everything about anything. Everyone learned to deal with him by either toning him out or making him look like a fool. But he was part of the platoon and part of the chain.

"Shut the mouth, fugly. Just let him work." Another recruit in the back had pushed his way forward and corrected Douglas.

It was Steven Bradly, a boy from the northern countryside who had grown up working on a farm and bailing hay for most of his childhood. He had a great work ethic, becoming good friends with Ethan from the start.

"Quit having a hissy fit, you frikin' girl, or I'll shove a tampon in your pie hole."

A couple of guys within the group chuckled. Ethan and Steve always had each other's backs, and each would defend the other.

"How about you masturbate a cow's titties!" Douglas retorted, attempting a better comeback, but it would be hard with his feminine voice.

Ethan looked up and saw Steve getting into Douglas's freckled face. Douglas's expression was stern, but he knew that Steve was serious. His expression dwindled as his eyes diverted left and right, staring at the rest of the platoon. He lowered his guard in defeat.

Steve was an intimidating guy, being one of the bigger recruits in boot camp. The only difference between Steve and Douglas was that Steve's weight came from his muscle. He was tall, but much of his weight came from his upper body. His face was chiseled and always had a five-o'clock shadow. With his short golden-brown hair and bright blue eyes, he had the looks, the brain, and the body. Everyone always questioned Steve about why he'd gone into the Marine Corps instead of getting a high-paying job in the civilian world. His reply was always the same, "That would mean I was wasting talents I should be using for my country."

Ethan carefully checked his work once more before standing and putting the map and other navigational tools into his bag. He pulled out his compass and walked toward the tree line. He then turned to face the group of recruits, who were waiting to hear how far they had to hike.

"I did the work and figured out that we have quite a ways to go. So, we're going to have to hike quickly."

One of the recruits within the middle of the pile asked, "How far?"

Ethan had anticipated the question, and he knew the response would not be well-received. "We have about two and half miles to the site, but if we set up into three teams and place ourselves in a wedge formation, we should get there fairly fast."

There were a couple of groans and mumbling under the recruits' breath. SSgt Hill placed himself in the back, quietly observing. He'd never really said much on previous missions, allowing the recruits to figure things out on their own. The only time he would jump in was to change up the scenario or paint a better picture of the situation.

"All right, that settles it. We have the coordinates and the distance, so now we just need three team leaders to control the teams. Any takers?"

Douglas was the first to step forward, jutting out his chest as he did. Ethan swore that if he stuck his chest out anymore, the two MRE's he'd eaten an hour before would burst out of him.

The second person to step forward was Jonathan Sunster, but everyone just called him Sunny. He was a smaller recruit, but he always kept up with the platoon. He also wasn't the smartest guy.

During one of the nights that Sunny had fire watch—two hours of patrolling a certain sector of the barracks—he had given the wrong report to a drill instructor. The instructor was so angry that he made Sunny take off his uniform and put everything on backward, including his cover and boots. He then made him stand facing the wall. The drill instructor told him no matter what to face that wall.

Fifteen minutes later, the Executive Officer walked in and passed by the stone recruit and immediately stopped in his tracks. He turned around and stared at the recruit for what seemed an eternity. The XO asked Sunny to turn around. Sunny did not respond or do what he was ordered. He then asked who did this and why his uniform was not within regulation. Again, Sunny did not speak or move.

Ethan didn't quite know what he would have done in that situation, but he was definitely curious to know what had gone through Sunny's mind at that given moment. The result was that Sunny had finally turned around and spilled the beans about the drill instructor's orders. Sunny was the first one up the next morning, sent to the sand pit by the instructor everyone knew had been reprimanded for messing with the recruit.

Steve could be seen waiting for the third to step forward and volunteer, but no one did. "Well, I guess I'll be the one to take the third team. So, everyone else split up into the three given teams and let's make a move on, we're on a time crunch."

Ethan threw his rifle over his back so it wouldn't interfere with the magnet. He placed his compass in front of his stomach and waited to see where the dial would turn. He was headed west toward the setting sun. He stared upward, toward a bundle of conifers, and set his eyes on one particular tree in the distance before stepping toward it and beginning his mission.

5

A PROMISE

Feeling lethargic, Ethan came to from what felt like an eternity in a coma. His body was numb, and his entire head pounded. He was warm but felt nauseated and wanted to vomit. He was feeling parched, his mouth was very dry, and his jaw quivered. He licked the top of his mouth, but his tongue felt like sandpaper. His lips were also dry, and he began to lick them.

He caught the strong, musty scent of hamster cages, reminding him of walking into pet stores and being blasted with that smell. Working construction, he realized it was obvious that the smell probably came from some sort of cedar, but he couldn't tell what type of cedar wood it was. He groaned as time passed and he became more aware. His body ached and felt very stiff, as though gravity pulled him harder to the ground. He was very uncomfortable and didn't want to move, or perhaps his body didn't want him to move.

He'd almost forgotten about the incident that had happened the day before, which he now regretted. But he also felt quite happy about being able to take down a giant that was more than twice his size. Ethan took pride in that, but not many people outside of the military knew that Marines cheated. He figured that

Tyler would not be so inclined to be happy with what he did.

Ethan managed to make a little smile appear, but he quickly frowned when he thought about what happened after the incident. The problem was...he couldn't remember. Ethan made a step-by-step account of what had occurred all the way until the blackout. Was it possible that he was dead?

"No, I don't think I would be feeling this horrible unless I somehow managed to end up in hell," chuckled Ethan.

However, he did remember the sound of tires sliding in the gravel and the high-pitched squeal of brakes that definitely needed to be changed.

"Maybe Tyler hit me with his car?" he muttered.

No, it couldn't be that either, he thought. *I had started to apologize to Tyler before I turned around, then...*

Ethan paused for a moment, and his heart skipped a beat. It was as if his body had finally found new video surveillance footage from that brief moment. Before he'd blacked out, he remembered two blurred figures who had long dangling black beards and wore some sort of blue jeans—the kind that every dad in the nineties wore—high watered and completely washed out. The moment was so quick, Ethan struggled to bring that memory into focus, fighting the pain in his head.

He paused the image of the two blurred figures in his mind, confident they were male. They came toward Ethan, presenting something to him. He tried to recall what it was but found nothing coming to light. It was just a black blob.

Come on, Miller, clean it up.... What was it? Ethan said to himself, confident he would figure it out.

Ethan finally had a eureka moment and saw it, then fear coursed through his body. His heart didn't bother to skip a beat, it just stopped beating for a moment. It had been a long time since he had felt that kind of fear.

He didn't have to clean the image in his head because he vaguely saw the shape of it. It was a hard object, used in the pocket of a shooter's shoulder—the buttstock of a gun. As soon as he figured it out, he wished he could forget it again. He knew why he had blacked out. He'd been hit in the head with a buttstock, which explained why he had a splitting headache.

He hesitated for a couple of minutes, scared to make any movements. His mind raced as he tried to understand all the questions that clawed at him. Finally, he struck up enough energy and decided to move for the first time to tend to his wound. He raised his hand toward his head, but before he could see how bad his head was, his fingers hit something hard above.

He felt so drunk, he thought he'd been lying down the entire time with his eyes closed, but his eyes had been open since he'd awoken.

"But why is it so dark, and what did I just hit?' Ethan stuttered.

His body became alert and went into defense mode. Fully awake, adrenaline pumped through his veins. Ethan rested his hand on his chest and felt skin. He began to pet his chest, feeling the sweat that evenly matched the clamminess of his palms. He now shifted focus to other parts of his body, directing his attention to his left hand, which was lying at his side. He placed his palm down and slid his fingers back and forth, wanting to feel sheets or blankets; something soft to bring comfort to what he believed was the makings of a nightmare. What his fingers touched told him two things. He was right about the smell of cedar, and what he felt was wood. He was lying on wood.

He breathed faster. Still lying frozen, fear took hold of him and left questions that he did not want to answer. The only way to know was if he built enough courage to move.

He tried to come up with excuses as to why he felt wood. He thought that it could be a joke. He forced his breathing to calm and took smaller gasps of air. He had to know for sure.

Ethan put both his hands to his side, palms facing down. He felt more wood. He scooted his fingers slowly out to the sides together, like a caterpillar moving inch by inch. He moved his hands outward, and both hands touched an object at the same time. His body recoiled in horror. He lost control of his breathing again, but this time, he couldn't stop it. Like a blind man, his hands crawled over the solid objects and felt them as quickly as he could. There was a wall on both sides, and he wildly moved his hands everywhere. Between gasps of air, he spit noises of nonsense. His body was out of control as his head flailed right and left, and his legs thrashed about. Fear was now the driving force behind his action. Fear was now the driver of Ethan.

His noises became louder and louder, and the fear that overtook him paused, directing his hands not to where he was lying or to the sides, but to the starless sky. Both hands rested no more than half an arm's distance from a platform of wood above him. His fear morphed into phobia, and his body completely fell silent, including his breathing and moans. He finally realized he was in a coffin.

He let out a bloodcurdling scream so horrid that he could taste the mix of saliva and blood spewing from his mouth. He pushed and scrambled to move his entire body anywhere he could. He screamed, crying and pleading for help. He begged for someone to come to his aid and let him out. Both arms and legs began to cramp, the muscles straining continuously without mercy.

Pushing outward and upward with his hands didn't seem to work. Ethan put his arms in front of his head, and he moved his body in a squatting position, lifting with his legs in an attempt to push the box out with his feet.

Still screaming, he lost all sense of his actions. He couldn't think straight. He punched the walls and the ceiling. Tears flowed from his eyes, and he became lightheaded. He moved as if he were drowning or going into cardiac arrest. He was having a panic attack; his fear of small spaces had never been this real.

"Let me *out!*"

Realizing that no one was going to free him, he knew he was

trapped. He gave one more scream and pushed the top of the coffin with all his strength before passing out.

"You got us lost, didn't you?" Douglas yelled. He came up from behind Ethan, leaving his team members in the back. Ethan rolled his eyes and marched toward another tree that he'd seen.

"Douglas, get back to your team and keep your voice down. That's all we need is to give away our position to the enemy."

Douglas ignored Ethan's directions, walking right next to him and having no respect for personal space. Mocking Ethan, Douglas whispered softly but with much exaggeration. "Miller, you're incompetent and shouldn't be point. Why don't you hand over the coordinates and map and I'll fix it? I won't even make a big deal about how you screwed it up. Not to mention we've been walking in the woods for more than forty-five minutes now." Douglas laughed and proceeded to taunt Ethan.

At that point, with the calculations and time elapsed, Ethan figured that they were coming close to the rescue site. He threw up a flat hand, giving the sign for halt. The entire platoon stopped and waited for direction. Taking a knee, Ethan gave the order to drop to the ground and wait. The team leaders surrounded Ethan.

"Hey there, Dougie boy, why don't you stay with your team next time? Don't want you getting lost out here in the woods." Steve gave Douglas's back a wild slap and grinned widely before nodding to Ethan.

"The pilots and their helicopter should be within the next hundred yards. I say we take a team for security to swoop around right, and one left. The third team will be the primary to go in and extract the two pilots." Ethan knew that all of them, including himself, were no more than twenty to twenty-five years old and all had very little experience with military tactics. In fact, they'd had only three months of any kind of training.

Ethan was confident that this was the right way to go, but he wanted to have the blessing of his team leaders.

Steve spoke up first. "I couldn't have come up with a better plan myself. Good on ya, bro."

Sunny just nodded and rolled his eyes, waiting to hear from Douglas.

Douglas looked toward the ground as he brushed the three or four peach hairs that somehow grew under his chin. "That's a pretty dumb idea, Miller. You guys really think that this kid's idea is going to get the job done?" Douglas spoke in a very high-pitched voice that seemed to echo throughout the trees.

A few hushing sounds were directed at Douglas, but he didn't seem to care as he continued to berate Ethan's plan.

Ethan took notice of SSgt Hill watching from a distance, his face steaming with frustration as he observed the platoon's lack of discipline. Douglas was going to ruin this mission for all of them.

"You think that splitting up teams is the best idea? It sounds ludicrous!"

Douglas had made such a commotion that the other recruits had started getting uncomfortable. They shuffled around, watching their surroundings anxiously.

SSgt Hill stepped out from behind the tree, yelling and waving his hands. He pointed toward the direction of the crash site. "You're receiving enemy fire from the west! You have one hour remaining."

Steve immediately ran back to take his team right, flanking the crash site. Sunny then followed in pursuit with his team and directed them left. This left Douglas, who stood in the same spot and yelled at his team.

Ethan, being point, was also part of Douglas's team. He ran behind a tree and waited for Douglas to give orders, but Douglas lay there motionless on the ground, aiming in with his rifle.

"Douglas, get us the hell online and start firing back!" Ethan shouted at him, but words were not getting any reaction.

At this point, every gun had been pointed toward the empty woods and all of the recruits shouted, "Bang! Bang!"

Douglas yelled at his team to keep firing, but he still made no effort to move the team closer to the fake enemy.

Ethan knew the other man was stalling because he didn't know what to do. He was caught off guard and confused. He couldn't bear to watch the sight of the frozen ginger any longer. He yelled toward the team to get online and fire.

The team already understood who was taking control, and no one seemed to have any objections.

Ethan's next job was to get Douglas behind some cover. He knew that it was all a drill, but his imagination helped him a lot in this scenario. He knew that Douglas would be called out as a wounded recruit or worse—dead—because he was still in the open. He grabbed Douglas and yanked him behind a nearby tree.

"Steve...Sunny!"

Both recruits looked up, waiting to hear from Ethan.

Ethan dropped his rifle and put his hand around his mouth to make his voice project even louder. "Buddy rushes!"

At that moment, all three team leaders had the recruits laying down suppressive fire while the others moved up five feet or so. This was the tactical way that the military put pressure on the enemy and closed in on them.

Ethan glanced back at SSgt Hill, whose demeanor indicated he was impressed with the platoon's methodical approach. He walked quietly behind the rushing platoon, looking and correcting anyone doing anything wrong.

What felt like forever finally came to a close when the instructor yelled, "Cease fire!"

The platoon stopped firing. Standing in front of Ethan was a full-size helicopter. The huge green bird rested in a circular section where all the trees had perished. Its nose had been dug halfway into the ground. The rotors were black and rusted, and three of the four were bent. All the doors were closed and lying beside it were two dummies.

Ethan noticed that the platoon had quickly let their guard down and was going to order them to post security, but Steve beat him to it.

"All right, everyone, I need one team for security to the right and one to the left. Ethan's team is going to be the medic team and get those dummies out of hell's acres and back to safety!" Steve said to the men.

Everyone did as he directed. Steve made his way back to his team, slapping Douglas on the butt and mumbling something about a cat catching his tongue.

Ethan was so thankful that he had Steve to back him up and support his decision. He was also glad that he was still going along with his previous idea. The two seemed to work very well together, and he hoped that they would be assigned the same unit once they graduated boot camp.

Ethan dismissed the thought and went to work while the other teams posted security. SSgt Hill painted a picture for both pilots. One needed a tourniquet to the right leg, and the other one had lost a lot of blood from his chest. The boys patched up the dummies as best they could. They waited for their instructor to give them a nod of acceptance before continuing their mission.

They were not given any gurney stretchers but were told to improvise. All of them gathered around, talking and discussing how to carry the dummies back to where they had started. They were not having much luck on finding a solution, and time was running out.

One of the recruits who barely ever spoke pulled out his poncho liner and grabbed two very long sticks that he had found near the woods. He placed the sticks on each side, close to the edge of the liner. He then rolled each side, wrapping the sticks like a burrito and allowing the edges to become handles. Four people could easily carry a person on it.

Ethan smiled and grabbed the recruit's shoulder to praise him for the brilliant idea. The team pulled one more poncho liner out and found sticks to make it just like the first one, placing the dummies on them. Both pilots were very heavy, and Ethan knew this would be a difficult return hike.

"You have thirty minutes remaining!" SSgt Hill quickly ran alongside the team that was struggling to keep the pilots off the ground.

The recruits sweated profusely through their uniforms. Ethan's fingers dug underneath the makeshift handle, squeezing it so tightly that his knuckles turned white.

Across from Ethan, Douglas dropped his side of the gurney as an expression of pain crossed his face.

"Keep going, guys! We got this! No one quits." Ethan, who never liked spitting out motivational phrases, yelled these words to his team, knowing they were hurting and every step they took caused more pain to their entire bodies.

"Ethan, let my team take over for you." Steve came rushing toward the struggling boys and offered to take one of the recruit's places.

SSgt Hill pushed Steve so hard that he lost balance and fell to the ground. "No! This team will carry these pilots back to the starting point. Not one person that isn't in this team will touch them!"

Steve looked up at Ethan and shook his head, giving him a nonverbal apology. He stood back up, brushed his knees off, and lifted his rifle before running ahead of Ethan's team.

A while later, Ethan noticed Douglas was barely holding onto his side anymore. This put more weight on the others, and they, too, started to drop. "Take a rest, guys. Stop right here." Ethan knew his team needed a break. They were so close. He'd bet they only had ten more minutes to go.

"You wanted to take a break. Well, let me tell you where that break has led you. The pilot with the sucking chest wound has progressed to a hemothorax. The thoracic cavity has filled with blood, causing pressure to the heart, putting the pilot in cardiac arrest and killing him. Because you wanted to feel better and catch your breath, that Marine is now dead. You also have ten more minutes to get your asses back!"

SSgt Hill had painted the picture so vividly that Ethan saw defeat mirrored in the other recruits' eyes. He had made the wrong call and now had to pay a price for it. The loss was on him, and the decision he'd made had cost the platoon that pilot. Guilt trickled over his body.

Douglas's face, flushed with exertion, stared down at what was now a dead pilot. "Let's leave him."

Ethan and the rest stared blankly at Douglas.

"I'm serious. Let's leave him. He's already dead. If we try and take him back, then we won't make it."

Everyone's mouth just dropped, and they stared in shock over the idea.

Ethan stepped in and defended the lifeless body. "Do you actually work that hard to be that dumb? You're so stuck-up, you couldn't drown in a flood. We are not leaving him!"

Ethan picked up one of the sides of the dummy and waited for the others to take the rest of the weight off the ground. As the recruits stared at the dead pilot, their eyes drifted toward the handles, and the thought of being in continuous pain kept them still. Douglas's idea became more sensible, and the only reason was because of the pain they didn't want to feel.

They all looked at the instructor, who stood next to them. His face did nothing to show whether the decision was right or wrong. That was all it took for the recruits to leave the pilot behind. They backed away from the dead body, including Douglas.

Ethan yelled at them to come back and pick him up, but they raced toward the evac point.

"Five more minutes!" SSgt Hill raised one eyebrow toward Ethan and tilted his head as he walked away.

If Ethan left now without the body, there was a good chance he could make it. No, he knew he could make it. The dummy weighed more than 150 pounds, and that was close to how much Ethan weighed. He used to be a lot heavier, but after three months of not getting enough protein and nutrition, he had lost a substantial amount of weight and muscle.

Ethan had to make a decision. He couldn't leave him behind; he didn't care if he was a dummy or not. Right or wrong, Ethan chose to take the hard way out, even if it meant not going home alive.

The security team that was behind him at the time was given orders to leave Ethan and continue to the evac point. It was Ethan and the pilot.

He grabbed his rifle and swung it over his back once more. Lifting the pilot over his back, he grabbed one leg and one hand in front and let the rest dangle. The weight was already unbearable, but Ethan pushed forward, tripping over the smaller twigs and bushes. The sun had gone down almost completely, and there was barely any light illuminating Ethan's path. He could see lots of movement in the distance between the trees. He knew he was almost there.

He tasted the sweat pouring from his forehead, and he huffed and puffed with every step he took. He was beginning to lose feeling in his hands and lower neck.

"One minute!"

It was all up to Ethan to break over that wall and push through. He heard the voices of the recruits talking and even laughing. That could have been him if he would have left the pilot.

Ethan jogged, and with every step, he picked up speed. Tears trailed from Ethan's eyes at the sheer amount of pain that tore through his legs and upper body. He questioned why he was doing this. Then he thought about the pilot and his family and friends. They would never be able to see him again. What if he had a wife and children? They deserved to see him one last time, even if it was at his funeral. He'd died protecting the country he loved. There was nothing that was going to stop Ethan from bringing him home now.

Ethan had come up with a full background for the pilot, using his imagination to bring him to life. The more Ethan humanized the dummy, the more Ethan wanted to make it. His legs pressed on even though they were numb. He thought his heart would jump out of his throat. Ethan was confident he was going to make it. At that very moment, Ethan's foot caught a branch that had fallen. He tried to break free of it, but as his body moved forward, the branch tangled about his feet. The branch had him beat. Ethan stumbled hard to the ground, taking the pilot with him.

Lying on the ground, he heard SSgt Hill approach from behind, saying, "Time! Congratulations, the pilot and you are dead!"

He then stepped back and watched as Ethan stared at the faceless pilot. But Ethan didn't see a faceless pilot. As he lay next to the dummy, he saw a man—a father of three and devoted husband to his wife. Ethan began to cry from the feeling of failure.

SSgt Hill, touched by Ethan's pain, removed his cover. He knelt down next to him and spoke in that normal voice he once had before the mission took off. "Son, what you did was suicidal and almost impossible. You carried a 150 lb dead-weight dummy a half a mile by yourself, knowing that the outcome might mean you wouldn't make it back. It's a dummy, you know…"

SSgt Hill paused a second and looked at the dummy, then back at Ethan, who wouldn't take his eyes off of it. "You didn't see a dummy at all, did you? You saw a human being, an American hero who gave his life for this great country. He deserves to be home with family, don't you think? What you did was honorable and heroic. It takes a Marine to do what you did."

With that, the tears stopped. Ethan looked at his instructor, who stood back up and placed his cover back on his head. "Get the hell up, recruit, and finish the job. I will not tell you again!"

As Ethan picked the dummy back up, he realized that the moment he'd shared with his drill instructor was rare. He knew he had made the right choice, whether he would have made it or not. What SSgt Hill taught him was that there may come a time with no chance of ever making it home, but this was the job every Marine signed up for, and it came at what might be great cost. The ultimate sacrifice.

As Ethan broke through the edge of the tree line with the pilot on his back, he made a promise that day. No matter what, he would bring all his men home, whether they were dead or alive, even if he died trying. Because that's what it meant to be a Marine.

6

A BROTHER IN ARMS

Ethan raised his heavy eyes, noticing the white streak of a sunray coming from between his legs. His vision was a little blurred, and he couldn't make out too much around him. Forgetting where he was for a moment, Ethan stretched his arms and legs. He didn't move more than a few inches before his hands and feet made contact with the coffin. His breathing became erratic as he remembered what had happened before he'd passed out.

So he wouldn't pass out again, Ethan closed his eyes and took a few deep breaths. Losing control of his body and heart rate would not do him any good. He needed to gain his composure and try to relax. He breathed like they used to teach pregnant woman while giving birth. Letting out a few breaths, he managed to chuckle in between. Even though he was in the worst of situations, never in a million years had he ever felt like he would ever have to use the Lamaze technique.

He tightly clenched his fists and held them at his sides. His toes curled, and he thought happy thoughts—thoughts of winning his high school football games and the time he'd made it to second base with Suzy Perkins during their senior prom. Ethan smiled at that one. Thinking further ahead, he pictured himself graduating boot camp and earning his Eagle, Globe, and Anchor. It gave him a proud feeling inside. After thinking these types of thoughts for an hour, Ethan realized his body had finally settled, and he opened his eyes.

As he did, he looked down and made a huge discovery. Because of the light that showed through, he could tell he wasn't wearing any clothes. Ethan whispered a defeated "shit" and calmly wiped some sweat from his chest. Being confused and in a panic, he hadn't thought of checking his pockets for a phone.

Scanning the small space, he noticed four plastic water bottles scattered on their sides near his head. In his panicked state, he must have missed them. He grabbed one of the bottles and hastily unscrewed it, dumping water into his mouth. He uncontrollably swallowed the water until he came to his senses and spit some of it back into the bottle.

"What am I doing?"

Ethan stared at the water, wanting to drink every last drop. Whoever had put him in there had added the bottles to play with him, allowing him to wither into a tormented death. Either that, or the coffin was not meant to be his final bed. He had to think wisely. If it was the latter of the two, he had no idea of the time he would spend in the coffin. He needed to ration his drinking.

He recalled a few survival classes taught to him while he had been in the Marine Corps. Rationing was no easy task, but this discipline was vital for surviving in harsh conditions. Ethan checked that box, for this most certainly qualified as a harsh condition.

Ethan thought for a moment, turning his question of how to ration into an equation. He had been given four standard 17 fl oz bottles of water. He had already drunk half of one owing to his stupidity and lack of discipline. If his kidnappers were smart and specifically gave him four, then they knew how many he would need to survive.

He had to err on the side of caution, believing that his time trapped in there might surpass the supply of water given. Ethan knew the average intake for a human was 32 oz of water daily. He had been given 68 oz of water altogether. In class, they had been taught that you could go a month with no food and seven days with no water. This water was important. Since they did not give him any food, he had to predict that he would be staying in there for at least that long, yet he hoped that wasn't the case. If he was able to maintain his discipline and self-control, each bottle of water could last him at least one seven-day interval.

The temperature was not unbearable, but it was hot enough for him to have trouble breathing normally.

Ethan had another thought. "How on earth do I go to the bathroom?"

Suddenly, he saw why there was light. He reached under his butt and felt a small hole. It was no bigger than the diameter of a coffee mug. So, the idea was that he must be higher than the ground and hung on a trailer of some sort.

"Is this how I'm supposed to shit and piss? This can't be happening."

The coffin was too small for him to try and switch sides so that he could see out the hole. He wanted to get a glimpse of where he was—some kind of idea, at least.

He tried to estimate the time he'd been in the coffin, but he could only tell that it was the middle of the day. He also could feel that he had been in the same position for a very long time. His arms and legs were beginning to cramp, and he very much wanted to move.

Since he knew that at some point, he was going to have to take a piss, he decided to attempt to turn around onto his stomach and see if he could do it without hurting himself or his jewels.

He reached over his stomach with his right arm and squished it under his left side. While doing so, he took his right leg and did the same. With one small movement, he turned around until his face was down, and his junk was thankfully fit snugly in the hole. Within a matter of seconds, he had drained his bladder. He didn't have the desire to go, but it just came out. As he pissed, he could hear his stream splatter hitting a solid object. He was becoming more aware of his surroundings. He knew that he had to be somewhat close to the floor. But he still couldn't make out where he was.

After a while of being face down, Ethan felt uncomfortable and decided to roll back over. It was much easier to roll to his back than the other way.

As Ethan rolled over, he noticed that his right arm was sore on the inside of his elbow. He pushed his body back so more light shined through. He barely made out a tiny red ring located over one of his bigger veins. "So, it looks like I was drugged to get me inside this cozy little coffin, awesome." It seemed as though the people who'd kidnapped him had thought a lot about the process.

Once Ethan had flipped on his back, his stomach growled and twisted. He tried to remember the last time he'd eaten. With everything that had happened, the last thing to cross his mind was food. However, now that Ethan could control his breathing, whenever another claustrophobic feeling attacked him, he'd close his eyes and think of happy thoughts. He had become more comfortable in the coffin. He didn't have a choice.

Ethan grabbed his stomach and pictured the delicious shrimp Alfredo his mom used to make with the big wet noodles and the Alfredo sauce that tasted like heaven. He wouldn't mind a medium-rare juicy steak or even some hot pizza. Ethan licked his dry lips. He couldn't bear to think of food anymore. He had to distract himself from feeling the emptiness in his stomach. He turned to his right and reached for his water, hoping to fill his stomach, but he stopped, knowing he couldn't give in to this temptation.

Ethan thought of the five W's to help him understand the situation. That should take his mind off dreaming of food or reaching for his water to satiate the hunger. He was curious as to the reason why he lay in a coffin, dying of hunger, completely nude.

No one would go as far as this to get back at Ethan for something that he had done. Ethan hadn't really interacted with anyone ever since leaving the Corps. No one, not even Tyler, would stoop this low to play a joke on him. Even as a joke, this was way too much. Ethan waited for someone to take the lid off the coffin and yell, "We got ya good!" But there was no surprise party.

Ethan thought of reasons why someone would kidnap him. So, he might have cut a few people off while driving or been in a few fistfights. Those were not good enough reasons to be put in a coffin and forced to piss out of a little hole. Sex trafficking passed through Ethan's thoughts.

"I'm stuck like a sardine and going to be put on display for someone to buy me, great. Hope they don't make me wear a dress if that's the case."

Trying to make light of the situation, Ethan went into a list of reasons he would make a horrible sex slave.

Hours went by, and Ethan suffered from hunger and boredom. The sun's rays had slowly faded and barely gave Ethan any light to see his feet in front of him. He attempted to hum familiar songs because he was horrible at remembering any of the lyrics. The only songs he could remember were "Bohemian Rhapsody" by Queen and little children's nursery rhymes.

As he continued to hold his stomach, Ethan quickly stopped humming, and his eyes became wide as his bowels made an alarming sound. The sound warned Ethan that his body would give way at a very quick pace. Ethan began to sweat and clenched his butt cheeks together. The hole wasn't big enough, and he knew that if he had any ounce of shit land in the coffin, then he would have to lie in it. Dealing with the smell was not on his to-do list at the moment. He couldn't possibly be able to lie in a tight space and handle the stench. His intestines growled in rebellion.

It wants to come out now, but what about the shit that does stay? These guys didn't provide any toilet paper for me, which means I'll be lying like a little baby boy with a mad rash.

He knew he had no choice but to give way because holding it in would be miserable and unbearable.

Ethan prepared himself for the next problem he had to endure in the box. He figured that it would be more watered down because of the drugs. It's possible that his body was trying to flush it all out, but this would also make him more dehydrated as well.

He felt for the hole and placed his butt directly over the top. He had to estimate where it would come out, knowing that if he pressed too hard, the crap would fly past the hole and back into the box. He steadied his body and pressed his feet against the base of the box, allowing his body to arch from his lower back and lift slightly so he had more room to drop his bomb. He then grabbed his butt cheeks, spreading them as far as he could so there was a lower chance of crap being stuck on him. He had no idea how long he would be in the box.

Ethan sweat as his cramps worsened, and heat swallowed the entire coffin. He couldn't hold it in any longer. He strained a few times and finally released everything he had.

To his surprise, the first wave came out very solid, and his aim seemed to have been right on target. He heard a thud as the stool made its way from him and through the hole. He was surely close to the ground. Two or three more times this reoccurred before the seizing cramps stopped.

He felt relieved as his body slumped. It had been difficult keeping his body in the air, but he felt a little bit of accomplishment—and also a little sense of ridiculousness—because of the situation he had just been put in.

During the time he'd spent dealing with the unforeseen challenge, Ethan had forgotten all about being in a box and the primary problem he endured. It had given him something else to think about. Now that the challenge was gone, the thought of being stuck in a box raised his blood pressure again.

He hummed songs and thought of anything to stay away from the thought of being claustrophobic.

After a while, he ran out of songs and replayed them. After what seemed like hours, it was starting to lose its calming effect. He actually wished he had to move his bowels or piss again so he would have something to do. He needed to come up with something else to take his mind away from going insane or raising his blood pressure.

Ethan got frustrated and hit the side of the box, which made a huge thudding sound. He perked up and came up with a brilliant idea.

With his right fist, he hit the box twice in a rhythmic order, followed by a slap with his left hand. He made a flow of drumbeats, using his right hand for the bass and left for the snare. He moved his head to the music that he created, sometimes adding beat boxing and trying to rap as well. He was so into the new idea that he was getting pretty good at it. He even heard extra beats he didn't know he was making.

Ethan lost himself in the music, forgetting about his jail cell. He built toward a crescendo, creating a loud drum roll before smacking the side of the box, ending on a cymbal crash created by his mouth.

Boom!

Ethan was startled. Did he just do that?

He had been playing for so long that there was no longer light shining through the hole. Maybe he'd accidentally hit the floor without realizing it. After all, he had been playing for a while.

Boom boom.

Fear rushed through his bones. He looked down, even though he couldn't see. His hands were folded together. He heard the noise again. It was a faded thud coming from outside.

Ethan waited in shocked silence for a minute. He balled his fist and made a similar noise twice.

He waited…nothing. He did it once more, nothing.

Was he just hearing things? Then out of the nowhere, the two booms happened once more.

Boom. Boom! Excitedly, he replied back to the mysterious noise. This went on for another minute or so.

There was someone else out there! He wasn't alone. They must have heard all of his drumming, and he was too busy to notice the person trying to reply back.

He smiled and hit the box once more, hoping for a reply. Again, the boom sounded, and Ethan kept responding back to the sounds.

An idea popped into his head. If they can hear my hits, then maybe they can hear me speak. After the mysterious noise replied back, he didn't hit the box but instead spoke. "Hello..." He said it again but louder. "Hello!"

Still no reply.

Ethan tried once more with a shout.

"Look, man, the drumming was fine. But screaming like that might get us in trouble. Just keep 'er down a smidge."

Ethan's eyes widened with joy and shock. "You can hear me?" he asked.

"Uh, yeah. I mean it's not pure as water, which I really need to stop slurping from these bottles. But yeah, I can hear ya."

There were so many questions that he wanted to ask this stranger, but fear made him wonder if it was an interrogation technique. He would approach with caution.

"So, where are you?" he asked.

"Welp, from the looks of this spacious and luxurious room, I'd say I'm in a cozy little coffin. Could have a little bit better accommodations, but I won't complain, he-he."

Ethan heard a muffled country accent coming from the stranger, and he figured this person had to be from the South. "Are you from America?" he asked.

"Sure am, come from good old Houston, Texas."

"And were you kidnapped just like me?"

"No, sir. Looked up 'fun vacations' online and booked this trip as soon as I saw it. Yeah, I was frikin' kidnapped!"

Ethan heard the sarcasm coming from the stranger's voice. He wasn't getting too many questions from the stranger, so he felt it was safe enough to at least swap names. "My name's Ethan, yours?"

"Trent."

"Well, Trent, do you have any idea what's going on?"

"I have a faint idea what might have happened to me. Last place I was at was the 'Chicken Coop,' a good country bar where I was having some drinks with the boys and checking out the gals. But unfortunately, I don't remember too much of it. Someone must have spiked my drink because I was passed out after three beers. And let me tell you, I can hold my liquor."

"Yeah, similar situation except I was knocked unconscious. Hey, do you have a sore around your vein in either arm?" Ethan waited a minute or two before Trent replied.

"Well, looky her', I was frikin' drugged. What the hell?!" Trent said with shock.

"Yeah, looks like that was the only way to get us into these boxes," Ethan replied. "I've been thinking it has to be a terrorist group. Taliban, Al-Qaeda, Boko Haram that are more located in Africa. I could go on for a while, but I was thinking of the ones that love the media and would do something extreme like—"

"Those frikin' goat humpers. My gosh, you're right!" Trent screamed. "ISIS just can't quit, can they? What are they up to?"

"My guess is they want to do what they always do. Kill Americans." When Ethan said that, he wasn't struck with fear. He had dealt with them before and had had enough of them. He guessed this was inevitable. If anything was to come of this, it would be a way to get back at them for everything they had done. Rage rose up his spine.

"But what in tarnation makes us so special?" Trent interrupted Ethan's thoughts.

They discussed their situations leading up to the moment they'd passed out. Ethan told what he could remember of the clouded figures with beards. Trent said he recalled a similar scene outside of the bar. It was all coming together and making perfect sense. But the information of who they were and how ISIS knew to look for them in those places stumped both Ethan and Trent.

"The pricks are probably mad that I blew their buddies up in the air, he-he. I loved watering the grass with their own blood!"

Ethan was shocked." Wait…say that again?"

"I'm saying when I was flying for the Air Force, I was blessed with plenty of opportunities to let those bastards see their insides." Trent laughed.

"Trent, I was in the Marine Corps Infantry. Do you think that perhaps they targeted us because we have fought them and now, they want revenge?" Ethan's revelation had opened up a whole new story addressing this huge question mark, bringing him closer to finding out the truth of why they were in coffins.

"Well, kick my boots! Look at that, we got a rodent from the ground! Y'all are pretty cool. Afghanistan, I'm guessing?"

"Yeah, same for you?" Ethan asked.

"Yes, sir, got out last year. I had enough of being shot at. Doesn't matter if I was in the air or not. Besides, I have a family that I would like to be a part of for a couple of long years. Got a nice smoking-hot wife and a baby girl who just turned one last month. This is a pretty shitty situation. Gosh, I miss 'em." Ethan could hear the tone of disappointment and sadness coming from Trent.

"Don't worry, man, we'll get out of this. Can't be that bad; we've been in worse." Ethan tried to cheer the conversation up and steer Trent away from any bad thoughts.

Ethan had a good feeling about Trent, confident that he was really in a coffin next to him and stuck in the same situation. Ethan had probably gone a day or so without talking to anyone, and he needed someone, even though he loved isolation. But this was the kind of isolation he didn't want.

Ethan asked Trent about his family, and Trent told Ethan stories of how he'd met Devon, his wife, and how they came to have their daughter Stephanie.

Ethan and Trent talked for what seemed like hours before they both were too tired to speak anymore.

"Look her', man, I got to get some rest. Even if I'm in this uncomfortable chest, my body is tired. You're an all right dude, you know that? We'll pick up tomorrow and figure out more of where we are and why we're here." With that, both of them turned in for the night.

Ethan, for the first time since he'd found himself in the coffin, felt some hope. But he didn't have any idea what lay ahead of him. For some odd reason, he was more awake. Not in the sense of a caffeine rush, but it was more like energy that he hadn't felt in a long time. He hummed "Amazing Grace" before drifting off to sleep.

7

IN THE BELLY
OF THE WHALE

The next few weeks, both Ethan and Trent spent most of their time talking about their lives in the military. What was odd for Ethan was that he couldn't believe the amount of openness he had with Trent. Back home, it had been different not being able to be next to another veteran. Maybe this was what he needed after all.

Of course, taking away the coffin and the kidnapping would have been much more preferred. However, Ethan knew what he was doing was venting to Trent. Even if Trent didn't know it, Ethan was happy in a weird sort of way. He had made a friend who knew something of his life from his own personal experience. He was entrusting Trent with a deeper level of himself, even though he had never met him or seen his face. It didn't take away the pain and regret of his past, but it seemed to mend it just enough for him to keep on moving. The longer he was able to keep his mind distracted, the less his thoughts wandered toward insanity. The two prisoners were keeping each other alive. If they were to stop their discussions, Ethan was afraid of losing the battle in his mind, which would result in death, meaning the coffin could end up his actual coffin.

Ethan figured that if ISIS were truly behind this, they would have more important plans for them than just keeping them in a box to rot. Although dying in a box was probably better and more merciful than what might be done to them outside of it.

But what were they waiting for? Why keep us stored in coffins? Ethan often thought to himself.

One thing was for sure. Every minute that went by was draining Ethan's energy and strength. He could feel that he had weakened a tremendous amount. But making light of the whole thing was something Ethan and Trent had been great at the past few days.

Ethan's skin, although he couldn't see it, was as thin as parchment paper, and any laceration in general would plague him in its inability to heal. He wondered how much weight he had lost. His strength had also dwindled as his muscles struggled to assist in any movement. Ethan had to shift his body to different sides every so often so his bed sores, which had developed after the first week, would not become severe. Ethan had to avoid the temptation to pour any bit of water on them to cool off the burning sensation of the sores. Although it was painful to move, it helped alleviate small panic attacks that would arise because he wasn't able to sit up. He had to keep focus on his breathing and on Trent. The two would stay up for hours on end, talking about their childhoods, their first crushes, and drunken mistakes.

"No shit, I was driving, and my friend was absolutely drunk hanging his head out the passenger window. I had another buddy in the back just tired and wanting to go home. Going sixty down the highway with a drunk man isn't the brightest idea. Especially if it's your own car." Ethan chuckled as he was finishing his story. "My buddy ended up puking out the window for what seemed like forever. But then I heard a disgusted moan in the back. I turned my head, still trying to keep one eye on the road, to see my buddy in the back with puke all over his shirt and a little that had flown in his mouth. I guess it's not smart to drive sixty miles per hour while someone is puking out the window. It just flies to the back of the car. I never let anyone smoke, but that time, I made an exception for my friend!" After finishing the story, Ethan heard Trent crying with laughter.

"Brother, that is a hilarious story. Well done on making me laugh while in the shittiest of situations."

Ethan was full of stories from his past. Marines were well known for their aggressive style and personalities that were exceptionally dark. At the time, it wasn't at all funny or exciting, but looking back afterward, it provided stories to tell while killing time.

They had guessed they were toward the end of their third week in the coffins. They also didn't know how long they had been out while drugged. Ethan supposed that Trent might have been out longer. This was because Trent had woken up and immediately heard Ethan's drumbeats. Also, it was possible that since Trent was from Texas, he had been sent to North Carolina, causing him to be drugged more than Ethan. But it was a guess.

His desire for food had left him after the first week, and his eyes only lay on his bottles of water. Thinking of food instead would make Ethan's stomach more upset. The two men would avoid talking about their mother's homemade dishes, or any talk of food for that matter. Their mouths were dry from dehydration. Ethan was now down to his very last bottle of water. He had only a few sips left. There was no way of knowing if they were going to survive once the water ran out.

"Hey, Trent, how much water you have left?"

"I, uh, finished two days ago. I couldn't help myself. I didn't want to say anything." Ethan could now hear Trent's words as raspy and faint. He was beginning to become despondent.

"Just hang in there. Any time now, we'll be out of these

boxes, and I can meet your ugly mug for the first time. Can't say I'm too excited about it."

Ethan could hear Trent work up a small chuckle followed by a few short coughs from his fun banter. He tried to keep Trent occupied and awake, having any discussions he could think of. The truth was clear, and Ethan knew there was not much time for his friend or him as well.

Drinking your own piss was an idea that came up in conversation, but to do that was impossible in the coffins they were in.

Trent had said, "You would have to have enough to shoot out like a water fountain and have perfect aim."

The faint light coming from the hole shined through the bottle that Ethan held. He stared at the last remaining drops of water, knowing it would give him a couple of days left. His body had deteriorated, and sometimes he could not form complete sentences. He tried to stay strong for Trent, but he struggled to stay awake, afraid that if he closed his eyes, it would be forever.

He unscrewed the cap from the bottle and lifted it to his dried lips. As the water touched his lips and moistened his mouth, only one droplet had managed to reach his throat, giving him one final comfort. That was it.

A few hours had gone by, and the two had stopped talking but would slam a fist into the side of the wood and wait for the other to respond, letting the other know they were still awake. They needed to conserve every ounce of energy, including not talking. Ethan heard a low rumble sound as if someone was rolling a bowling ball, but the sound was faint.

"Hey, Ethan, did you hear that?" Trent asked.

"Yeah…yeah, I did. Is that what I think it was?"

"I've heard that plenty of times. That there was thunder." Trent managed to say with surprise.

Ethan wasn't confused that there was thunder. He knew they were outside from the sunlight, but something about the thunder was off. It could be because he was in a wooden coffin, and it muffled the sound. But Ethan couldn't quite put his finger on it.

"Hey, Ethan, ya think we might be able to grab some water if it rains and seeps through this wood?" Trent hoped.

"I'm going to be completely honest with you, Trent. This is some kind of strong cedar, and I really don't see it happening. With the thickness of it, water won't get through."

"I was afraid you were going to say that," Trent said with disappointment.

Ethan heard raindrops hitting the top of his coffin. The thunder became louder, and even cracks of lightning chimed in. He became excited that something new was happening. However, he had trouble hearing Trent.

"Ethan, brother. I ain't feelin too great."

The raindrops had gone from little ticks on the coffins to loud thuds.

"What do you mean, Trent?" Ethan fought to hear him over the rain drops.

"I mean I got a funny taste in my mouth, and I'm all cold. Need to light a fire in here or somethin'. My head is spinnin' like I got a bull tryin' ta kick me off."

The sun had completely gone away from the hole between Ethan's legs, and only shots of white light revealed itself when the lightning struck, followed quickly by a loud crack of thunder. Hearing Trent now was almost impossible.

Ethan leaned his right ear against the wood, trying to hear if Trent spoke to him. He heard noises from Trent's direction. They sounded like he was beating the side of his coffin. He called out to Trent, but the same sounds kept coming.

Ethan realized that Trent wasn't trying to get ahold of him. He recalled what Trent had said earlier about not feeling well and having a funny taste in his mouth. He had seen this plenty of times while he was deployed when his boys wouldn't drink enough water. It was dehydration. Trent was having a seizure.

"Trent...Trent!"

Ethan's only friend wasn't responding, but he heard shouts of commands from a distance. They were muffled, but they also were not English. A number of voices were responding to each other.

Ethan banged on the coffin, yelling and screaming. "Hey! Hey! We're in here! We're in here! Help...Help us, please. He's having a seizure!" Ethan screamed with all his might, trying to yell over the thunder.

Voices got closer as he continued to scream for help. "Trent! Yell for them," Ethan pleaded.

He received no response from Trent or the mysterious voices. His own voice weakened and became raspy from the exertion of yelling. Ethan, fighting over the sound of the rain, slammed the side of the box and screamed with barely a voice left. The men were right on top of him.

With no warning, Ethan felt his box move and shift, and people around him were screaming. Objects were hitting the sides and the top. Ethan, with little voice left, kept calling for them, but it was no use. These people were in a rush for reasons unknown to him.

He gave all his energy into three last slaps of the box until he stopped. His hands were numb, and his throat burned. It hurt to swallow.

The box stopped moving, and the voices were gone.

If they didn't help, then they had to have been the people who put me in here. They knew we were here.

Then Ethan remembered Trent. But the rain came down hard, and there was no way to reach him. He had no voice left. His mind felt like it moved at a million miles, and he didn't know what to focus on. Until something pushed his body from the center of the box to the right side. The impact caused his bedsores to feel like they were on fire, and he yelped in pain.

An invisible force moved Ethan from one side of the box to

the other. Confused, he shifted himself to the center.

Are the people back? Ethan thought to himself.

A crack of lightning struck, and Ethan felt the thunder as if it were right on top of him. As though he were in the middle of a car accident, his entire body slammed to the right side and then launched to the top of the coffin.

What the heck is going on?

Ethan concentrated really hard. Again, he was shoved back and forth. For a brief moment, there was silence between the cracks of thunder, and Ethan heard the crash of waves.

"We're on a boat."

8

DEFIANCE

Ethan awoke to the sound of nails being taken out of wood in the distance. Men shouted, their tone both directing and demanding. Ethan listened closely and knew it wasn't English, but he also didn't know what language they spoke. He could only assume that whoever had taken him had reached their final destination.

Ethan wondered how long he had been out from the fierce storm. He couldn't tell the time, but by the look of the hole, it was daylight.

He had no chance of fighting his way out of what seemed to be almost a month in the small enclosed box. He was thirsty and weak. His lips were chapped, dry, and filled with pain. He just lay on his back, staring at the wood and waiting to be next. All he craved was pure water.

The sounds of the men and wood being broken were getting closer. He was finally going to meet the ones who had kidnapped him. At this point, he was no longer scared or nervous. His body had given up.

With no warning, a loud noise sounded. Ethan felt his coffin being raised and dropped with a big bang. He heard a screeching sound as the nails were ripped apart from the enclosure. The top came off, and he was suddenly blinded by a bright light. His eyes immediately shut, but the light still burned through his eyelids. He attempted to cover them with his arms, but his body lay there motionless.

Both of his arms were grabbed by strong, firm hands. The amount of force from being lifted pushed back his head, giving him whiplash. He was thrown over the coffin and slammed on his stomach with shouts above him. The impact was hard against Ethan's knees and arms. It felt like rustic metal, which was not forgiving. The shouts became angrier, and he could only assume they wanted him to get up. Eyelids still closed, Ethan tried with all his might to push up, but it was no use.

"Astayqiz! Astayqiz!"

It was the first time Ethan had heard their language clearly. He looked over and saw a small patch hanging half out of the guard's pocket that showed a black flag with Arabic symbols. His body filled with shock as his prediction became true. The guard saw what he was looking at and tucked the small patch back into his pocket. Ethan knew exactly who they were.

They lifted him aggressively, and after getting his footing, he slowly opened his eyes. His body felt like a brick, and all his bones were concrete. He was so stiff, he couldn't bring his hands over his eyes to block out the sun. His arms just stayed to his side.

It was hot and very humid. Even though Ethan was still naked, he could feel the heat covering his entire body. Sweat dripped profusely down his forehead and arms. The humidity was thick enough to use a knife and cut a nice chunk of it. His body needed time to adapt to the new climate.

His vision was blurry as his eyes adapted to the light, but he could see a black figure in front of him with what seemed to be a white turban on top of the figure's head.

He looked around a little more, squinting at the nearby structure. Frames of beams were side by side, keeping around five coffins each in three layers. Straps were placed across some of the coffins that were still hoisted on them. It looked like they were all strapped in pretty well. Ethan saw more blurry figures unstrapping the coffin next to him and lift it off the shelf before slamming it down. Ethan wondered if Trent was in that one.

Trent! Was he dead or alive?

The last time Ethan had made contact with him was right before the storm broke out. He could only assume that Trent had passed out after his seizure. Ethan attempted to look at the coffin being taken apart to see if the body in the coffin was still moving or if the coffin was his final resting place.

Ethan was given a harsh push and, attempting to maintain his balance with his noodled legs, he grabbed ahold of the person in front of him—another guard who was keeping watch, most likely. He was immediately struck in the gut by the gun the guard held. Ethan fell to his knees.

"All right! Give me a break."

Ethan continued to look at the ground, trying to catch his breath. A boot stepped left of his face. Ethan raised one arm in defeat, then he realized he had a little more mobility in his arms. He brought down his arm, taking a second to contemplate an idea.

"Get up!" The guard nudged Ethan with his boot.

Oh, they speak some English too, thought Ethan to himself.

He waited for the guard to bend down to grab his arm before taking one pathetic swing at him. The guard stepped back from the slow-motion swing, hitting Ethan in the back with his gun and chuckling.

Ethan stumbled a few steps, only to be stopped by a rail. The top half of his body slumped over the rail, and he saw dark blue water pressed against the side of a dirty white ship. He looked to the right to see the ship had levels. On the other levels were livestock sticking their heads out from the side. Mostly sheep and pigs were among the livestock that he noticed. The wood he was in must have been so thick that even the animals' smell didn't reach his nose. That made sense how his captors were able to smuggle him and the others across the ocean without being questioned.

Ethan faced ahead, seeing a coast of smooth dark sand following gigantic rocky cliffs that ran along the coast for miles. He thought it was a smaller version of the Grand Canyon. It was so beautiful with the waves crashing upon the sand and the sun attacking the side of the cliff from an angle, allowing the view to be captivating. As he scrutinized the beauty in the worst of times there was a certain spot that stood out for him. It was a crevice in the cliff that ran as a switchback road all the way up to the top. He calculated it would take a good two to three miles of walking just to make it up the steep hill.

As he stared further out along the coast, he saw part of a building with two pillars. On the tip of the pillars were two round balls reflecting a beam of white light from the sun. He couldn't make out any more of the building's features other than the two pillars. Ethan was still trying to figure out what country he was in, but he had an idea. Immediately, he was grabbed by the neck and thrown backward.

He was turned around by the guard who had hit him not too long ago. Ethan looked past him and saw human skeletons. Their skin was gauntly stretched over their bones and riddled by sores and scrapes. Ethan could count every rib on the prisoners. Some were barely able to stand, while others were lying on the ground, lifeless. Each one looked as though they were dead mummies walking among the living.

Is this what I look like?

There was yelling coming from beyond the few coffins ahead of Ethan. He saw a man who was refusing to move forward from the commands of one of the guards. He looked young and afraid, and he panicked, flailing with what strength he had left in his arms. The guard came closer to him, shouting louder than before as he lost his patience.

Ethan stared, wondering how it would play out. He saw absolute hopelessness in the young man's eyes as he looked from the guard to the water. Ethan took a weakened step forward, knowing what the other man was going to do. The man took one leap, only managing to get half his body over the railing. He allowed the rest to follow from his weight as he dropped to the murky water below.

In shock, some of the others moved toward the railing to see the man attempting to swim with all his might. He slapped the water only a few times, allowing himself to stay afloat. Within a few moments, the man was pulled under as a current took him to his final resting place.

Ethan could only stare as he witnessed a choice of death rather than more suffering. He felt the railing under his weak hands, and he had a moment to take the dive as well. It was his chance to end any more suffering that would come to him. For a brief moment, it felt heavenly. He had a choice. He pressed down, feeling his body raise only inches when a hand grabbed his arm before any more thought could come of it. He was yanked away from the railing to face the same guard who had lifted him from his coffin.

He looked straight at the man, and with a sarcastic smirk, he said, "Hey! Don't I know you? Oh, yeah, that's right, I killed a lot of you goat lovers."

Ethan saw the figure bring his butt stock over his head.

He let out a sigh of regret, "Shi…" Ethan was hit in the head and lost consciousness…again.

Ethan crept on his knees, passing bunk after bunk. He had to take each step carefully, afraid that any careless movement could create a loud enough sound to be heard.

Steve was right behind him in the same kneeling position, looking behind to see if anyone had come into the hut. All Steve could see was a couple Marine heads peeking in from the door. He couldn't tell which heads were which because they were all silhouetted. Curious, they too wanted to see the outcome.

Sweat dripped down Ethan's forehead and around his eyes, making its way to his lips. He dared not wipe it away. Time was of the essence, and if he was going to complete this mission, he had to do it quickly.

Steve held an orange extension cord. He quietly pulled it in front of him, leaving around two feet of length for Ethan. The cord ran all the way to the door next to the peeping Marines. Ethan continued to crawl, holding the weighted object in his right hand. The cord attached to it made it difficult to maneuver with stealth, but he knew Steve was giving him enough slack to work with.

Suddenly, Ethan halted next to a bunk that had a strange noise coming from on top of the bed.

"Sounds like a damn wildebeest gasping for air!" Steve whispered, struggling to hold his laughter.

Ethan brought his finger to his mouth, gesturing for Steve to hush. Ethan waved Steve around him and met him at the edge of the bed on the other side. Once both boys were set on each side of the bunk, they slowly raised their heads above the top of the bed. Their noses rested flushed against the green quilt. They looked at Douglas Woods, the one and only orange haired, freckled Marine.

He was completely passed out and roaring like a lion.

Steve and Ethan looked at each other. Steve gave him a nod. Ethan nodded back and raised the hair clippers. One of the Marines giggled behind them as they watched the entire situation unfold. Steve glanced sternly at the door, even though he couldn't make out any faces or who had giggled in the first place.

Ethan turned on the clippers, which made a loud vibrating

noise. Everyone in the room held their breath as Douglas moved only an inch or so to readjust. The Marines in the back had moved even closer to get a better look. After a moment of total quiet, everyone let out a sigh of relief.

Ethan looked down for a moment to gain his composure and realized that the snoring had stopped. He looked up at Douglas, who still lay there but stared directly at Ethan, his eyes wide open. Both faces turned to surprise before Douglas made any sudden moves.

Steve jumped on him, holding him down. "Go, Ethan! Do it now!"

Ethan didn't hesitate, grabbing a huge chunk of Douglas's orange curly hair and running the clippers straight through it, leaving one long airstrip of a bald lane. Ethan held the victory handful of hair in the air. The Marines in the back cheered and screamed.

"You're dead, Ethan!" Douglas elbowed Steve in the face and knocked him backward, then jumped for Ethan.

Ethan dropped the clippers and the handful of hair and darted for the exit. He turned his head around to see if Douglas had gained on him, but he was still trying to put on his pants, mumbling and grumbling about chopping Ethan into a billion pieces. Ethan slowed down, making his way through the exit as he slapped all the Marines' hands who had witnessed him take on such a daring feat.

Ethan got cocky and brought his hands out wide in the shape of a T and faced his palms up in the air as if asking for all the glory in the world.

At that moment, Douglas surprise-tackled him from behind, his pants half on. "I'm so sick of your games, you prick!" Douglas wailed on Ethan, who kept his head covered by using his arms to protect his head from being beaten in.

The Marines crowded around the two boys wrestling in the sand, yelling and cheering them on.

After a minute or two of fighting, an officer emerged from the group, wearing digital desert camouflage. The cheering quickly faded away.

The officer stood silently for a moment, watching the two grapple each other. "That is enough!" The officer placed his hands behind his back, taking a breath to compose himself. "Cpl Miller, I will never understand why you think pranks and fighting in this godforsaken country are the answer to your boredom. Afghanistan is a place of fighting and shenanigans all on its own, and here you are creating more of it."

First Lieutenant Smith was Ethan's platoon officer in charge of him and thirty other Marines.

Lt. Smith was a thinner man compared to other lieutenants, but his physical fitness was astounding. He could outrun anyone in the entire battalion. His squared jawline was always clean shaven, and he had more of a country look about him. His smile drove all the girls to drool over him, and he knew it. But when it came to work, his ethic was second to none.

"Grab the other squad leaders and meet me in the OCC at 1600. We have a briefing to go over." Lt. Smith shook his head and turned around.

The circle opened a hole for him to leave, and the energy of the fight died. Everyone went back to their own huts, and Douglas finally had a moment to pull up his pants.

"You're a piece of shit, Miller, you know that? You're going to regret this, I promise you."

Ethan just smiled at Douglas's comment and walked away, meeting up with Steve, who had grabbed an ice-cold soda to place on his jaw.

"How's the jaw feelin?" Ethan got a close glance at it, noticing that it was going to bruise like a peach. "It's not as bad as I thought it was going to be. At least mine will heal in about a day or two. Dougy boy has to wait an entire month before his wound grows back!"

Both boys laughed and went to their can, leaning against it outside.

They paused for a moment and looked over the entire base. Camp Dwyer was a dry and desolate place, its perimeter protected by a chain of huge bags filled with sand and wire. Twenty clicks in the distance were mountains and more sand. The cans were mostly where the Marines would hang out when they weren't on patrol or guarding the base, and most of them would just sleep the entire time they were off. They called their huts 'cans' because it literally looked as if someone had cut half a can of corn and stuck it in the ground, making it thirty times bigger. No one really minded the can, but it was a burning sauna in the daytime.

"Can you believe that we've been here almost ten months and within three weeks, we're finally going to go home?"

Ethan thought on Steve's words for a bit. They had been fighting ISIS for such a long time, he was tired and excited to go home. But he didn't want that to blind him from the rest of the work they still had to do. Ethan took a deep breath and looked at Steve. "As far as I'm concerned, we still have a lot more work to do, and I expect to stay here till it's done and over with."

Steve grunted while stepping out from the can and facing Ethan. "Bro, did you hear me? We get to leave in three weeks! We get to go home and see our families, drink as much beer as we want, and enjoy the freedom we so willingly fought for!"

With that, Ethan grabbed the soda Steve held and popped it open, taking a long drink. After he chugged it, he took a relaxing gasp and handed it back to Steve. "And that's what scares me."

Steve, now holding the soda, was left speechless with his jaw wide open.

Ethan retreated back into the scalding hut to get changed for the briefing.

9

IN THE SHADOW
OF ENEMIES

Ethan awoke with a massive headache, and a jolt of pain
ran from his head to his feet. There was a lot of tension in
his neck. He attempted to massage it, but his hand would
not move. He tried to move another part of his body. No luck.
Gaining more feeling, he realized his body was swinging from
left to right. He felt nauseous.

Opening his eyes, he was greeted by a starry night sky. He
chuckled to himself, *A change of scenery for once.* He was shivering from the cold, and every hair on his body stood at attention.
Ethan felt pain in his wrists and ankles. As his eyes widened, he
saw a naked figure upside down walking, his butt close to his
face. Confused and disgusted, he gained his bearing and noticed
his head was hanging. He slowly raised it and looked down at his
thin body, finally understanding where all the pain came from.

A rope bound Ethan's hands and feet around a pole, and the
naked man he'd already met carried him—or at least, he'd met
his behind. A man by his feet was naked as well. He couldn't see
many details because it was almost completely dark.

"Ah, nuts." Ethan moaned as he dropped his head in frustration.

"Nuts is right. This is not how I pictured officially meetin' you." A soft whispered voice came from the man holding the pole by his feet.

Ethan raised his head, thinking hard about the voice he'd just heard. He had heard it before and quickly pieced it together. "Trent?" Ethan shouted with excitement.

"Shh. Keep it down or we gonna get caught, and I plan on survivin' just a few more days, so hush your voice." Trent bent his legs and shot up, pushing the pole above his head and setting it down on the other side of his shoulder.

"I'll tell ya what. If it ain't your body weight that's heavy, then it surely are them nuts of yours." Trent laughed as he let out a painful breath.

Trent's voice had a masculine Southern drawl that was pure yet rugged at the end of every word. It was different than the muffled voice he was used to. Ethan was glad that he had survived the coffin and seizure.

"I see you survived your cruise. Where are we now?" Ethan whispered as he looked around.

"Well…I was being lifted out of my box when you caused an uproar. Quite a sight to see, he-he. After you were knocked out, they grabbed another man and tied our hands on the end of this here pole. Getting on the small boats to get to shore was quite an experience with you attached to us. They gave us a little bit of water and bread once we had reached shore. Unfortunately, you being unconscious, they didn't bother. After that, we had a long hike up the cliff in one long single-file line. Now we're here, walking on some hilly path. There are around twenty of us prisoners and between every eight or so are two guards, one on each side. So far I've only seen them with AKs." Trent was still trying to keep his voice down, so they didn't get caught.

"Can we take them?" Ethan asked.

"If you have any bright ideas or a knife to cut off these ropes from our hands, I'm all ears. Until then you just hang there like a pig being prepped for roastin'." Trent breathed heavily again.

Ethan could tell he was tired, and he felt guilty for having him carry the pole and the extra weight. He wondered where Trent got the strength.

"Have any idea where they are taking us?" Ethan whispered, struggling as he tried to break free from the rope tied to his wrists.

The man carrying him from the front chimed in, his tone aggressive and rude. "Boy, you better shut your mouth unless you want to be the next one to get an early release to eternal damnation. These men are working for ISIS. They have the wardrobe to prove it and the language to confirm it." The man had an older but higher-pitched voice. He didn't bother to whisper.

"How many died?" Ethan questioned.

Trent sucked in a lot of air before answering. "A few so far. Most of them didn't even make it out of their coffins. One even jumped overboard once he was out of the coffin. Tried to swim to shore, but he didn't make no more than a few yards before he couldn't find the strength in his body. Sank faster than a 500-pound anchor. He didn't have a chance."

Ethan lowered his head as he played the scene over.

"Lord knows we have done something to deserve this. We've sinned, and we are paying the consequences. You just shut up and hang on to your first-class ride to hell." The strange man raised his voice even higher than before, causing one of the guards up front to yell.

Ethan lowered his neck again to see a black figure pointing to another guard to check on him.

"Abu." The black figure doing the pointing yelled to grab the guard's attention.

Hearing his name, a guard turned his head to find a finger pointing toward Ethan. Abu nodded and left his current spot.

"Mahlaan! 'Iinah mustayquiz!" Abu noticed that Ethan was awake. "You bastard troublemaker, eh!" The guard took out a knife, pressing it to Ethan's neck. As he pressed harder, Ethan lowered his neck more, but it did not stop the guard from continuing to press down harder.

Ethan became nervous about the amount of weight from the knife on his throat. He broke into a sweat, and blood dripped down his neck. Every time the two men holding him took a step, his body would shift, causing the blade to break more of the skin.

"Ahh haa. The boy fears." The guard laughed as he moved the knife lower down his chest, using the dull side of the blade.

Ethan prayed that he would not take this any further. But without hesitation, the guard switched the knife back to the sharp end and placed it horizontal to Ethan's manhood.

Ethan had no control over what the guard planned on doing. The guard smiled at him. Even though it was dark, Ethan saw his teeth glimmering in the moonlight. The knife reflected off the moon, and the guard swiped sideways, breaking skin. He let out a small yelp. The cut was shallow, but he feared more about how deep this man was planning to go.

Laughing more, the terrorist positioned himself to make yet another, deeper cut. Ethan closed his eyes and held his breath. Ethan's body free fell for a quick second before he hit the cold and stony floor. The guard, whose head was under the pole, fell face first into Ethan's crotch and dropped the knife. The man holding Ethan from the front quickly dropped the wood and bent down just like Trent, who was attached to the pole in the same way. Trent had purposely dropped the pole, making it seem like an accident.

Once the guard regained his composure, he searched for the knife and wailed in fury. The entire group stopped at the commotion. The guard pulled his hand back to strike at Trent, who attempted to protect himself. Stuck to Ethan, Trent had no way of defending himself. He closed his eyes and waited for the guard to lunge with the knife.

A stone came out of thin air and hit Abu in the head. Another guard, who cast a bigger shadow, raced toward the scene, causing

Abu to freeze in place. Breathing heavily, Abu didn't turn around, keeping his deadly gaze on Trent. Ethan stared at the two men, still in shock.

Ethan mentally named this particular guard the Shadow. He struggled to see what he looked like in the darkness. From the moonlight, Ethan saw a man who was fully clothed in black and had his entire face covered, apart from his eyes. Ethan couldn't see much of him or what he looked like.

The Shadow only looked Abu in the eyes, nothing more. The anger in Abu faded away as he slowly lowered the knife. Abu turned the knife toward Trent.. He raised it and leaned close to Trent, cutting his ropes. Trent released a sigh of relief. Abu walked to the other side of Ethan and cut the ropes of the other man who carried him. Both of them freed, they were approached by another guard who tied their hands together, but without the pole attached to them.

Ethan struggled to lift the heavy pole to the side. Abu knelt down next to him, staring at Ethan for what seemed like an eternity. Smiling, Abu took the rope attached to his wrists and cut it, then he did the same for Ethan's ankles. Immediately, Ethan rubbed his wrists and ankles, already feeling the lacerations where the ropes had cut his skin.

The same guard that tied Trent and the other man quickly made his way to Ethan, where he was lifted up. His wrists were covered again by a rope and tied tightly.

At least his ankles were free of the rope, thought Ethan to himself.

The Shadow pushed a prisoner in front to start walking. Once again, the prisoners followed the person in front.

Naked, Ethan quickly realized that the ground was not soft dirt under the soles of his feet. Every few steps, his foot would step on a small pebble or sharp stone, causing him to trip or go limp on that leg. He could already feel his feet blistering, and he couldn't imagine the amount of pain Trent or anyone else had gone through walking longer.

In the moonlight, the men and women kept silent as they hiked for miles. Ethan wanted to continue his conversation with Trent, but he didn't dare speak a word because of Abu, who was walking right alongside of him. It felt to Ethan that he and Trent had created a grudge from Abu. Ethan definitely did not want to be on anyone's radar, seeing he had no idea what was to become of him and the others. He was in self-preservation mode.

As they continued to walk, Ethan noticed the sun rising. Layers of silhouettes formed as Ethan saw mountains in the distance. They were not just regular mountains but the biggest mountains he had ever seen. It looked as if the black shapes ran across the entire earth for miles. They were so high that they seemed to touch the stars.

As the sun reached higher in the sky, Ethan beheld the sight of the mountains. At the summit sat a frame of white. Below that was a rocky formation with scratches of indented shadows that blended into the snow. The sun pressed against Ethan's body, sending a feeling of warmth through his veins. He closed his eyes and inhaled the cold breeze of fresh air. For a moment, Ethan felt the presence of God's beauty.

They had been walking all night, and Ethan guessed the number of miles traveled was close to thirty-five or forty. It had been awhile since having to hike for such a long time. The military had taught them how to move continually through any given terrain. Even then, there was always an accurate calculation of the miles hiked, and they had food and water in their stomachs.

Speaking of food and water, since he had not been given any, his energy was drained. He breathed heavily with every step he took. Looking down, Ethan tried to avoid any possible obstacle that would cause him to trip. His health was draining every minute, making Ethan ponder how much longer he could walk without water or food. His face was numb, his lips dry, and his throat stung with every swallow he took. His walk slowed, and his mindset started to fade away.

"Oh, no. You're not hittin' the grave yet, cowboy. You better get a move on before I kick ya right in that tiny bubble ass of yours." Trent said under his breath.

Ethan had been zoned out for so long that he'd forgotten about who had been behind him the entire time. A little bit of excitement coursed through Ethan. Seeing the sun meant that at any point in time, he could turn around and finally see the man who had been placed in the coffin next to him.

It was not that Ethan longed to know what the man looked like, but he wanted to know who had been there to keep him calm in the box, who had become Ethan's companion. It had been a month since their capture. Within the first few days, it had become apparent that Trent was willing to sacrifice himself for a brother he barely knew. Ethan felt the same way. With that, a new sort of strength was created in Ethan, a strength not of survival but of protection and family.

Ethan made one long exhale before turning around. Behind him, looking down and walking with a lethargic pace, was a man with a narrow face. He had a discrete bulge at the top of his eyebrows and a full beard that was blond. Ethan could tell that even though his body was emaciated, he could picture what his original body type had been. His lithe frame would have contained broad shoulders and a defined chest. He had veins that covered every inch of his body. His dark blond hair was short, messy, and dirty. His cheeks were rosy red and bubbly. With the structure of his face, Ethan could tell that Trent would have large dimples if he smiled.

Ethan smirked a little, knowing that he had made a friend through this incredibly unfortunate journey. "How are you holding up?" he mumbled, his words making it seem as though he exhaled with a hum. Abu was still a little way ahead, and Ethan didn't want to attract the guard, causing the same situation that had occurred last night. He also was not looking forward to seeing what Abu looked like either.

"I'm holdin'. My feet could sure use a nice rubbin' if you're up for the job?" Trent let out a small painful laugh.

Ethan's feet were raw and cut. The dirt ground they were walking on became more rugged with stone as they approached the mountains. Every so often Ethan would step on a small family of scrub brushes that were strong as barbed wire, causing puncture wounds as well. Focusing on avoiding the rocks and brush kept Ethan busy as they walked, but it didn't prevent him from feeling his painful feet.

His body was sore and ached all around. The cuts around Ethan's neck and pelvic area were scabbed, making Ethan very grateful that they were not deep cuts. Unfortunately, there could always be a possibility of infection, which Ethan knew could cause trouble down the line.

His energy was low, but he continued to walk. Ethan licked his lips almost every moment he could, attempting to keep them from drying out, knowing it would only make it worse. Pain pulsed through his lips. The temperature became warmer as each minute passed. Ethan knew that the temperature wouldn't be a problem anymore, but he had to fight against the sun to prevent his lips from burning.

"How many guards have you counted?" Ethan softly spoke under his breath.

"I've counted twelve. All armed. Ethan, don't even think about doing anything. We're hungry, tired, and we have no energy to overtake even three men. I've been watching them eat from their packs and drink water. They are strong. We are not." There was fear in Trent's words, and Ethan knew that he wasn't a hand-to-hand fighter. He was a pilot who knew how to attack from a distance.

The group came to a horseshoe hill that looked as though it was entirely made up of stone.

"Listen, with tactics and the right timing, we could overtake them all. We just…" Ethan was cut off by a guard he heard from

IN THE SHADOW OF ENEMIES

the front of the line, and everyone came to a halt.

A big guard came down the side of their single-file line and started speaking in Arabic while looking at all the guards. Then he gave the prisoners a look of disgust. "We need all alive, although we can't help if you weak."

Ethan watched as the big man hopped off a horse and walked down the line, demeaning the prisoners. A burly man who was covered from head to toe in black sat on another horse. His shoulders were broad, and his eyes were as dark as the night. Ethan could only guess that this was the Shadow who had saved him from Abu. He continued to sit on his horse and watch as the guard below explain to the prisoners the need for survival.

"We reached Shalka Pasture. Below is river to drink. You have short time, do not stop or we will kill you. Run," the guard, who was obviously second in command, yelled with hatred in his voice.

The Shadow stood next to him and clapped his hands, and all the guards kicked the prisoners and hit their butt stocks against everyone's backs, screaming and wailing. The line in front began jogging. Once the man in front of Ethan jogged, Ethan picked up his heavy legs to follow.

As Ethan ran, his breathing became raspy. His throat was dry, and there was not much saliva being produced to keep up with his breathing. Every time he swallowed, it felt like razors going down his throat. He held his mouth shut and breathed from his nose, trying not to swallow.

His legs felt like bricks as he ascended the base of the stony mountain. As he moved further up the hill, it became steeper. Looking up, a lot of the prisoners were on their tied hands, using all fours to push themselves up. Everyone struggled over the boulders and loose gravel.

Ethan finally had no energy left. Lowering his front half down, he placed his tied hands in front and pulled, allowing his legs to shuffle to the front. His hands followed, moving past his

107

legs to pull again. The prisoners were no longer in a line but scattered all around, trying to make it to the top. The guards were able to keep their balance and walk around the mountain, keeping tabs on everyone. They laughed and sometimes tripped a prisoner, watching them fall face first on the gravel.

Ethan was in a routine of climbing the mountain. He didn't dare look up, afraid to lose his confidence about how much more he had to go.

Trent was able to gain more speed up the mountain, passing Ethan. "Come on, brother. We're almost to the top. We've gotten this far, and we can get farther." Trent spoke with motivation, giving Ethan the ability to find the strength to stay behind him.

As they moved, they surpassed all the prisoners. Ethan and Trent were in full focus, and their bodies moved on autopilot. Ethan saw that they had about fifty more yards to go. The hill was now at its steepest.

Shots rang out as guards fired around the prisoners who straggled behind. Ethan looked down and saw that some prisoners had stopped to catch their breath and regain their energy. Guards beat them, yelling and pointing to the top.

There was nothing Ethan could do to help them. They had to do what was told of them and reach the top. It was a game to the guards to torture them. He saw the fun they were having, and he saw for the first time the fear and struggle in some of the prisoners' eyes.

He turned back around, seeing that Trent was a couple feet from the top. Ethan smiled as Trent climbed to flat land, continuing to stay on all fours, and let out an accomplished breath.

As Trent looked forward, he saw a guard with a blue rope and white turban already waiting at the top. The man had scruff around his tan face. A scar in the shape of a moon crossed his left cheek. He let out a smile, showing yellow, crooked teeth. He tilted his head just a tad before leaning back and lifting his leg, striking Trent in the face. The force of the strike pushed Trent backward, down the mountain.

Ethan quickly grabbed ahold of a boulder, grasping for leverage as he extended his arms perpendicular from his body. He opened his elbows to create a pocket, aligning himself with Trent's trajectory.

As Trent traveled down, he flipped around, and his chest landed into the area Ethan had created. He closed his eyes and yelled. Stopping the momentum of Trent's fall caused Ethan's feet to anchor themselves in response. The pressure was excruciating as the gravel pierced deeper into his open wounds.

Both men lay on the side of the hill for a moment. Trent seemed to have been knocked out, blood dripping from the top of his head. Ethan regained his composure, looking at his feet and wincing. The guards and prisoners had caught up to them. More of the guards who did not see what had happened kicked Ethan and Trent, yelling at them to move.

He noticed a different look and tone in the guards as they saw Trent passed out. They argued with each other and pointed their gun at Trent's head. One of the guards racked his gun, preparing to end Trent's life. Ethan painfully raised a hand and looked at the ground, trying to find the power. The guards stopped at Ethan's movement.

"Come on, Trent. Wake up, buddy!" Ethan grabbed Trent's hands and raised them above his head to painfully squirm underneath him. "Trent! Wake up!" Ethan yelled, fearful that he wouldn't have the strength to carry him up.

Trent let out a moan, and Ethan smiled hopefully. The guard that was about to execute Trent lowered his rifle in amusement.

"All right, no homo, but we're about to get to know each other really well." Ethan grabbed Trent's tied hands and put them around his neck, turning Trent into a backpack. Ethan lifted one foot, followed by the other as he slowly inched up the mountain. The guards watched in amazement. They took bets with each other as to whether Ethan would make it to the top.

Ethan had no idea what he was doing, but he couldn't think anymore. All he could do was let his body take over. The blood from Ethan's feet accumulated pebbles that stuck to him every time he picked up his feet. Pain rose from the bottom of his soles to the top of his pounding head as he continued up the hill. All he could do was focus on his breathing.

Trent helped Ethan more and more as they reached the top.

Once Ethan's top half passed over the edge of the hill, he dropped Trent to the side, both of their bottom halves sticking over. "If it's not your body weight that's heavy, it's surely your nuts." Ethan said between gasps of air.

Trent and Ethan looked at each other and started laughing before the guards lifted both of them up and pushed them toward an astonishing view.

A large pasture lay in front of them, filled with bright green grass that swayed back and forth. A perimeter of stony hills protected the pasture as if it were a hidden gem. The sun's rays ran past the area, creating a small spotlight of heaven. The intensified colors left a lukewarm feeling. A cool breeze that came from the white mountains swept past both the men.

Farther down the field was a pond filled with dark blue water where they saw prisoners dunking themselves into it. The guards spoke a few demanding words and pushed the two into joining the rest of the prisoners. Ethan allowed Trent to place some of his body weight on him so that he had more time to recover.

He hastily went to the pond, where he dipped his feet in first and felt a cold wave shoot throughout his body as well as a strong sting from all his wounds. He raised his head and closed his eyes. His body cooled, and each of his hairs lifted in praise. He continued to walk until the water was up to his chest. He scooped up the water and drank like a horse. He immediately felt his chest rise, and energy fed into his body.

It felt like he'd only experienced a second of peace before

the guards shouted. Ethan awoke from his dream and turned around to see that a few of the men had dumped what had been in the horses' packs. There were different kinds of sandals and robes. One by one, prisoners' ropes were cut, and they were given sandals and a robe. Some fit perfectly and some were too big or too small. The guards didn't seem to care. Once you had been given your items and they were put on, the guards would tie them back up again.

Ethan was the last to get his stuff. He came upon the guard with the blue rope and scar.

"Troublemaker wants clothes and shoes?"

The voice Ethan had heard last night was Abu's voice. Ethan now understood why Trent had been kicked off the top of the hill. Abu was getting back at him for what had happened. Startled at understanding what Abu was capable of, he let out a sigh.

As Ethan grabbed the robe, Abu dropped it so Ethan had to pick it up. Ethan bent down, only to be kneed in the head by Abu. The guards close by chuckled, giving affirmation to Abu. Ethan got up with the robe and put it on. It luckily fit him fine. His robe had a dark blend of red and blue hues. It was thick and comfortable.

Abu then grabbed Ethan's sandals and waved them in his face before smiling that crooked smile and tilting his head. He put them back into the bag and yelled for the Shadow. He turned around, and for the first time, Ethan really saw the Shadow.

He looked distinctly different than the others. His stance was stiff and showed authority. His body was bigger and puffy, as if he wore a lot more layers. Ethan figured that he was definitely hot under all of that, unless these guys were used to wearing so much. As Ethan studied the Shadow, he managed to look at the only part he could see, and it sent chills down his spine. His eyes were completely black, as if there was nothing but two black holes.

Those couldn't be real.

The Shadow noticed Ethan looking at him, and he quickly averted his eyes to the ground. At this point, Ethan understood that the Shadow was the leader of this expedition.

Abu raised his shoulders, and the leader nodded his head. Abu looked back at Ethan smiling.

As Abu began to tie his hands again, he whispered into Ethan's ear, "Looks like we lost your shoes. Ha-ha!"

Ethan was going to have to travel with nothing under his feet.

Abu pushed Ethan back in line, this time behind a yellow robed man. He turned around and Ethan saw that it was Trent. The wound on his forehead was cleaned off from the water, and thankfully, it was a little cut that didn't look detrimental.

"Yellow looks good on you. You should keep it," Ethan said, trying to make light of the situation.

"Those feet look good on you; I wouldn't wear anything if I were you." Trent saw Ethan's smile leave after he had cracked the joke. "I'm just messing with ya. I saw Abu put the sandals back in the bag. We can switch on and off if we ever stop."

Ethan nodded in agreement.

10

KNOCKING ON DEATH'S DOOR

The group trudged closer to the base of a mountain. Ethan noticed they had a lot of miles to go as he lethargically made his way over another hill. Once on top, they told the prisoners to sit.

About a mile ahead, a road slithered across the path they took to get to the mountain. Ethan's excitement grew as he saw lights from cars passing back and forth on the road. Trent's eyes met Ethan's, and hope sparked in them both. Ethan smiled.

The guards waited until the sun had completely set before they took four prisoners down the hill toward the road. Ethan watched as one guard waited ten minutes before taking the next set of four. They were being cautious so they wouldn't draw the eyes of the drivers.

Ethan and Trent were part of the middle group of four to leave the hill. Frustration filled Ethan when he realized Abu would take them across. This would be harder than he expected. Abu would have his eyes on both of the men like a hawk. Ethan didn't know what he was going to do or if Trent would agree.

The only luck they would have is if a car passed on the road. The road ran for miles. Ethan prayed that a car would emerge from the darkness.

As the four came closer, Ethan held his breath as lights came from the right side of the road. They were only a hundred yards away from crossing. Adrenaline rushed through his body, and his mind raced. He didn't know what to do, but he had to do something.

Abu raised his hand above his head and made a fist, which told the group of four to lay flat against the ground. All four complied, Ethan's breathing became heavier. He focused on inhaling and exhaling, hoping to have a fresher mind. He knew he had a window of time to make a move before the group behind him caught up. The car would also soon pass the section they were crossing.

Ethan's body twitched as Abu's sole attention remained on the car.

He leapt from his position and jumped on Abu. Surprised by the attack, Abu tried to break free from Ethan's grasp. Ethan had barely any strength to fight, but he figured the surprise would be enough.

Wailing, Abu managed to get to his feet, his AK breaking free of Ethan. As Abu turned his rifle toward Ethan, Ethan lifted his tied hands into the air, scared and disappointed that he had failed. He waited for the shot to ring out, but a shadow came from the black abyss and tackled Abu. The AK fell into the distance.

"Ethan, head toward the car!" Trent yelled as he struggled to keep Abu on the ground.

The other two prisoners kept still and watched in horror. Ethan turned around, hearing a commotion from the other guards.

He headed toward the road until he was only fifty yards away. The driver sped along, having no idea what was happening. Adrenaline pumped madly throughout Ethan's body, keeping his legs running like a machine. His heart beat like a drum, wanting to break free from his chest. Ethan reached the road, out of breath. He ran into the middle of the road and waved his arms.

"Stop! Please! Help us!" Ethan screamed in horror.

The lights covered Ethan, quickly blinding him like a deer in headlights, and he stayed frozen in front of the beams. It didn't seem like the car was slowing down. Did the driver see Ethan, or were they not willing to stop?

The sound of loud screeching tires sliding against the pavement echoed around him. Ethan held out his tied hands, panting and relieved that the car actually stopped. He slowly walked toward the side of the car. A man yelled as he got out of the car, his eyes turning to shock and horror as he looked at Ethan.

The car lights gave stark detail of what Ethan looked like. His thin and frail body was covered in bruises around his arms, neck, and face that began as dark blue and faded into black in the middle. Dried blood covered him from his neck to his ankles from his wounds never having a chance to seal. Ethan gazed at him, feeling the despair of the past month. The man walked toward Ethan with outstretched arms as if to give aid, but a loud crack echoed through the darkness.

Ethan watched the life leave the man's eyes as they turned into a blank stare. A splatter of blood exited his head as he fell limp to the ground.

Ethan stayed frozen as his body went into complete shock. A ringing overpowered any sound that came after. Everything seemed to go out of focus as muffled yelling came from a distance, and he stared at the dead man. What had he done? Abu reached Ethan, taking him to the ground and beating him with the rifle. Ethan didn't defend himself. He only lay there, his eyes focused on the dead man. After running out of breath from beating Ethan, Abu grabbed him and hauled him to his feet.

Trent joined Ethan with another guard, who yelled at Abu. Abu fired back, and both prisoners bowed their heads, expecting the worst to happen.

A guard quickly dragged the dead stranger into the trunk of his car. Turning off the lights, he drove it off the road and toward the mountain. The rest of the group crossed and walked about a mile from the scene. Once the entire group was gathered, the guards sat them all in a circle.

Ethan and Trent sat side by side, and they waited to see what would become of them. The guard who was second in command grabbed Abu, and the few other guards who had been close by—including the Shadow—awaited an explanation. They talked and screamed as they pointed toward Abu and the runaway prisoners.

As they spoke, Ethan's thoughts traveled back to what had happened. It was his fault that an innocent man had died. Why hadn't he thought before acting? What was his plan once he got the driver to stop the car? Ethan mourned and became angry with himself.

Trent nudged him, shaking his head. It was as if Trent knew what Ethan felt. Trent was trying to bring comfort to Ethan, but Ethan wanted none of it. It was his fault a man lay dead in the trunk of his car. He could have had a wife and children who waited for him at home, and he would never return.

The Shadow came near Abu. He said nothing, only looking at Abu with anger written in his eyes before striking him across the head. Abu placed his fingers across his cheek and directed his disgusted gaze at Ethan and Trent. He then walked toward them and spat in their faces.

Abu spoke calmly, but his voice sent a disturbing chill throughout all the prisoners. "We sleep here. You are out of strikes. Do anything else, you die."

Ethan felt the hate from each prisoners' eyes. He had put himself and everyone else in a terrible position. He closed his eyes, recreating the scene of the man being shot over and over again until he exhausted himself into a deep sleep.

Ethan neared the gate at the compound, guarded by a Marine. Lt. Smith waited for him and the other two squad leaders. Sergeant Rodriguez was also beside the lieutenant, waiting patiently.

Sergeant Rodriguez had been Ethan's platoon sergeant since he had graduated boot camp. He was known as the 'Mexican above all Mexicans,' with dark tan skin and short black hair. He loved his tacos and celebrated the Day of the Dead. Kind and lighthearted, Sergeant Rodriguez took care of the platoon, and the platoon took care of him. His slick and sharp voice carried a smooth melody.

"You seem to always cut it close to these briefings, you three. Can we at least attempt to show the CO that we care about our last three weeks?"

The boys nodded as each one greeted the guard with their credentials, which allowed them to enter the small building that was protected by a large fence and barbed wire. This particular building had all the important information and intel on the enemy they fought. It was also where they gave all the briefings for missions and patrols.

Ethan took off his cover and entered the building to head straight for the briefing room. After months of patrolling and missions, he knew his way around. Steve walked next to him. They looked into other rooms, filled with stacks of paper and computers that had wires running along the walls. The area was in constant movement as men and women discussed plans and crossed the hall to complete tasks. Ethan called it the 'building that never slept' because it was always alive with people who didn't stop. He also always smelled cheap chew and energy drinks, which caused Ethan to yak in his mouth.

"What do you think we'll be doing this time? I bet it's our last patrol, and we can start turning it over to the next battalion," Steve said curiously, turning around to see a female Marine walking out of a room.

"Well, I guess we'll find out in a moment," Ethan said, his

tone bland. He was never excited to get a briefing, and it was because of one man, the CO.

Captain Holtzway, the commanding officer, was a clean-shaven man who had short brown hair. He resembled the same type of look as actors in Hollywood films about the military. His athletic build was proof of the workouts he did with the battalion.

Ethan had never liked the man because of how he did things while in command. The negativity from the boys in the cans was because of the Commanding Officer, and morale was low, if not gone. He treated the Marines like children and never gave them the respect they deserved.

When all the Marines' showers had broken, Captain Holtzway told the Marines that it was not in their budget at the time to fix them, instructing that they focus on the mission at hand. The Marines were furious, and he may have broken their morale with something as simple as not fixing showers, but he didn't break their spirit.

Ethan and Steve had come up with a great solution to the problem. Ethan grabbed a knife, a chair, and a box of plastic water bottles. He then poked a hole in the water bottle cap, using the knife, and stood on a chair. Steve would then remove his clothing, and Ethan would squeeze the bottle over Steve. Water left the bottle in a single long jet stream, which allowed Steve to bathe himself quickly.

Once others took notice of the idea, they came together, discussing how to save enough water to drink and to use for showers. The men had fun with it, and it helped in boosting their morale. Once word made its way higher up, Captain Holtzway shut down the bottled water shower operation and ordered the base to have the showers fixed.

He was also a big structural officer who did everything by the book, never straying from it. As much as that was honorable, it also took out the common sense that paper didn't have.

When it came down to discussions, Ethan argued with

Captain Holtzway in the most respectful way, but he always got as close to the line as possible. To Ethan, it was a challenge, but it was also him trying to protect his platoon as well.

Once the group entered the briefing room, Captain Holtzway was already next to the board. A white tarp hung there, and a PowerPoint slide reflected off it.

"Good evening, gentleman, just in time for your briefing." Captain Holtzway had a deep but nasal voice that made every man in the room cringe. "This will be very simple, and I do not want to spend too much time on this, as I have a meeting with the colonel later on this evening. Please hold all questions till the end. I am happy to say this will be your last mission before turning it over to the new battalion taking over in a few weeks."

Steve leaned over and whispered to Ethan, "I told ya so." Steve elbowed Ethan once and leaned back against the wall to pay attention to the rest of Captain Holtzway's briefing.

Ethan smirked.

"I'll be going over the entire order for this mission, but first, I want to explain the situation. I've been given word that the elders in the village north of here are having much difficulty with receiving food and water supplies from outside sources. ISIS seems to be the cause of this problem. Our job is to make contact with them and have a nice little chat to see what we can do to make the Afghan people happy." Captain Holtzway rubbed his hands together and paced as he shifted through the slide show.

"Our mission does not call for any confrontation with enemy hostiles. However, we will always come prepared and fully loaded. From previous encounters with ISIS, we know that they have obtained skills from their sister ally group, Boko Haram, which is trained in guerrilla tactics. If encountered by hostile activity, expect a small number of them—with at least half an hour of fight and possible AT4 rocket launchers—to come from the north." Captain Holtzway grabbed some cards off the table and looked at Steve, who stared out the window. "Cpl. Bradley, would you mind telling me what EMLCOA stands for, just to refresh everyone's memory?"

Steve froze for a second to process that the CO had called on him, as he hadn't been paying attention. He finally dropped his arms, which had been folded, and stuttered as his eyes moved left and right, trying to come up with the words that were not forming.

"Enemy's most likely course of action, sir," Ethan answered for Steve.

Captain Holtzway looked at Ethan. "Oh, thank you for answering the question I specifically asked Cpl. Bradley."

Steve's face turned bright red, embarrassed that he hadn't been able to answer a simple question, but being caught off guard had made his mind go blank.

"You're welcome, sir, figured since you have that meeting coming up you wouldn't want us wasting any of your time." Ethan stared at Captain Holtzway and grinned.

Captain Holtzway, still looking at Ethan, began speaking for a beat before breaking eye contact and moving forward with his order. "We will have first platoon leaving the compound. First squad will take front, Cpl. Miller and I will be in the middle with his squad, and third squad will be taking the rear."

Ethan's eyes widened. "Sir, I'm sorry for interrupting. Did you say that you were coming on the mission as well?"

Captain Holtzway grinned back before answering him. "I was honored to be offered a spot at the table of elders for a meeting to discuss possible choices to move forward with helping in their struggle, as well as protection for them and the supply routes that are being seized by ISIS. So yes, I will be taking part in this mission alongside first platoon. I hope that you are okay with that, Cpl., since you seem to have authority to ask me anything and to interrupt me."

Ethan did not want to bring the CO on their last mission, and he had valid reasons why.

After hearing that Captain Holtzway was going, Ethan felt

a surge of frustration. He no longer paid attention to the meeting. Ethan had been on patrol before with the captain, however, and it had been a nightmare. He rarely ever left the compound. When he did, it was for only an hour or two. The platoon had to be on their best behavior and follow the rules in the book, which could be dangerous at times. Ethan followed his gut, and when it came to firefights, he would make decisions that protected his boys but went against the rules of engagement. Ethan knew having the CO with them would prevent him from protecting his men. His actions now could be questioned, causing him to be at risk. He could face being court-martialed and kicked out of the Marine Corps.

"We will come up from the north in an admin-style patrol to the town and meet the elders at the entrance. We will follow them to building A, which is a two-story building. I will have Cpl. Miller's squad inside with me while the other two squads set up a perimeter of security around the building with minimal distance between each Marine. Note that the area will be filled with civilians and many markets along the streets. We will be alert at all times due to the heavy traffic ar..."

"Sir?" Ethan interrupted.

Steve nudged Ethan to tell him he had crossed the line.

Captain stopped what he was doing and looked at Ethan, annoyance written plainly across his face.

Ethan couldn't stand to listen to the CO knowing that there could be a possible chance to save his men from having a horrible mission with him.

The captain let out a sigh and spoke to him as if he were talking to a six-year-old. "What is it, Corporal Miller?"

"Sir, why don't we invite the elders over for the meeting instead of going there? This would in turn save us a trip protecting you from any possible danger. You wouldn't even have to leave the wire. We can arrange a proper meal set out for them to show respect. I'm sure they would enjoy..."

Ethan stopped at the captain's expression of disgust.

The officer looked at Ethan for a moment, then around the room. Everyone was shocked at Cpl. Miller's words, and all waited in suspense for what the CO would do next.

Ethan knew he'd stepped over the line.

Captain Holtzway's face changed from disgust to false cheeriness. He spoke in a high sing-song voice. "I'm sorry, Corporal, I hadn't thought of that. With your wisdom and knowledge, I think it would only be fair to have you stand up here and give the briefings from now on. In fact, I think I should take my rank off right now and hand it over to you. Promoted right on the spot, ha-ha!" His cheerful voice quickly changed into a shrill one while his expression morphed back into disgust. "Tell me, Cpl. Miller, what are the Afghan traditions when it comes to offering a seat at the table?"

Ethan hesitated to enter the trap, but he spoke with confidence, "It is an honor in their culture to receive an invitation to the table. It would be rude and insulting if you were to decline their offer and ask them to come here instead."

As Ethan said the words, he understood that he was wrong. He'd allowed his mind to become clouded because he'd wanted to avoid taking the CO on the trip. But he knew that the captain was right. It would cause a fray in the relationship that the Marines had been working so hard to build.

"Cpl. Miller, the Afghan people are intolerant of such diversity and change. They hold their traditions high and their values higher. Such nonsense in trying to change their beliefs would lead to high consequence. They will stay in their conservative box, and we will do no such thing to destroy their law and order or destroy what we have worked to salvage from this long and devastating war."

The entire room was quiet, and only the sound of typing from other rooms could be heard echoing through the halls outside.

"I understand you have such high concerns for my safety and

health. But you will stand there and listen to the rest of the order without saying another word. You will go back and brief your men. Do you understand? You are talented in killing and tactics, I'll give you that. But your mouth and actions may get you in trouble one day." Captain Holtzway turned his eyes to Ethan's superiors. "As for you two, maybe we should tug on the leash just a little bit harder, eh?" the captain said before readjusting himself and continuing the briefing.

Ethan felt the stares from every eye in the room. He turned his head to see the look of disappointment on Lt. Smith's face. Ethan, still frustrated, tried to hide himself against the wall to mope.

After the briefing, the group of men exited the building.

Once outside, Sgt. Rodriguez tore into Ethan. "What in the hell were you thinking, Miller? Puto, are you trying to get written up, or do you just want to make it harder for the Lt. and me? You have a lot of nerve doing that. If you try that shit again, we're going to have problems. Do I make myself clear? Now go and get ready; we leave at 1300 hours."

Ethan kept his head down and didn't look at anyone. He gave a discouraged nod, notifying his platoon sergeant and platoon officer that he was out of line. Sgt. Rodriguez and the lieutenant both gave Ethan one last disappointed look and headed toward their barracks. Ethan and Steve made their way back to the cans and gave the boys their own briefing before they prepared for their last mission.

"Just couldn't keep your mouth closed, could ya?" Steve chuckled through his words.

Ethan kept walking with his head down. He knew that he and the boys wouldn't be able to work the way they normally did.

"You know why I pushed for the elders to come here. And you know once the boys find out that the CO is coming, they are going to flip the cans inside out and be in a pissy mood. We're going to have to be extra careful the entire time we are out there."

"It's only an admin mission. That's basically the simplest mission 'slash' patrol we could be on. We're not engaging anyone, and we're not going to get engaged in any fights! It's so easy."

Ethan slowly stopped, and Steve turned around to see why. Ethan took a deep breath and looked over the perimeter of the camp at the mountains.

The sun had set, and the yellow rays gleamed off the tips of the mountains, revealing layers of rock and true height. He thought to himself that he'd been able to do extraordinary things and see extraordinary places, yet he'd never been able to climb the mountains. He didn't know why that thought had entered his mind, but he always thought the mountains were so beautiful. Even in a dangerous place.

"Steve, a leader never leads behind his men. How can he if all of his men cover his view of what's in front? No, a true leader will lead from the front and see with his own eyes. And what do the men see?" Ethan questioned him.

Steve looked at Ethan, then away at what he thought Ethan was staring at. "Men see the leader?" Steve answered him.

"They see a man not full of fear but full of bravery and compassion for them. A man not afraid to face it alone because he knows that in return, they stand alongside him. Not in front, not behind. They fight as one. Captain Holtzway is blinded sometimes by being behind the men who sacrifice their lives every day. He just doesn't understand that. The common sense isn't there. That's why I spoke out of turn." Ethan walked again as Steve listened carefully to his words.

Steve furrowed his brow and, being deep in thought, asked, "What do you fear, Ethan?"

Ethan thought of his friend's question for a moment before answering. "Fear is only what could happen. It can never live in the present. I'm a man who decided to live in each step that I take, not letting fear dictate my path. I'll make that choice, not fear. If my choice is wrong, I'll live with the consequences."

Steve smirked at Ethan, asking, "What if it's death at the door?"

Ethan looked at Steve with squared shoulders and boldly said, "Then I'll let myself in."

11

INFERIOR

Ethan awoke to a sharp pain in his side and quickly came out of his deep sleep. Abu had awakened him with a strong kick to his ribs. Ethan let out a loud gasp. He knew that the guards would be keeping a close eye on him. They must really want everyone alive for them not to kill him after what he'd done yesterday. He knew that the prisoners had other feelings, and it made him wonder if he was dead either way.

The guards demanded that they tighten up the line and continue walking toward the mountain. Abu specifically walked next to Ethan, staring him down with hatred. He'd hit Ethan in the ribs or back every now and then if he was caught slowing down the pace of the line. They had also split him and Trent up, putting Trent close to the front of the line. He too had a guard close by.

After a few hours they finally made it to the base of the mountains. Ethan noticed a hanging valley, an indent between the mountains filled with nothing but stone. His eyes wandered upward until they rested upon the peak of the mountain. He felt like an ant compared to it.

Before they started their climb, with the prisoners' hands still tied and Ethan's feet naked of shoes, the guards gave out little pieces of stale bread and sips of water. The nourishment provided by a small bit of food allowed Ethan to think back on a brief conversation he'd had with Trent while still in the coffins about the nature of terrorists. They did as little as possible to keep their prisoners alive. The fact that they still kept them alive led them both to believe that they were needed for a certain purpose. Ethan just didn't know what.

Ethan pondered over why the terrorists needed them. ISIS was a very aggressive militia group that had little respect for any other beliefs. It was a one-way street if you came upon them. You either joined their cause or died alongside each and every one of your family members. Sometimes, if a husband turned down their offer to join, they would make the husband watch as they killed each member of his family before killing him.

They are a sick group, thought Ethan to himself. If Ethan ever believed that it was possible for a human to have no soul, it was surely them.

ISIS taught their young to obey and sacrifice themselves in the name of the Sunni Islam doctrine, following the prophet Muhammed.

Ethan understood very little about the culture itself, let alone the religious aspect of Islam. He did remember having a few classes on Islam and how it all came about:

Muhammed had been raised by his uncle in what is now Saudi Arabia. He followed in his uncle's footsteps as a camel caravan guide, carrying passengers from point A to point B. He was known as a very faithful and trustworthy man.

Being very religious, he made many pilgrimages to various places across Saudi Arabia. During one of his travels, he meditated by a cave and was greeted by the Angel Gabriel. There, he was given a message to preach as a prophet, and thus Islam was born in 610 A.D. For years, Muhammed's religion grew. Some followed, but many ignored or mocked him.

Through all the trials and wars that broke out between 624

to 628 A.D., Muhammed, his followers, and his allies finally established peace in 630 A.D.

However, what confused Ethan so much was the fact that there was not one religion of Islam but many that broke apart from the original beliefs and practices taught by Muhammed himself. Ethan's friend in class helped him to better understand this reasoning by using an analogy of his own religion, Christianity.

Christianity does not have one group and one teaching. Instead, there are different denominations that have their own teachings of the same book, the Bible. Even though each denomination has something slightly different to teach than the other, they all mostly teach from the same foundation.

That is exactly how Islam works, and there are tons of different denominations that follow Islam and Muhammed. There were two that stood out to Ethan, and those two were explained in detail because Ethan was told that, when deploying to Afghanistan, there was a possibility of being caught within a religious war.

The two groups were Sunni and Shia. They both came about when Muhammed the prophet passed, and Islam needed a new leader. Sunni, which stands for "way," elected Abu Bakr, who was a friend of Muhammed and one of the first to believe in Muhammed and his prophecy. The other group, Shia, also known as "partisans of Ali," believed in Ali ibn Abi Talib. Ali was a cousin of Muhammed, and the Shia believed that there was a divine order in his bloodline, but the Sunni disagreed.

Ali was elected and continued leading them for five years until his assassination. Since then, the division had been mostly based on questions of authority and politics. The religious fight over Islam has continued with constant bloodshed and war. Unfortunately, with ISIS, Ethan believed there was extra bloodshed apart from the religious war.

Ethan guessed that ISIS followed the doctrine of the Sunni, as a large percentage of the world's Muslims were Sunni. He also knew of Muhammed's radical teaching, which was explained by the Quran.

The Quran actually means "recitation," which is what the Muslims believed to be true. They lived their life through reciting, acting, and prayer. The text follows everything from what the Angel Gabriel recited to Muhammed. Readers studied among the divisions of chapters from the stories of Allah and his miraculous signs, the day of judgment, and how to live their everyday lives. The Quran is the foundation of a Muslim's life.

However, Ethan always thought it was funny how a lot of Muslims never admitted to the acts of violence that Islam has pushed for. They say that Islam is peace, but is it?

They call it jihad, or "holy war." They felt their acts of violence were justified because the Quran speaks of reaching out to those who do not believe. If they do not believe the same teachings of Islam, then the messenger has done all he can, and the nonbeliever must die. Just like those who sacrifice themselves and kill innocent people, they believe they will be rewarded in paradise.

Ethan remembered looking into the Quran and reading a few of the texts. Some commanded to, "Kill the disbeliever...or treat them harshly." So, these men were brainwashed from day one. These terrorists were powerful.

What Ethan feared was what ISIS was most known for. The beheadings of people in front of the camera. That was ISIS's scare tactic. ISIS used the media to control people and place fear in them. Ethan figured this would be what they wanted them kept for, but death wasn't Ethan's sole fear. As he looked ahead, he saw each of the prisoners' heads sunk deep below their chest. Defeat had marred each of their faces, and he knew that even trying to fight would be helpless and pathetic because of the lack of strength they had, even if they outnumbered the guards. Then Ethan laid his eyes on Trent.

Trent looked more defeated than anyone from the group, and Ethan knew why. It was also what Ethan feared the most. Trent was a father, a husband, and Ethan's friend. His mind and body were wired to protect himself and others, and he knew he was doing a horrible job at it. His ideas and choices were in an attempt to free them, but it started to seem like it was time for an alternate route, which meant breaking the pride Ethan had. He was going to help the others survive.

The front of the line reached a ginormous crevice within the mountain. It was a tight fit. Only two or three stood next to each other while walking through it.

Once Ethan stepped in, he took a moment to let his eyes adjust to the new lighting that reflected from the stone.

"Wow," he whispered to himself.

The walls of the mountain stood all around him, acting as protectors of something mysterious and magical. Ethan felt as though they looked down on him, running vertical for miles until Ethan tilted his head back and felt the scabs from his neck break.

He was in a canyon of rocky waves that formed different tones from light and shade. Shades of red, yellow, gray, and black blended amongst the strata. The sediments look like either salt or sulfur.

He ran the tips of his fingers along the walls, feeling a cold, smooth, yet rugged texture. It was as if he were the only human alive to ever touch such a sacred stone.

After a few hours of hiking through the snakelike crevice of the mountain, the second in command demanded that the other terrorists make camp as the sun set.

Ethan still found himself separated from Trent and most of the other prisoners. No one wanted to be near him, afraid that they would be caught associating themselves with him.

They were all told to sit down and rest. Ethan took to a small corner, where he laid his back against the stone wall and slid down to sit. He began to search his body and tend to his wounds.

He rubbed the back of his neck and ran his hands down his legs to feel the tough and weak skin that had been damaged from being out in the sun. He lifted his robe to see the cuts that had been made by Abu. They were already in the process of healing, and Ethan thanked God that the cuts had been shallow.

He raised a foot and rested it on his other leg to see the bottom of his feet. Ethan was shocked to finally see how bad his feet looked. Blisters that had been formed were cut open, leaving a clear wet liquid to wash over his foot, which blended with the deeper cuts that had fresh blood slowly pouring out. Ethan felt the pain, and his foot pulsated. His pain became more unbearable as his feet swelled from resting.

He put his tied hands to one side of his hips and lifted up, shifting his weight to hopefully be distracted from the pain. He squinted his eyes and gasped as the pain spread from his feet to his knees. He slid farther back and hit the wall. When Ethan felt the wall, he noticed the loose rocks.

He turned, seeing a section of the giant rock, which had eroded away and left a bit of rubble. Ethan put his tied hands under his feet and moved them behind him. He picked at the rock until he was able to pull out a shard that was in the shape of a blade. The blade portion was rugged but felt sharp enough to cut.

Ethan noticed a guard who walked by, and he slowly lifted his butt forward while placing the shard of rock under him. Ethan just stared at his legs until the guard walked past him.

He moved his hands back in front of him, holding the rock and grabbing the edge of his robe, slicing it until it frayed. Still watching around him to make sure no one could see him, Ethan slowly ripped off a strip of material from around his body. He quickly wrapped one of his feet and tied the end off at his ankle. He repeated the step one more time for the other foot.

After tending to his feet, he placed the rock behind his butt. He noticed Abu walking toward him. He put his legs in a crisscross style, preventing Abu from noticing what he had just done with his feet.

Abu approached Ethan and looked at him in a sick morbid way. Ethan sensed that Abu wanted nothing but to torture him, but as long as the Shadow was around then Ethan was safe, or so he hoped.

Abu got into a combat stance and kicked Ethan in the face, knocking him to the ground. Ethan stayed there for a moment, then spit out the blood that accumulated in his mouth. He sat back up, putting his back against the wall and raising his chin, showing no sign of pain from the hit.

Abu, shocked at the pride on Ethan's face, repeated the kick to his mouth. It knocked Ethan to the ground again, but he kept his face pressed against the cold stone floor that time. Lightheaded, Ethan didn't have the ability to spit out the blood, and he let the blood flow from his numb mouth. A nasty smile formed across Abu's face, and he laughed victoriously.

Trent, who was farther up from Ethan, sat around a group of prisoners. He lifted his head to see the commotion. He could only look on helplessly and watch the entire scene.

Ethan got himself under control and sat back up again, which wiped the smile off of Abu's face. The pain in Ethan's face was sharp and piercing, but he decided not to show any of it to Abu.

Abu's eyes filled with anger, and he drew his foot back to kick Ethan again.

Ethan braced for the kick.

"AHH!" a voice hollered.

It was first time that Ethan had heard the Shadow say anything.

The mysterious man stood like a strong, authoritative statue, and he stared at Abu. Everyone watched to see if Abu would heed the Shadow's demand to stop.

Abu breathed deeply, not taking his eyes off of Ethan. He then bent down and placed his hand on Ethan's jaw. The two foes locked eyes, neither of them breaking contact. Ethan could feel the hatred flowing from the terrorist's eyes. It radiated through the hand that touched his skin.

Ethan had an enemy within the enemy, and it wasn't something he had intended to create. The rock that Ethan had placed underneath his butt now settled directly between his legs because of the hits he'd taken. Ethan slowly took his strapped hands and moved them closer between his legs without Abu noticing. Adrenaline coursed through him, and his heart pounded.

Abu's face changed into a questioning expression, and Ethan thought for a moment that Abu knew what Ethan was going to do. Ethan waited half a second, thinking about how he wanted to grab the rock and slice Abu's throat.

Ethan quietly chuckled to Abu before whispering, "Inferior."

Abu leaned in closer to understand the word Ethan had said. He didn't know it, and he couldn't describe what it sounded like. But Abu heard the tone. Abu's eyes widened when Ethan managed to give a small smile, letting Abu know that he was under someone's authority. He had no power to kill him. Ethan wanted him to know he couldn't do the one thing he wanted to do.

Trent huffed a laugh when he saw what Ethan had just done.

Abu shook his head, letting Ethan know it wasn't over. He let out a wisp of air before pushing Ethan's head into the wall. Everyone started to breathe again, and Ethan raised his hands away from the shard and closer to his stomach. Ethan waited for something to happen. Nothing did. As he waited, his adrenaline died down, causing him to feel the pain in his feet.

The sun had settled, creating a black cover over the entire group. The temperature dropped low, and everyone could feel it. Ethan heard teeth chattering throughout the area, and he even caught himself shivering. He was happy he'd decided to wrap his feet with his robe.

As Ethan sat and stared into complete darkness, cold and alone, he felt the need to look up. He rested his eyes on yet another beautiful sight.

Above him, past the giant slithering walls, lay a black cloak with billions of white sparkly freckles. Overwhelmed, Ethan stared, open-mouthed. An intermix of colors blended from blue into a bright purple. It was as if Ethan were watching the ocean of the night sky slowly float away. Ethan couldn't understand how he could watch this beautiful sight and feel free yet be so trapped.

He saw God's beauty right in front of him. The waves of the stars and oceanic colors flowed like a current that was more distinct in the night sky. He questioned, if God can create such beauty in the eyes of His creation, then where is He right now? Why does he open Pandora's box to someone who has endured enough hell? He uses this majestic scene to tease the sinner to pay for the consequences of his past. Salvation only comes to those whom God chooses. Ethan's enraged feelings caused by his thoughts made him shiver more than before, and his bones began to ache. He cursed God for his life, his pain, and his suffering.

At that moment, the giant walls growled, echoing a low rumbling sound throughout the mountains. The terrorists all spoke in their tongue. Ethan couldn't understand them; however, they sounded scared. He heard their panic as the growl got louder and closer. Not being able to see anything but darkness, even Ethan trembled at the mysterious noise. It sounded like a giant beast had awakened from a deep slumber. The Shadow became restless with his men and their cries of terror. All the screams competed with the beast.

Ethan used this chance to imagine the area at daytime. He closed his eyes, concentrating so he could map out the spot where Trent had sat before it became dark. He grabbed his rock and stood. He maneuvered alongside the wall and guessed he needed to go at least ten yards before turning forty-five degrees to the left and walking straight.

Ethan knew that one yard was three feet. Using yards to Ethan was always easier for him because of football in high school. But to measure it out, he did the math to figure he needed to take thirty steps to the left. He placed one foot in front of the other, always touching toe to heel to make it as accurate as he could.

The men were still yelling, but Ethan tried to ignore it so he could worry about the counting. Ethan was startled when he ran into an object that he thought was one of the prisoners. He quickly moved around, subtracting three from the total amount of steps he needed to take. The growling was now almost on top of the group. He needed to work faster.

As he counted down to one, he turned forty-five degrees to the left and pictured another ten yards plus some. He took one long breath before quickly placing his feet one after another. The yells and the growling made Ethan look around for a dog or a monster, but he still couldn't see anything. His mind wandered off from counting and focused on the beast that neared ever closer to its prey. One of the terrorists, who had been running around and swinging his rifle in the air, pushed by Ethan. Ethan landed on the ground, losing his bearings. He panicked through the constant cries for help and screams in Arabic.

Ethan was startled once more with a flash of light and a crack from a gun not too far away. One of the men had lost control and fired a shot at the sky.

"Devil!" screamed one of the terrorists.

Another shot rang out, allowing Ethan to catch a glimpse of Trent. He took quick action and crawled on all fours, making the best of his hands being tied. Ethan crawled a few yards before running into someone.

"Trent?"

"Ethan?"

"So, is this a regular night out in Texas?" asked Ethan.

"You had a beer under that robe of yours, then I would say this is exactly a night out in Texas. How the hell you manage to get over here without gettin' shot?"

"Well, it seems like the guards are a little preoccupied right now." Ethan raised his voice over the yelling and noise of the beast. "Any idea what that is?" Ethan was a little restless with the mysterious growling. He took his rock and sliced at his restraints. It didn't take long to cut the rope. Ethan cut Trent's as well.

"Ha, that noise is of a beast that can fly. It's an American Eagle searching for her babies, they call her a Boeing AH-64 Apache. Attack helicopter with twin-turboshaft that packs quite a bit of heat. Someone knows we're lost, and they lookin' for us." As Trent finished speaking, a bright light shined above their heads.

The terrorists began to cover their arms over their faces and hid against the stone walls.

"Maybe they found the car they had pitched by the side of that road? Either way, our captors show fear." Trent smiled at Ethan.

"They show vulnerability, a weakness that will be their downfall if they are not careful. Until then, we all work together to survive, and we can only count on ourselves. No one else is going to look over us." Ethan stared up at the sky as though waiting for something to happen.

The Shadow through the middle of the path grabbed at the guards to get up. He gestured to them, flapping his arms to rise. He pointed with a stiff arm, giving them directions on where to go.

The terrorists all moved slowly, checking above their heads while they moved around, pulling everyone up and putting them in a single-file line. Ethan was grabbed along with Trent and forced into the line. It was very difficult to see as everyone bumped into the rocks and other prisoners. Even the terrorists had trouble keeping themselves from running into things.

They were quick to get a move on. Ethan thought for a minute and held onto the rock. The sound of the bird faded, calming all of the terrorists down. They always called helicopters birds, mostly because of the rotors that needed to be used for thrust and lift.

He had opportunities that he could have jumped at during this very moment to escape. However, it was not just his life in the hands of these maniacs. He needed them, and they needed him.

Ethan never expected the helicopter to find them, so the feeling of hope had never sparked in him. He pressed on, finalizing his decision. He was playing a whole new game he'd never thought he would have to play. He squeezed his arrowhead-shaped rock as if he were giving up everything he had as a person. He then loosened his hand, dropping the weapon and allowing it to turn back into just a rock.

12

AN ENEMY
AMONG THE ENEMY

O nce the sun broke over the mountains, the rays covered
everyone with a blanket of heat, and the cold temperature slowly slipped away.

Ethan and Trent had been walking alongside each other,
and no one had noticed the entire night. The terrorists had been
recovering from the chaotic scene with the helicopter. Most of
them had been quiet as they all traveled through the mountain.
Ethan figured they were pretty embarrassed. Not one prisoner,
including Ethan, had been tortured.

Ethan's feet, even though cut up, had felt better against
the tough earth after he'd wrapped the material around them.
The energy of the prisoners quickly faded, and Ethan noticed a
lot of them stumbling and tripping over the smallest of rocks.
Ethan himself had little motivation of survival left. He would
just put one foot in front of the other in the hope that the next
foot would follow.

The group made it to an open escarpment as the sun rose.
The light revealed the prisoners were walking along a narrow

path elevated miles above the canyon. Ethan moved closer to Trent's side, nudging him and nodding his head to the side, making him aware of the drop-off. He took notice as he leaned over a little to get a better perspective. Once Trent had a good look at what was over the edge, he took a quick step to the stone wall, and fear crossed his face.

Ethan could see that the side of the mountain was only big enough for five men abreast. It wasn't a lot. Ethan's chances of falling off the side were pretty good given that one small trip could turn into a flight down the mountain.

Ethan moved closer to the edge for a second out of curiosity to see what was down below.

At the base of the canyon, Ethan saw a basin formed by years of erosion. An aggressive river ran through, leading the way to whatever Ethan figured would be their destination. Ethan noticed that the rock strata had moved from a gray tone to more of a sandstone base, almost similar to that of the Grand Canyon. There was barely any green around, but Ethan noticed the occasional brush here and there.

Abu finally made his way up the line, giving Ethan a hateful glare. Ethan noticed his expression and the fact that height didn't seem to bother him. He knew that Abu wanted to kill him, and at this point, Ethan almost would let him.

Ethan was in a lot of pain from the hike, and not getting enough food or water didn't help either. His body was slowly shutting down. As both made eye contact with each other, another presence was made known. They both looked ahead, noticing the Shadow staring back at them before the two wrestled with their eyes once more. Ethan was safe as long as the Shadow was around. Ethan raised his untied hands, creating two thumbs-up with a winning smirk. Abu could only stare at Ethan in disbelief. Ethan couldn't help but chuckle with what little energy he had left as he looked at Abu's confused face.

It took a moment before Abu processed what he was looking

at. He ran to Ethan and struck him in the gut. The line stopped as Ethan fell straight to the ground, landing on his side. His body wasn't able to keep him on his knees.

Abu yelled over to the other guards to tie him back up. Trent slowly bent one knee, trying to help Ethan. Once Abu saw that Trent had untied hands as well, the entire line of prisoners watching the scene broke into laughter. Abu's mouth dropped wide open, large enough to catch flies. For a moment, his demeanor was defeated, and he spun around in the small space he was given as though he was surrounded by hyenas. He was the butt of the joke.

Abu yelled, spitting on Ethan and kicking him in the gut as the guards tied Trent's hands again.

The kicking didn't stop. Abu had lost his mind and wouldn't listen to anyone, including the second in command who yelled at him to stop. Ethan lay there, taking each kick and wanting it to end. He clenched his eyes shut and held his breath.

The prisoners stood there where they could see, silent as the air, watching their fellow brother get beaten to death. No one was laughing anymore. Trent had two guards on him, so he couldn't help his friend this time. Ethan's head seemed light, and his organs felt like needles internally stabbed him from the inside out. He tightened his body, preparing for the next kick, but nothing happened. All the commotion stopped.

Ethan opened his eyes and saw that the Shadow held a knife to Abu's throat. He couldn't believe he was still alive. His body ached all over. He had been saved again by the Shadow.

Abu had a look of betrayal on his face but kept completely still. The Shadow looked at both parties with disgust. Ethan could see he was contemplating, but what?

"Traitor," Abu had whispered.

A fierce expression crossed the Shadow's face as he heard the mutinous words. He stared at Ethan for a long period of time before he released his rutted brow. The Shadow then dropped the knife to the ground in front of Ethan. He then looked from Ethan to Abu, giving a slight nod. The most devious smile ran across Ethan's face as he took his eyes off the leader and back to his enemy. The guards backed up all of the prisoners, leaving a space for Abu and Ethan.

Ethan turned, watching as the Shadow walked through the cluster of guards and prisoners before mounting his horse. He took one last look at Abu and Ethan before riding away. Something was different in the air. Ethan was left alone, to fend for himself.

"You are at a duel, my good sir. Seems like they made the decision…a fight to the death," one of the prisoners said.

Ethan couldn't believe what was happening. He had pushed the cards too much, and now he must reap the consequences. He looked at Trent, who looked a figure of helplessness.

"You can do this, buddy," his friend said.

Ethan heard the lie in his tone. He looked around, noticing every prisoners' head was down as if the battle were already lost. He knew they had no strength left in their bodies. They were defeated and had been trained to do what they were told since the trip had started. They just wanted to live. All they could do was watch in horror.

Ethan's body could barely move, let alone stand up. Every inch was bruised and blistered. Ethan already believed he was as good as dead. His heart raced as Abu made his way toward the knife.

Ethan didn't want to die. There was something inside of him that told him to fight. To keep going and to continue the journey he had started. An unseen force pushed him to grab the knife with his tied hands and jump from his side, swiping at Abu and pushing him back in surprise. Ethan landed on his side a with a sharp pain. Trent looked up with wide eyes, and a small smile appeared.

The prisoners cheered as Ethan slowly stood, leaning against the wall for support, the knife facing Abu. Ethan breathed with adrenaline and fear while Abu only looked at Ethan with disgust and a lust to kill.

Both stayed on their ends for a moment. Abu knew that he had more power and energy than Ethan, but Ethan had the upper hand knowing he had the wall and the knife. Unfortunately, he had very little strength left. He knew only a few strong moves could be made before he would lose it all. He had to think smart about this.

He knew that going toward Abu would be the wrong move. Abu had wanted to kill Ethan since the start of the trip.

Let Abu come to me, Ethan thought.

Sure enough, Abu sprinted toward Ethan, screaming at the top of his lungs. Ethan went to one knee on the ground and stepped forward with the other leg. He maneuvered around Abu and sliced the femoral artery close to the other man's upper thigh. Abu let out a loud, agonizing scream.

The entire group of prisoners hollered out encouragement for Ethan, and the guards stretched their arms out to block the prisoners from intervening. Ethan used it for motivation and the strength needed for self-preservation. As long as adrenaline coursed throughout his body, he had a chance. Abu turned around, limping on the left leg, realizing his hatred for Ethan had temporarily swallowed his logic.

Abu again came at Ethan, who was still on one knee. Ethan aimed for Abu's chest, but he saw it coming. Deflecting Ethan's hands over his head, Abu knocked the knife over the edge.

Ethan's fear increased tenfold as he lost his only savior. The knife had been his only advantage to winning.

Abu straddled Ethan, hitting him in the face with every ounce of fury. Ethan kept his hands up and blocked the punches as best he could.

"Come on, Ethan, fight! Don't give up!" Trent shouted above the commotion on both sides.

Ethan barely heard Trent over the punches and screams from Abu.

He looked back and saw how close he was to the edge. It was his only shot of making it out alive.

Abu was lost in his lust for Ethan to die, and as he continued to punch, Ethan hip-tossed Abu just a smidge. It was so weak that Abu never realized Ethan was moving closer to the edge. Ethan didn't want it to look too aggressive in case Abu snapped out of his tunnel vision and realized what Ethan was doing.

"There ya go, little by little." Trent noticed what Ethan's plan was and encouraged him to continue.

Ethan inched ever closer to the edge, taking a few last punches before he gave all he had. His feet firmly planted, he jerked his hips up and thrust Abu forward.

Caught off balance, Abu was thrown over Ethan's head. Realizing he had made another fatal mistake, the man released a frustrated yell. Ethan took advantage of Abu's loss of dominance and thrust him farther over his head.

Abu instinctively, out of an act of desperation, stretched out his arm to stop his forward momentum into the abyss below. Ethan noticed that Abu had stopped just shy of the cliff. His face, however, was wracked with fear as he noticed what he had almost fallen into, what Ethan had been trying to do.

Abu regained his throne as he overpowered Ethan, straddling him and locking his legs so Ethan would not try that again. This time, as Abu was in no rush or immediate danger, he took his time relishing a more intimate attack. He grabbed Ethan's neck and pushed his head over the side of the cliff, choking him.

Ethan struggled to reach for Abu's face, but he was out of breath and energy. There was nothing left in him, and he felt himself getting lightheaded.

"Ethan, hit them elbows!" Trent yelled.

Ethan had started to lose his sight before he heard Trent. With both hands tied, Ethan lifted his hands above his face

144

and slammed down on Abu's right elbow, making Abu shift his weight toward the left side of Ethan's head. Ethan punched him in the nose, and Abu released his grasp on Ethan's neck. Ethan let out a large gasp of air before he slammed a knee into Abu's crotch. The terrorist let out a very large squeal as the kick sent Abu off balance. This gave Ethan enough space to push Abu off him.

Both of the fighters gained their composure. Ethan stayed near the edge, not realizing where he was as he caught his breath. Abu wandered toward the wall and used it to stand back up, cupping his balls to make sure they were still there. His leg bled profusely, leaving a trail straight to the culprit whose robe was covered in his blood. Sweat poured from Abu's face, and it was obvious the man was in pain. He was bleeding out quickly. Ethan knew that it wouldn't be long until Abu fell completely.

Ethan saw Abu tend to his wound; Abu's breathing was becoming hoarse. His weakened body told everyone that he was a goner as the lifeblood leeched out of the wound.

The two looked at each other. Abu had underestimated Ethan, not giving him enough credit. Ethan had maybe one more minute of fight in him before he had absolutely nothing left. The prisoners and guards were together, each screaming for their own to win the fight.

Ethan had made it this far and couldn't lose now. There was still a chance to end this. Abu yelled once more and sprinted toward Ethan. Ethan screamed, working with every ounce of energy he had left, and lunged with one foot forward. Bending down, he kept his head to the right side of Abu. Ethan reached through the terrorist's legs and lifted, throwing Abu directly above his body. Ethan fell backward as his body turned, his stomach cutting over the edge of the cliff. Ethan watched as Abu's body sank to the depth of the basin. His bloodcurdling scream echoed until it was forever silenced by the abyss.

Ethan heard shouting from behind him. There was no way

he could pull himself back up. He lay there for a second, looking at the spot where Abu had landed. He couldn't believe that he'd just won. He couldn't believe he was still alive, for that matter.

The adrenaline faded. Ethan felt his body slip, and he panicked.

The prisoners were crowded around so much that Trent was able to yank free of the guards and help Ethan back with the hands of another prisoner. The guards struggled to get everyone in line.

Trent helped Ethan to his feet and yelled over the chaos of the other prisoners, "You look like shit, ya know that?"

"You should see the other guy," Ethan commented back with a serious face before both of them broke out in laughter.

The Shadow pointed, directing the prisoners where to go, and the guards moved around, making sure the line was clean. Ethan's gaze locked with the Shadow for just a moment, and Ethan was lost in his dark soulless eyes. What confused Ethan was that it seemed the Shadow was giving him a sympathetic stare, but Ethan couldn't know for sure. He was too tired.

Trent was able to stay next to Ethan and help him along the thin road. It didn't seem to bother any of the other guards that the two were together.

"Boy, you are one crazy son of a bitch," Trent said. "I can't believe what my eyes just saw."

"I can't believe what I just did, to be honest. That shouldn't have happened the way that it did. You know, I heard you a few times. Thank you," Ethan said gratefully.

"Well, I'm just glad that varmint is gone."

For the next few hours, a couple prisoners took turns holding Ethan up along the mountain side. He couldn't walk on his own because of some of the injuries he'd received during the fight with Abu. His eyes were also nearly swollen shut, so Ethan couldn't see much anymore.

Ethan's feet were now one whole blister each. He tried not to pop it on any sharp rocks, afraid that it would cause an immediate infection. He had to be careful because he doubted there would be any medical staff to take care of him.

The day was coming to a close, and it became cold again. Ethan wanted to give up. His body was numb and full of aches and pains. The prisoners were defeated from the nonstop walking. After Abu died, the Shadow had made no more stops for anyone. Even the guards were tired and keeping their heads down, not paying attention to the prisoners as much as they should.

"Trent, I need to lie down. I don't think I can go any further. This is really sucking right now." Ethan's voice was raspy.

"Come on, Cowboy, we're almost there. I can smell something new and fresh over yonder."

"Yeah, that would be rotting corpses you're smelling from the future just up ahead." Ethan spit out some dust he'd accumulated from his lips.

"Ha, even on death's bed ya sure do got some humor. Hey, let me ask you a question. Why do you think God be giving us this life? Why do we have to endure this sort of thing?" Trent spoke with a desire for Ethan to have the answer.

"We deserve what is coming to us. I deserve every bit of the godforsaken hell trip that He put me on. Honestly, I've been waiting for this a long time." Ethan at that moment felt acceptance for what he had endured and would endure.

Trent looked at Ethan as if he were absolutely crazy. Trent continued to study Ethan, but he didn't try to push the subject anymore. There was more to Ethan than Trent had realized.

"Holy mother-trucking shit." Trent spoke with awe.

Ethan looked up and saw that as the sun hid its rays behind the peak, there was a certain mountain off into the distance that looked different than the rest, very much like it was out of place. He couldn't quite understand why he had made that observation. It was as though the mountainside had a tumor sticking out of its side. Beside it ran the river that was once so far below. It beckoned its new guests with its refreshing smell and the sound of the rushing current. As the sun lowered itself below the tip, the entire mountainside became dark. Within that moment, the bulged section lit up like millions of lightning bugs had gathered together. Ethan struggled to keep an eye open to view the marvelous sight. Once more, there was serenity to be found in the worst of circumstances.

"Looks like God isn't done with us just yet." Trent chuckled.

Ethan ignored the comment and continued to walk, waiting to find out what was in store next.

13

THANATOS

After another full day's walk, motivated by the sheer will of survival, the prisoners finally reached their unfortunate destination. Ethan and the rest came upon a gigantic deformed boulder that was the same color as the mountain and gravel it sat upon. The top of it had a hole that looked like someone had taken a giant spoon and scooped the top out. The same thing was done on the side of it. As Ethan approached closer, he noticed it wasn't stone but built with material not from the environment and camouflaged to blend in with the sloping mountainside. The walls had indentations and weirdly placed gashes as though someone had scooped out portions of the walls just like the top of the boulder.

After laughing at the strange rock formation, he looked up at the fireflies. They clung to the corners of other different sized boulders, each with different indents and shapes just like the one he was next to. It was like nothing he had ever seen before. Throughout this strange arrangement were paths leading in and around them. They were mostly flat, but Ethan noticed that the "roads" sometimes had a random bump or curve that bellowed in. It didn't seem to add up because it was planted on an incline. There was no sign of natural run-off from the mountain, and he thought it would erode any pathways through this strange mountainside. From the look of it, he thought the rocks could very easily have been there since time immemorial, untouched by the modern era. Ethan felt an uneasiness settle into his stomach, but he had no idea why.

He could see no walls around the perimeter, but it was also fairly dark and only the light from the moon allowed him to see where to step. The lights around the family of rocks were still too far away to use for moving. Navigating the darkness was made even more difficult by the fact that he could barely open his eyes from the swelling that had resulted after the beating he'd taken the day before.

Suddenly, as Ethan began to move center of the boulder, he watched as the mountain from behind filled in the gaps with its color and natural shape. The angle of where he stood had made no sense, but as he moved, he began to see a normal squared building. He heard himself whisper an awe sound. There was an opening closer to the left side of the building that took on the shape of a door frame and, one by one, the prisoners' ropes that had bound them for so long were cut and they were taken into the deformed building.

As Ethan approached, the structure looked like it was constructed of all man-made materials. However, when he observed it at an arms distance, the material looked like a facade that covered a hidden secret within its walls. Although fascinating at night, he wondered what it would look like in the daytime.

He finally reached the entrance, and Trent had to stop holding him up so he could be taken inside. The guards cut Ethan's rope last and threw him inside.

Torches every few feet were mounted, giving light to the entire place. To Ethan's amazement, it looked like a normal interior building. He'd been expecting to see deformed walls and holes within the floors. Along the walls on each side were small cells that could hold roughly the size of an adult man. The cells ran parallel along the narrow hallway he was being pushed down. To his left and right were prisoners he had never seen before, as if there were already other captives who'd been taken from other places.

We are not the only ones, thought Ethan to himself.

All the prisoners had only a robe in their cell. Each one looked tired, dirty, and hungry. Most of them were emaciated, so much so that Ethan could see their skeletal features prominently in the torches' flickering light. The smell of the cells was musty, and it pierced Ethan's nostrils. There was no draft to hide the scent of fear leeching from the pores of the defeated prisoners.

Ethan only attempted to mask the smell with his hand a few times before he resigned himself. He tried not to make eye contact with anyone as he walked down the hallway. All of them had a look of death and despair in their eyes. He accidentally locked eyes with a large man that looked like he was a Greek giant. He was almost too big for the cell. As they both gazed at each other, Ethan could only see anger and a desire for revenge. There was a sharp scar that crossed over the man's left temple. Ethan wondered if it was from this trip or if it was an old scar.

Down the hallway and through an open door a chamber was revealed similar to the one he'd just left. More prisoners filled each cell, and the more he searched, the more he realized he had to have seen more than a hundred men and women there. They continued through yet another door, which made Ethan picture the building in his head as a labyrinth. This amazed Ethan, as he had not thought this building had such depth. It was as though they pushed deeper into the mountain. Finally, they reached the last chamber, which dead-ended into at least two dozen more cells, although these were empty. Ethan and Trent were the last to be placed inside them. Luckily, Ethan was imprisoned once more next to his friend.

One of the guards shoved Ethan into his small cell, and the door closed and locked behind him. Stone and dirt created the ground, and a brick wall lay behind him. Ethan looked around for windows but did not find any. The only light came from the torches sporadically placed throughout the room, hanging above the pillars.

"This just gets more and more interesting as time goes on." Ethan slouched down and put his knees up to rest his arms.

"Yeah, brother, I would have to agree with ya. I'm just as curious as you. Think they here to use us as media bait or maybe to get ransom?"

Ethan pondered on Trent's question. "Nah, there are too many men and women in this place. Not to mention, there were a lot I didn't recognize. It seems we're not the only group to make the journey."

"Hey! Come on. Let me out of zeer!" a man with a Russian accent a few cells down screamed at the top of his lungs.

He was a bigger man that you could see still had some meat left on his bones. The trip for him didn't seem to have taken its toll as it did on the others and Ethan. There were a lot of bruises on his face, which indicated that he must have been a trouble-maker throughout the trip.

He stared at the ground but continued to scream. "I'm tired of diz' place! Feed me at least, you crazy baboons!"

Ethan knew that this wasn't going to end well if he kept screaming.

Sure enough, after a minute of screaming for food and water, guards rushed in with AKs and posted themselves throughout the room with their backs facing the cells. Ethan and Trent looked at each other, knowing very well that someone was about to make their entrance.

A minute later the Shadow walked into the room. He had a clean black robe with a hood that hovered above his head. A white cloth covered his face except for his eyes. They were still as black as Ethan remembered, resembling the eyes of a shark. A white belt covered his waist.

The Shadow held a silver plate of food. It had some shiny green grapes still attached to the vine. Next to it were four or five different kinds of meats that Ethan couldn't pick out. On the plate closest to the guard was a full loaf of bread that looked a lot like ciabatta. Ethan's stomach growled as the fresh aroma of the delicious smelling assortments entered his nose.

"Hey! Now zhat's more like it. You wiz the silver plate need to hand me zhat food." The Russian stood and held the cell bars, beckoning the Shadow to come closer.

The Shadow walked to the Russian's cell and placed the silver platter close enough for the Russian to grab.

The boisterous prisoner suddenly became cautious. He looked at the Shadow with suspicion. Hunger took over, and he quickly grabbed some grapes and a few pieces of meat, devouring every bit he had in his hands.

The other prisoners, shocked by what they had just seen, yelled and screamed, wanting to grab anything they could from the Shadow's plate.

Ethan's stomach began to ache as he realized how long it had been since he had an actual meal. He forced himself to stay quiet and sat against the wall, watching the whole scene unfold. As hungry as he was, he knew it was too good to be true and that something wasn't right. He even noticed Trent trying to grab the plate that was a hand's length out of reach. Down the line were desperate hands, reaching and begging for any scrap of food. It was as though their stomachs had taken over their minds and caused them to act like zombies.

The Russian ate the remaining food in his hands, laughing at the other prisoners. He gave a small dance and showboated like he was better than everyone.

The guards suddenly stiffened, and the Shadow moved to the entrance. The reaching arms slowly died down and retreated back into the cells. Their voices carried off into complete silence. Everyone watched the entrance as clicks of footsteps were heard from a distance. The sound increased as another step was taken. It was as though someone wore dress shoes.

Ethan couldn't see. The prisoners still clung onto their cells, waiting to witness the new person. He noticed that everyone seemed to have the same feeling as him, that someone important was about to make an entrance.

The clicks grew louder until they stopped at the entrance of the room.

"Good evening, ladies and gentlemen," a soft warm male voice said, piercing the room. It somehow brought comfort, sounding like a pleasant host.

"I'm sure all of you have had quite an amazing trip, and I apologize for any inconvenience that it caused you. Transportation in this terrain is very hard to come by. The only means is simply by foot or horseback. See it from my viewpoint as, in a sense, taking the scenic route." The man chuckled. His articulate words showed he carefully formulated his thoughts before he continued. "My real name is not important. However, knowing how everyone operates, I do not wish to be given a name that I would most likely not agree with. For now, you may call me Eubulus. I will be taking care of you all as your most humble host."

Shocked, Ethan realized the mystery voice was American. It had a little bit of a northwest accent to it.

He spoke as he walked slowly down the aisle. "Now, let us move to the question you have been asking yourself this entire trip. The wait is over. I will answer it for you. All of you have been summoned to partake in a once-in-a-lifetime opportunity. An opportunity to find out who you truly are inside. To dig to the deepest depths of your soul and encounter a sad worthless being...or a legendary god who was molded into the form of man. The greatest gift I could give you as your host is the path to find out which of the two you are. Fact is, you already started your journey when you came off the boat."

The man, who'd been previously hidden by all of the

prisoners, suddenly revealed the mysterious visage behind the voice. He was a much older gentleman who ranged from the late fifties to the early sixties. His narrow face held a goatee that was white as snow. His head was proportionately round with no hair, causing the flickering flames from the torches to reflect off of it. The deep and heavy bags under his brown eyes revealed a man who had seen better days. The wrinkles around his face and forehead moved as he spoke. A very tan Caucasian man, his complexion told the story of many years beneath the sun's rays, indicating that he must have been here awhile.

He wore a silver suit with a blue tie that was neatly ironed and looked as though it came right from Savile Row. The black oxfords he wore shone as bright as his bald head, and not one bit of dirt or scuff could be seen on them.

"I want there to be no confusion within this room. You may leave whenever you want. You are, of course, guests here, and I would certainly not want to keep you against your will. You would then be stopping your journey short of the opportunity I have bestowed upon you. It would crush my heart to see you leave so soon when you have only just arrived, but I understand."

There was a brief moment of silence. No one moved or dared breathe. At that moment, there were no answers as to why they had been brought there or who Eubulus was, and Ethan was more puzzled than before.

"Screw your fauncy speech. I vant out of here!" The Russian banged his hands against the cell and pushed his face past the bars.

The old man looked toward the Shadow, who nodded to Eubulus, confirming that this was the specific prisoner mentioned in a previous conversation.

"Dear sir, I have given you shelter from the wind, the rain, and the scorching sun. I have gifted you with food from a silver platter. Why would you want to give up a chance of attainting greatness?"

"Zu puny old hag has held us against our vill. Notzing but cowardly dogs hiding with zour guns." The Russian spit at Eubulus like a snake spits at its prey, and it landed in the old man's eye.

Eubulus stood there, seemingly taken aback, and slowly pulled out a handkerchief from his breast pocket to wipe himself clean. "I regret your ignorance and stupidity. You are of course free to go as I promised."

The Shadow opened his cell, and the Russian just stood there looking baffled. He took a step but was stopped by the voice of Eubulus.

"Before you go, know that it is a long trip. May I offer you the loaf of bread?" The old man held his hand out to the silver platter still being held by the Shadow.

The Russian thought for a moment, then reached for the loaf of bread.

As he reached for the loaf, two guards grabbed him and forced him to his knees. The Russian began to struggle, dropping the loaf of bread, and the Shadow helped hold the Russian in place. The three guards worked together, stopping him from escaping their grasp. He screamed as he fought to break free.

Eubulus walked to the loaf of bread, ignoring the struggle behind him. Bending down, he picked it up, brushing off the small particles of dirt clinging to it.

The prisoners leaned in closer, and Ethan's heart sank. He looked at Trent, who had the same fear on his face.

"I'm quite disappointed in the decision you chose. I am here to bring not only greatness to each and every one of you, but with your help, we will illuminate the entire world about who you all are." Eubulus stared into the distance and past the walls like he could see through them. His brown eyes gleamed with a daydream. He had a vision, and he was infatuated with it.

Ethan could only imagine what lay behind those eyes.

Eubulus's voice went from soft to a screeching pitch of anger.

"I gave you a door to fulfill your name and place it at the top of the pedestal, yet you slam it in my face and make me look like a fool in front of everyone. I will keep my word, and I will let you leave. You will leave to the afterlife." He broke his thousand-yard stare and turned to face the Russian.

The Shadow grabbed the Russian's hair and pulled it back, lifting his head to the ceiling.

Eubulus clenched the frightened man's jaw like a vice. The strength of his hand outmatched what little strength the Russian had as he struggled to keep his mouth closed. Using the bread like a crowbar, Eubulus worked the tip of the loaf into the Russian's mouth. Little by little, the loaf disappeared into the man's esophagus. His eyes began to water, and tears flowed down his cheeks. Everyone in the area heard pockets of air gurgle from his throat as he struggled to breathe. A sound of the mandible detaching from its socket sprang a popping noise that echoed throughout the cell.

Ethan watched as Eubulus's expression remained unfazed, and he stared into the eyes of a helpless victim being used as an example. Ethan's gaze then switched from the man at death's door to the man who was sending him there. The expression on Eubulus's face was not one of anger or enjoyment. But it was not one ever accredited to that of a killer. It was rather like the countenance of an artist in the midst of sculpting. In that moment, he was a potter using the bread like clay and molding his intentions.

No matter how much the Russian begged with his sounds and eyes, Eubulus continued to shove the bread farther and farther down his throat. All the while, his face remained stoic and purposeful.

The entire room had gone silent, and all of the prisoners retreated back against the walls, trying to get as far away as they could and realizing there was not an option to leave. This was evident as Eubulus had made his point quite clear. Their only choice was to accept his offer if they wished to survive.

The Russian gave up the struggle, and his eyes rolled to the back of his head. He seized for a few seconds before the guards dropped his lifeless body to the floor, his face landing toward Ethan.

Ethan stared at it as his own face remained frozen with no expression. His mind couldn't complete a full thought. He'd just watched a whole other level of death. It was almost like out of a movie.

Taking his handkerchief once more, Eubulus cleaned his hands of the saliva that had foamed up on them as though he had finished a delightful meal.

"All of you take note that there will only be one way out of this, and I'm very happy you were able to see it firsthand. Of course, it will not always be by my hand. I've been informed that some of you have already made it difficult for my men. Some going as far as taking it into your own hands to alleviate what you think is a problem. You have not seen problems yet. It has been a walk in the park. As much as it kills me to let those disciplines slide past, let me be clear that from here on out, there will be no more escapes, munities, or disobedience. You will do what you are told." Eubulus stared right at Ethan for an uncomfortably long moment.

Ethan understood right away that he had put himself in a larger spotlight than the others. His body shuttered as their eyes connected for the first time. He stared at a nightmare.

He'd known that he was going to be on the guards' radar, but now his name was at the top of Eubulus's list. Ethan kept his sight on Eubulus scrutinizing him, trying to ask himself all the questions about him specifically.

What was he planning on doing with them? Ethan wondered as Eubulus made his exit, followed by the Shadow and the remaining guards.

Still silent, the prisoners didn't say a word. Each one slowly sat down and attempted to get comfortable. Some placed their backs against the walls and just stared in front. Some tried investigating their cells for any means of escape. Some were so tired that they just lay on the ground and dozed off. Since getting off the ship, they had been on the move, always being watched and never having any time to speak to one another. Now that everyone was alone together without any supervision, no one wanted to speak.

"Ethan, what are you thinking?" Trent moved to the side of Ethan's cell and waited for a response.

The truth was, Ethan didn't know what to think. Even though his mind raced, it seemed completely blank, not knowing where to start.

Ethan looked at Trent, saying, "Brother, we just might be screwed on this one."

Trent's face went from hope to devastation, and Ethan noticed. He needed to come up with something to ease the illness coming from within both of their stomachs.

"Listen, we've made it this far. And it seems that they have us here for a particular reason. They have something else in mind more than just fun and games. If we stick together as much as possible, we can try and survive. We just have to wait for the right opening. We'll watch each other's back and go from there. Take one moment at a time. Right now, we need to keep up our strength and get some sleep."

Trent nodded, agreeing with Ethan.

Both tried to get comfortable. Ethan was still hungry and contemplated grabbing the loaf that protruded from the Russian's mouth. It felt to Ethan that no matter what happened, they would soon join the lifeless body that lay on the floor in the middle of the aisle. Ethan put his hands under his cheek to try and make a softer pillow. Staring at the dead body, Ethan tried to sleep. They had left the dead man where he lay. Ethan guessed it was to make clear what could happen if they did try to escape. How would they escape?

Ethan graciously stepped inside the house with two of his men. At the front of the line was Captain Holtzway, being led to a room filled with pillows and carpet. Men wearing turbans and robes gathered in a circle.

They must be important elders of the village or the surrounding villages, Ethan thought.

As the group of Marines entered, the elders stood, and one specific elder left the circle to greet Captain Holtzway and Lt. Smith. Muhammed Patan, the head elder of the village, wore a white robe and turban. His face was filled with wrinkles, and he moved very slowly. Looking like he might be in his nineties, his dark skin contrasted sharply with his long, grayish beard. They exchanged a handshake and placed their hands over their heart once they were done.

The elder gestured for them to take off their boots, but Captain Holtzway explained that they could not owing to safety reasons and hoped that they would understand. The elders nodded, giving them the okay to sit on the cushions.

Before Lt. Smith sat, he turned to Ethan, asking, "Is everyone set up outside and in position?"

"Yes, sir, half of my team is supporting Steve outside, and they have the perimeter covered. Douglas has his squad right outside of the village overlooking the compound as well as keeping a few eyes outward."

The lieutenant confirmed with a nod and turned to sit down. Ethan could tell that his platoon commander was just as uneasy as he was. Having the CO on this mission was impractical and made everyone stay on their toes.

Patan took his own pillow and switched it out with the pillow that Captain Holtzway would have used. This was a huge sign of respect from the Afghan people, especially from an elder. Ethan knew this from the classes he had taken before deploying to Afghanistan.

Everyone sat down, crisscrossing their legs and getting settled. Ethan chuckled under his breath when he noticed Captain

Holtzway struggling to get his legs crossed. Lt. Smith, who had no problem getting to that position, turned around and noticed the small smirk across Ethan's face. The lieutenant's stern expression quickly turned Ethan's face neutral. Ethan had been caught red-handed laughing at his CO, but when Ethan noticed a wink from his platoon commander, it allowed Ethan to ease up.

"Mother of my son, please bring in the food." Patan gestured to a woman who came in with a few others, carrying plates of food.

The aroma was different and unique, and the new spices stood out to Ethan the most. Each man received a plate of rice and lamb. It was a very delicate dish that was made for special occasions. Ethan tried to remember what the dish was called.

He placed one of his men at the door and another across the room from him. Ethan went back to his corner and was greeted by one of the women who had a plate for him. Ethan kept his eyes away from hers and put his hand out to gesture 'no' but saw that Captain Holtzway was giving him a nod to take the plate.

Ethan didn't hesitate as he did not want to insult the host. He took the plate and waited for further instructions. This was past his comfort level—not only being placed within the room of the elders but also alongside his higher-ranking officers.

As he looked closely at the plate, he remembered the dish's name. It was called kabuli palaw, a dish made of rice and lamb. He smiled, proud that he remembered a lot of the history of these people.

The men made small talk and asked all of the polite questions first, then Ethan took it upon himself to scope out much of the room's layout and the closest way to the exits. The room was fairly large, and the chipped and worn stucco was plastered over in a light teal color from top to bottom. Several fine colorful woolen tapestries hung from each of the walls, draping the room with warm hues. There was one window on the right side of the wall, where Ethan saw his Marines patrolling back and forth, occasionally being nosey and attempting to peek in without anyone taking notice.

* * *

Outside, an entirely different scene unfolded. Steve spoke with his men about some of the delicious food that he had when he was in Germany. Surrounding them were a lot of the villagers doing their daily tasks and chores. Some had carts of goods from food to brightly colored clothes. A group of small kids played with a ball on the street, laughing and giggling. Steve kept an eye on the buildings that surrounded the area.

Ten yards away, a boy in a tan robe and a blue vest walked toward Steve, and a ball lay next to the child's feet. The boy reminded Steve of a very young Aladdin with his beautiful black hair and smooth Arabian skin. When the boy smiled and looked curiously at Steve, the Marine thought, *He is such an innocent kid.*

The boy's blue eyes were bright as the ocean on a sunny day. His face had a whole bunch of dirt on it from playing. The other kids were behind him in a group, waiting to see what the boy would do. The boy looked at Steve for a moment like he was trying to figure him out. He turned toward his friends, then looked back to Steve before kicking the ball.

Steve stopped the ball with his foot, and the boy waited to see if he would kick it back. Steve laughed as he looked at the other Marines. He was greeted by a few smiles from them before he kicked it back to the boy. They played for a little bit before the other kids chanted for the boy to come back over with the ball.

* * *

"How's it looking out there, guys?" Ethan whispered into his radio.

"Second squad is doing fine." Steve laughed after having a special moment with the blue-eyed boy. "All set in their positions, patrolling a little bit and making sure everything in the surrounding area is being cleared every so often. Kicked the ball a few times to the kids. They seem to be enjoying our company." Steve chuckled again over the radio.

Still holding onto the plate, Ethan held his hand over the radio so it didn't make too much noise to distract the meeting.

"Third squad has eyes over village and beyond. No movement can be seen coming in or out. Also, why does Third squad get the boring part of all this? Everyone else gets shade, and I'm out here getting my ass fried?" Douglas continued to complain over the radio until there was a window of opportunity for Steve to jump in.

"Because you're an orange-haired albino freckled kid. You could use the tan."

Ethan knew there was too much chatter going on, and he told the platoon to only use the radio when necessary.

Back in the room with the elders, Patan waited for the guests to start eating. As soon as Captain Holtzway ate with his right hand, so did Lt. Smith. Ethan followed suit and took his glove off to begin eating. The food was actually very good, tasting like a homemade meal back home. He wanted to brag over the radio to everyone else, but he knew that would be poor form. It would definitely piss off Douglas.

After everyone finished their food, the women came back in to take the dishes away. Ethan handed his plate back over to the same woman who had given him the food. Keeping his eyes away from hers, he bowed his head in gratitude. After the last women left the room and everyone had readjusted themselves, the meeting began.

"Captain, on behalf of the village, I would like to thank you for what you have done for us. It has surely been an amazing journey with you coming here and helping us with the problems that we have endured. We are grateful, and we thank Allah for bringing you to us. However, we think that it is time for you to go."

Captain Holtzway's eyes widened, and the energy of the room changed.

"I don't quite understand, Patan? We have so much more to offer the village. We have built a great relationship with each other, and I would hate for that to go away." Captain Holtzway looked toward Lt. Smith, who was just as shocked as the other Marines.

Patan looked around at the group of elders. Ethan noticed that their faces had become crestfallen. Clearly something was wrong. There was more to this change of pace than what was being said.

"The United States is committed to helping you strive for a healthier life as well as protection. I understand that it can be overwhelming for a new group of people that do not have the same beliefs as you to come in and direct your life into another realm of change you were not expecting. I assure you that we have your best interests in mind and wish to continue working together. If we have offended you in any way, causing you to want to discontinue our relationship, please tell me so that I can make it right."

The captain might have some horrible leadership skills when it came to his own Marines, Ethan thought, but he was making a very great argument to win the elders back.

"We owe you no explanation of reasons why you need to go. You have barged into our territory without our permission, and we let it go for the time that you have been here. We have humored your presence and allowed you to come through here using what little resources we have, and we have traded as well. We thank you for your kindness and care, but the elders and I have spoken. You are no longer welcomed in the village."

Patan's tone had become more agitated as Captain Holtzway attempted to work with him, seeing if they could find a solution together. The elders shifted around, seeming antsier.

"Hey, Miller," Steve said over the radio.

"Not now, man. Things aren't going the way that we were expecting," Ethan whispered to Steve, trying not to cause a distraction.

"Yeah, umm. Well, let's just say there is a shift in the wind out here as well."

Ethan furrowed his brow, trying to process what was happening both inside and outside.

* * *

Outside, the Marines suddenly became aware of the weight of the heat pressing down upon them. An oppressive stillness shrouded the streets. Steve held the radio near his chest as he glanced around the area. Within a minute of the locals laughing and talking, everything went quiet. The villagers had disappeared from sight. The carts had either been moved or closed. The kids were nowhere to be seen except for the ball that lay in the middle of the road. Shutters to windows that had been open were now shut. Steve shook his head as his heart raced. His men and the rest of the platoon outside slowly raised their rifles to the ready position.

Every Marine's eyes watched for any and all detail and movement. Something was not right, and Steve and his men knew it. A gust of wind swept through the street, and Steve turned his head, watching as dust blew across the road. Near the other side of the street in the alleyway was a small human figure, hidden in the dark. Steve raised his rifle toward the shadow. He squinted to get a better view through the sun.

Slowly the mysterious figure walked out. It was the blue-eyed kid that Steve had played ball with just a while ago. All the Marines slightly lowered their rifles. There was no need to feel threatened by the boy.

Steve stared at him before gesturing for him to go home or go play ball with the kids. Instead, the boy came out from the shadows until he was a quarter of the way into the street. Steve saw the boy's face clearly as he stepped into the sun. Unlike before when he had smiled and laughed, his body was mechanical as his hands were to his side. He looked stiff as a pole. He walked toward Steve, causing the Marines to raise their rifles once more.

Steve's mouth became dry, and his heart pounded before he spoke under his breath, "Turn around, kid…turn around." A million decisions crossed through Steve's mind. He didn't know what to do. The boy couldn't be more than ten years old. "Get out of here! Go home, ya hear!"

The boy stopped in his tracks. He was about thirty yards away. Steve and the Marines backed up along the side of the building as he directed everyone not to shoot.

* * *

Ethan was still inside, and the argument had escalated to yelling between the captain and Patan. No one else engaged either of them, but Ethan could see that everyone was on edge. He wanted the captain to give up and come back to this at a later time. He could tell that this group was not going to have any more of his talk, but the captain was starting to lose his temper and his professionalism.

"You need us to protect you, and your safety is the concern of the United States. Without us, you will be taken under the control of ISIS, and we will not allow it! They cannot hurt you if…"

"They have our children!" Patan cut off the captain, tears flowing from his eyes.

It was as if there had been a built-up pressure that was finally released. The other elders dropped their heads in embarrassment and defeat.

"They have captured our sons and have taken them to their training camps. There is nothing you can do. If they are to survive, we have to comply with them and rid you from our village. Please! I beg of you. Just leave."

For once, Captain Holtzway sat speechless. Ethan knew this had taken a turn for the worse. He wouldn't even know what to do in this situation, and he was relieved not to be in Captain Holtzway's position.

Ethan looked around the room, noticing one elder who did not seem to be fazed by what Patan had just said. Ethan squinted at the man as he stared at Patan with anger in his expression.

* * *

As the tension continued to mount outside, Steve continued to direct the boy and his men not to do anything. He was trying to keep everyone where they were until he could figure out what to do next. Steve reached down to grab his radio, but the boy took a step closer. Steve dropped his hand from the radio and picked up the rifle again. The boy stopped.

Steve had to think of his men and the mission at hand. He had the CO in the building next to him. He had to protect him at all cost. But there was also an innocent child. He didn't want what was going through his mind to be true.

As Steve looked at the boy's eyes, he noticed that they stared off into the distance. He wasn't present. Something reflected off of the boy's cheek. Steve attempted to get a closer look at it. Then he noticed it was a tear.

Steve screamed.

* * *

Simultaneously, Ethan witnessed a horrific pivotal moment as the angry-looking man slowly reached inside his pocket.

A loud explosion sounded outside.

Ethan reacted quickly, grabbing the lieutenant by the back of his flak jacket and sliding him into the other room. They were immediately pushed to the ground by a second explosion that went off in the room where Captain Holtzway had been.

14

AWAKENING OF AN EMPIRE

E than awoke sweating profusely. He attempted to move a few of his limbs but the effort was halted as pain shot through his body. He let out a gruesome moan. The wounds had finally been able to catch up and start healing. Ethan put a hand on his head, rubbing it to relieve the pounding headache. The smell of the rotting corpse on the ground seeped through Ethan's nose. Its stench stung with every inhalation Ethan took.

"Did you know you yell in your sleep? It makes it very hard for others to get any shut-eye 'round here. I'd complain to the front desk but can't seem to get ahold of anyone." Trent was sitting with his back against the wall. He stared up at the ceiling, looking as though he'd been up for a while.

Ethan noticed Trent's hand move to cover his nose often, like a tick. He, too, was attempting to mask the stench. The flies had already taken hold of the body and were enjoying the feast.

"No, how would I know if I yell in my sleep if I'm sleeping?" Ethan moved his back against the wall.

Trent nodded, and his face reacted to Ethan's words as if to say, 'good point.'

They stared at the ceiling together.

"Any idea of what we're in for after that nutbag came through?" Trent questioned.

"I don't have a clue. Eubulus is not like the rest of the terrorists. He isn't a part of their culture, yet here he is. It seems like he could be the leader, but he might be a middleman or someone that possibly has a skill set no one in the group can manage. What it could be, I have no idea." Ethan unwrapped his feet, relieved to see the blisters finally going down.

"Looks like we won't have to wait too long to find out." Trent nodded toward the door as a couple of guards walked in holding rifles.

After the guards were spread throughout the hallway, the Shadow walked in, wearing the same outfit as the day before. He stopped a few feet from the front and turned his back to the cells, facing the doorway.

A thin man with a tan cotton robe came through. He had a younger look about him, and Ethan guessed he was in his late twenties or early thirties. His skin was dark and he had a smooth narrow face, showing distinguished cheekbones. He wore a clay-colored turban and walked with his back slightly slouched. His arms waved back and forth with no coordination, showing a lack of confidence.

"I swear I'm done with these video game bosses coming through. I feel like I'm in a never-ending Mario game with hundreds of Bowsers." Trent whispered under his breath as the new stranger walked to the center of the cells.

The young man continued to walk until he was met by the dead body. Startled, he put his hand out as though to block the sight from his eyes. He diverted his focus and looked around at the group of dying souls. After a minute of looking at each and every one of them, he smiled. Upon seeing this, Ethan and Trent were taken aback and threw their heads against the wall. The young man's teeth were crooked and jumbled together.

"It's your turn." Trent spoke softly to Ethan.

Ethan looked back at Trent. "When you try to lie through your teeth but can't because it's blocked and can't handle the tooths."

Both men laughed uncontrollably.

Their noise grabbed the attention of the stranger, and he walked toward them. "What is...so...funny...gentlemen," the man spoke with pauses and a Middle East accent. His English wasn't bad, but it apparently just took him some time to think of the words before he spoke them, and his tone wasn't aggressive or out of authority.

Ethan and Trent stared at the smiling man and didn't move.

"My name is Akhilesh. I will...be taking care...of you all. I must first...take you...to orientation...is how you say it."

Akhilesh nodded to the Shadow, who then gestured to the other guards. They all proceeded to drop their weapons to the side and unlock the cells. Every prisoner, including Ethan and Trent, stood completely still.

Akhilesh looked around and seemed to wonder why no one was moving. He noticed that everyone was hesitant, so he waved everyone out. "We will not kill...you. Please cooperate. Don't be...scared." He waved a few more times.

Cautiously and one by one, each prisoner came out and queued into a straight line. Ethan and Trent followed suit. Once everyone was situated, the first one in the line moved, following Akhilesh out the door.

As they made their way out of the jail past the previous chambers, Ethan noticed that all the torches in the other rooms were not lit. The biggest change was that the cells had no one in them anymore. They were completely empty.

Where did they all go?

Trent had a sense of horror as he tapped Ethan on the shoulder, confirming that he saw the same thing. Were they walking on death row?

Once Ethan made it outside, the sun attacked his eyes the same way it did when he was removed from the coffin. He placed his arm over his eyes as he slowly adjusted to the sun's bright rays. Ethan breathed in heavily, and the freedom of fresh air gave him a second wind to keep moving forward.

Being locked in that filthy prison had dulled his sense of smell. He had not realized how bad it was until he stepped outside and breathed in clean air. It was dry and hot, but there was still a light breeze that cooled Ethan and everyone else off. The prisoners did not hesitate to enjoy the moment provided by nature's freedom.

When Ethan's eyes finally adapted, his jaw dropped.

His eyes took in the full scale of what was hidden before he was put into the prison. On the side of the mountain sat a small town. Its different sized huts and multi storied buildings shaped almost like stone structures integrated into the mountain, which ran almost half a mile up in elevation. Some streets seemed to be dead ends while others descended to the lower levels of what Ethan could only believe to be a town. Narrow alleys traversed throughout the village, and they all connected to the main switchback road that led to the summit.

As they marched in a single file line, Ethan noticed that each structure was built differently than the other and each held its own unique style of mismatched angles. They were similar to the boulder building that he and the rest were held in overnight. Every time Ethan centered himself with a building, he would see its true form and, as he walked away, it turned back into a stone structure. What intrigued Ethan the most was the material used in the architecture. Even though it seemed to be built using sandstone and clay, the foundation of the homes appeared to be rooted deep within the bedrock, which could only be accomplished through the use of a machine.

At the tail of the village ran the river Ethan had been traveling alongside for the past few days. It coursed through the bottom of the town, where a few smaller houses sat.

That's where they get their water supply, thought Ethan. The river ran with haste as the current could be seen with the naked eye; it was clear enough that he thought he was able to gauge its depth.

Ethan found himself both overwhelmed and captivated by the level of engineering required to construct such a complex village in that harsh of a landscape.

"Please…please…come this way…and do not fall behind." Akhilesh waved everyone along as though excited to take them on a school field trip.

Although relieved that someone wasn't trying to kill them right off the bat, Ethan wondered if it was all just an act. He hoped the next place they went was not their final resting place.

The village was empty. They saw no guards, families, or kids. The only sound they heard was the wind rushing between the alleys and over the dusty streets. It sent an eerie vibe, penetrating the bones of the prisoners. It was a complete ghost town.

How can a place with no people be so well assembled? Ethan wondered.

As they walked down one of the streets, two random men in Arabic attire strode along the road. They didn't pay any attention or even seem bothered by the group of thin and disgusting men and women walking in a line. They went right through the line of prisoners as if they were ghosts before continuing toward their destination. The other prisoners also seemed astonished that the village breathed life. They stared at the men, hoping they would rescue them from their captivity, but they were sorely mistaken.

Akhilesh stopped at a three-story that had looked like a massive stone wall until Ethan moved closer to its center. The house had a wall that looked like an unorganized wave running adjacent to the mountain. Over it, Ethan noticed parts of a wooden roof that angled down and sloped toward the front. Even the roofs of the houses were made in different shapes. Some sloping down until a certain point where it would swirl left and drip back down. Other points of the roof sometimes shot toward the sky. He wondered what laid on the other side of the wall. The house was camouflaged to be the same color as the mountain and there was an opening similar to the prison boulder they were held in.

Ethan gave up on listening to all the strange signs and weird feelings in his gut. There was no way he was going to figure out the answers on his own. He would have to go with the punches, and he was feeling them.

Akhilesh walked farther into the rock and opened the door, waving for a guard to walk through before looking at the first prisoner to follow. One by one each prisoner made their way in.

When it came time for Ethan to walk through, he hesitated. He was worried that this would be his last stop. He thought to himself that there was going to be a gas chamber or a butcher shop waiting for him on the inside. He looked at Akhilesh, who only smiled with his crooked teeth and nodded, his face seemingly innocent. Did he even have a choice? Ethan took one last gulp of fresh air before pushing through.

Ethan was greeted by a regular foyer that opened toward a wide living room on his left. Several empty picture frames decorated the walls, which were a light teal color above a concrete floor.

Every room had tapestries of different designs, showing carnivores and other wild beasts elegantly posed in aggressive stances. Each room was furnished with complimentary animal patterns associated with the tapestries.

Ethan caught a glimpse of the kitchen, which had pots and pans hanging above an island that looked as though it was made of marble. Ethan smelled fresh paint coming from the walls. It looked as though all the finishing touches had been completed.

"I cannot tell you how confused I am right now," Trent spoke softly to Ethan.

Ethan only nodded, feeling the same.

"Hey, what's the deal, ay? Why are we here?" A man in the front spoke to the leader of their trip.

Akhilesh kindly pushed his way through the dozen or so captives, saying, "Pardon me."

Every face showed various degrees of bewilderment.

"Oh, that is…what…orientation is for." Akhilesh smiled and walked toward an empty mantle suspended over a fireplace. He turned his back to the mantle and looked at all of the prisoners.

At the same moment, the fireplace shifted from the inside and the noise of movement emanated throughout the room. The slab located at the back of the hearth dropped with quickness as the fireplace receded down into the floor, revealing an opening to a secret chamber.

Ethan and everyone remained motionless and speechless. It was pitch black inside. Everyone would have to bend down to make their way through.

"Is orientation in the pits of hell because that's where you seem to be taking us?" the same man who had talked previously asked, breaking everyone's trance.

"Oh…that was a…joke…ha-ha. Follow me, please." Akhilesh snorted a bit and then bent down, crawling underneath the mantle and vanishing into the darkness. The guards pushed each prisoner through. No one had any choice as to whether to proceed into the unknown.

When it came time for Ethan, he put his hand on the mantle and bent down to look in. He was met by a draft that was caught within the passageway. A guard stood right next to him and pushed him with his rifle. He got down on his knees and shook his head before crawling through.

Once on the other side, Ethan stood up and noticed how much cooler it was. It was still pitch black, and he kept bumping into the person in front of him. There was a very earthy smell to the area. He actually enjoyed it. He reached out his arms on both sides and felt the moisture seep from the stone. They were inside the mountain.

He moved a couple of feet, trying to follow the line of prisoners. There wasn't much room for them to walk since the walls were tight. Ethan didn't like that he had to walk on sharp stones once again. He could tell that it was reopening his blisters even though they were swollen and numb from this morning.

A light formed in front of the group. It ran to the back, revealing the carved-out stone. It was amazing to Ethan that someone had taken the time to dig through the mountain. Rugged and eroded, the stone contained bits of fungus living on its inorganic surface. The cavern didn't extend too far above their heads, maybe only a foot or two. As far as Ethan could tell, everything seemed to be man-made. Akhilesh, who held the lit torch, told the few in front to follow him.

As they moved deeper into the mountain, the cavern widened. The narrow path soon culminated in a large T-shaped hallway. Ethan barely made out the ceiling, which was partly illuminated based on how Akhilesh held the torch.

The floor also changed. The uneven cobblestone was smooth and a relief to Ethan's feet. They turned to the right, and Ethan swore they'd walked in a circle.

Funneled through the hallway, Ethan saw huge chamber doors located to the right of the passageway. In between were the same corridors that Ethan and the rest had just come out of.

What the hell is this place? Ethan thought to himself.

They were met with a huge metal gate similar to something one would have seen in medieval times. Ethan remembered learning in sophomore history class that they were called portcullises, and they were generally used in front of castles and were raised or lowered vertically. The massive gate had a lattice grille and must have weighed thousands of pounds.

"I have a bad feeling about this," Ethan said as light flickered on Trent from the torch.

Trent's expression showed that he felt the same way.

Akhilesh beckoned a guard to the side of the gate, where a button was placed. The guard held down the button and the gate rose, making a deep groan. The prisoners stared as they all realized there was electricity in the mountain.

The gate thudded to the top. The base of it had teeth-like spears that would copulate into the matching orifice in the ground.

"You all have...cooperated. So, well...and I can't thank you...you...enough. I will wait here...please...go in." Akhilesh bowed his head as the group made its way past the giant barrier and into another area that was also pitch black.

Ethan stepped over the gaping hole and placed his foot on something soft. It took him a second to process what he felt and if it was real. Were his feet that numb? His toes dug into fine-grained sand, and he grabbed a pinch before releasing it. With the group, he slowly trudged to the top. Everyone's frayed nerves became palpable to Ethan, making his heart pump faster. The blind prisoners had their hands up, trying to feel what was in front of them.

Ethan had so many questions. Was this where they were going to die? In a mountain, in the dark.

"The earliest amphitheater in Rome was inaugurated in 29 B.C. in Campus Martius by Titus Statilius Taurus."

Everyone froze as they heard the voice echoing throughout the darkness.

"Unfortunately, it was destroyed by the great fire of Rome in 64 A.D. Nero Claudius Caesar Augustus Germanicus was delighted to build himself a monumental castle after that devastating fire. He was a fool. The only intelligent decision he made was committing suicide in 68 A.D. Did you know that the colosseum was called the Flavian Amphitheatre, which was built during the Flavian Dynasty? It could seat 45,000 people with another 5,000 standing."

Ethan couldn't stop his heart from beating uncontrollably. Eubulus's dark sirenic song made Ethan believe fear was necessary.

"For centuries, Rome would conquer the world and place fear into the hearts of those who opposed it. Within its walls resided a community that took pleasure in festivals. Those festivals filled the colosseum with joy, pride for their own blood, and legendary stories that we still remember today. We have lied to ourselves that we are now civilized and that our hearts have softened. We only see stories of the games as though they are a tumulus. But the faint heartbeat still lies dormant within our very souls. We have just buried it at an immeasurable depth. I have spent years formulating a proposal that would help us ascend toward our true nature as human beings. I have built what no one thought could ever be built again. Life will draw breath within this very spot, and I will stand above Vespasian and his sons, Titus and Domitian."

Eubulus's voice grew louder, and his passion waved through the thickness of the dark abyss.

"Once again, the humans of the world will cheer for the bloodshed of their own kind. Money will be traded among them for the sport that was lost for centuries. I will exhume what was buried through my resurrection. And for you...You will play the most glorious of roles. You will stand against one another, looking each other in the eye moments before taking the other's life. These sands will be fertilized by your very own blood. Deep within this mountain, the games will spark fire within each and every one of your spirits. I told you that you would have the opportunity to find out whether you are just a man or a god among men. You will fight for family, for self-preservation, and you will fight because it is your calling. The world is going to watch you. Watch you fight as a gladiator in Hades' Colosseum."

All was silent as Eubulus made their future known. Ethan waited for the nightmare to be over with and for him to finally wake up.

What sick joke is God playing on me?

Eubulus commanded, "And God said, 'Let there be light... and there was light.'"

The mountain screamed with an awakened call, and the earth trembled as a beam of light shot from above and landed directly over Eubulus, showcasing him. Ethan saw eight mast-shaped sections breaking apart from the center. The entire ceiling opened, revealing the bright blue sky. Each mast had a huge hinge, holding it from deep within the corners of the mountain. It was as though each one had an arm that lowered it. Once lowered, they retracted back, and a huge clunk indicated that the mast had locked in its open position.

There was a perfect oval around the top. Dust particles slowly descended and sparkled within the sunbeams. He shifted his eyes from the sky, gasping with awe and trepidation at the sight before him.

Ethan stood in the center of a colosseum that was also the inside of a mountain. Imprisoned within an oval-shaped wall that ran the perimeter of the colosseum, it towered roughly twenty-five feet high with four doors placed equidistant from one another on each side. Wrapping around the circumference of the wall was an elegant white marble band, illustrating what Ethan believed were gladiators fighting each other with spears and nets. Some had swords and some had tridents. Bears and lions were roaring or tearing apart a man. Ethan even saw gladiators that had long hair and exposed breasts fighting men. As he moved along the band, it shifted to water, boats and arrows being shot from one ship to the next. These were actual stories of gladiators and the history of Rome.

Above the wall, seats wrapped around the entire arena where spectators could sit and cheer on the games that Eubulus spoke of. Two sets of stairs on each side of the colosseum ran up at a forty-five-degree angle, almost reaching the top of the masts.

Behind him, a split of the two walls had seats on both sides and the bridge where they'd entered. The gate was still lifted, and Ethan wanted to make a run for it, but two guards stood on either side holding rifles. Ethan then returned his gaze ahead and past Eubulus, where a distinct protrusion in the wall stuck out farther and taller than the surrounding supporting wall. It was like a press box that had an awning built over it. In Roman times, it was known both as a cubiculum and a pulvinus. Comfy red and green seats were placed in the box, with a black leather chair that sat front and center. These ornate chairs were known as biselliums, a place of honor for those running the games. Behind the seats was something that Ethan couldn't figure out.

A huge screen hung on the wall above. The top of the frame held a sword with a snake wrapped around it. It looked as though the snake had squeezed itself around the sword, but it reached down the pommel and ate another snake's tail. Ethan followed the figure of the snake downward until it met with another sword's hilt. The snake being eaten also had his body wrapped around this sword and intertwined itself, squeezing and slithering up that sword's pommel and eating the first snake's tail, completing the rectangle. Both snakes bled, and everything was silver and black except for the screen itself.

Ethan directed his focus to Eubulus, who was enjoying the faces of the frightened prisoners. One prisoner dropped to his knees and mumbled some prayer that Ethan couldn't understand.

"What if we don't fight for you?" A bigger man that looked as though he had done some bodybuilding in the past spoke up.

Eubulus didn't look at him. Instead, he admired his creation. "I am only here to delegate, manage the money, and oversee this work to its fruition for our dear organization. I am merely the middleman who is getting paid numbers that shouldn't exist. It's the investors and the world you will be fighting for. I might have forgotten to mention that there are cameras all over the colosseum, training grounds, and other areas. We have been able to hack into every possible screen connected to the internet. When the games begin, that is when the human race shall liberate from its dormant shell, no matter how many times they change the channel. But of course, do not worry. At all times, we will have a fully functioning city of people coming in and out, acting as if they've lived here for decades. But they are here to be spectators of the games and to have a little bit of fun. My investors have revered the Roman Empire as a prosperous and properly organized society. One that they hope to cultivate and nurture toward globalization once again.

"I have overstayed my time, and I'm growing quite bored of your presence. Akhilesh will take care of you from here on out. He will be what the Romans would call a lanista. The next time I see you could be your last. Good day." With that, Eubulus turned around and exited through one of the side doors, disappearing from view.

"Ethan?" Trent choked as he looked over at his friend.

There was nothing Ethan could do but stare at the closed door.

Ethan's mind moved so fast it was as if he were living inside a movie. His mind couldn't process that this was reality. He was suspended in a state between denial and fear. He didn't want to be standing barefoot on sand in a colosseum but rather on a sandy beach somewhere along the Carolina coast.

"Trent, we're screwed."

15

GETTING ACQUAINTED

A few guards and Akhilesh ushered the prisoners back through the vaulted hallway in the mountain before maneuvering through the small passageway to the hidden mantle.

Once through, Ethan noticed that there were more guards in the house, all carrying weapons. They were escorted through the kitchen to another room painted with the same teal color as the living room. One small window on the right brightened the room, revealing pillows that were placed in a circular pattern. Ethan had a feeling that he had seen this room before, but he couldn't remember where. One of the guards pushed him to exit the room and placed him outside with everyone else.

Ethan went through the doorway, met by the sun's rays once more. He squinted in an attempt to adapt from being in the dark mountain for so long. He raised his arm to ease the sharp pain in his eyes. Heat covered his entire body, and he felt the humidity attach to his dry skin. His lungs opened to inhale the fresh air that came with a gust of wind over the mountain top. He smelled the water from the river that continued to race down the hill. He noticed others having similar feelings. As Ethan began to see better, he scouted the area in front of him. His body stiffened and he took one step forward onto dirt, looking at what was to become his new home.

In front of him lay an open area of what Ethan could only assume was a training ground, but not what you would see at an MMA or boxing gym. It was something Ethan had seen in the movies and history books. He noticed a few things in common with the Roman times.

In the corner to the right was a thick wooden post with a crossbeam, rising about eight feet high. Called a palus, it was used to take the place of a human. Ethan knew this because for a while, he had been fascinated with how the Romans would train. This was one way fighters would better their sword skills without the opponent or enemy trying to kill them. But that was as far as he had ever learned.

There was an area where he was sure everyone would learn as a group. Beyond that was a structure of wooden beams criss-crossing in an oval shape, forming a skeletal scaffolding like that of an arena under construction. He could make out a few bleacher seats that formed the perimeter on the inside. Ethan questioned why they would use them.

As others walked onto the dirt, Ethan noticed that they too had stopped in their tracks and were staring across the huge training grounds. He knew they were to be tried on every level of emotion, strength, and physical durability. He attempted to block any form of fear regarding what was to come. He had to hold his fear down to keep his mind clear.

Four walls blocked them in. One L-shaped wall, facing away from the mountain, ran higher than the other sides. On top was a walking platform where guards roamed back and forth, all carrying AKs. A post sat in a corner, where a machine gun was mounted on a tripod. Behind it sat another guard. The wall connected to a second level where there were doors every few feet. Ethan guessed that they would stay in those rooms. There were stairs at the end that led down to the first floor. Under the second floor's long shadow sat brown wooden tables.

Trent tapped Ethan on the arm and showed him different areas of the training grounds that had cameras attached to the walls and corners of the yard. Eubulus wasn't kidding about the cameras being everywhere. Ethan counted at least ten. They were small and white and must have included material that protected them from the elements. Every move they made would be monitored by Eubulus and his investors.

Ethan continued to scan the area, looking for any avenues of escape. Even if he or anyone else wanted to, it would be impossible. Their bodies were weak and fragile from lack of food and water. Their bones were brittle, and there was no way to fight their way out, which was why it struck Ethan as strange that they had posted more guards around them.

"Please...take a...seat and prepare...to eat. Your training... starts soon." Akhilesh held his hand toward what Ethan could only call picnic benches.

Ethan sat, and Trent followed suit. As the two sat down, a few others that had been in the group joined them. Others gathered at the remaining tables, waiting in fear for any kind of surprise. It seemed everyone was still unsettled about what had been revealed in the mountain.

One by one, people came out of the kitchen door with silver platters, carrying black bowls with silver utensils sticking out of them. Others came out with platters holding solid brown cups and pitchers. Ethan thought they might be servants because their clothes were almost as dirty as the ones that he and the other prisoners wore. They moved behind everyone that had taken a seat and started placing the items in front of them.

Ethan immediately knew the dish they were serving. The aroma of lamb and the scent of rice and cooked vegetables filled his nostrils with hunger and memories. It was kabuli palaw. The dish that was served right before everything went to hell in Afghanistan. Ethan tossed the painful memory aside, trying to mask the effect it had, causing his stomach to turn. This had been the only solid and nutritional food that had been in front of him for weeks. He was so hungry. Everyone else was drooling over the dish, but no one made a move.

Akhilesh gestured for them to eat. "Please eat as much...as you want. You must regain your...strength, it is a...how should you say...delicacy to...eat kabuli and is...very healthy for...you."

Akhilesh stood close to Ethan's table like a mother would when she first makes a new dish for her family to try. Everyone looked across the table at each other, waiting for the other to try it first. Ethan observed the shifting glances among the prisoners as each was waiting to see who would make the first move. The fear of being poisoned or possibly meeting the same gruesome end as that ill-fated Russian overruled their hunger. Was this some sort of sick joke?

Trent seemed to be filled with a sudden confidence. It could have been hunger or bravery to test it before anyone else. He grabbed his spoon with intensity and jabbed at the bowl of food, shoving it in his mouth and inhaling it without chewing. Everyone stared at Trent intently, waiting to see if he had any sort of reaction. Trent stopped for a moment after eating two scoops to see if anything would happen. His eyes widened, and a smirk crossed his face. His hands raced toward the bowl again, bringing it to his mouth and nearly shoving the kabuli down his throat. Everyone looked at each other before mirroring Trent.

They ate their food like savages, and the servants continued to fill their bowls.

After half an hour of eating, they all stopped because the servants had no more to hand out. Everyone took their cups and washed down what taste of the kabuli they had left. No one had talked for the duration of dinner. You could hear the moans from a few of the prisoners who felt the aftershock of overeating. It had been nearly a month since eating a full meal, and everyone's stomach had shrunk. After being expanded at a rapid rate, the group started to feel the effect of their choice. Many of the prisoners were off to the side on all fours, crying in agony as they vomited their entire meal.

Ethan's heart physically burned with regret from gorging himself, He too wanted to vomit. He struggled to look at Trent, who moved like a newly succumbed zombie. Trent looked back at Ethan, squinting his eyes and making a very painful face. With no warning, he let out a crackling fart. It echoed throughout the training yard and stopped everyone in their drunken state.

A burst of laughter exploded across the yard. Some fell over and others pounded the tables with their fists. Ethan and Trent were laughing to the point of tears. Even though they were in a very painful state after eating more than they should have, it was the first time they had laughed in a very long time.

"That vas very funny!" a man with a mild German accent said. He was around his late thirties and had been laughing at the edge of the table. He'd fallen over and was picking himself up. His long and narrow face had very little stubble around the jawline, and it ended in a prominent butt-chin. His hair had remained short, even through weeks without grooming. "Listen, I sink it is very important to learn about everyone here. Since we vill die, I don't vant to die a stranger."

Ethan's and Trent's laughter faded with the rest of the table. He had made a decent point. Ever since they'd started on this horrible journey, Ethan hadn't looked at anyone else or really cared to know about them. Trent was the only friend that he had clung to since being in the coffin on the boat. Maybe it was time that he saw someone else for who they were instead of just another prisoner. Eyes moved from one person to another. Ethan could feel everyone scrutinizing each other.

"I shall go first. My name iz Leon Müller, German, of course. I am thirty-seven years old. I vas in zee KSK Kommando Spezialkräfte German special forces for over seven years." He had a stiff posture to him with his back straight to the sky, but he was still loose in his tone. He smiled as he spoke. "I have a vife with two beautiful baby girls, Ava and Amori. They are my... life." Leon started getting emotional thinking about his family. The man next to him spoke to ease up the sadness.

"I'm Jason Murphy, Irish Army Ranger, specialized in a lot of explosives, if you catch my meaning. Not too much to me really. This is the bulk of what ya get."

Ethan could tell that Jason was a talkative man as he described himself as a taller leprechaun but without the gold. He said he didn't come with much luck either, or else he would be back in Ireland with his beautiful blonde lass.

Jason's long black curly hair ran down his large forehead and covered his ears. His bright blue eyes contrasted against his long black beard, which had grown around the entire lower portion of his face. Even with all of the long hair, he still looked like a handsome model one would see on the cover of a men's magazine. Not having had a lot of food handed out, he looked as though he was still in good shape.

"Isn't quite remarkable how you can make something so small combust from small particles of tiny atoms that form such a beautiful relationship with chemical bonds only to have them ripped apart..." Jason was saying.

Ethan noticed how the Irishman kept moving his hands around as he talked about different type of bombs and their structure. His voice had an Irish lilt that was sometimes hard to keep up with as he talked.

"Hey, you, what about you? You seem like a pleasant guy to get to know." Jason pointed toward a man across from him, giving a little bit of a chuckle.

Jason must have been trying to make a joke because the man he pointed to wouldn't look at anything but his empty bowl, his face stern and angry. It was almost as though he was trying to make more food appear before his eyes. He had golden brown skin and a lean body. His hair was at the point of growing an afro, but it had not quite reached its full potential.

"Oh, come on now, lad, nothin to fret about here. Go on, tell us something," Jason pressed.

Everyone seemed eager to know more about him.

"My name is Jake, Jake Williams. Grew up in L.A. I was in the military."

"Which branch?" Trent asked.

"Does it matter? I served and now I'm here, so it really doesn't solve anything now, does it?" Jake snapped. He looked up then, seeing an older gentleman at the corner of the other side of the table. "What about you, old man? How the hell have you made it this far without crawling over and croaking?" Jake nodded to an older gentleman who looked as though he was close to a hundred.

The older man had thin gray hair that still covered most of his head, and wrinkles ran down his forehead in a vertical motion. His wrinkled neck looked as though it could be mistaken for a turtle's neck. He had a fierce expression, staring back at Jake without batting an eye.

Trent leaned over and whispered, "Is that Clint Eastwood?"

Ethan just shook his head and tried not to smile.

"My name son...is Doc Brown. A retired Army medic who maneuvered his bony ass through the trenches of 'Nam. My eyes have seen more shit than you will ever see in your lifetime, boy. As far as croaking goes, I'll leave that to you. Lord knows you'll be the first one to cry for your momma."

Jake's jaw was about an inch lower, and his intense look had been wiped away.

"I'm sure this guy can get you to sing a few tunes." Doc pointed his thumb to the tanklike man next to him.

"HA-HA." The man's laughter slammed through the table like thunder.

If a hammer had human features, this man would be it, thought Ethan to himself. His head was naturally bald, and a brown beard covered his face. His nose stuck out a little more than the average nose, but his face was so big that it balanced the rest. Veins branched out from his neck under his jaw. He looked like a gentle giant, but Ethan didn't want to test his strength or skill.

He'd only been given yellowish baggy Arabic pants that you could see Aladdin wearing. The robes were probably too small for his broad shoulders, so the guards had to resort to just giving him bottoms. Each of his pectorals looked like small tractor tires, and every time he laughed, they looked as though they tensed into steel. His arms were as big as Ethan's head. Even with the lack of food, he still had meat to him. He looked as though he towered over everyone. Ethan guessed he stood at 6'9" and weighed in around 250.

"Nah, Doc, I wouldn't do that to him. He seems like he can hold his own. I'm Daniel Aarons. Retired Army Ranger having served for twenty-five years. I have a daughter back home. You know, she is getting married this week. I've been counting the days till her wedding day. All I wanted to do was walk my little girl down the aisle and hand her off. At least I know she is safe." Daniel's voice was deep as the mountain, but when he talked about his daughter, it was obvious that he was a very sensitive man. Still, Ethan didn't want to get on his bad side.

Trent spoke next, saying, "It seems our good partner Eubulus had good reasoning to kidnap just the veterans who had some sort of skill set in fighting. Although, Doc, I'm not quite sure why he rounded you up."

Doc tilted his head at the question.

"Now, it seems that we don't have a choice but to follow through with his games. Also, my name's Trent, U.S Air Force. I flew, and I don't have much fighting background so I might be hollerin' first." Trent laughed toward Doc to lighten the mood a little bit more.

Daniel, the giant, ended up laughing, getting a knuckle-pound from Trent for following up on an old joke. Everyone had gone through and said a few short things about themselves except for Ethan. All eyes shifted toward the last person at the table.

"My name is Ethan, and I'm…"

A sudden thud split through the air, cutting Ethan off as well as the other tables. Everyone jumped back into reality and started searching for the source of the sound.

In front of Ethan on the table was a solid wooden rod indented into one of the table's planks. His eyes ran up and along the pole to see who held the other end.

The sun had gone down and was setting around the golden hour. Its rays shone down upon Ethan, making him bring up his arm up to block out the sun and see clearly.

A human silhouette held the staff. Ethan squinted his eyes a little more, and the mystery person transformed into a beautiful angel. Golden rays shone around black wavy hair that ran past her shoulders. Even with her back against the sun, her eyes lit up like yellow fire and her face was strong like a black panther's. She had tan skin that sparkled and sharp cheekbones that accentuated her round lips, which in themselves could arouse a man. Fit like a goddess, she wore a black tunic that cut off at the stomach. Black pants, wrapped with a black and silver skirt, adorned the top half of her legs, and white ropes tied around her slender waist.

The men's jaws dropped to the ground, except for Doc Brown, who enjoyed the boys' flabbergasted reaction.

"So, did I kick the bucket?" Trent stuttered.

"You're married, remember," Ethan said in awe.

"Yeah, I'm married…I ain`t dead," Trent retorted.

A disgusted expression suddenly marred the woman's face, and within a second, she sliced the rod across the table and through Ethan's forehead. It knocked him off the bench and onto his back. Daniel, the giant, threw his head back from this unexpected attack from such a petite woman. He whipped his head around to see if anyone else had just seen what he'd seen.

Ethan rolled around on his back a few times as he held his

head, attempting to whisk away the pain as much as he could. He took his arms away to see that Akhilesh hovered over him.

"Ah, I see...you met...your doctore. She will...be training everyone...in gladiator combat. The other lanistas did not...want her because she...is a woman. But I found...out...that she is not... what she seems. Please, all follow me...and I will show you...to your rooms. There you will dress...for training." Akhilesh led everyone with a snicker.

Ethan rose slowly, rubbing his forehead while looking at the mystery woman. She still remained in the same position he'd seen her in earlier, only now she stood straight with the rod placed beside her. She stared at Ethan with hatred, and he could only follow suit as everyone else dismissed what had just happened.

Guards were in front and behind the group as Akhilesh led them to their chambers. As he neared the doors, each one opened when he swiped his wrist across a black box that hung midway along the wall near each door. They heard the sound of air being released before the door slid sideways into the wall.

Everyone's eyes widened at the surprising sight. One by one, they walked into their rooms and the door slashed closed behind them. Ethan was led to the one farthest to the left.

Akhilesh opened his door, and Ethan stepped in as the door closed behind him.

This was the first time that he had been alone since the coffin. There was a sense of liberty in this prison cell. The absence of anyone around him gave him a sense of peace. He awoke from this because he knew it was only going to be temporary. He looked up to examine his new quarters.

In front of him was a narrow room not much bigger than a walk-in closet with brown brick walls. A window with bars stood opposite him, around seven feet high, and a bed with a white frame to his right connected to the wall. On it was a blue mattress and a pillow, and lying on top was attire that he assumed he needed to change into.

He walked further into the room and was met with a white sink across from the bed. Ethan went and turned the right silver knob, and cold water came out. Ethan shut it off and turned the left knob. Cold water again.

Ethan huffed a humorous laugh. "Figured it would be just cold."

Another way Eubulus would humiliate them.

He cupped his hand under the water and lifted it to his mouth. He took a sip before spitting it back out. It tasted halfway between well water and calcium buildup. Ethan didn't know if it was safe to drink or just to clean himself. After all, he hadn't taken a shower since the day he dipped himself into the pond.

He could smell himself reeking of death. It was like smelling ammonia that cut through his nostrils. Next to the sink was a toilet with one knob. At least he didn't have to sleep in his own shit anymore. Ethan took off his robe. It was all tattered and torn and still covered with his dead opponent's blood. He threw it near the corner of the door.

From the clothes on the bed, he put on a tan canvas loin-cloth that fit like a diaper. It was thick and comfortable, but it made him feel like a callow man. Eubulus must really want us to play the part of a gladiator for him and all of his suitors, as well as the world.

He decided to wave his hand, hoping the door would magically open. Nothing. Ethan put both hands on the rustic door and tried to slide it, but it wouldn't budge. He placed one knee on the ground and breathed in deeply, letting out all his air with a sigh. He tried to figure out if there was a way to get this door open, but how?

"Open sesame?" Ethan spoke.

The door opened, startling Ethan into jumping backward, and Akhilesh stood there.

"You look...astonishing in your...subligaria...are you ready for...your first training session?" he giggled, showing his jumbled teeth. He waved for Ethan to move in front of him out of the door.

Ethan took a second to gain his composure and get to his feet. Once he stood, Ethan moved out of the room and back downstairs to gather with the others.

As Ethan descended the steps, he noticed that the group of prisoners had all formed in the open area where he'd guessed, earlier, they would train. They created a formation with columns and rows. Everyone stood at attention, and no one moved a muscle. Ethan saw each prisoner with a sword in his hand. A sword lay on the ground in a spot up front, and Ethan assumed that was where he needed to be since there were no other spots available.

He ran over and picked up the unused wooden sword. It was surprisingly heavy. How was he supposed to hold it?

Ethan stood up and looked around. He counted four guards on the platform walking back and forth. A fifth one who kept to himself was stationed behind the machine gun. On the ground, a few more stood with their backs against the wall as they watched the prisoners.

By this time, darkness had settled onto the ground, and the moon cast an eerie light over the training yard. A cold breeze swept through, cooling the ground below his bare feet. The evening dew traveled up his legs to his spine, and every hair particle stood at attention. Ethan became agitated about standing in formation with no instruction as they all stood outside shivering.

Ethan broke away from the group and turned his head to see where Trent was. He found his friend three people down in the front row. "Hey, Trent, what are we doing?"

Trent kept his face straight and talked through his lips, "We were told to stand straight, don't move, and keep our eyes forward."

"So, we're just expected to stand here and let ourselves freeze?" Ethan turned to look for Akhilesh and was met with a rod in the forehead, the same spot that had been hit earlier at the table.

Ethan fell backward, dropping his sword and landing on his butt once more. He yelled with frustration and pain. He patted his head to check for blood. The rod suddenly came within inches of his face. Once again, Ethan's eyes followed the rod up to the same woman he'd seen earlier. Her expression was stern as her face glowed in the moonlight, but at that point, Ethan only saw a pain in his ass.

He slowly stood before shooting out his hand to grab the rod and pull it toward him. The woman countered his force with a mouline move, encircling the staff around his arm, causing Ethan to lose his grip and balance. The woman spun, using the other side of her staff to punch it in the same spot on Ethan's forehead as before.

Ethan fell to his back, blood dripping from his head. He wiped it away as he processed the last minute.

The group of prisoners stayed where they were, but their eyes were all directed on the scene in front of them. A few of the guards had stopped their patrol to watch. Some snickered.

"What is your problem woman? That's the third time you've hit me!" Ethan wiped himself off as he stood, attempting to hide his embarrassment from the others.

The lady straightened her arm behind her, extending the rod toward the open gap where Ethan had once stood.

"What, you want me to go and stand there? You want me to adhere to your silent command? Why don't you just tell me? You haven't spoken one word, and all you've done is hit me." Flustered and not wanting to succumb to authority—much less from a female—Ethan stepped closer to her, his expression challenging. "What are you going to teach us that will prevent us from dying? How are you any better than us, apart from the fact that you know your way around a staff? Do you think keeping us out here at night to freeze is going to help us? Why don't you just tell us that we are as good as dead?"

The woman clenched her teeth. Ethan could see that he was

hitting a nerve, and he wanted to push it more.

"Tell us, speak the truth." Ethan stepped around her, picking up his sword and staying a few feet from the line. Ethan held his arms out like a bird with his back turned to the formation, adding, "What are you, mute? Talk!"

The woman turned around and looked at Ethan and the others. She stood there for a moment as though waiting for something to happen. Flipping the staff around her arm, she let it rest behind her on her shoulder blade. She slowly placed one hand on her chest, then placed both middle and index fingers together on both hands, forming an x, and tapped them twice. She released and held up one hand, making signs with her fingers.

"Shit, you are mute." Ethan dropped his arms and let out a sigh. He didn't think that there could be anything more disquieting than the silence moving through the air. He felt more than embarrassed, he felt ashamed.

"I bet you feel like a dick." Trent let out an uncontrolled snort.

She looked at Ethan, pointing to him, and then to her head. Her hands then came together before moving apart as one hand lifted up in the air.

"Ha-ha." Jake, who stood in the middle row, gave a boisterous laughed.

Everyone looked at the black man, who was still laughing.

The lady aggressively signed to Jake with a questioning look.

"Yeah, I know what you're sayin'," Jake said as he also signed with his hands "My sister is deaf, and I taught myself when I was younger. My parents never cared to learn for her." Jake signed, his expression and tone sincere. "If anyone wants to know. Her name is Aeliana."

"Oh, that name, 'tis beautiful. Ee-lee-AHN-ah." Jason spoke with a thicker Irish accent as he pronounced her name. "You know it be meaning sun in Latin?"

Jake interrupted. "Yeah, whatever, anyways. Ethan, she wanted me to tell you that she thinks you are shit for brains."

The entire group laughed uproariously, and Ethan could do nothing but laugh with them at the entire situation. He'd kept his head down, but his eyes lifted to look at Aeliana. He nodded discreetly and walked back into formation.

"All right Aeliana, let's see what you have to offer."

16

GLIMPSING A PREMONITION

E than and the rest of the prisoners stayed in formation the entire night, learning a fighting stance with a wooden sword called a rudis. Already a heavy sword, it got even heavier as the night continued.

Aeliana walked by Jake, who held a number one defense with his sword, and signed to him.

"Move to the number two defense stance." Jake watched her sign and gave the command to everyone aloud.

Leon lethargically pressed his sword across his body. As he did, Aeliana came by and pushed her staff to the center of his body. Not prepared, Leon failed to defend himself against the attack. The sword flew out of his hand, and the staff plowed into the German's stomach, knocking the breath out of him. Leon dropped to the floor, coughing and gasping for air.

"Oy!" Jason tilted his head at Leon.

For hours, Aeliana made them stand in different positions for long periods of time, correcting their stance and technique.

"Move to number five defense stance." Jake placed his sword above his head.

Behind Jake, Doc struggled to lift the sword. He was sweating profusely.

Others had already puked on themselves a few times because of the dinner they'd previously had. Most of their stomachs had expanded too rapidly, causing acid to build up and making them regurgitate their meal.

With no sleep and hours of holding their positions, their bodies cramped. Some dropped their swords and scurried to pick them up before Aeliana caught them. If they were too slow, Aeliana would snap their hand with her staff or trip their feet, sending them crashing to the ground.

Ethan's arm was tired. After long weeks of torture and lack of nourishment had caused his body to become feeble, the sword felt very heavy. Sharp pains ripped through his shoulder blade and right arm. His wrist tilted, and the tip of his sword bent toward the ground as he lost his grip.

Aeliana came out of nowhere and threw a strike down toward Ethan's head. With instinct guiding him, Ethan grabbed the sword with his other hand and held it parallel above his head.

A huge thud echoed throughout the yard as the wood of the staff hit his sword. Ethan closed his eyes, thinking the staff would reach his head. Ethan forced them back open and saw the doctore's eyes through the window created by the crossed weapons. He could almost hear her telling him to always be prepared for a surprise attack, especially when someone is at their most vulnerable. She retracted the staff and continued to walk through the lines.

A dim light behind them grew brighter as the early morning hours passed. Ethan realized that the sun had started to rise, and they had been training since the night before. There was not much energy left in them.

"Hey, excuse me, Aelia...doctore, ahh...*dia dhuit*. We've been going at this quite a bit. Shouldn't we be taking a break or maybe g' a quick bite ta eat?" Jason kept his talk short in fear of getting swatted in the back of the head from the staff.

Ethan sighed with relief alongside everyone else that Jason had said what they were all feeling. Ethan could hear his and others' stomachs growling.

Their doctore went to the front of the formation, the sun shining brightly in her face. All the men were mesmerized by her eyes. She moved her hand in the shape of a C and slid it down from the top of her chest to her stomach and continued to sign in sharp movements. Her face showed disappointment.

Jake spoke with what little breath he had from holding the sword and a number-eight defense. "She says that you all are foolish to think of food when your survival depends on how well you learn to fight."

"But all ve has learned iz how to move our sword in eight different spots." Leon mustered up the courage to drop the sword and speak, backing up Jason's rebellion.

A guard walked toward the group. Aeliana made the motion for the guard to stop, letting him know she had it under control.

"I am the best shot you have at living longer than if I wasn't here. You must trust me." She signed with urgency, nearly pleading with the men.

"Ma'am, with all due respect, I don't think there will be much you could help me on. You look like my daughter, and I couldn't imagine ending your life. I'm three times bigger than you." Daniel, the giant, spoke in his deep rugged tone, his voice emanating with confidence and sincerity. He was one of the few who hadn't seemed to struggle as much as the others throughout the night.

Everyone nodded in agreement with Daniel. There was no way she would be able to take down Daniel.

A huge smirk crossed Aeliana's face at the spoken challenge.

Doc read her facial expression and turned around. Still in pain, he managed to trudge through the formation. He passed by the onlookers, their eyes widening at his sudden casual action.

He sat down on the bench nearest to him and chuckled as if he were going to witness the greatest scene of the decade.

"She says everyone stand back except for Daniel," Jake yelled.

Aeliana walked toward a table near one of the walls close to the palus and set her staff down. There were a few other wooden weapons lying around the table, and she took a moment to scout the variety of weapons in front of her.

Meanwhile, the entire group stood back with Doc, still seeming confused. Daniel continued to stand in place, sword in hand and as dazed as the others. Ethan thought he looked pretty funny just standing there and not knowing what to do.

Once Aeliana found her weapon of choice, she picked it up and walked back to the area, standing across from Daniel roughly fifteen yards apart. It was a simple wooden knife.

Daniel tilted his head forward and his eyes widened. He questioned whether she asked him to do what he had begun to suspect.

She made a quick sign to Daniel, and Jake's mouth dropped open before he said, "Yo, bro, she said try and hit her."

Daniel looked from Jake to Aeliana. Ethan knew the giant did not want to hurt the innocent woman. He looked at everyone else. The group whispered to each other about how Aeliana was crazy to go up against an actual beast of a man. She would be crushed and then killed, although Ethan somehow knew that it was going to have a different outcome just by how Doc waited for something incredible to happen.

"Prove to her that she's not capable of instructin' you," Jake translated.

Daniel stood there for a solid minute with a puzzled look on his face. He seemed to be inwardly fighting with himself. Even if it was a wooden sword, a blow by him could leave any full-grown man in a coma for the rest of his life. He looked to the other prisoners for their blessing as his face showed concern for the woman begging him to strike at her. He turned his eyes back to her. His innocent expression vanished, and he stood tall as his muscles constricted. He had made up his mind. His loose skin morphed into a tense and stern scowl. His smile turned venomous. He would hold nothing back. He wanted to know the truth.

Ethan's heart raced, and he was more awake than he had been the past couple of hours. No one made a sound or dared blink in case of missing anything.

Daniel took a step forward, and Ethan could have sworn he felt the ground move. The giant took another one, and another, and soon, Daniel was running full speed. His mouth opened, he clenched his teeth and held the sword to his side as he ran. It was like looking at a locomotive increasing its speed toward a tiny ant.

Aeliana just stood and smiled with the knife at her side.

Is she going to just let him plow her over? thought Ethan.

Daniel was eight yards away from her when the doctore took a step back and charged forward. Her steps were quick and light as a cloud. They were only a couple yards away from each other. Daniel raised his sword and slashed it down. Aeliana didn't seem bothered by his movements and continued to run toward him.

Only a few feet away from each other, Daniel threw his sword toward her at a diagonal angle while releasing a thunderous cry. Aeliana took one last step before she dropped to a knee and evaded the strike. In the same motion, her other foot pushed past the side of him and planted on the ground while taking two incredibly quick strikes. One was to the front of his groin area, and the other strike went behind the lower part of his heel. Daniel was still attempting to finish his strike when Aeliana stood to deliver the blow to his side. Dirt flew into the air, swirling into a puff of dust.

Each of Aeliana's strikes was so quick that it was hard for everyone else to track. However, they must have hurt because Daniel reacted to them with a frustrated growl.

Daniel transformed into someone else completely. His eyes filled with rage and anger. Without looking, he swung his sword around, attempting to hit the target behind him. Aeliana was quicker, maneuvering under his extended arm and cutting his wrist. She then followed through with a gouging slash in his side. The sharp wooden knife drew blood in all the spots that she made contact.

Again, she had the upper hand as she swung herself behind Daniel. She tapped him on the back, and he turned around before she backed away from him.

She toyed with him while retaining complete control of the fight. Ethan held his breath, amazed at what he saw.

Daniel did not see her as a daughter or a woman anymore. He only saw her as the enemy. He sliced at Aeliana like a ferocious animal, but no matter where she stood and how hard he swung, she moved before the sword reached her.

"Look at him swatting at a fly that's too quick for him. Ha, he's out of breath." Doc had sat and crossed his legs, grinning from ear to ear.

Doc was right. Daniel had lost his speed and his breath, but the doctore still hadn't broken a sweat.

Daniel limped forward, trying not to drop his eyes from his opponent. Everyone heard the whimpering short breaths of the giant. He was low on fumes and frustrated.

He looked at Aeliana for a brief moment before he gathered all the strength he had left. Lifting his sword behind him as far as his muscles would allow, he threw his sword at a forty-five-degree angle. Aeliana flicked her wrist and let go of the knife, allowing it to freely spin. She caught it again, the tip facing down while the butt of the handle faced upward. She rammed the butt into Daniel's wrist while twisting his hand. His sword fell, and Aeliana swung her leg around like a crescent moon, catching the dropped sword and returning to her beginning position.

She was now in the combat stance that everyone had learned that very morning, sword drawn and pointing directly at Daniel. What no one had noticed was that she didn't have the knife any longer. As the dust settled from the fight, Daniel was on one knee, out of breath and holding what he thought was his sword. When everyone looked at it, they realized that instead, it was Aeliana's knife.

The entire group of men murmured in disbelief. All the guards around the yard had stopped and talked among themselves, nodding their heads and laughing at the fallen giant. No one had expected that outcome.

Aeliana dropped her guard and walked toward Daniel. Without having broken a sweat, she stuck out her hand. Her smile had turned sweet. Daniel's eyes, which bowed in defeat, had started to glisten, and his frown diminished as he regained his breath. The giant gave a short, gentle laugh while moving the knife to his other hand and stuck out his right to grab his doctore's offered hand.

Ethan and the others walked toward the two fighters. The sun pressed their backs with warmth, and a slight cold breeze greeted their faces.

Aeliana faced the group to sign while Jake spoke for her.

"I am not your enemy. I'm the only chance you have between life and death. This training is what could get you back to your families. If you do not listen, then you will die."

"Well, that is short, sweet, and to the point." Jason broke the silence once again.

"Your doctore specializes...in many forms...of fighting. Such as hapkido, karate, and Kyushu jujitsu...but most importantly...she is trained in all...areas of gladiator combat."

Akhilesh had walked out from the kitchen door. As he came through talking, a scent of hot oatmeal trailed behind him. It entered everyone's noses and immediately, Ethan's stomach growled with hunger.

"What is Kyushu?" Jake crossed his arms, curious about the martial art he'd never heard about.

Leon spoke through the group, "Kyushu iz zee art of pressure-point fighting. You basically force your opponent to break zeir grips, lose consciousness, and even paralyze them for brief or long periods of time."

"She knew she could handle Daniel the entire time, no matter how big he is. There is more to her than meets the eye," Trent said, awe coloring his voice.

Ethan had never seen such fluidity and danger in anyone else's movement. Her style of fighting had more than one variety, just like Akhilesh had said. He was more intrigued as to how she'd learned it and where she came from. Trent was right, there was more to her than met the eye. However, Ethan still had other unanswered questions.

Ethan ended the group's giddy mood when he asked, "Akhilesh, earlier you said that Aeliana wasn't chosen by the other lanistas and so you ended up with her. Who are they?"

The lanista looked at Ethan shyly, then looked away. He seemed like he tried to get his thoughts in order before speaking. The question intrigued everyone, including Doc, who had returned to his feet. The group moved closer and listened to Akhilesh.

"I am…but one lanista of a few…that have a group of men and women…like you. We are spread throughout…the village. We are in charge of handling…the doctore as well as…overseeing the progress…of the gladiators. In the beginning, before… all of you arrived, all the lanistas were gathered…to see the doctores and choose. I was last to choose. Aeliana was the last one left." Akhilesh looked at the faces around him.

"So, you're telling us that we are going to fight—" Ethan started.

"We're going to fight others like us?" Trent finished.

The area was silent except for the faint whisper of the river. Everyone stood still as they absorbed the sickening idea. At some point, they had all wondered if they would really be fighting each other, but no one had wanted to believe it.

Ethan's thoughts raced. They ran through his head as he tried to think of escape routes, communication to the outside world for help, sabotage. He wanted to find a way to prevent standing across from another man, fighting to take a life and save his own.

"And what is so special about her other than she's a Jedi?" Jake asked as he pointed to the doctore.

Aeliana glanced at Akhilesh, who reacted with a smile.

"That I cannot...say. Please...sit down and...enjoy your breakfast." He held out his arm, gesturing to the men to sit at the tables and wait to be served.

Aeliana departed from them and left through the kitchen door.

She must not be a prisoner, thought Ethan.

No one pressed the matter any further. Their stomachs overruled each of them, and one by one, they sat down where they had the day before.

Simultaneously, the servers came out with the same kind of trays and cups, only this time there was oatmeal in the bowls. Ethan was surprised to find it still hot. It was gooey and a little dry, but it still had a sweet grainy taste. There were short conversations here and there, but no one talked about the reality of having to fight others like themselves, possibly even in the same military branch.

The sun had almost filled the entire yard, and Akhilesh came back as most of them had finished their last bowl of oatmeal. Again, almost everyone had eaten more than their stomachs could handle. Ethan had been in his head so much that he had barely eaten an entire bowl.

"I want all of you...to rest...next training will start...soon."

Everyone didn't fully acknowledge him but did as he commanded. He might not have shown authority, but he was kind and in no way wanted to show any aggression toward them. It was something they didn't want to change. Besides, the guards had a more persuasive hand than they did.

Again, Ethan was the last to enter his room. As the door closed behind him, he immediately walked to the bed and sat down on the edge.

The bed was stiff and there was little to no budge when he applied weight to the mattress. It felt like it was made from the synthetic leather used to make a soccer ball. There was a thick black knitted blanket folded in the corner of the bed. He slowly petted the mattress, waving his hand over the blanket to get a better feeling for it. Ethan guessed it was made of woolen yarn. It was rough but would keep in the warmth when it got cold in the night.

Running his hands through his hair, he felt the dry follicles filled with dirt and a lack of hygiene. Ethan took one hand, grabbed a handful, and pulled with medium force. For some reason, he thought that all his hair would come out because of how dead it felt to him.

His beard had grown expediently within the weeks since being kidnapped. He wondered what he looked like after not having been groomed.

Ethan decided to lie down and reflect on the situation for a moment. It felt odd to know that even though he was in the worst of situations, he wasn't who he was a week ago.

He'd been a man who wanted to live the rest of his miserable life with no acceptance from anyone, continuing to live in the shadows and not be heard from again. He truly believed being loved or being happy was a gift that he wasn't allowed to have. His wounds never fully became scars, only lacerations that seeped out the truth when he remembered—a pain that had lived in him since that fateful day.

He hadn't felt that pain for an entire week, and he felt guilty for loving the absence of it.

He lay his head on the pillow and faced the stone ceiling. Under his breath, he whispered, "I'm sorry."

A tear fell from his eyes as he drifted into a deep sleep.

Ethan woke to the muffle of loud screams and crying through the ringing of his ears. His head felt swollen, and his body hung heavy like a ten-ton bus had hit him square in the chest. He opened his eyes to see a blur of light. As he came to, his eyes adjusted. He found himself face down on the floor. He pushed himself off the ground, debris falling off his back.

His senses came back slowly. Still dazed, he noticed pieces of ceiling and blocks scattered about him. As he became more aware, the ringing went away, but he heard a popping noise all around him. He tried to take in some air, but halfway through his inhalation, something clogged his airway.

Ethan coughed uncontrollably and gasped for air. Coughing didn't seem to clear it. He fell to the floor and turned onto his back. His body wasn't responding, making it difficult to move or think.

His sight blurred, and he noticed a shadow in the corner of his eye. Ethan's heart beat faster. He tried to pull himself away, but the strong shadow grabbed him.

Ethan attempted to fight, but it was no use without his senses. He was slowly dying from lack of air, and his hands went to his side. He felt the top half of his body being lifted, and the shock of cold ran down his head to his face and neck. Chills sliced through his body. He felt his head being propped back and his jaw opened. Cool liquid entered his mouth and down his throat. It ran through, clearing the blockage. He was placed on his side to cough, thus clearing his airway.

He heard the faint mumble of someone talking to him. "Miller, rink som mor whater. Yourrr gowing to be okay."

The words of the stranger were deep and ran together. Still, Ethan continued to drink. The ringing had died down, and his vison became clearer.

Ethan looked around at the debris of walls and ceiling around him. His eyes wandered for a brief minute before everything came to him again. He whipped his head to where the meeting had been conducted with the elders and yelled, "Captain!"

"Captain is gone, Miller. We have to link up with the platoon and make our way back to the base. Get up and grab your rifle."

Lt. Smith was the blurry figure who had saved his life. Ethan did not have time to think about what had happened. The lieutenant was right, he had to get out of there. They were in no position to fight off the terrorists, but they were going to have to fight their way out.

Ethan lifted himself up and looked around to find his rifle, which was not too far away. He crawled over and grabbed it, doing a quick once over to see if it was still operational. He took out the mag to check the ammo. It was full. He popped it back in, turned his safety off, and gave the lieutenant a nod.

Ethan grabbed his radio as the lieutenant closed a window.

"Miller to anyone, Miller to anyone. Can you read?" Ethan heard gunshots popping close by. He didn't know anyone's position or if they were even still alive. He had to hope. Ethan reached out on the radio once more, but there was no response—only static.

"They must have some kind of radio frequency jammer. I wasn't able to get ahold of the C.O.C." The lieutenant kept his head down and slid his face slightly out of the window, getting a better view of the situation outside.

"If they were smart enough, they would go to the highest point they could to transmit the block."

Ethan had an idea and reached inside his backpack. Pulling out his map, he unfolded it and laid it flat on the floor, wiping it of any wrinkles. Using his finger, he traced some of the alleyways and pointed at some buildings. He then took out a pen and quickly drew a circle around a building.

"This building here is the highest in the town..."

The lieutenant moved toward Ethan to look at what he had found.

"Me and the others had already mapped out some of the important landmarks before leaving. If we were to predict that they are blocking our frequency from the highest building, it would have to be this one. It's about a click away. If we run this path through some of the buildings and alleys, we can make it there."

The lieutenant's face hardened as he contemplated Ethan's plan. "I like it. It's realistic, Miller. What does G1001 on the building next to it mean?"

"That's my next issue I was going to talk about. Before we left, I coordinated with heavy artillery, coded certain areas of the town that I thought would be important and their exact position. I have the M777 Howitzer on standby, ready to blow up any of these buildings. We just have to get in contact with them."

The lieutenant stood there for a moment, and a smirk slid across his face. He laughed and patted Ethan on the back as they gathered their things. "All right, Corporal Miller, lead the way."

Ethan felt a surge of adrenaline and confidence as the lieutenant praised him. He gave the lieutenant one last look before moving quickly past him and toward the door.

Ethan's idea had them running across the road to the other side. This would place them in a very open and vulnerable spot, but if they made it, they would have much more cover and concealment. Ethan took one big breath and held it. He closed his eyes and counted to three before releasing his breath and bursting through the door.

His heart racing, Ethan immediately raised his weapon, his senses highly tuned. Off in the distance, shots and screams could be heard.

Methodically, the two men made a quick pace across the road. Ethan scanned the right side of the road, and Lieutenant Smith took the left. As they moved across, Ethan caught sight of objects on fire and debris from fallen buildings in his peripheral vision. He caught the scent of blood mixed with burnt rubber and wood. Ethan couldn't really tell what the smell was, but as it filled his nostrils, it made him want to puke. He tried not to let it distract him from any sort of movement that could give their presence away.

They noticed a giant crater in the middle of the road.

Another bomb must have gone off around the same time the one in the house did, thought Ethan to himself.

He hoped that Steve and rest were okay and still fighting. For a brief moment, Ethan prayed that they would run into them if they had made it through the initial blast.

Halfway to the other side, they heard a laugh followed by the sound of a ball being kicked. Ethan and the lieutenant turned their muzzles toward the sound and froze. A soccer ball came into view. Two men in robes with AKs, not worried about the battle taking place, laughed together as one kicked the ball.

It took the terrorists a moment to realize they had two Marines aiming their rifles down on them. The one doing the kicking saw Ethan first and stopped, and the other did the same. For a moment, all four stared at each other.

Ethan had no time to think. Four shots rang out within a second, and both men dropped to the ground. Lieutenant Smith quickly turned his eyes back to his side of the road.

The sound of shots firing would notify someone of activity in their vicinity and give their position away.

Ethan dashed into the alley, running along one wall of a building and keeping some distance from Lt. Smith, who made his way to the opposite side and scanned around Ethan. The sound of grenades and shots became louder as they moved closer to their objective.

At a window roughly head height, Ethan dropped underneath it as the lieutenant moved past it, scanning quickly with his muzzle. Ethan did the same for the lieutenant when he came to his window. They both moved with haste, not missing a beat with each other. They moved like they had done this thousands of times before. Ethan controlled his breathing, and his eyes were sharp as a hawk.

They reached a door, and the map showed that it would cut their time by a quarter of the way if they ran through that particular building. Ethan pressed his back against the wall next to the door, his gun facing a nearby road. He hoped no one ran into his view. As the lieutenant worked on the door to see if it was locked, they heard an explosion coming from a hundred meters off.

He knew that the men were nearby, but his job was not to join them. His objective would be able to help them all. His heart began to hurt, and he wanted to tend to his brothers, but this was no time to think irrationally.

The lieutenant pushed on the doorknob, but nothing budged. They knew they couldn't stand there for long or else they would be sitting ducks. The lieutenant shook his head, notifying Ethan that the door was locked. Ethan noticed the placement of the hinges to the door, which meant it opened from the inside.

Quickly Ethan raised himself in front of the door like a raging bull and gave a strong kick, smashing the door in. Ethan gathered his balance as the lieutenant entered first.

Ethan rushed inside, noticing an open room with carpet in the center and pillows in a circle on top of it. An open stairwell ran up the wall and to the right, and the stairs led to some beautiful brown double doors. Below the stairs sat an archway, which led to another room.

The lieutenant probed the front and the double doors while Ethan buttonhooked straight ahead and then turned abruptly left to scan a door hidden in the corner. Ethan's priority was to watch their backs as they moved forward, clearing the house.

Ethan was very surprised to see such a large room that could be described as almost having vaulted ceilings. As he kept his eyes on the door he had busted, he took notice of a closet to the side. At the same time, he heard a creak coming from the double doors above.

A man jumped out in a surprise attack, screaming as he sprayed a few shots from his AK-47. Ethan quickly rolled under the stairs as the shots spit at him. The terrorist didn't see

Lieutenant Smith in time, and as the man recoiled with one bullet in the chest, his weight caused him to lean forward. Before the man hit the railing, Lieutenant Smith popped one more in his head. The lifeless body wrapped itself over the railing and dropped to the ground with a thud. Ethan looked at Smith, silently thanking him. Ethan then took lead and pushed through the archway to the next room; he pied every corner, window, and wall, which allowed him to cover all areas of potential danger. Ready to shoot at the slightest movement.

Ethan and Lt. Smith had danced themselves into a rhythm. The two moved slowly and smoothly as they went in and out of the houses. Moving closer to the G1001 building, they caught a few others off guard, dispatching them quietly so as not to stir attention.

As they passed through a hallway upstairs, Ethan noticed through the window on the opposite side of the road a few Marines fighting from one house to another. They were being pushed back. He could see Sunny and a few others trying to carry a Marine into a building. They were directly parallel to the main fight. The terrorists seemed to be pushing them away from the building that the lieutenant and he were trying to reach. Ethan could just pop those terrorists from where he stood. He had the perfect vantage point.

He knelt down and looked through his scope, seeing the easy targets and calculating how fast he could shoot them before revealing himself. He lined up a perfect shot on a man who stood on the second story.

"Ethan! Stop!" The lieutenant grabbed Ethan by the flak jacket and pulled him to the floor. "I understand where your head is at, but pull it out of your ass. The way you can help them is by bringing the building down." The lieutenant pointed toward the building.

Ethan lay there for a brief moment, gathering his thoughts. The pain subsided from his chest, pulling him away from the opportunity presented to him.

The lieutenant grabbed Ethan's hair and ruffled it like a father would to a son. He quickly then pressed on his head to push him toward the stairs, leading them to the door across from building G1001.

Before Ethan turned to walk away, he saw the lieutenant look out of the window, a pained expression etched over his face.

Ethan and the lieutenant lined themselves up with the door, and the lieutenant slightly opened it to look outside. They were only a few feet from the building.

"So how do we want to go about this?" Ethan whispered as sweat trickled down both of their faces.

The lieutenant wiped his salty eyes, trying to see more clearly, and grinned at Ethan. "Did they ever teach you about the bunny in infantry school?"

Ethan stared back, trying to figure out what the lieutenant was trying to say. Once Ethan realized what he wanted to do, he tilted his head and sighed. "Aww, come on, Lieutenant. Are you serious? Haven't I been more than enough of a target today?"

"Terrorists love bunnies ...just run straight to the back, and I'll come in behind you and clean house. Besides, I'm a better shot than you!"

They laughed.

As Ethan walked inside and turned his head, he immediately pushed the lieutenant with all his might. A loud shot rang out, and Ethan fell to the floor, his right shoulder in serious pain. The lieutenant fell to the floor from Ethan's push, and he managed to get two shots off at an infidel who had quietly entered the house without their knowing. Two more men came from the other room. They hopped over their dead companion and attacked both Marines.

Ethan reached for his weapon, but it was kicked out of the way by a man who wore a black turban and robe. The turban hid his entire face except for his cold brown eyes. The other was the same, but he showed his entire face, which was filled with a mass of moles.

Ethan realized that the man who had kicked his weapon was carrying a machete. He raised his arm and struck down at Ethan while calling out to Allah. Ethan didn't hesitate and rolled quickly out of the way, pumping his legs at the man and trying to distance himself from being sliced by him.

The lieutenant had a similar situation, as the man with the moles made very fast strikes at him. Both men's guns sat in the center of the room, protected by an oblivious terrorist who luckily was not smart enough to pick them up.

Ethan grabbed a large knife, known as a Kabar, attached to his flak jacket. He wrenched it from his sheath and yelled from the pain in his shoulder. He glanced down, noticing the blood that soaked around his wound. Ethan pushed the pain away and moved into a fighting stance, focused on his enemy.

Ethan's heart pounded like a beast. His body numbed, and self-preservation took over. He lunged and struck at the other man, but his opponent stepped back to dodge the attack. Ethan remained where he had lunged, anticipating a strike from above. Sure enough, the attacker followed through with the strike, which enabled Ethan to catch the wrist before slicing into the assailant's brachial artery. A hoarse scream came from the wounded man, and Ethan didn't hesitate. He lunged as the veiled stranger attacked with his machete. Ethan quickly moved past the long opened-arm strike, blocking it with his left hand, and made contact like a cross. Ethan cut the man's arm again and switched the Kabar from his right hand to his left, plunging it into the man's shoulder and leaving it there. His opponent gave another cry.

Ethan no longer felt any pain from his shoulder wound. He turned his back into the terrorist, grabbing the Kabar and part of the man's robe as leverage, and threw the man over his shoulder. Ethan straddled him then, yanking the Kabar back to give a final blow.

Ethan breathed heavily, and adrenaline surged throughout his body. He turned to see the lieutenant on the ground, wrestling with the man who had all the moles. Ethan felt like he flipped a switch as he forgot the rules of engagement and lusted for blood. Walking past the rifles, Kabar still in hand, he grabbed the man by the neck. Spinning him around and to his feet, Ethan stabbed him continuously while pushing him back into the window.

Ethan held onto the man's neck, and every stab came with more force than the one before. They both stared into each other's eyes. The only difference between them was that the man had already departed the earth, and his eyes were dead and cold. Ethan's were just cold.

"Ethan! *Ethan!* Stop, it's okay. It's okay." The lieutenant grabbed his rifle and cautiously walked toward Ethan, who still held the Kabar in the man's stomach.

Ethan felt the warmth of a hand gently touching his shoulder. Sounds of fire from outside and screams filtered into his ears, and his shoulder began to sting again.

As though Ethan had not breathed during the entire fight, he gave an exhalation that seemed to last a whole minute. Ethan turned to the lieutenant and nodded, feeling himself again, and his guileful eyes sank back into their abyss to reveal a warm, innocent gaze that greeted his lieutenant.

Ethan looked away from the lieutenant and down at his hand, which still held the knife in his enemy's lifeless body. Tears streamed down his face, and his mind drifted to the monster he had become. He held in the feeling and pulled out the knife.

As he did so, the man gave a large screech, and his eyes bulged from their sockets.

He awoke.

17

CLASSES OF CONFLICT

Ethan shot up from his cot, escaping his horrible vivid dream. Sweat poured from the top of his head while he hyperventilated. His beating heart continued in arrhythmia. He quickly turned to his side, putting his feet on the ground, and gasped.

The soles of his feet had begun to heal along with his other previous wounds. However, because of where they were now living, wherever that might be, the environment was drying his skin so fast it made it difficult for the wounds to stay sealed.

Ethan's hand pressed against his forehead, where Aeliana had hit him not once but three times in the exact same spot. It throbbed, but it did not hurt as much as the horrible nightmares he'd been experiencing since the beginning of his ordeal.

The guilt that had been absent since the beginning of his captivity had finally caught back up with him. The demons that had leeched on to him for so long had been swept away by new pain, only to have them lust after him once more. How was it fair for him to carry such a burden on shoulders that were so weak?

Ethan could only think of one Man that would allow such cruelty. The only questions Ethan had were: Why was he still alive? Why did he still want to live? What was there to live for while continuing to humor a crazy lunatic?

He gathered his clouded thoughts and shoved them in the back of his mind. He took a deep breath—starting from his pelvis, through his stomach, and passing his neck to the top of his head—and held it. He closed his eyes, and when he couldn't hold it in any longer, he released it.

Ethan stood, feeling every bone in his body ache with stiffness. He arched his back and paced back and forth, warming up his body. Light from his window came into the room. He thought of hoisting himself up to see outside, but it was too high, and he still didn't have the strength to reach it. Once he got stronger, he would try it.

The door swished opened, and a guard with an AK stood on the other side. He said nothing, but Ethan could only assume it was time for him to get his butt kicked.

The scalding heat from the sun's rays shot through any cloud that dared give the men some shade. It made training challenging, not for the sake of stamina but to remain focused on what the doctore told them. Jake did his best to explain it verbatim, but when it came to sign language, Jake said it doesn't always translate to proper English. Sometimes it's broken up and doesn't make a lick of sense. The language of fighting was sometimes hard for him to explain.

They were taught how to defend certain strikes and how to attack when they were on the offense. At this point, it was all very basic, but Ethan knew that forming the foundation of gladiator training was crucial to survive any bit of this devasting game that Eubulus had created.

While training, Ethan found it oddly soothing and easy, as if he had already been trained once before. With certain strikes, it might take him a bit to understand, but once his form was accepted by the doctore, his brain didn't stop there. He broke away from the book and developed newfound techniques, forming different ways to work with other techniques and scenarios.

After days of learning the foundation of the sword (rudis) and a hoplon shield—mostly made of wood, leather lining, and leather straps—the gladiators were then trained with a combination of movement and strikes. Leon was especially good with his shield. Because his posture was so straight and militaristic, he maneuvered in ways that made him a hard target. His eye never left his opponent.

Ethan, on the other hand, always looked for the weakness in what seemed strong. Even a tower built to last for centuries could still be knocked down. You just had to find the right weak point to it. Ethan never dismissed this instinct. In fact, when one of the men received praise for learning a new ability of the rudis or hoplon shield, he incorporated that style of fighting into his own bank for later.

Ethan soaked up every bit of the gladiatorial style of fighting. As the days went on and they continued to provide nourishment and water for the men, Ethan regained his strength very quickly. Most everyone else did as well, though there was a smaller percentage of prisoners who had a more difficult time recovering after the harsh conditions they'd endured. He could move faster and strike harder. His reactions were getting quick like a snake.

When the day was over and they were brought back to their rooms, Ethan continued practicing his footwork or doing conditioning exercises to increase his strength. He was becoming a machine, and he didn't want to stop. It was addicting.

After two weeks of training, Aeliana came to the front of the formation and signed for Jake to join her.

"Aye, I think we might have reached graduation, wouldn't you say, lads?" Jason used a very thick accent to make a joke about how well they had been doing.

No one paid attention to Jason as he rambled.

Aeliana was silhouetted in the sunlight behind her, and a soft breeze swept through the yard. It was one of those days the men had learned not to take for granted, especially when it was a west wind. From that direction, they were gifted with the smell of the water coming from the river.

Jake watched as the doctore signed. Ethan didn't just soak up the training, but he was also starting to learn sign language as well. He remembered a lot of the words used for anything that involved offense, defense, and basic fighting terms.

"You all have successfully accomplished not sucking at the training you have received so far. But it is just the beginning. You have only scratched the surface of what you need to know. All of you have learned the basics of what is called a ..." Jake stopped talking because it was a word that he didn't know.

Aeliana spelled it out for him, letter by letter.

Jake's eyes widened once she finished signing.

Everyone in formation instinctively leaned forward, waiting for Jake to speak.

"All right, guys, so I'm just going to put this into my own words. Basically, doctore has been teaching us only one style of fighting for the games. It was necessary to learn this structure, as it is the foundation of gladiator fighting. We have been learning the style of Samnite, where it is just a sword and shield. When we go out there, we will have been given our own type of gladiator style based on what our doctore thinks will suit us best. Today, she will choose for us, and we will then split up to learn that certain style. We all have to fight against these styles, so we need to know how to defend against them. Strengths and weaknesses." Jake's shoulders slumped with the weight of this newfound information.

Ethan looked around, and all heads were bowed. They seemed defeated to know that this was only the beginning of the training. Every bit of information being thrown at them needed to be learned or else it could be their life because they had missed a little detail. Ethan had a sudden surge of adrenaline and excitement, but he pushed it deep down to contain it.

"How's come ve have to have you chose for us? Vat if ze disagree?"

Aeliana listened to Leon's question but ignored it. She turned and beckoned a few ISIS guards to bring out some chests. They seemed decently heavy, if the way the guards carried them was any indication.

She walked to the first chest, which was the size of a table. They were mostly all black except for the silver screws and hinges that held the boxes together. Aeliana opened the chest and pulled out what seemed to be a net for fishing.

A guard came from behind, holding a three-pronged iron trident and a small dagger. He handed it to Aeliana, who then handed it off to Jake, who inspected the weapon with a dumbfounded look.

"This is the gladiator known as Retiarius. His style of fighting is what some would call a fisherman."

Everyone soaked in everything Jake said as Aeliana lifted the net and showed the little details of the weapon. She passed it off to Jake like she had done with the previous weapon.

"First, we have the net that has a meshlike material. On the end of the net are iron weights to allow for a farther throw. It will also help with tangling your opponent. There is a rope tied to the net that will go around the gladiator's wrist."

She then grabbed the trident, explaining through Jake that the trident acted as both weapon and shield. Even though someone could throw it as a spear, it was unwise unless the person knew that they were going to hit their target. Without it, they were left with a small dagger known as a pugio.

Ethan's mind raced through the pros and cons of that fighting style. He looked the net up and down, thinking he wouldn't mind getting his hands on it to feel how it worked.

"You will be given no shield or helmet, just as they didn't in ancient Rome. Eubulus would like this to be as original as possible."

"How about not at all, lassie?" Jason of course spoke out of turn once more.

Aeliana scolded him with her piercing eyes as she continued signing.

"You will be given a left shoulder guard with a bronze plate shielding your left side," Jake translated. "Your body is more vulnerable as well as your face. However, you have less weight and therefore can move around more quickly."

She grabbed the armor out of the chest and dropped it in front of her.

"Jason, you will be a Retiarius."

Jason lifted his head slightly and gave a fearful gulp. He was caught off guard for once.

"I hope you can run just as fast as you talk," Aeliana signed.

Jason moved past the men in the formation with a slow trudge. He slouched as he walked past the row in front. He stood in front of Aeliana and grabbed the net and trident. His arms retracted to the ground as if they were magnetized, but everyone knew that it was heavy. Jason grabbed the rest of the gear and was sent to an area in the yard, along with a few others who were called out to learn about the Retiarius. He mumbled to himself as he left formation.

Aeliana moved to the next chest and reached in, pulling out two swords. She flourished both of them before stabbing them into the ground so she could continue signing. "These two swords are called gladius swords. If you are wielding these, then you are considered to be a Dimachaerus. There is not much to be said about this gladiator except that he must be exceptionally ambidextrous. His fighting style needs to be dependent on moving quickly and adapting to any given situation. His shield is his sword. Reactions need to be quick. His body armor will most of the time be determined by the investor. They are a close quarter fighter and are highly recommended to learn all of the different fighting styles." She ripped them from the sand and swirled both of them around her body, ending with a defensive pose.

Everyone seemed impressed by how fluidly she moved with both swords. Ethan was more amused when she spoke about the abilities that a Dimachaerus had. He perked up when she mentioned being able to adapt to any given circumstance.

"Leon, come up here and grab these, along with a balteus—leather belt—and a leather shoulder guard."

Leon didn't seem to mind the decision of the doctore. He moved forward, grabbing the two swords, and went away with five others that Aeliana had called.

Ethan noticed Leon having a difficult time moving or striking with his left hand. Others also had the same problem, most likely because of the fact that everyone had been taught to use a shield in their left arm instead of a sword. Ethan was disappointed that Aeliana had not chosen him to be a Dimachaerus. He knew he didn't have a choice, and he was not going to make it an issue.

The next chest contained a very large shield. Jake's face was blown away by seeing just how large it was. A large rectangular shape with rounded edges and a green base, gold trim lined it. In the center, a golden serpent struck from the shield. Aeliana pulled out a gladius sword and a few other pieces of protective equipment. She handed it to a nearby prisoner to hold.

"A Murmillo will need to be big and strong, like a raging tank that is patient and knows when it's his opportune time to strike. He must understand that he is a defensive class and cannot be hasty to make a move. He waits for a mistake and for fatigue to set in. Daniel, this is your class."

Daniel looked around at everyone and accepted his fate before grabbing his shield and sword. There were only a few selected for that class.

Moving about must be very difficult, thought Ethan.

There were only a few chests left, and the group dwindled down. Ethan thought that some classes seemed like the better deal, and others were completely suicidal.

Jake was called for the Thraex class, along with Doc, Trent, and a few others. It was the obvious lightweight style given to those who wouldn't be able to hold up a heavier shield like the Murmillo class. Included in it was the small circular shield, a little bit of armor, and a gladius sword.

Jake would do well with this class given his strength and speed. He would be a very difficult opponent to face. However, Ethan knew that Doc would not fare well. Others also had an expression of sympathy and pain for Doc. It wasn't fair for him to fight. There was no advantage for him. Ethan hoped that no one would spend money to invest in him. No one would want to waste money on Doc.

Ethan looked at how fragile Doc was as their group walked away. Jake remained next to Aeliana and yelled for him to come up with the rest of the group and grab the remaining gear from the last chest.

Ethan held his breath to receive his deathly surprise. Aeliana pulled out a smaller rectangular shield, one smaller than the Murmillo. Round at the edges, the trim was silver, and there was no symbol in the center. It was plain black. Aeliana grabbed a gladius sword. Ethan picked both of them up, and his arms immediately went to the floor just like Jason's did when he'd lifted his. The weight was almost unbearable to keep above his waist. How on earth would he be able to fight with this?

Jake stood next to Aeliana, who signed to Ethan. Her body language seemed very empathic toward him.

"Don't worry, man," Jake said. "She says with time, you will be able to wield the sword like the wind."

Ethan looked at her and didn't want to have a lie told directly to his face. Even with all the practice he was doing, it wasn't going to be enough to survive. He knew when the time came, he wasn't going to use any of these items. He never had any intention of killing one of his own. Now, if they put Eubulus in the arena, he'd be happy to give that man his last breath.

He ignored the comment and didn't respond back. Accepting this would be letting Eubulus get what he wanted. He couldn't believe that one man could be so evil and heartless, yet so brilliant.

"It's called the Secutor class, like a step down from the Murmillo. You'll be able to be more mobile yet take some heavy hits. The rectangular shield has round edges in case you come in contact with a Retiarius class. The net could get stuck if the shield wasn't made to be round." Jake patted Ethan on the shoulder and walked away to join his group.

As Ethan began to leave, he accidentally locked eyes with Aeliana, and they had a moment of silent conversation. It threw Ethan off. He could have sworn that her eyes told him one thing, yet her body language still remained as the doctore.

It confused Ethan enough that he caught himself in an awkward moment with his trainer. He struggled to remain masculine and wanted to tell her anything that came to his mind, but his thoughts went blank.

It had to have been the lack of water or even the time being spent out in the sun. He knew it was time to walk away from her. Trying to move, he dropped a leather greave that went on his leg. He struggled to pick it up.

Aeliana stood still, no emotion showing on her face. The guards must have seen what was happening because they went by and kicked the back of his legs to get moving. In the middle of nowhere, sentenced to face death in an arena, Ethan still managed to embarrass himself. He walked to his group, hoping no one had seen that little scene.

"Hey, cowboy, I don't think I've seen a smoother ride in my entire life. Unless you count that forty-year-old single mom who got drunk on a mechanical bull and fell off within .5 seconds." Trent had seen the entire run-in, and the men in the back had laughed along with Trent.

Ethan squinted like a child and continued walking. His face was as red as their sunburns.

A system had been established to expedite the process of training without limiting Jake's time. Each group was taught the basics of their role, the foundation on which each class worked, their strengths and weaknesses, and the basics of defense. Jake walked around with Aeliana, explaining to them how each move worked, then he would go back to his own group and train on his own.

After the groups understood all of what Aeliana wanted to teach them, she would go from group to group, fixing their technique and showing them what she wanted. She rarely had to ask Jake to come and help her.

The yard was big enough to hold everyone. Even the Retiarius class could move about, swinging their nets without getting in anyone's way.

Ethan was told to work on a few basics with his shield and sword, but he couldn't help exploring the shield and what he could and could not do with it. He understood that something not working then didn't mean he couldn't make it work later. He knew that he and the others were still very weak and not used to that type of weight. He wasn't as mobile as he wished, but he knew that after a week or so of using the actual sword and shield, he might be able to come back and try different methods.

The struggle of going down on one knee and placing the shield over his head was very difficult for Ethan. Just as he thought earlier, his mobility and strength were not where he knew he needed to be.

He got back up and fell immediately to the ground with a slow ugly throw. He put the shield above his head and imitated receiving a blow from above. He pushed the imaginary sword with his shield and pierced the wind with his sword.

As he worked, he noticed a red dot on a few of the cameras that he had never seen before. Had the red lights always been on? Ethan attempted to remember any possible red dot. He came up with nothing.

A red light must mean Eubulus or some possible investors watched them.

His eyes scanned the entire yard and noticed that everyone put all of their effort into their training. They all had military experience of some sort, but no one had gladiator training. Yet, they were putting all of their energy into trying to survive and keep their heads above water.

What Eubulus had built was working like clockwork. Every day, more guards roamed around the area more often, meaning that prisoners were becoming more and more like actual gladiators. He had a schedule to keep, Ethan was sure of it. It was only a matter of time before the first game arrived.

The mastermind was building an empire from within, and no one could do anything about it.

He looked at Trent, who was helping Doc with a simple dodge attack. Doc studied Trent's footing, but he was still not able to apply it when he tried it himself. It was very ugly, and there wasn't much that was suave about his fighting. He was lucky, though. Investors were going to take one look and not waste the time of day on him.

Ethan froze, his eyes fixed on the interrupted sand. He thought to himself, *Eubulus needs all of the elements to make his plan work, but what if one of the elements is missing?*

Ethan snapped out of his frozen state and worked on advances and retreats, moving through various strikes.

He had many ideas running through his mind, but he didn't want that to be noticed. He needed to keep his thoughts a secret. He would wait until dinner and discuss his idea with the rest of the table.

Many frustrations and struggles occurred with every class. Daniel the giant had trouble guarding a few areas that Jake or someone in his class could easily strike. Aeliana made it clear that he would have to start stretching in uncomfortable positions to reach those important spots. She also showed Daniel what to look for when the weak points were in harm's way.

Ethan paid close attention to the placement that Aeliana would teach others regarding where to strike or what to avoid. Ethan especially noticed that when she showed the exact spot to hit, she would be a little off or sometimes strike differently than how she had previously taught. Could she be holding back at teaching everything she knew? Akhilesh did mention that she was proficient at a couple of different forms of fighting, including pressure points. Ethan made sure to keep a close eye on Aeliana and study her fighting, even if it was in small doses.

Leon's left arm was not as smooth or fast as his right. Aeliana quickly showed the Dimachearus group how they would have to switch back and forth from offense to defense like a light switch. It was a very rare and hard class to master, but if they learned the dance, then they would be a force to be reckoned with. Sometimes, Leon would get so frustrated that he would throw the sword and walk away with his hands on his hips. His frustration swirled throughout the entire training yard, and others swore or dropped their technique and lunged at the palus or another man.

By the end of the night, Akhilesh finally presented himself like he always did, and they all thanked Aeliana for her time before she headed out. Ethan was eager to get to the table and tell everyone his idea.

While everyone consumed the same dish they'd had for the past few weeks, Ethan worked on a way to tell everyone at the table his idea.

No one ever decided to leave the tables that they were at after day one, and everyone seemed to prefer it that way.

"Hey, man, you okay? You've barely touched your dinner," Trent said.

Trent had also managed to get everyone else's attention. They continued eating, but their ears perked up, wondering what was wrong with Ethan.

Ethan stopped playing with his food and sighed. "Did anyone notice while training today that the cameras had a red light? Did anyone notice this before today?" Ethan watched as everyone replayed the entire day in their heads and farther back.

Once he figured no one had an answer and probably couldn't remember a time, he spoke quietly in fear of the guards or the other table hearing him. "Neither did I, at least not before today. I think those lights indicate that the cameras are on and they are watching. I think it's maybe Eubulus or the investors. They might also be there to tell the guards and anyone else that are not being held captive to be on their best behavior. Why else would Eubulus have them? He wants everyone...everything to look immaculate."

Everyone at the table was now more at a loss than when Ethan had started. Even Doc had a dumbfounded look on his face.

"Eubulus has found a system...an equation that if all the numbers line up, they equal out to him being successful in more than one way. He needs a group of men who would be willing to stop at nothing to wipe humanity from existence, to keep guard, and to do his hard work for him. He needs a secret arena that cannot be found with a river that will provide electricity. He needs investors to bring in the money. And lastly, he needs gladiators either willing or forced to provide entertainment."

Ethan got more excited, and his voice softened.

Everyone concentrated intently on hearing Ethan's next words. They leaned into the center of the table, their nostrils clogged by the vile stench of sweat from working all day in the sun.

"Eubulus needs great gladiators to fight in the arena, and he needs investors to put money on us. But what if every time those camera lights come on, the investors see something other than great gladiators?"

Doc and Jake seemed to understand what Ethan was saying, and they both smirked. A few of the others still didn't quite understand it.

"What I'm saying is that we fight horribly. We make the investors move on to someone else other than us. If we show them that we are going to lose severely in the arena, then no one is going to want to pay. We then get to stay here without fighting." Ethan was very proud to get that all out without having brought too much attention to the table. He sat back and waited for a response.

"Gosh, I don't know about that, Ethan. That's a mighty risky shot." Trent shook his head, still processing the idea.

"Doc isn't going to have any wee problem with that now, is he?" Jason somehow managed to make another joke in light of the serious risk they would be taking.

Ethan knew that someone at the table wasn't going to agree.

"I don't know about you guys, but that's dope. Count me in on that." Jake folded his arms and looked around.

"Well, even though leprechaun over here tells better jokes than he fights, I have to agree with him. I won't be able to change how much I suck already."

A few chuckles erupted from a few of the men.

"I don't like ze idea of zat. You will all make yourselves look like idiots and zell catch on," Leon disagreed, but Ethan was prepared for it.

"Listen, we will still train hard and work to help the others. It's only when those camera lights go." Ethan began to fight for his idea.

"But what if someone catches on, like Leon said?" Trent was being the devil's advocate, trying to look at the consequences of their actions if they were to go through with Ethan's idea.

"If we don't make it obvious, then I think it will be able to give us more time to heal, train, and get stronger. Maybe some investor is crazy enough to take on one of us after being horrible at this, but what if we get spared more than if we were to show off in front of those cameras?"

Akhilesh came into the room then, pushed everyone to head into their cells.

Ethan saw that everyone wanted to continue the conversation, but it would have to wait until morning breakfast. The guards came over and pushed the men upstairs. Ethan was aggressively forced into his room, where he immediately went to his bed.

He hoped that no one would rat him out, although he couldn't see any reason for any of them to tell Akhilesh or Aeliana. They were all part of the same team, men who are all trying to stay alive as long as possible. Ethan knew that this was an individual game, but that didn't mean he couldn't help those men in any way possible. He tried not to think of it anymore. The more he worried or thought about it, the more his eyes stayed open.

Ethan plopped onto his bed face first with one leg on the bed and the other off. He reeked of sweat not only from himself but others. He wished they would at least understand that if they wanted warriors, they needed to have them healthy. Living in their own filth and sweat wasn't going to help them in any way.

Looking over, Ethan noticed a plastic hook on the side of the sink. A rag and towel hung from it. On the sink was a white bar of soap.

Ethan's heart rang with happiness, as it was the first time he'd seen soap in what seemed like forever. The smile across his face then faded back to his neutral expression, and he shoved his happiness into the back of his mind.

Ethan just lay there and looked at the bar of soap. Why was it so hard for him to accept happiness and welcome it instead of always welcoming suffering? His mind wouldn't stop wandering, but he needed to stay clean so he wouldn't get sick. It would make his day more troublesome if he didn't wash.

He decided to clean himself while he had the chance, even if he ended up in the same revolting state the next day. He used his arm to push his body up like a jack. Lifting himself onto his feet, he headed toward the sink. He grabbed the bar of soap on the side and wet it, then he rubbed it over his hands.

His mind drifted away from his horrible smell and onto his family. He wondered if they were worried about where he had gone. He'd left on horrible terms with every one of them.

Tyler most likely still worked at his gym, happy that there was no one there to darken his life with brush-offs and unreplied text messages and phone calls. Ethan's family was probably also able to enjoy a peaceful meal without experiencing an argument or the complete ghosting of his presence. It was much better that he had been taken away. He was toxic to the people who loved him the most.

He hadn't been the best family member or friend. They also couldn't understand where he came from and why he needed to be left alone. The more love that was given to him, the less he wanted it. If he'd only remembered to take the safety off of his pistol in his room that night, he wouldn't be here.

Ethan took off his subligaria to clean every spot of his body. *It is possible that this is God's way of punishment. Wire my brain to work the way it does and to feel the way I feel to torment my soul. And to put a cherry on top, He puts me in the middle of nowhere to face what I've been living with for the past two years. So, I can agree that this is what I truly deserve.*

Ethan was almost done cleaning himself as he chastised the Big Man upstairs. He had so many questions as to what would happen if he was put in that arena and told to fight an innocent man or woman. Even though he wanted to put to rest his haunted past, why did he still fight for life?

When the time comes, even if my plan works, it won't work forever.

Ethan hoped that he would do what was right and that his body wouldn't take over.

The only positive thoughts Ethan had were that his family and friends were safe, and it was him instead of them. Ethan moved back to his bed, clean and refreshed. He was quite happy that he had made the decision to clean himself. His skin felt smooth and his scent was not traceable by his nose. It gave him peace of mind to finally be washed and clean. On the bed, Ethan covered his body with the wool blanket. He drifted off to sleep and waited for the next day.

18

SUBTERFUGE

The next morning during breakfast, everyone at the table looked at the metal bowls under their chins. Some scooped around the edges, creating a clinking sound for a few passes before making the effort to eat a bite. Most of the men struggled to lift the spoons to their mouths. Jake moaned a few times, shifting his body to adjust himself on the wooden seat.

Ethan's body was stiff as a doornail. With every movement, he became convinced that he needed WD-40 just to move an inch. He hoped that it would go away soon.

Yesterday was the first day they'd used the actual weapons. These were the same ones they would use in the arena. Their environment was cold and silent, and it got more realistic as time moved forward. Fear sunk into the imagination of everyone. They knew that one mistake could end their life. However, it wasn't the worst fear that some had.

Daniel the giant mentioned his daughter and how he would love to hold her again even though she was an adult. He said that she would always be his little girl. A lot of the men were taken away from their families and loved ones.

Doc had spoken of his beautiful wife, Margret, who happened to have the same birthday as him. He described her as being a beautiful angel who never aged. "You would think she was still in her mid-forties the way her smile lights up the room."

Margret would be proud of Doc and all that he had done to survive this horrible nightmare. Ethan knew that he missed her dearly.

He could tell that no one wanted to bring up the conversation from the night before. Ethan didn't dare bring it up himself in fear of beating a dead horse. Ethan might be the reason why everyone was sulking the way they were. Bringing up that idea might have struck a nerve, opening the door to more fear, but this was a chance to break the chain and survive for even longer.

Ethan couldn't think of any other plan to keep him and the others safe. He wished that he could tell everyone in this darkened place, but it would give away the plan too easily. They were running out of time before everything came to fruition.

The guards came over to end the silent meal, pushing everyone to start training.

Over the past few weeks, Aeliana and the guards had been more lenient, allowing the men to warm up using the rudis swords since they were wooden. They did whatever they wished before the actual training day started.

They still kept plenty of guards around to make sure no one thought of overthrowing them. Ethan always counted around two that roamed up top on the promenade and another that stood in the guard tower. Another three or four generally guarded the lower doors, and two remained near Aeliana. Since the men were beginning to gain back their strength, the guards had to be careful. These were still trained military men and women.

Ethan went to the palus in an effort to train his strikes and strengthen his attacks. He took one swing, and as the sword hit the wooden pole, painful vibrations charged through Ethan's body.

"Gosh dang it!" Ethan spewed a few curse words and tried to

---

roll his shoulder a few times, making a few slashes in the air to distract himself from the pain.

"Gosh dang it? You're startin' to sound more like me now, he-he." Trent approached with a rudis sword to work the opposite side of the palus.

"You know, Ethan, I've noticed we haven't really been able to talk much since our first encounter. I'm sure you've been able to figure me out by now. Family guy works in the mud with the pigs and has that good southern drawl with good southern looks. I'm what others would call a basic cowboy. But I can't seem to figure you out. I mean, one moment you are quiet as a church mouse, and the next you have this aggressive drive that's as loud as church bells." Trent sliced the wooden stake lightly to not draw any attention to their conversation.

Ethan knew where this was headed, and he continued to work on his strikes, avoiding eye contact with Trent.

"I mean, you've had some crazy ideas already of tryin' to get out of here. And you continue to come up with some. The men and I have talked it over, and it's pretty risky to drop this training that could help all of us survive. I think we are going to pass on this. I'm not sayin' we aren't impressed by your will to live, but don't ya think it might be putting others in danger?"

Ethan got a burning sensation in the pit of his stomach, but he pushed it down. Why was he getting frustrated with Trent? His idea was the only one that might actually work.

He pondered on Trent's words for a bit and decided to look at the man across from him. "Trent, why are you okay with letting a man put you in an arena to fight another human being? You're letting Eubulus dictate how you will die. The real fight should be against him, not against ourselves. Don't you want to see your family again?" Ethan shifted his eyes back to the palus before softly hitting it once more.

Ethan could tell that Trent needed to think about that for a little bit. He didn't want to cause any strife between him and his friend. Trent was right about one thing: Ethan had been confusing to all of them. His emotions and mind played tricks on himself, causing him to flirt with conflict. He didn't know what he was doing. Ethan cooled down from his earlier frustration with Trent. His friend was only trying to understand him better.

"Trent, there is still much about me that you don't know or understand. In fact, I don't quite know myself. But what I'm doing is what my body is telling me to do. I don't want anyone to get hurt, but we are in a whole other world, and I'm allowing myself to do what we all know how to do. Adapt." Ethan tried to explain as best he could without having to open up to Trent.

It seemed like Trent understood. His eyes softened, and he smirked, showing his agreement about their odd prisoner-of-war situation. "Yeah, okay. But you can't steal the word tarnation. That's strictly for me."

The two laughed at Trent's lame joke before continuing to practice in silence, and there was a new cheerful vibe to their hits.

Ethan was happy that he didn't have to explain any more than he had. He knew what he really wanted to say. 'Let me validate my reason for still living. Give me the chance to figure out why I'm still here.'

The two worked on their strikes, helping each other out as much as they could before Aeliana came through the door. At the sight of her, everyone rushed into formation to find out what training would consist of that day. The sun was blocked by quite a few clouds, and the breeze made it chillier than what the trainees were used to. Happily, they knew they would be training all day, which should keep them warm. Jake routinely stood in front to translate for Aeliana.

"Doctore wants everyone to go to their respective groups once more and continue working on what we learned yesterday." That was that. Everyone departed to their groups.

Ethan walked to his group, where their weapons and shields waited for them. He picked up his sword and shield, and as he did, he nearly lost his grip on both. He was in a lot of pain from the previous day, and everyone else also seemed to have difficulty raising their shield above their heads.

Ethan had been working on that specific move when Aeliana came over to watch him. He didn't notice her at the time. As he lifted his shield, the pain caused him to only partially raise it. He held it there before he noticed a silhouette of a staff coming down on top of him. If it weren't for Leon and his technique of always keeping a squared stance, Ethan would not have had any vision of this attack.

He raised it above his head in spite of his body's objection. The staff plunged deep into the top of Ethan's shield, tossing him backward and to the ground. Gaining his composure from the surprise hit, he looked up to see another attack coming. Aeliana threw down her staff as hard as she could. Ethan quickly rolled on top of his shield and off of it, grabbing it and covering himself to hide in case of another quick attack.

"Are you insane, woman?" The words spewed from Ethan's mouth as he attempted to stand.

Aeliana pierced Ethan's soul with her dagger-like eyes.

All the men, women, and guards watched them. Some snickered, knowing that Ethan had made the doctore furious.

Ethan wished he would have kept his mouth shut.

She took two steps toward Ethan, warning him that there would be another strike. The twist of her hip with her staff indicated to Ethan that it would come from her side. Ethan reacted, placing his shield in that direction and leaving his body open from the front and other side.

Aeliana continued to twist her body, but her front half moved parallel to the ground and her front leg came up into a chamber. Ethan didn't see her kick land right into his chest, putting him back down on the ground. He could have sworn his lungs popped from the force of her kick.

It was blatantly obvious to everyone through Aeliana's body

language that she was still angry about being called a woman. Meanwhile, Ethan was still recovering from the kick to his chest. The doctore held out her staff to one of the men who held a sword. With a dumbfounded expression, the man slowly took the staff. She then quickly reached for the man's sword and looked directly at Ethan.

Ethan's squinted and huffed while he shook his head, watching her grab a real sword. *She wouldn't dare come at me with it,* he thought. *That could kill me.*

She turned her face toward the ground, her beautiful, vicious eyes staring down on an abysmal failure of a man.

Ethan stood, getting into an en garde position, his feet tiptoeing back and forth. He couldn't seem to stay grounded. He knew that she was going to come at him full force like a raging bull. His breathing became unsettled, and a surge of energy shot through each of his limbs. The pain he'd felt that morning vanished as adrenaline raced through his veins. The hand on his shield gripped tightly, and his sword seemed to morph into an extension of his hand. His pupils were dilatated and full of fury. His excitement grew enough to project a deep bellow within his body as he pushed off the ground toward his trainer.

Ethan threw himself at her with a strike from the side, aiming for her neck. If Aeliana hadn't squatted underneath it, she would have lost her head. She moved around Ethan, who whipped himself around to send another piercing strike straight to her stomach. Using her wrist, she lowered the tip of her sword toward the ground to push that strike away. Ethan left his face open, and Aeliana jabbed at it. She made contact, sending him back a foot.

Ethan heard a few happy oohs from the group of men.

Aeliana struck at Ethan, and he threw his shield up to counter her strike. When her sword hit, it was such a heavy blow that it shook Ethan's core. Something else also struck at Ethan, apart from her sword. It was as though Ethan could see everything from the outside in. He felt comfortable knowing where that sword was and felt as if he was in control. He didn't know how, but it felt amazing knowing he could make contact, not get hurt, and still be able to be in control of not only his own actions but hers as well.

She struck again and again on Ethan's shield. Pushing back with every hit, Ethan lost his energy as she crashed down on his shield without giving him a chance to retaliate. He made a decision that on the next strike, he would attempt to break away.

Ethan waited for the right time, and as he felt the sword touch his shield, he pushed away her sword. Leaving his entire body open, he followed through with a strike to her shoulder. She met steel with steel once again, grinding the swords against one another.

She was wiser and stronger than Ethan, and he knew that he was in her domain. They struck back and forth as Ethan attempted to avoid contact with her sword. She was too quick and knew her way around any of the basic attacks.

He didn't know how to best her without trying something that wasn't taught by her. His fatigue dampened the hold on his shield. The adrenaline was still there, but he felt it fading. He needed to act fast.

He waited for her to strike and moved forward with his shield in front and gladius sword to the side. She plowed on his shield as he wanted her to do, and he waved it out of the way, twisting his body. As he did so, he placed his sword toward his opposite hip as though sheathing it, then drew it out toward Aeliana's face.

The move threw Aeliana off, and she moved her upper body back, the tip of the sword just missing her nose by a few inches. While Ethan was quite pleased with the idea of throwing her off, he didn't see her hand come up from below, moving between his shield and sword. The edge of her blade kissed his right shoulder, causing blood to well from his skin.

Ethan became intoxicated over the feeling of her sword cutting his skin. It was so sharp and clean. He felt the air cover his newly opened wound, and his chest spread wide as Ethan took in a deep breath from this over-the-top feeling. Did he enjoy the pain, or was he in shock from it?

Aeliana's strike did not stop there. As her sword left Ethan's shoulder, she continued to move with fluidity. Like a dancer, she moved downward and twisted her body, stretching her leg out to sweep Ethan off his feet.

Ethan landed on his back, knocking the breath out of him. His head hit the ground and flashing lights went off in his head. By the time the lights were gone, the tip of Aeliana's sword was on his neck. Making any movement would push his skin into the sword.

The adrenaline faded away, and all the pain came back to him, including a sharper pain from the new cut that Aeliana had given him. It wasn't as pleasant as he remembered it a minute ago.

Aeliana then raised her sword with one hand, and Ethan closed his eyes, thinking that she was about to finish him off. He heard the sound of metal penetrating sand, and he could feel the sand particles jump onto the side of his face. He opened his eyes to see that she had driven her sword into the sand inches away.

She looked at Ethan and everyone else. Her hands came up to her chest, and she signed to everyone. Jake stood in the distance, but he translated for her as he stepped through the group of prisoners.

"There is a sign that could possibly save you, if you are willing to drop your pride. The investor might spare you. The sign is called *missio*. Back then, if you fought bravely, this was what you signed to the emperor to ask for mercy." Aeliana then extended her middle and pointer finger, clutching the rest in a fist.

Ethan watched this while still on the ground.

"There is no hope for you, if you are to be lazy. Investors are not here to watch children play with sticks. You are fighting for your life. Remember that next time you want to half-ass anything. Within the next week, you all will start fighting each other and learning from each other's classes. Show's over. Get back to work." Aeliana took one last look at Ethan. Her expression remained disdainful as she left him to lie and think about his choices.

Jake and Doc came over to help Ethan stand.

"That was actually a pretty intense fight, wow! I'm really impressed. I mean you got yo butt whooped, but you did it in style." Jake laughed as Doc looked at Ethan's wound.

"Even though she could have done worse, that cut is still going to leave a scar. We need to get that cleaned; I'll see if they have a medic room." Doc looked at the wound a few more seconds before walking away to find out what to do if someone got hurt, as it hadn't really happened before Ethan.

"Look man, what you said earlier about that idea of playing dumb. I still kinda like that, and when the time comes, I'm down, all right." Jake bobbed his head a few times before slapping him on the back.

Doc had grabbed someone that escorted him to a room near the tables where they ate. They actually had a doctor who was there to treat his wound. To his surprise, it didn't need stitches, but it did need to be cleaned. As the doctor gathered his supplies to clean it, Ethan couldn't help but think back over what had just happened.

He reviewed the fight in his mind and how he felt. He might have gotten his ass kicked in Jake's terms, but he was very happy with his new findings.

His body was naturally good at determining his environment and the opponent. Even though he knew very little about the craft, he was able to understand the concept and mechanics. As time went on, he knew he could get even better at it. He wasn't even mad about the cut Aeliana had given him.

It was strange to finally know what a little cut could do to you during a fight. It wasn't what Ethan had expected. Of course, the idea was not to get sliced like a New York pizza. Ethan chuckled at his own inner joke as peroxide poured over his shoulder, and he gasped as the doctor cleaned and bandaged it.

In the clear, he headed back out to train with the rest of the group.

For the next two weeks, the men fought against each other. Sometimes they used the rudis swords, and other times they used the real thing. They mastered their own class and adopted their own fighting styles. Even though there was a certain form to each class, each individual added their own finesse to it. Ethan was exceptionally good at adapting to any of the styles, no matter who or what class he fought against.

By the end of the second week, no one showed a lack of confidence in any aspect of their training. The food had given them enough nourishment to build back up their strength plus some. Their bodies had been molded like Greek sculptors made by Polykleitos himself. Owing to all the activities done out in the sun, their skin now held a bronze hue. They were stronger, faster, and no longer sore from the unfamiliar movements.

Ethan's body was well-known throughout the yard to be perfectly conditioned as to what everyone expected a gladiator to look like. No one knew that he spent extra time in his cell working on anything he could to improve his chances of becoming a better fighter. He worked on his footing, kicks, and punches and even stretched to increase his mobility and strength. His six-foot body had golden brown skin. The scars, including the one Aeliana had created, showed brighter.

Ethan would hear from Trent upon seeing his more prominent scars that there was more to Ethan than met the eye. Ethan's muscles were much more linear but stronger than when he was back home. His stomach showed a distinguished six pack, and his curves helped outline his muscles. His chest was wider, and his traps spun out like two wings. The shape from his chest to his hips created a V. His calves were plump and bold, and any time

Ethan moved, hundreds of tiny muscles moved about with him. His hair was cut off, as well as everyone else's, to show uniformity and help their helmets fit more securely.

Each time they picked up their shield and sword, it was with purpose and assailment. They knew that the next time could be their time to fight for their life. Aeliana had engrained that into their minds very purposefully. If they were to survive, everyone had to be willing to believe they would.

They had reached a standard that even Aeliana was impressed with. If she saw something that made her happy, she would give an accepting nod before moving on, and that was what the men strived for. Sometimes she would step in and try and push the individual. It was never the same as the day that Ethan fought with her, but it was still enough to put someone into a real-life scenario without being threatened.

"Listen, y'all. You guys have done very well and damn have we been slappin'…" Jake stopped his joking laughter as he could feel a stern stare coming from Aeliana. "Okay, those aren't her exact words, but she did say that you guys have done well. Today, the cameras are going to be open for investors to view their selection and place their bets. This is the time that we show off our skills. The more the investors like you, the more money they are willing to put down for you."

Ethan's mind raced back to a few weeks ago when he'd proposed that the table dumb down their skills so that no one would want them to fight. If it could spare them a few fights, then it would be worth it.

"Everyone will move to the practice stadium over there and sit in the bleachers. First two up are Jake and Wilson. Actual weapons will be used."

A couple heads turned, their eyes widening at the thought of using the real thing.

Everyone moved to the bleachers inside the practice arena. When Ethan walked around the outer edge, he was met with two large, open doors. They were whitewashed with craters in them. As he moved past the doors, there indeed was an oval-shaped stadium and a wall circling the entire arena. As Ethan viewed the area, it looked as though fifteen cameras had been set up around the top edges of the wall, sitting five feet apart. Red lights shone brightly on each one.

The stadium was much bigger than Ethan had imagined. The walls were not as high as the stadium in the mountain, but it was high enough that he wouldn't be able to reach the top if he attempted to jump. He guessed that it was around twelve feet high.

Everything looked as though it was made of the same wood that came from the surrounding landscape, although he had no idea of the actual type of wood. Ethan noticed a pulvinus that was just smaller than the one in Hades' Colosseum. Two regular wooden chairs sat side by side, a door right behind them.

Stairs to the right and left greeted Ethan when they walked inside, and the guards steered them to walk up and take their place. Ethan sat next to Trent on the first level to get a good view of Jake and Wilson.

Wilson was a scrawnier man, and like Jake, he was a Thraex class. Although he wasn't as bright, he'd picked up on his fighting quickly.

The two had suited up and faced each other from either side. Jake held his silver helmet with his sword in hand. It would be the first time they wore helmets that were fitted for their heads. His helmet was specially made to be lightweight, although it looked heavy. The visor spun round 360 degrees, and it looked sharp. The front of the mask had plenty of holes like a mesh to see most of his surrounding and still be protected. The top of his helmet had an antenna on top, similar to an anglerfish's light.

Everyone's eyes moved to the door when the podium opened to see Akhilesh and Aeliana. Both wore exotic clothing.

Akhilesh had dressed in a fully white robe. A blue strap ran around his left shoulder and crossed his chest to wrap around his waist. Aeliana wore all black, and Ethan thought it was her favorite color. She wore a black top with see-through material that covered her shoulders. Her baggy pants had a golden trim that ran along the seams. Their expressions were serious, and they paid no attention to any of the prisoners as they walked around the wooden chairs and sat down. An awning the color of dirt shielded them from the sun.

Jake moved about to warm himself up, and his right arm had scaled leather gauntlets that ran up his arms. Strips of leather straps to hold them in place hung below his arms. He also wore the leather greaves and woolen straps around his legs. The greaves only covered a little past his knee.

Jake looked prepared and focused, but only for a minute. He looked around the bleachers and tried to find someone. He finally spotted Ethan and gave a nod. He put on his helmet and faced Wilson.

"Why did he nod to you?" Trent asked curiously.

"Beats me." Ethan was sure he knew what the nod meant. He leaned in even closer to get a better view of the fight.

There was a low eerie sound that came out of God only knew where. To Ethan, it sounded like a mix between a low tuba sound and electricity.

That must have been the sound to start because both men headed toward each other.

Jake made the first move, putting his front leg out to the right before pressing off of it and moving to the left, making a football juke to Wilson, who took the bait. Jake threw his sword down on Wilson's vulnerable side. He parried Jake's strike just in time, pushing it away from him.

The two circled each other and closed in again. They bantered back and forth for a few hits. Jake would try to use his shield for most of Wilson's hits. The shield was small and circular, so Jake had to be precise and make sure the sword hit where he wanted it to.

As Wilson tried to uppercut with his sword, Jake stopped it with his shield followed by an elbow to Wilson's face.

While he was unbalanced, Jake ran toward his opponent, but that time, he charged his shield into him. This was never taught in training, and it made a few people talk on the purpose of that decision. Ethan looked up at Aeliana, whose expression showed confusion on the move as well. He pressed Wilson into the wall, slamming his back against it. Wilson recovered quickly, punching Jake directly across the helmet three times with the pommel of his sword before Jake let go, backing off.

Jake discreetly opened up his shield, which allowed for Wilson to kick Jake to the ground. He lay there on his back, his shield a few feet away from him. Wilson struck Jake each time, being deflected but getting closer as Jake lost his stamina. There were perhaps a few more strikes left before Jake got sliced.

Many of the men and women had already started talking about who was going to win this fight. Ethan had overheard most of them making jokes about how Wilson wasn't ever going to the arena. What they watched seemed to shock a lot of people. Ethan knew what Jake was trying to do, and it actually might work. The question was whether everyone else at the table was going to do the same. Ethan's final question would be answered in a couple of seconds.

Just as Ethan turned his head to look back at the two fighting, Jake lost his grip from his sword and was left lying there helpless. Wilson toppled over him, sword pulled back and waiting to pierce Jake right through his heart. He instantly looked up at his lanista and doctore for direction.

Helplessly, Jake looked at Ethan and Trent. Ethan could sense that he was nervous. He knew that Jake hoped this would work, and he had put all his trust in Ethan. Jake dropped his pride enough to move his hand slowly, not to provoke Wilson, but to make the sign of *missio*.

The arena filled with gasps at how the fight had ended. Aeliana's expression was furious, but it didn't seem like she'd caught on to what Jake had done. It was more a look of disappointment. She knew what he was capable of, but the investors and hopefully Eubulus did not.

Akhilesh stood. "What a...wonderful fight. Well done. You may now take off your....gear...and sit down. I believe Daniel and Hensley...are up next," he said, looking toward the two ginormous men who were both Murmillo fighters.

A deep sounding whisper came between Ethan and Trent, and Ethan realized that Daniel had been sitting behind them the entire time.

"This better work, my friend." With that, the giant stood and went down to join a guard who had all his gear for him.

Another guard waited for Hensley.

Ethan noticed Trent staring at him as if he had done something behind his back. Ethan just shrugged his shoulders and looked at him as if he had no idea what was going on. The point was that he really didn't know what was happening. Ethan wondered if the men had talked without his knowing.

Daniel put a leather greave on his left foot. His helmet was similar to that of a Thraex, but it was much thicker and made of bronze. His grill, covering the front of his face, had a mesh look like Jake's.

Daniel grabbed the large shield that leaned against the doors, which were closed. He turned around and faced Hensley, who had mirrored him in all aspects of armor and weaponry.

Ethan was nervous that his plan was going to cause some uproar. He had been watching Daniel and his fighting. The bigger man had worked really hard and listened to everything Aeliana had taught him. He knew he wasn't fast, and when he first learned about his class, he didn't ignore that fact. He learned to be patient. He had also conditioned himself to take a blow and not shut his eyes or lose his technique.

The sound of the low electrical tuba noise moved through

the air, and two men ran toward each other. The bleachers trembled as both men bashed their steel against each other's shield. No one was in a hurry to throw the next one.

Daniel made a quick stab to Hensley's knee, and his blade scraped the side of it, causing a little laceration to form. Hensley seemed to lose control for a moment, and he panicked, letting out a tiny cry. He backed up, forming a little distance to regain his composure.

That was a brilliant move by Daniel, thought Ethan to himself.

If he could show that he was actually trying to win the fight, then no one would think twice about someone rigging it. There was a change in the wind, however. It was the first time someone had seen bloodshed in an arena. Daniel was the first to do it. Ethan looked around and saw that some men had turned pale as they'd watched.

As Ethan looked into the pulvinus, he noticed that both leaders seemed pleased, and their faces didn't show that they suspected anyone of rigging the fight.

Hensley looked at his leg, then stretched his back out before returning to Daniel. The injured fighter grabbed his shield and rested his sword on top of it as he came forward. He was much lower to the ground, and his legs bent as he pushed forward. His stance seemed more tactical.

Hensley acted like he was going to stab Daniel, but he instead opened up his body and raised his back foot, delivering an explosive kick and sending him back. Hensley didn't stop there. He raised his arm above his head and swung his sword down on Daniel's right shoulder. The sword was stopped by only a few inches because of Daniel's shield, which he'd raised just in time.

Ethan caught a slight change in Daniel's posture as he dipped his shield. It was just enough to where Hensley kept his sword on the shield and pressed through. The sharp blade sliced through Daniel's shoulder. A louder cry came from Daniel, as the wound was deeper than the one Daniel had inflicted on his opponent.

Ethan closed his eyes for a second, knowing this was his doing. He imagined Trent looking at him disdainfully.

"It'll work," Ethan whispered under his breath.

Daniel broke the sword away, using his shield and exposing his entire left side. Ethan knew that Daniel had done all of this on purpose, and he wanted to give an open spot for Hensley to use. He just didn't know if anyone would go so far as to kill someone. Hensley raised his sword quickly, leaving the tip under Daniel's neck. *Missio* was then used from Daniel's hand, and the match was done as quickly as it had started.

Aeliana stood and paced around the chair. It didn't seem as though she had caught on to what the men were doing, but she seemed to be questioning herself and her teaching. She grabbed one of her fingernails and chewed on it as she sat back in her chair.

Akhilesh called the next group.

One by one, the men at the table had done what Ethan had proposed. It was quite astonishing to see how each one did it and how discreet they were about it. No one seemed to catch on.

Leon and Trent both did well in their round, not having trouble throwing their fight. Doc made everyone nervous, but even giving it his all, he would still be bested. No one was nervous for him because everyone expected him to lose on his turn.

These were the first fights in front of their peers and investors. The pressure to do this for the first time weighed on everyone.

The strange psychological issue running through Ethan's mind was that almost every fighter did put all their effort into the fights. It was as though they were trying to show off or prove that they were the best. This truly shocked Ethan, as it was not morally right.

Are we wired deep down inside to be the best and do whatever it takes to be the alpha male? If it came time for a man to end another innocent man's life, would they be able to do it?

"Ethan and.... Jason, please." Akhilesh yelled.

Ethan's heart raced, and a nervous tingling sensation ran

throughout his body. The two names called lifted their heads and looked at each other; their features were twin images of shock. How was this going to work? They didn't have any time to think this through. It was a minor detail that no one, especially Ethan, had thought about.

`Ethan rose slowly and made his way down to the front, where the guards had their gear waiting for them. As he put on his equipment, he looked across to the other side and saw Jason having a mini-heart attack. He stumbled over while trying to put on sandals. He was a Retiarius, which meant that he was not to be covered with much armor. All he would be given was his trident and net. He did have a manica, but it only covered his left side and unfortunately, Ethan saw that Jason's manica was only leather and could be easily penetrated.

What is he planning on doing since we have to go head to head with each other? Ethan thought.

Ethan was given his rectangular shield and oval helmet. He placed the helmet on and noticed that it only had two small eye holes for him to see. His sight was limited to a large degree. He had to move his body just to get a better view of his left and right side. It was very uncomfortable and gave him a little bit of anxiety because it reminded him of the coffin.

He was handed his gladius sword and did windmills to try and loosen the leather straps that tightened his manica, which was also made of leather. Ethan didn't get a plate that covered his left side like Jason did.

Ethan was ready to fight, and as he stood there in a fighting stance, the sun beat down on him. The sun's rays again showed how defined his body had grown with all his distinct lines throughout his arms and stomach. He might not have known it, but he looked like a gladiator.

The brutal deathly sound went off, telling the fighters that it was time to begin. Ethan had to plan this out because it was the first time that two different classes had gone up against each other. With Jason, Ethan had to be careful of the net and trident that extended farther than Ethan's gladius sword.

Ethan moved forward but kept a fair distance away from the net's throw. Jason was already swinging it around and around, waiting for Ethan to move closer and get caught in it.

Ethan's focus was solely on Jason's net. He needed to entice him to throw it but still be able to have the speed to move quickly out of the way. Wearing the helmet was making Ethan frustrated. It hindered so much of his view. It was also getting hot inside, making it harder for Ethan to breathe.

His pounding heart throbbed as he made the bold choice to move in closer. Jason took the bait and threw his net as hard as he could, his body flailing as the net left his hand. It spread open, revealing a larger distance than he had anticipated. Ethan ducked and rolled to the ground just shy of the net catching his foot. He got back onto his feet and ran toward Jason, who quickly attempted to pull in the net. Ethan was too quick for him to pull it in all the way. Once Jason realized this, he grabbed the rope and released a foot or so more, diving around Ethan.

Ethan lost sight of Jason and didn't have enough time to catch where he went before the rope slipped around his legs and swept him off his feet. He landed face first, the bronze helmet smashing into Ethan's head. He lost his heading and his sword.

He turned around to see Jason thrusting the trident at his head. Ethan let go of his body and let gravity take him to the ground, and the trident skimmed the side of his face. If Ethan was right, Jason was trying to beat him so he didn't win, which meant that the investors would favor him instead of Ethan. Why else was Jason being so aggressive on the offense?

Ethan couldn't let that happen.

Reaching behind him, Ethan felt for the trident. As he felt for the pole, he looked up to see Jason's hand on top of it. He tried to pull it up, but Ethan got ahold of it. Fighting with all his might, he kept it stuck in the sand.

Ethan could barely breathe as he used all his energy keeping the trident in the ground. Without thinking, he removed his helmet and grabbed a breath of fresh air. His chest opened wide to receive it, and he quickly let go of the trident to roll toward Jason. He wrapped his legs around him, sending him hard to the ground with the trident fleeing to another part of the arena.

Both men were on the ground without any of their weapons. Ethan made the first move to hop on Jason, straddling him with his knees and putting his hands around his throat, squeezing as hard as he could. Jason floundered about, trying to hump Ethan off, but Ethan was better grounded.

All eyes were on the men grappling with each other without any weapons. Jason struggled, knowing he was losing. Ethan noticed him look at his trident, which lay only a few feet in the other direction of Ethan's sword. As Ethan and Jason looked at the same target, Jason capitalized on that distraction by slamming his elbows down on Ethan's arms, buckling them. Jason managed to buck Ethan off and scurried to his trident. Ethan had no choice but to go for his gladius sword. They grabbed their weapons at the same time and spun around, only to freeze when they realized their weapons were inches from each other's throats.

"It seems that...we have a...draw."

Ethan collapsed to the ground, not realizing how much strength it took to fight another person. He'd thought he had more stamina, but this was a wakeup call.

"Guess you didn't get the memo, huh." Ethan huffed, laughing and facing his opponent who also lay on his back exhausted as they seemed to morph back into friends.

"Nah, mate, I was in on it as well, but I really wanted to see where I stood. And you seem to be a high standard to go up against; you fought well. You can't be havin' all the fun now." With that, Jason stood up and offered a hand to Ethan, who accepted it with grace.

Ethan looked up at Aeliana. She wore an expression that seemed all too familiar to Ethan. He had a gut feeling that she might have caught on. Only seconds later, she turned and walked out of the door.

Jason had put up an excellent fight. They couldn't ask for anything better than a draw. Akhilesh stood up and moved to the head of the pulvinus.

"Thank you all. That is all we....will do...today. Head toward...the tables for...dinner. You've earned it," Akhilesh said, exiting from the same door as Aeliana.

The group of men all let out a sigh of relief as their tests were over. As they left through the two open doors, laughter and jabs were exchanged as groups of men and women waddled to the tables to eat.

"Woo, I thought Daniel was going to slice Hensley's foot right off," Jake slapped the giant's back, retrieving his hand immediately and shaking it vigorously.

"No, I wouldn't have done that. I guess I just got caught up in the moment, he-he," Daniel defended himself in a joking way.

Ethan crowded around the cheerful men. Daniel wrapped his arms around Jason, giving him an old-fashioned noogie.

It was weird to sense all this affection circling around from a bunch of masculine men. Ethan was happy for a bit, and he felt as if he were back in Afghanistan with the boys. It quickly faded away as Ethan knew where they were. What they were doing was going to destroy all of this happiness.

"Mr. Miller."

Ethan and the rest of the men stopped in their tracks. They all turned around to see Akhilesh, Aeliana, and three armed guards standing a few feet away. Ethan's smile withered to a fearful frown.

"You need...to come...with us."

A guard pulled out an empty brown sandbag and extended his arm.

Ethan didn't dare look at anyone around him. He stiffly stepped out.

"Turn around," a guard said.

It could have been a sense of pride, but Ethan didn't turn around when he was told. He didn't know if it was his pride against the people who had kidnapped him and forced him to fight others or because he had to face the men he'd put in danger.

Ethan didn't do what was asked of him. He wasn't ready to submit. The guard pointed aggressively for him to turn around once again, but Ethan stood still, staring blankly at the guard.

The guard reached over him and forced him to turn. His eyes settled on Doc, who held the deepest expression of lost hope. That was the last vision he saw before it went dark.

19

THE MIND'S EYE

Ethan was blindly led outside the yard and through the house. Two guards held each arm, directing him where they wanted him to go. They decided to cuff his hands, using the rope that he knew all too well. It was the straw rope that had cut his skin with every little movement during his trip into this place.

The guards had to be careful now that he had regained his strength and was being taught how to be a gladiator.

His hands remained near his groin area, where he rested them on his balteus belt, which was a strip of thick leather used to protect the abdomen and could hold small weapons. He only wore the loincloth they had provided and still had woolen straps around his legs.

He remembered from watching TV that people who were being brought somewhere blindfolded could count their steps and remember the directions they turned. Then you could just turn it around and do the opposite when you returned to the first place. Ethan, however, could not accomplish this feat, as he was having a hard time doing both at the same time.

After being dragged around for five minutes outside, he

was halted by the guards. He heard a large door open. A gust of cold wind blew past Ethan, giving him the best feeling of chills. The door sounded like a ginormous vault scraping itself against metal, and Ethan tilted his head as he focused on it.

A smack came across the back of his head. He took the blow and came back up. They must have sensed his investigating where he was.

He humorously looked left then right, barely able to see anything but two figures still grasping onto him. "Okay, which one of you did that?" Ethan looked back to his left and spoke to the guard holding him. "Yeah, look, I know it can't be you 'cause your hands are as small as a newborn baby's. And my, may I ask what lotion you use because they are soft as a baby's bottom."

The guard must have understood or wanted him to shut up. He took his hand off of Ethan and took a swing at him.

Ethan sensed the right timing and quickly ducked, letting the hand swipe across the other guard's face.

This made the first guard speak a quick apology in Arabic; then an unexpected punch exploded into Ethan's stomach. The punch knocked the wind out of him.

Ethan couldn't help but snicker as he gasped for air, "Yeah… that was worth it."

They continued to move him, but with more aggression since Ethan had pulled the little stunt to embarrass the guards.

The sun that had been beating down on his body instantly vanished as Ethan was met with shadows. They brought him through the vaulted door, and his bare skin was blanketed with air conditioning for the first time in months. It felt so great to walk with the feeling of the cold washing over his skin. He didn't dare take one second for granted.

As he traveled inside, a florescent light would descend through his sackcloth every few feet before fading away as he moved past it. He could tell that the floor wasn't natural but manmade. Ethan guessed it was tile.

Doors were also easy to recognize, as one guard would have to let go. They would twist him so there was one hand on Ethan at all times.

The lemon scent that roamed the halls was clean and pure. Ethan's nostrils opened wide and received the smell warmly.

The walk was incredibly long and tiring. Ethan was surprised at the number of stairs he had to climb. It was as if they were climbing a skyscraper in downtown Raleigh.

Finally, after walking for a few minutes, the guards halted once more and pushed him a few feet forward. Ethan's feet rested on a hard-bushy square that was elevated off of the floor. He could only guess it was a doormat.

The guards yelled something that Ethan couldn't understand. He continued to not move. A guard reached down, grabbing Ethan's ankle and pushing it back and forth with strain. Ethan knew they wanted him to rub his feet on the mat, but he just stood there clueless. They yelled at him. Ethan let out another smirk as he wiped his feet like they asked, only he bucked both of them out like a horse. He laughed as both of them yelped.

Ethan felt a sharp pain in his side, followed by a very hard hit on his back. As he bent over to tend to his side, which hurt much more than his back, he heard a door in front of him open. Without any warning, he was thrown through the doorway. Ethan was already off balance and wasn't ready for the push. His whole body was sent flying to the floor.

Ethan hit face first against the hard ground, creating an immediate bump to his left temple. He sent out a cry of laughter. Ethan lay there for a moment trying to guess his whereabouts while being blinded.

"You're a very difficult man, Ethan Miller. That is all, gentlemen. You may go."

The voice sent chills down Ethan's spine, and he shuddered at hearing it. The door slammed behind him, startling Ethan. He knew that voice. It was the northwest American accent that talked with low warm tones.

Ethan sensed movement as Eubulus walked closer to him. He heard the clicks of Eubulus's shoes against the floor. His muscles tensed up, and he held his breath. The other man's presence hung only inches away. Ethan heard the slight sound of his breathing sucking in and blowing out, like a kid playing with a plastic straw. Suddenly, Ethan saw a movement coming toward him. He squinted his eyes and waited for pain.

The sack was pulled off his head, and Ethan's face was exposed with his eyes closed.

"Mr. Miller, I'm not going to inflict any harm. You are here so that we can simply have a decent conversation."

Ethan opened one eye, scouting the room and seeing Eubulus, who stood two feet from him. He opened the other eye when he saw that no harm was being done to him. Ethan loosened his muscles, let out a sigh of relief, and allowed his breathing to go back to normal.

The creator of Hades' Colosseum and the reason why he was in this mess gave Ethan a sincere welcoming smile as though there were no conflict between them. Ethan could only give a fake smirk to convey some sort of communication.

It had been over two months since he'd last seen Eubulus. He was dressed in a gray tuxedo, which looked tailored. A white handkerchief peeked above his breast pocket, and his tie, a lighter hint of gray, rested on his white dress shirt. Ethan looked down to see his oxfords black as night. The man knew how to dress fashionably.

The lights from above formed a glare on the tip of Eubulus's head. It was quite distracting to Ethan, but he tried not to stare. Eubulus had a perfect silver beard that wrapped around his mouth and under his chin. He must have been growing it out since the last time they were in the same room. Put some white hair on top, and Ethan could picture the KFC chicken guy.

Eubulus circled Ethan like a shark would before he took him

for his dinner. His eyes looked Ethan up and down as though he were checking his cattle for a show. He looked like he was most pleased with the work he had done. He nodded a few times after looking at Ethan, then turned around to walk back to his desk.

Ethan stood there half-naked with his jaw to the ground. What he saw was astonishing and majestic.

The floor stretching from both ends was made of Calacatta gold marble. The white was pure and bright, and the gold tint highlighted the gray veining, which sparkled from the lights that bounced off of it.

Ethan looked past the floors and to each side of the walls, which were made from the mountain. Ethan now figured out that they had been walking into the mountain.

The walls had craters and divots that crashed against each other like crystals, resembling waves splashing onto the beach floor.

Every few feet, spaces had been carved out to display Eubulus's suits of armor and weapons. LED lights lit the perimeter of each slot. Ethan saw the familiar classes, such as the Murmillo and Secutor, each with its armor that looked much older than the armor he or anyone else had put on. This was starting to look like the bat cave.

Ethan walked forward, noticing four pillars. Two were aligned on each side with the corresponding sibling. They stood fifteen feet from one another and were carved from the cave itself. He followed the pillars all the way up, craning his neck so far back to take in the spectacle above him that he fell slightly off balance. Above him was a vaulted ceiling, but it wasn't that in itself that surprised Ethan. It was the breathtaking artwork, looking like something out of the Sistine chapel and painted by Michelangelo himself.

It was done like they did it back then with the fresco painting, using a chemical reaction to fuse the paint into the ceiling. The colors made the murals come to life as if they were really there.

One section had striking young naked women playing in the pond and splashing at each other, and angels with the cleanest white robes looked down from above with a smile. Another had a few chubby babies with wings. They pranced in the air as they struggled to keep their feet off the ground, flapping their tiny wings. One baby specifically was cradled in the arms of a woman wearing a blue robe. She looked down on him, giving comfort.

Farther away in another mural, a man with a silver scythe cut the long yellow wheat in the field. His expression showed determination and fatigue. There were even specks of sweat that caught Ethan's eye. The detail was incredible. In the distance stood a small house with a child and a mother. They watched their father and husband work to provide for his family.

Ethan looked above the house, noticing a dark storm brewing far away. As he searched the storm, it grew bigger with lighting striking every so often. Ethan's heartbeat intensified as his senses uncovered the story. Ethan stopped when he reached the eye of the storm.

A large muscular man with lengthy white hair stood there, his face showing great distress and hatred. His white robe wrapped around him and swirled past his feet. Little demon children with tails and long fingers chomped and tore at the man's robes and visage. The black storm turned to red as Ethan gazed upon a man with a white suit and yellowish orange eyes. He stood across from the other man with a bold and modern look. That man was different than any of the other artwork displayed on the ceiling. It was such a devilish mural that it gave Ethan an upset stomach.

Eubulus saw Ethan's eyes wandering the ceiling for more time than he had wanted and broke the silence.

"I see we both have a taste in the Greco-Roman Renaissance era. You know, it's a very rare art form and truly a dying skill to have. It took me over a year just to find someone who was able to perfect it the way I had envisioned. Why don't you come closer so we can discuss a few minor muddles?"

Ethan forced himself to turn away from the art. He noticed that he was emotionally attached to this painting, and he couldn't figure out why. It creeped him out that he enjoyed the same thing as his enemy.

Ethan turned to confront Eubulus behind his massive granite desk. The stone was different to look at. Inside the slab was what looked like yellow, glowing lava that maneuvered throughout the table. It gave off a luminescent light that didn't seem to bother the eyes. It caught Ethan in a trance when he stared at it.

Ethan knew that there was a certain reason for Eubulus to bring him to this room. It was a change from his lifestyle in the training yard with dirt and mud. There was more than bragging going on.

Eubulus sat down on a comfortable black chair that matched with the color of the mountain. Behind him was a large-screen TV mounted from both ends of the room. The screen projected what looked to be a live shot from Greece. The view was set on a mountain with shrubs and grass waving to and fro in the wind. Ethan could see himself lying on that grass overlooking the stunning scene. Near another mountain in the distance stood a half-demolished old stone temple. Looking below, Ethan saw the Aegean Sea, its waves crashing onto the nearby shore. As the ocean moved with no pattern, the sun's rays sent sharp crystal-like particles floating in every direction.

Ethan observed the noises of different exotic birds singing. He even heard the grass blades rustling against each other as the wind passed. The waves below crashed every so often, as though they were really there by the sounds reaching a full 360 degrees in the room. There was an invisible breeze with the scent of salty water brushing against Ethan's body and face. His mouth was slightly open, drawn back in a youthful smile, as his head gently moved back and forth. His senses were fully engaged.

"You've made quite a name for yourself here. You've even managed to kill one of my men and still stand before me breathing."

Ethan sensed that he was more impressed than angry. Ethan kept silent and continued to listen intently.

"You know, Ethan, I knew you were going to be trouble from the start, but I didn't know you were going to be such a headache. I am thankful you were able to accept one of many friend requests that we sent out. I think you had Jessica Marshall, was it?"

Ethan stood there for a moment, struggling to understand why that name seemed familiar. Then it hit him. His eyes spread wide as he remembered the beautiful woman on Facebook that he had stared at on his laptop. He must have clicked accept when he'd heard Tyler in the closet. How stupid could he be? Now everything made more sense with the van apparently trying to run him over, only they had been trying to kidnap him.

Eubulus continued talking, full of glee from the little surprise he'd given Ethan. "Ahh, yes, how else do we find out where you veterans are? Social media has helped us find almost every one of you. I have a group of very highly educated men who distribute those messages everywhere in the world. Sometimes encrypted messages, images, and other forms of bait. ISIS knows a lot about social media."

Ethan stared at Eubulus, who continued bragging about the means of baiting all of the veterans across the world.

"But, as I was saying, I have one full page of problems you've caused. I could list them off but—Wait, now that I think of it, you've killed two people so far. Having to clean up that mess on the road was more of a hassle than I thought." Eubulus's voice was firm when he spoke about the incident in which Ethan had tried to make a run for the road and stopped that poor innocent man.

Ethan felt a deep guilt from inside remembering that night.

"I can't continue to have you running about, freely killing men, building mutinies against me, and getting away with it. It just doesn't help with my reputation, and it surely doesn't help with my objective," Eubulus said, getting down to the reason he had brought Ethan into the room.

Eubulus reached for a tan wooden box that carried long thick cigars inside. He took one out, trimmed one end, and pulled a lighter from his suit pocket to inflame the end of the cigar. Eubulus then sucked into it, rotating it back and forth to heat it evenly. He took a few puffs before lowering the cigar slightly and turning away from Ethan to exhale the first full breath of smoke, savoring it. The sweet musty aroma of the tobacco danced its way into Ethan's nostrils. Eubulus put the lighter back once he was satisfied.

"I see great things in you, Ethan. Listen, there is another person deep down in your soul fighting to get out. I've seen it in your eyes, the way you fight. It's who you really are, Ethan, and I've created this new world for men just like you. Make a name for yourself here and out there. The entire world is going to see you conquer death. I'm here to provide you purpose for your lonely and miserable life. Fight for me and claim your throne!" Eubulus spoke to Ethan as a father would his son, holding his arms out with excitement.

Ethan could only stand across the table as he tried to hold on to the other man's words. As much as Ethan didn't want to admit it, he was shocked to understand the offer that Eubulus had given him. He wanted him to become his protégé just like Palpatine wanted Anakin Skywalker. But Ethan knew the ending to that story, and he didn't want to go down that road.

Eubulus was a brilliant man, a mastermind. Ethan chuckled to himself, knowing Eubulus had been psychologically changing all of them—molding them the way he wanted them to be molded.

It was exactly how the military did it. They would break them down by taking away their name and self-identity. They would take away everything they had loved and held onto. They were left with nothing but the shirts on their backs. When you had nothing left to live for, that was when you were reset back to your basic instincts.

Eubulus had done just that with his own style. Instead of making military men that worked as a team, he built the men from the ground up to be selfish and to survive solely focusing on keeping their lives.

The others had so much to hold on to more than their lives. They had their families and loved ones that were praying for them to get home. That was exactly what drove them to fight. Eubulus didn't have to work too hard on them to get them to do what he said. The equation still worked. But there was something different with Ethan, and Eubulus knew it.

Ethan had nothing to live for. He had already been broken down to his core, and he wasn't afraid of death.

He knew what it felt like when he sparred against his fellow gladiators or even when he had fought Aeliana. The adrenaline and fire that lifted his feet off the ground when linking their swords together. The exhilaration of cheating death was as if Ethan was intimate with it.

Listening to Eubulus speak of all those rewards wasn't what attracted him. It was something more than fame or fortune, it was liberation. Ethan knew that Eubulus saw that.

Ethan snapped out of the spell and mentally pushed those feelings away. He had to be careful not to let Eubulus control his inner thoughts. He had already been molded by him before he was kidnapped. The unsettling part was that Ethan thought Eubulus had stalked his life before all of this began. How was it possible that Eubulus knew what Ethan felt unless he knew him better than he knew himself? Ethan couldn't let himself be influenced.

"No one is going to fight for you." Ethan held his last word for a moment, seeing what would happen.

Eubulus looked past Ethan, ignoring what he had just heard. He gave a few puffs before flicking some ash on the end of the butt to a nearby tray.

"Ethan, have you ever heard of Stockholm Syndrome?"

Ethan shook his head.

"In 1973, there was a bank in Stockholm. I believe it was called the Kreditbanken. Well, on August 23, a man by the name of Jan-Erik Olsson went in there to rob the bank. He ended up taking four hostages and held himself in a vault for six days. Quite a long time to be cooped up in a vault with four mouths to feed. He did of course have help from another captor who later joined him."

Ethan stood there, trying to figure out what this story had to do with anything.

Eubulus continued smoking his cigar as he told the story. "Come to find out, during that time the captives formed a positive and heartfelt feeling toward their captors. One, specifically, named Kristin Enmark. At the end of it all, she even asked the police if she could go with them, telling the officers that they didn't harm her in any way. Some say that she even fell in love with Olsson. See, the trick was that she was conditioned to something traumatizing and threatening done by Olsson. However, because Olsson never did those things and took care of her, she transformed her mind, almost like a defense mechanism. Start with something horrible, such as a threat, and anything nice after that is viewed as a courtesy and kindness. Your morals change and your mind is wired completely different and…voilà, you have Stockholm Syndrome."

Ethan could only stand there, his head slightly tilted. "So, you're saying that we are going to fall madly in love with you?"

"No, Ethan. What I'm saying is that you have a primitive base inside of you. You all do. Given a threatening situation, it can start the spark at that primitive core." Eubulus flicked his cigar before setting it on his tray and clapping his hands together one time.

The screen behind him changed to hundreds of screens displaying all of the training yards. Ethan saw every angle of every yard Eubulus had built. Each box showed men fighting each other, training to kill each other in the colosseum.

Ethan glared at the screen with Trent and Leon fighting each other. Their faces said it all. They lunged at each other with a fierce hunger and clenched teeth. What Eubulus had done was exactly what he said he would. They were hypnotized or under some spell as they fought like savage animals.

"Followed by positive feedback from the captors, and you have a creation of something beautiful. Those men and you are going to bring back what has been kept buried deep within. I'm just helping it reach the surface. Come over here." Eubulus stood, grabbed his cigar, and beckoned Ethan toward the screen.

Ethan did what he was asked and stood beside his captor, shocked by what Eubulus had been viewing in the luxury of this room.

With the snap of his finger, Eubulus changed the screen of the men to Hades' Colosseum. They were above the awning, where seats were placed for what Ethan could only guess was Eubulus and his guests.

He viewed some people cleaning the wall, and others combed the sand in the center. The masts that connected to the mountain had been retracted back, and the stadium was fully open, leaving access for the light to enter. Ethan thought it was a beautiful site. He looked at Eubulus, who admired his own work.

"Very soon, the entire world will see the games live once more. At first, they will be appalled by it, and they should. They've been taught from birth what is right and what is wrong. But only for a while. They will soon welcome the games, and people will bet and laugh, and joy will come from them."

Ethan despised what he heard from the man. "Eventually, someone will fly over here and see what you're doing. They are going to come looking for us."

Eubulus smiled and looked down as though Ethan had told a lie. "No, I don't think they will. You see, I have not only built this stadium, but I have built this town. The buildings are designed and painted to conform to the landscape. From an aerial view, it will look like a bunch of rocks and land. There is no fear of anyone finding us. We have control over every Satellite in space. We will know if any eyes are looking our way before they come within 100 miles of this area. We are simply, invisible."

Ethan was blown away with what he'd just heard. Eubulus had seemingly thought of everything.

"Look at it! Don't you want fame and fortune, Ethan?"

"I'm not going to kill for wrong morals and wealth."

"On the contrary, you will do what I have brought you here to do. There will be no question about that." Eubulus's voice changed to annoyance, and his body became stiffer.

"I'd rather die than kill another innocent." Ethan remained calm as he continued to stare at the men working the stadium.

Eubulus turned to Ethan. "You are going to kill whether you like it or not. Soon you will be conditioned just like the others. You can see it in their bloodthirsty eyes, in their body language, the way they attack each other with pride. It's in their blood to be the alpha male, and they will become gladiators. It will be how it was back then. We are not going to have any more ideas about trying to sabotage my games, now, are we?" Eubulus moved in closer, leaning as he looked straight into Ethan's eyes.

He seemed to reach past Ethan's guard, and he saw that what Eubulus said was true. He knew what he was doing. It was as though there was some algorithm to it.

"This mountain runs in my veins. I see and hear everything, and I will not stand for any mutiny on my mountain or in Hades' Colosseum. Do I make myself clear?"

Ethan surpassed his fear of the man that stood in front of him, building enough courage to speak. "I will not play your games, Eubulus."

Eubulus straightened and looked at him again, contemplating if Ethan was stronger than he had thought. He smiled, taking a few puffs once more from his cigar, but this time he blew a wave of smoke toward Ethan and watched it crash upon his face.

Ethan boldly kept his gaze fixed upon Eubulus, fighting the urge to succumb to the smoke as it clawed at his eyes. Eubulus, not breaking eye contact, furrowed his brow and took a step closer. He slowly lowered the cigar and placed the burning embers directly onto Ethan's chest, twisting it over his heart. Eubulus's face changed, showing no remorse or any other expression.

The pain was heart-wrenching for Ethan as the burn singed his skin. The feeling began to sprout from the cigar and stir throughout his body, but he didn't dare make a noise. He fought the urge to scream, denying what Eubulus wanted out of him. He stared at Eubulus, fighting with every ounce of energy.

Eubulus continued looking into Ethan's eyes. "I don't play games, Mr. Miller, I create them." He pressed harder for the next two seconds and pulled away, and Ethan's wound throbbed. Eubulus snapped his fingers, and the screen changed back to its original live feed of Greece. Eubulus sat back down, ignoring Ethan and tapping a button on a nearby electronic box.

Two men came in and picked up the sack. Ethan understood the message that Eubulus was finished with him. He walked back around toward the guards who had taken him into the mountain. They seemed jollier than last time.

As they shoved the straw sack over his face, he heard Eubulus's voice from behind. "Your get-out-of-jail-free card has expired. Consequences to follow, Mr. Miller. You will do what I ask whether you want to or not."

Ethan didn't quite understand what that meant, but as Eubulus finished his sentence, the string around the sack was cinched tight, causing Ethan to struggle for air. The guards pushed him out the door and continued to play with him.

They kicked him from behind and pulled back on the sack, throwing him off balance. They teased him by placing their feet in front of his, causing him to fall. They even tripped him while going down the stairs. It didn't hurt as much as it was humiliating to Ethan.

The sad part was that Ethan was used to this sort of treatment. He knew, of course, that he'd instigated a lot of it. The reason he felt he could get away with any of it was because he knew that the guards couldn't touch him, at least not kill him. Abu was a different circumstance.

The Shadow had to have told Eubulus how out of control he was. This time, the guards were acting different. The beatings were more brutal, and they didn't care, as though they were no longer nervous of extremely harming him. He knew he had reached his line, and he had no more liberty to mess with the guards now.

The noise of the vault door cracked open, and as soon as Ethan passed through it, the sun beat down on him. He wished he could have enjoyed the last bit of air conditioning and lemon scent, but it was now back to the desolate heat with a bunch of sweaty men and death knocking on their door.

They led him the rest of the way to the yard where the other men were training. Ethan was kicked in the butt hard enough to travel a few feet before losing his footing and falling face first in the dirt. By that time, Ethan's string had synched tight enough around his neck that his airway was closed, and Trent quickly came over to his aid.

Trent took the gladius sword he had been training with and carefully poked a hole in a loose end before slicing it off along with the string. Ethan stretched out his neck, opening his airway that was begging for oxygen. The rest of the men walked over to see all the commotion.

As both guards walked away, one of them returned quickly to give Ethan one last heavy kick in his side, followed by spitting on the ground. Trent and the others gave the guards a disgusted look, knowing they weren't able to do anything about it.

Ethan gave a thankful nod to Trent as he was lifted from the ground and cut free from his bonds. Ethan brushed off the dirt sticking to him. As the others gathered close, they saw Ethan's bruised body. A few lacerations marred his face and arms from being sent to the ground. A larger gash on Ethan's left knee was from the time he'd been sent down the stairs. And, of course, there was the burn on his chest from the cigar.

Ethan ignored the wounds as he looked at the men and smiled. "So, what did I miss?"

"What did they do in there, interrogate you or something?" Jake crossed his arms, not showing any bit of surprise about the incident.

Most of the others wanted to know the same thing.

Ethan just stood there like he had when he first saw Eubulus's room for the first time. He seemed to always be in the middle of everything, but a lot of it was his fault. Should he tell them everything? Or should he keep silent? Would keeping silent help? Ethan couldn't stand there for too much longer or else they would begin to suspect something negative and harmful. If that was the case, then telling them what Eubulus told him would result in a negative effect.

These men needed to stay alive, and what they were doing at this moment was training for how to do exactly that. But that was exactly what Eubulus wanted. Ethan was trapped in a corner, but then again, all of them were. He also couldn't tell the table his idea about throwing the games because of investors. Eubulus had complete control of everything.

"I guess I'm just that good. Apparently, I have great potential to be a star." Ethan lied right through his teeth, and he was sure Trent knew it, the way he stared at him.

"Psh, you didn't even win your fight! You lost to leprechaun over there," hollered a man in the back who had watched Ethan and Jason fight.

Ethan had created his choice and his demise by saying the dumbest thing that could have come from his mouth. He felt that he was creating so many enemies that there would be no one left as allies.

He knew he would eat his words later. "Well, technically it was a tie, but I just need a little bit more time, and I'll be fine."

Ethan walked away from the center of the group, trying to avoid any more of the subject. He passed by a few men and caught a glimpse of Aeliana training them. She hesitated for a few moments, still standing square with the men, but her head turned to follow Ethan. Her face indicated that she knew the answer Ethan had given Eubulus. Ethan realized that she knew what had happened up there in that office. He didn't know if she was going to tell anyone or leave it alone, but she seemed as though she watched a dead man walk. Ethan grabbed his weapon and shield to start training by the palus.

"You going to tell me what's really goin' on?" Trent had come over with his gladius sword and slammed it over the wood.

Ethan could tell the other man was frustrated and wanted to know the truth.

Tension mounted between the two men, and only the palus kept them apart. Trent was not dumb, and he had been the closest to Ethan since day one. If anyone could figure him out, it would be Trent.

"Look, man, can't you see I've been pretty beat up already? Just leave it alone."

"Nah, it doesn't work like that. There might be some stuff shoved deep down I might not know about, but I know when you fibbin'. Is that a cigarette burn on your chest?" Trent was really pushing for the truth, and he struck harder against the palus.

Ethan knew he needed to be direct with him while staying away from any conflict. "Trent, I've been at war with myself before I even got here, wherever the hell we are." Ethan dropped his sword and walked around the palus. He attempted to be sincere and open, something he hadn't done in a long time. "Do you wake up every day asking God what the heck your purpose in life is? Because I've done nothing but become a waste of space. Trent, I'm struggling to find a reason to still exist. And here I am, trying to survive, the opposite of what my mind is telling me. So, forgive me for doing what I believe gives me some kind of temporary resolution."

Trent backed down once he saw that he'd hit a nerve. He looked down at his feet and kicked some loose dirt, thinking about what Ethan had just said to him. He then nodded and looked at Ethan. No words were spoken, just a moment between two lost souls in an unsettling time. Trent smiled and raised a closed hand, offering a fist bump. Ethan smiled as well and accepted the truce.

The two smashed their fists together, and as they did, a loud roar echoed throughout the yard and past the walls. The sound swirled through the entire village and bounced off the mountain. Both men looked around, trying to find the source of the sound.

A loud eerie siren raised its pitch from low to high. Chills ran down the back of Ethan's neck and down his arm, and every hair on his body raised before the siren silenced.

All the men had stopped training and looked around.

The sun dipped low in the sky, creating one of the most perfect sunsets Ethan had ever seen. Its orange and yellow mixed with sapphire and red, inflaming the other colors with a brilliant glow. The lukewarm temperature and gentle breeze created a moment of pure bliss. He had always been told that if someone were to survive the beginning of a catastrophic hurricane and make it to the eye, it would be one of the most heavenly sights they would ever see. He believed it would look something like this.

Ethan closed his eyes for a brief moment before hearing a most frightful and familiar sound.

A man over a speaker system mumbled his words together, and each word blended in a long low hum. "Nismillah-ir-Rahman-ir-Raheem…"

The invisible man continued to recite what Ethan knew to be one of the five daily prayers. This specific one was called the

Salat Al Asr. Ethan had heard it constantly throughout the villages or mosques in Afghanistan as it blared over the P.A system. Within the next few moments, Ethan heard an ensemble of men praying with the loudspeaker.

Trent looked over the outer wall of the ludus before he turned to Ethan, his expression hopeless. "Eubulus's guests have arrived."

20

A WELCOMING OF DEATH'S HAND

The energy in the yard seemed to drain as sounds of the Islamic prayer rang in all of the men's minds. No one could concentrate on what Aeliana attempted to teach them.

The sun had left the men in complete darkness, and clouds covered the silver moonlight. The wind had stopped altogether, leaving behind thick humidity. If the men were not slashing at a shield, they slashed at the air.

Trent and Ethan stood alongside each other as two other men were asked to step into the center of the yard and fight using their metal gladius swords. As they went at each other, they struggled to see any of the strikes, resulting in one of them jumping back in fear of being hit blindly. This made Aeliana furious, and she pushed him back into the circle.

"So, what is your next plan of action, Ethan?" Trent kept his eyes toward the fight, trying not to draw any attention to their conversation.

Ethan pondered the question, thinking Trent might still be trying to figure out what happened to him when they'd taken him away. Ethan had been processing the conversation he'd had with the evil mastermind. He was confronted with a proposition and possibly an ultimatum. Fight to survive, enjoying the glorious fortunes to come, or continue down the road of rebellion and perish. It was ridiculous to think about killing an innocent life for one's own. At least, that was what Ethan thought. But why did he love the idea of flirting with death?

Eubulus spoke with connection and had given facts about the internal structure of Ethan. Not even his family had been able to understand how he felt or why he acted the way he did. He himself didn't even fully understand. Everything about Eubulus pointed toward relating to him in some dark and twisted way, and Ethan couldn't keep his mind on the objective at hand.

Ethan observed both men's fighting style, critiquing their movements and how awry they were in the dark. He spoke to Trent, his voice soft. "Have you ever been confronted with a choice that no matter what you choose, it will be wrong in someone's eyes?"

Trent pondered on it for a moment. "Yeah, sure. I mean all choices will be seen as wrong in someone's eyes, I guess, but what's the point?"

"How do you know which one is the right choice?"

"Well, do what your heart says is what I would ride with."

Ethan absorbed Trent's answer. He looked up into the night sky, wishing he could see through the clouds and to the moon. He turned to Trent. "The mind is a clock consisting of little gears grinding each other to make it all work. The blood pumping through your veins is the key to keeping the little pieces moving. The heart is the pendulum in charge of maintaining alignment and focus for our morally good choices. The heart is the core of the clock, because it moves everything in time. Who you are as a person drives you to make a choice whether it is bad or good. The farther the pendulum is out of time, the farther you are from making the right choice. All these pieces combined give you the ability to make a thought that leads to a choice."

Trent lowered his voice as a guard walked past them. "Okay, but I'm still not following here."

Ethan waited for the clash of swords and a few grunts before speaking, "What if my pendulum is broken?"

Trent turned to Ethan and tilted his head, trying to understand.

Aeliana stomped toward the fighting men whose skills seem to be getting worse, and Ethan vaguely thought that she was not in a good mood. She kicked one man over who was already half on the ground from jumping away from a strike he couldn't see. She followed through with picking up the sword, wielding it in a way to defend herself when blinded.

"Doctore, I cannot see where his sword is coming from. He has the advantage as the little light from the moon shines on me, but he becomes a silhouette," the man explained in a way that made her more furious.

Aeliana swiped the sword at the man who had given her an excuse, causing him to retreat. However, she flourished the sword directly into the sand, then turned around to sign in a fiercely sharp way.

Jake moved closer to see her better. "She says that the mind is weak to those who do not breathe fighting. They can be manipulated; they can be your puppet."

She beckoned the other man to come at her. He jumped into his fighting stance and flung his sword at Aeliana, and she grabbed the sword she had impaled into the ground. She diverted her body away from the sword and committed an overhead strike that pressured the amateur to place his shield above his head. Within two seconds, the doctore had feinted her opponent, all while turning her sword to a supinated position and placing the tip of her sword against the man's side.

Ethan noticed something about Aeliana's actions. She had moved her nonwielding arm in a direction that made the opponent focus on it without them realizing. In doing so, the opponent robotically placed himself where she wanted him. *Amazing,* he thought.

She returned to her natural stance and threw her sword into the ground. She bowed her head in defeat and paced back and forth, which seemed to confuse everyone. She looked at each man as though she looked at her children. It was a strange moment for everyone.

She finally stopped pacing and looked at the men before signing, "I cannot help you in the arena. I can't stop them from ending your life. I've done all I can to prepare you with the amount of time I've been given." Aeliana paced back and forth once more, looking at the guards and the doors.

Something is going to happen, thought Ethan.

"Were you...giving them...a victory speech, doctore?" Akhilesh laughed as he came out of the dark with one hand holding onto a piece of paper and the other clutching his wrist in a shy manner.

It startled a few people, including Aeliana, for he seemed to come out of nowhere.

Akhilesh came to the center as Aeliana moved out of the way. He unfolded the piece of paper and looked closely at it.

"You have done...such a great job...training. It is time. Tomorrow is...the big day...the big...opening...and I have the...list of fighters...who were chosen...from the investors..."

Ethan could almost feel the tension rise in the men. This was it. This was what they had been kidnapped for, and this was why they had been training. It made sense why Aeliana was acting unlike herself. She had been spending days after days training them and striving to train the best. There was a lot of pressure on her as well as the fighters. The final moment had come, and no one wanted to hear their name called.

"Hensley...you'll be facing...a Murmillo named...Felix."

Hensley's eyes turned blank as he gazed past the faces staring at him. Ethan knew the thousand-yard stare when he saw it.

"Wilson…a Thraex named…Pho."

Wilson pushed past some of the men and stood in front of Akhilesh. He dropped to his knees, bringing his hands together like a prayer and begged, "Please don't send me out there. I'm not ready. I'm not ready!" Tears flowed from the massive man as he continued to plead with the Lanista.

Akhilesh stood, seemingly taken off guard. He looked as though he didn't know what to do. A couple guards came over and pulled Wilson from the ground. He squirmed and yelled. Heads in the group lowered while some men and women turned their bodies away out of discomfort. A part of Ethan understood Wilson not wanting to go, as most of this had been a nightmare for the men, but time had always been against them.

Ethan also felt a lack of sympathy. He wanted to go over there and slap him in the face to wake him up from being an embarrassment. Ethan was appalled by his own thoughts as he watched the miserable man cry for help.

Wilson had pushed one of the guards to the ground, alerting more guards to come in and help. They began to beat on Wilson in any way they could to keep him on the ground.

Cries for help turned into screams of pain and agony. The man was emotionally and physically hurt. His fear was more than his physical strength. The men off to the side continued to stand and watch, and some bowed their heads in shame and sadness. A couple men turned around so they wouldn't see their friend suffer.

As the guards beat Wilson down with whips and buttstocks, something caught Ethan's eye. Aeliana stood to the side, hidden in the dark with her arms crossed. He squinted, trying to zoom in on her face. He could have sworn that he saw a glimmer of a tear fall down her cheek. The moon was still covered by the clouds and he wasn't sure, but he wondered if Aeliana was not who she seemed to be.

Ethan's attention was diverted to Wilson's yelp as he was struck in the head by a gun. A splat of dark liquid formed around his forehead. It got to be too much for anyone to see, and the guards were not letting up. His feelings changed from sympathy to something else.

As he watched the guards tear into Wilson, he observed the smiles on their faces as they enjoyed and took pleasure in every hit. Ethan's blood boiled as he took one small step forward. Not thinking of what he was going to do, his body worked against what he should be doing. Eubulus was in the back of his mind. His mind screamed at him that he was not safe anymore. If he did something, there was no guarantee that he would be protected.

He couldn't stay and watch this happen. He took another step. A hand grabbed his arm tightly, and Ethan turned to see Trent shaking his head in disagreement.

Ethan could only look at his friend. He took Trent's hand and slid it off of him as he turned around and ran toward the group of guards.

He busted inside the ball of men playing with their food like a bunch of hyenas. A couple of the guards flew backward, landing on their butts. Some just stopped and froze from the surprise attack.

The men gasped in shock as they watched Ethan plow everyone over, covering Wilson's body with his own.

Ethan didn't strike a guard or try to defend himself. He simply wrapped his arms around Wilson's body, keeping his head under his chest like a mother would a child. He hooked his hands together and waited for anything to happen. Ethan heard appalled shouts from the guards.

"How dare you? You little piece of shit." One of the guards who had been pushed aside took his gun and flipped it around like a baseball bat. He chambered around his shoulder and swung through, hitting Ethan in the back.

A shock of pain went through Ethan's back and throughout his body. He let out a small bark but held Wilson even tighter as another blow came down on his back.

"There is no one protecting you anymore," the guards screamed.

* * *

While this horrible event continued, Jake saw the men, including Akhilesh, watch in disbelief as the guards beat Ethan.

Trent, Jake, and a few other men stepped forward. A guard farther away noticed and pointed his gun, alarming a few others to do the same. The situation was getting out of control, and someone would die if it was not resolved.

Aeliana moved between the men and the guards as she signed.

Jake saw her, but he didn't say anything, for fear of getting shot.

She signed again with more urgency as she looked at Jake.

The guards beating Ethan stopped and seemed to regain their minds.

Jake fearfully translated as he put up his hands. "She says you need to stop or else Eubulus will be furious. Both of these men are going to the arena tomorrow, and if the investors find out what you did here tonight, then you'll pay for it with your life." Jake slid back into the group, hoping to be dismissed from the guards' attention.

The guard who had taken his gun like a bat moved toward Aeliana with a distasteful look. Checking her up and down like a piece of meat, he held up the back of his hand to slap her. He swiped but stopped himself from making contact at the last moment. Slowly and discreetly, he turned to look around at the walls as though trying to see if someone watched him. Trent noticed but didn't seem to understand what was happening.

"You are no better than these worms." He lowered his hand and called off the guards, who broke away from Ethan and Wilson.

As they all went back to their original areas and patrols, a few men in the crowd heaved a sigh of relief.

A guard passed by, giving Ethan one last kick in the side.

* * *

Ethan loosened his muscles and unfolded his arms from around Wilson. The other man seemed to be in his own world, gazing at the clouds like a child seeing them for the first time. His breath was shallow, and his hands were clenched tightly.

Trent and Jason came over to look at him and take him back to his room with a guard that had remained to the side.

Ethan stood, stretching his back and rubbing his side. He was lucky they hadn't hit him in the head or else he would have been in another dimension.

"You ded a heroic act, my friend," Leon praised, slapping Ethan on the back. He pulled his hand back, wincing when he remembered that Ethan had just been beaten in the same spot. "Sorry." Leon smiled and looked at Akhilesh, who turned to the crowd.

"Please...no more fighting...save your strength...for tomorrow."

The group of men once more made a crescent moon to hear the rest of the names as Trent came back down with the guard and Jason.

"I will continue...with the names." Akhilesh read them off, and each person named accepted their fate and retreated to the tables, either sitting or talking with someone who attempted to console them.

"These are all...the names...good luck...tomorrow."

Trent stepped forward.

Akhilesh's face filled with horror. A few guards came toward them, and a lot of the men seemed on edge as they waited for another outbreak.

"Excuse me, Akhilesh," Trent said, "but Jake translated earlier from Aeliana that both Wilson and Ethan would fight tomorrow?"

Akhilesh and Aeliana looked at each other as though guilty of a crime. Ethan hadn't heard this because of all the activity that happened with him and Wilson. He was caught off guard by what Trent had asked.

Akhilesh paused a moment before speaking with a calm voice. "We were to wait…but now that…you know…Ethan is to fight in…what we call…a….Prolusio."

Everyone around Ethan looked at him to see if he understood the word.

"I think I speak for every mate here, what does that mean?" Jason, being nosy, wanted to know as much as the next man.

"It means that Ethan…will be the first…to warm up…the crowd."

All eyes widened, and they looked at Ethan.

Ethan accepted this just like every other man that had been called. He expected that this was Eubulus's consequence. It was time for him to go, and he felt pride and strength to get it over with. This was where the line of his life had been drawn. He knew that he wasn't going to lift his sword in the arena. He dared not take another life while he lived, and he knew Eubulus would put him up to the test.

"One more thing…you will fight…alongside another fighter." The lanista looked around in the crowd, narrowing in on a face that was merged with the other men. He pointed. "Doc Brown… you are to compete as well…alongside Ethan." Akhilesh spoke in a tone that wasn't congratulatory.

Ethan lost his breath for a moment before looking at Doc.

His face was rugged and torn. He just continued to stare at Akhilesh, avoiding any contact with anyone. He seemed to be processing his thoughts and trying to put them together. He put his hands on his hips, looking down, then back up. Pressing his lips together, he struggled to form a smile before nodding and retreating to sit at the table.

Ethan, infuriated with Eubulus, could only watch as his new fighting partner left to be by himself. The evil man had planned this, and Ethan would be put in a predicament where he had to make a choice. So many thoughts ran through Ethan's mind that he hadn't moved a muscle. He eventually looked back at Akhilesh and Aeliana, and both stared back at him as though displeased.

Aeliana had crossed her arms and squared her body. She stared at Ethan as she had the first time they'd locked eyes. Ethan sensed that she wanted to tell him she was disappointed or possibly mad at him. He couldn't read her very well, and the darkness made it worse.

There was something about her that told Ethan she wasn't who she seemed to be. Like she wanted to tell him to run, escape, or that he should have never been born.

She turned her eyes away and signed to Jake.

"Y'all had a rough day and need your sleep, especially those who are fighting tomorrow. You may stay out for a few more minutes before the guards take us back to the rooms."

She and Akhilesh broke away, leaving all the men to wallow in their doom. Most of the men had gone back to their rooms, followed by the guards. Some had stayed back.

The men at Ethan's table all came forward to support him. Daniel put a hand around his neck and pushed him around a little bit, trying to lighten the mood. Trent and Jason smiled at the scene.

"You'll be fine, mate, you're one of the best fighters out here." Jason nodded before heading to his room.

"Kick their ass for us, man." Jake reached out for a handshake, pulling him in for a quick one-handed hug.

"Don't give up, friend. Survive." Daniel's low voice rumbled through the yard, and he gave Ethan a big hug before leaving with Jake.

Trent was the last to approach Ethan, his expression neutral. Ethan expected to get a speech telling him to survive or that he'd be fine in the arena, but Trent stood there and said nothing.

Finally, Trent broke the silence. "I've stepped in a lot of animal shit in my life, but you, my friend, have stepped in the biggest pile I've ever seen."

The two friends stared at each other for a few more moments before they broke into laughter.

"I can't help it, man, it just seems like I'm the patch of grass they all like to go on."

Their laugher died down enough for Trent to wipe away his mirthful tears. "Listen, I'm gonna need ya to come back now so I have someone to mess with. These other scouts can't take a joke."

Ethan managed to give Trent a small smile as he looked over Trent's shoulder. Doc still sat at the table.

Trent noticed it as well. "You should go talk to him. Give him security." He raised his fist.

Ethan accepted by pounding his own against it. The two parted ways, and Ethan walked slowly to Doc.

Ethan was filled with so many questions and little answers. With the snap of a finger, Ethan had been left with someone who couldn't fend for himself. Now Ethan was his only protector against the other opponents. He didn't know how he would he manage this. He had been determined to go into that arena and perish. He knew exactly what Eubulus was doing, and Ethan was trying so hard to not let it happen.

"Can I sit?"

Doc looked up and gave Ethan a small nod. Ethan wrapped one foot around the bench and sat across from Doc, and the two gentlemen sat there mute, both contemplating their inner questions. Ethan had never expected for something like this to happen. He had always wondered why Doc had been a victim, but the answer didn't matter now. The two were bound to die together tomorrow. Ethan wanted to just sit with Doc and keep him company whether they spoke or not.

Only a little light from the moon shone through the clouds, and Ethan only saw a few of Doc's facial features. His wrinkles looked as though they had drooped extra low, and his face seemed like it had sunk into his body. His hands remained folded together as they rested on the table. Ethan's nose took in the cool breeze that carried the fresh scent from the river. It was complete silence except for the rushing water that could be heard in the distance.

"Do you know Death?" Doc said.

Ethan was shocked by the words. It was a loaded question, and he wasn't sure how to answer. He sat and looked at Doc, not knowing how to respond. "In some way, I guess, yeah." That was the best answer he could give at the moment.

The older man looked Ethan in the eye, his sight seemingly unhindered by the night. "My entire life, I've worked alongside him. I was never scared of him being there. In fact, it was a comfort." Doc's voice became sincere as if he were talking about an old friend. "I tried so hard to save everyone. To keep their heart beating so they could go home to their family and grow old with their loved ones. It was my job to keep them alive. But without Death, there is only suffering, and that was something I couldn't control. Although people fear Death, I had to learn to work with him rather than fear him. I gave my all, and even though I live with their lives on my hands, I thanked Death for ending their suffering."

Ethan had never viewed it that way. It was mind-boggling to hear someone who had seen more death than anyone, including himself, speak like he was a friend. "So, if you're not afraid of him, then what are you afraid of?"

There was no room for silence, and Doc volleyed it right back to Ethan. "If you are not afraid of Death, then what are you afraid of, Ethan?"

Ethan sat boldly upward like he was in front of an important king. He wanted to sound brave and full of courage, but in truth, Ethan was far from both of those.

This entire time, he'd been looking for anything to give. He had to take a moment and think about what he had been fearing the entire time since the incident. Ethan tried to focus on the running water coming from the river, the only godly music that made him calm and alive since being captive in this godforsaken place. He gathered his thoughts, which swam in all directions, and homed in on one answer—an answer that folded all the broken pieces together.

He looked into Doc's eyes and answered with honesty, "Life."

Doc pulled back at the unexpected answer. He then smiled and turned to look into the distance. The two sat together in silence before the guards took them away to their separate rooms.

Ethan entered his room, happy knowing that he understood how Doc felt. He had been afraid that Doc would want to live longer and possibly be fearful of his life ending, but the way he talked, he seemed as though he was ready to die.

There had been something missing from him, Ethan realized. He never did get an answer on if Doc was scared of something. Ethan reviewed the short conversation he had with the old man.

Doc treated Death as a friend, and Ethan looked at Death as if it were an enemy. But the common factor was that Doc and Ethan viewed Death as a person. To them, it was not a cessation of life, but an actual being that went about doing its job of taking life and sending people to the afterlife.

Ethan chuckled as he saw a clean towel, washrag, and soap bar ready for him to clean himself. If this were a hotel, he would rate it a minus-two star. He insisted on being clean before the next day, thinking it would be the last time he would ever be clean again, at least physically.

After Ethan washed, he lay himself down on the uncomfortable bed and wrapped the blanket over him. He looked outside through the bar window high on the wall. There was no moon present, but he knew it was there.

Even though he wanted to enjoy the moon for the last time, he was still at peace. His heart was calm, and his blood flowed like a soft river deep in the land.

He'd tried so hard to keep the time he had left, but that was the thing about time. It continued whether you wanted it to or not. And for tomorrow, time would finally be over for him. He was ready to go. It was time for him to go. He had lived long past when he wanted to live. He should thank Eubulus for this, even though he was an evil man. Eventually, he would get what was coming to him, but Ethan wouldn't be the one to bring him to justice.

Like any other night, his thoughts wandered until they reached his family and friends. It had been a while since he had seen his mother's smile or heard his sister's laughter.

When he thought about their faces, his smile widened. He remembered all the times they spent together enjoying food, beer, and happiness. It was the first time in a long while that he was able to take in the joy and feel love from them.

To Ethan, it was as if these memories were a last meal. Something that he could splurge on before taking the last plunge of life.

All of a sudden, Ethan's fist tightened just like Wilson's had. His eyes drifted from the window to the ceiling, where he could only see blackness. His smile faded.

His mind left the faces of his family and the good memories. He saw flashes of faces from the past, but these were faces from the other side. Gnashing and groaning noises filled Ethan's diminutive cell. The happiness that had filled Ethan's heart had diminished.

He lay with an unsettled mind and eyes that chose not to sleep. He shuddered from a cold breeze that randomly swept through.

The haunting continued. He felt Death next to him, breathing, taunting him. He was no friend of his. He was a cheater and a thief.

"Take me away like you did the others. I deserve it."

Ethan spoke softly but with a sense of presence. He spoke like Death was really there, standing in the corner with his scythe in hand.

"You have joked with me and kept me alive for your own entertainment. I've tried so many times to do your job but failed..." Ethan took a moment to gather his emotions. "I'm not afraid of you. I welcome you. I don't want to suffer anymore. I beg of you to take me."

Ethan wept tears as he wandered off into what he hoped would be his final slumber.

21

THE GAME OF PURPOSE

A gleam of light shone on Ethan's face from the morning sun. He opened his eyes, then moved a few inches out of the sunray to see the window. There didn't seem to be a cloud in the sky, unlike the night before.

He humped his front half up so he could set his feet on the ground. Stooping his back, Ethan felt like cement had been poured over him from his neck to his tailbone.

Ethan sat up and sent both his elbows around his side to pop his back. A couple crackling noises blew through his spine. He snickered at how he consistently put himself in situations where he felt sore the next day.

He hoped that Wilson would be calmer and more collected. The theme was survival, and the more they had their wits about them, the longer they could stay alive. If not, they would be killed before even entering the arena.

He rested his arms over his legs, looking at the ground and his feet. He wiggled a few of his toes. For over the past few months, he'd noticed that his feet had become so calloused, his skin had formed a barrier like a shoe. The sand or small pebbles in the yard no longer seemed to bother him.

His eyes traced up his feet to his calves. They were shaped like two heavy teardrops connecting to his legs. He gave them a small massage as he admired the transformation. He wondered why he had taken notice of these things at an unusual time.

Ethan lifted his head ever so slightly to look in the corner, expecting to see him—the one waiting for the right time to do his job. No one was there. Just a corner full of bricks. He stared at it for some time, trying to picture what Death would look like.

If Death was a friend like Doc had said last night, then he would have heard what was spoken to him. He would take control of what was to become of today. Ethan was ready.

Reality sank into Ethan's mind, and he knew there was not much time left before he stepped into that horrid pit.

Imagining what it would be like made Ethan nervous, almost like the feeling a player would get before a game. What an odd feeling to have when you compared it to something like a simple sports game.

Ethan looked around, figuring they would have brought him his gear or something to put on to get ready for the fight, but all he had was his loincloth. He was surprised that he had actually felt comfortable in the diaper, although he felt he looked ridiculous with it on, but everyone else was in the same boat with their gladiatorial attire.

The morning prayer Fajr shook Ethan as it was blasted through the entire village.

"Subhana Rabbiyal al-Adheem." The same man who had recited the evening prayer the day before was doing the morning. Ethan heard chanting from outside as the Arabic people participated.

If there was any worse torture than physical pain, it would be listening to this prayer over and over again. He toyed with the idea of sticking his fingers so far into his ears that he would be able to clean out his brain.

The door suddenly opened, and a gust of wind came through,

whipping past Ethan's face. A figured stood in front of the door. It was Aeliana.

She wore a thin silky tunic that covered her entire top half. It was fitted to her body perfectly, showing her true physical appearance. She was indeed a very athletic woman. Her black hair looked just as smooth as her tunic, running straight along her back like a waterfall. She wore the Jasmine-style pants that fluffed out, and they too were black.

Ethan saw light form around her. For the first time, Ethan really looked at her as someone other than a doctore and an enemy. She was a beautiful woman who had the skills to take care of herself, and that was attractive to Ethan.

Aeliana caught him admiring her. She stepped in and grabbed his jaw, pulling him up from his bed. She took a second to stare back at Ethan and look him over, then forced the disgusted look back on her face.

Ethan investigated her face and saw that her pupils were dilated. He made a peaceful smile to her, creating a brief moment between the two.

Aeliana whipped her hands up as her fingers intertwined together to form the word. "Ready?"

Ethan knew what she had signed. Shaking his head, he followed her out of the room.

Walking downstairs, he moved toward the table where everyone sat and waited for their meal. He found his open spot next to Trent. Aeliana left his side and walked away, entering the house.

Ethan sat and observed the group, who acted as if nothing were wrong. They said good morning to Ethan and continued talking. They spoke to each other as if it were another typical day being held captive. Ethan looked at Doc, who sat at the end of the table on the opposite side. He was quiet and reserved. The conversation flowed around him as well.

Akhilesh exited the door closest to the kitchen. He wore a

white turban with a blue robe, and his red scarf wrapped around his shoulder and left arm.

"Akhilesh, you lookin' pretty fly, my man," Jake commented with a joking laugh.

Akhilesh gave a small smile and a nod. "Thank you, Eubulus would...like all of the lanistas...in formal attire...just like Roman times. It is the opening...day."

Jake's smile quickly departed when Akhilesh mentioned what would happen. All the men, especially the ones who were to fight that day, had an uneasy feeling in their stomachs.

As the food was brought out, all conversation stopped. Only the ones not fighting were able to eat all of their oatmeal and water. One man who was being sent to the arena had quickly left the table, puking on the dirt nearby. Many wanted to do the same.

Ethan could only sit and look at his food. He did not wish to eat either. His stomach was upset, and his mind had wandered to what was going to happen and how he was going to do it. He had made up so many scenarios of what it was going to be like stepping into the arena. He tried to tear it from his mind.

"Mr. Miller...Doc Brown. It is time. Please...follow me." Akhilesh beckoned them to where he stood next to three other guards, fully armed with AKs.

Ethan took one last look at the table of friends he had formed since being there. They were all good men, and he was happy he could see them with care in their eyes as he left the table.

"Hey, Ethan."

Ethan turned, seeing that Trent had leaned away from the table as he yelled at him.

"Today is not the day to be a patch of grass."

Ethan huffed and gave a small smirk. In reply, Trent grinned before returning to the table.

Ethan guessed this was the behavior the men went with owing to the circumstances. There was no cake or happy send-off.

They acted as though he were going to return. He watched as they started up a random conversation. Ethan viewed it as a sign of respect and honor. He took a mental snapshot of the group before turning around to follow Akhilesh through the door.

They went the same way they did the first time they had gone to meet Eubulus in the arena. The door underneath the mantle vanished, and they stepped through. Akhilesh grabbed a torch that sat in a metal device mounted to the cave wall. He took out a lighter and lit it, forming a small circumference of light.

The line they formed held both Ethan and Doc in the center as they pushed through the narrow cavern. Fire flickered on the wet stone on each side. Coldness washed over his body from being so tight and close to both sides of the wall. Ethan didn't notice the uneven ground with the sharp rocks that had cut his feet the first time he walked through. He was coming through as a different man.

The same musty and damp smell he remembered from before clung to the rocks. It was refreshing to Ethan, and he held that scent as long as he could.

Ethan noticed buzzing sounds as they came closer to the opening. When he looked over the shoulders of Akhilesh and a guard, he saw a few figures walking in white robes, passing each other every so often.

As they walked through the opening, Ethan's ears were pierced with the loud noises of the crowd who talked and chanted. Hundreds of men came and went, pushing Ethan and Doc in different directions.

The noise echoed throughout the entire mountain. It sent chills down his spine, and seemed to do the same to Doc, who enclosed himself at the sound. They looked at each other, sharing looks of astonishment at what they saw.

Torches hooked to the side of the wall above their heads separated every few feet. It gave a medieval appearance as the glare of the fire bounced off the stone brick.

Ethan gazed at the circular hallway that raised itself up at least fifty feet. Square tiles of stone covered the ground and walls. Open doors led to the colosseum, reminding Ethan of the outside of a football stadium. He wondered if there were going to be concession stands with food and drink. Just as the thought entered his mind, in the distance, he noticed some men in a line, grabbing plates full of food and cups. Ethan raised an eyebrow and smirked at his own joke.

As they moved along, more men in white robes stared at both of the fighters in disgust. One came by, and as he talked to another man, he stopped to spit on Doc. Ethan watched in disbelief as the two continued to walk. The guards and Akhilesh ignored this encounter as they trudged through the crowd.

Eubulus must have painted the picture of the men as criminals and monsters the way they were already being treated. Not only did he brainwash the people he kidnapped, but he had also brainwashed the crowd as well.

They were taken into a door on the opposite side of the arena, where Ethan and Doc were met with two more guards who stood behind a table. Behind the guards were different class types of armor and their designated weapons. Each had their own section, with their racks and shelves holding different types of material such as cloth, metal, bronze, and leather.

"These two men…are here for…the Prolusio."

The guard seemed to understand what that meant because he immediately turned around with the other guard. They grabbed two Secutor shields and two gladius swords.

The guards handed them their weapons and shields. Ethan stood there, waiting to receive the rest of his armor. The guard looked back at him like he was an idiot.

"What are you staring at?" the guard asked, his tone demeaning.

Ethan was sure he had a dumbfounded look on his face, and he spoke to the guard as if he was the idiot. "I'm staring at you, waiting to get the rest of my armor."

The guard stood in place for a moment before laughing uncontrollably with his friend. Ethan and Doc looked around, trying to understand what was so funny with what Ethan had said.

"You are not...permitted to wear...any armor...per the rules...of a Prolusio." Akhilesh gave a smile, seeming to try and ease Ethan's questioning expression.

"So, we are to go out there helpless only to be sacrificed. Is that what you're saying?" Doc asked the question that he already knew the answer to.

"Yes...I'm afraid so." Akhilesh said the words as if he didn't fully agree with them.

Ethan and Doc looked at each other once more. They knew what their outcome was to be, and Ethan felt that both of them might not be as ready as he had hoped.

The fighters were taken out of the room and back to the hallway. There was not one person in sight this time. Everyone had disappeared to go to their seats, which meant that it was almost time. A guard pushed Ethan toward the gate where they were supposed to enter.

Ethan struggled to keep out the noises of the crowd on the other side of the stone wall. As he traveled in a circle, he saw in the distance the frame of light, its shadows in the shape of the latticed grill. It was the portcullis gate they'd stood in front of the first time they entered the mountain.

Ethan's hands were already sweaty as he gripped the leather strap connected to his shield. The pommel of his sword was laced with what felt like bone. He looked over the only two objects he possessed. It would be the last he carried before he left the world.

His body now aligned with Doc's, and their eyes gazed through the open square tiles showing the white sand. Ethan saw the sides of the arena, along with its stone sketches of gladiators and their stories.

His eyes landed on the canopy, its seats filled with men in different colored robes. The middle seat, which was covered in all black and bigger than the rest, sat empty. Ethan knew who was to take that chair, and he had yet to show himself.

Above was the mast, separated into eight awnings. They had been retracted back, opening up to the blue sky as they allowed the sun to enter and give the arena natural light.

Ethan had to hand it to Eubulus for accomplishing such a feat that no other man could possibly have pulled off. He had created Hades' Colosseum for the world to witness. Ethan shook his head, knowing that he was going to get what he wanted in more than one way. His nerves began to take control, and his breathing became light.

"Ethan, there was something I wanted to tell you." Doc kept his face forward as he spoke in a calm voice. "There was this… one dumb boy who had made up his mind to join the military at fifteen. I guess he wanted to follow suit just like his older brother. He had such courage, and he thought what he was doing was an honorable sacrifice for his country. He lied his way through medical inspection and acted like he was ten years older. Little did he know what he was in store for.

"He had made it to his platoon and got to know everyone there. He had formed a family and an unbreakable bond with them."

Ethan looked at Doc, who smiled as he told his story.

"I came to know this boy more personally than I had ever expected. He had a strong spirit and a wise mind. I never knew where he had found it, but it kept him alive."

"Slowly that boy became a man as he was faced with new scenes he never could get out of his mind. The horrible things he saw and did ate at him from the inside out. It tore at him, making him ill. The platoon noticed this and tried so hard to bring him back to reality, showing him the good in the world, but he ignored it and continued down a path of darkness." Doc had to raise his voice a little louder as the crowd had become unsettled and restless.

"One day, part of the platoon went on a normal patrol but was soon ambushed by the enemy. The man was shot twice, once in the shoulder and once in the leg. He was of no help to anyone. He lay there on the ground and watched as his friends perished in front of his eyes. He wept, waiting to be next. But there was one gentleman in the platoon who knew the man better than anyone. He had jumped on him, covering his entire body. As shots whizzed past both of them, the gentleman whispered in his ear, 'Your time has not yet come. You have so much to live for.'"

Doc had that thousand-yard stare as he looked through the gate. "The rest of the platoon reached them in time to push away the enemy. He was treated for his wounds on the spot. And all he could do was just stare at the gentleman who had saved his life. He kept saying 'It should have been me; it should have been me.' That man was never the same after that."

Ethan was stunned by the personal story that Doc told him. He also did not know why he was being told this before they both were about to die.

Doc finally turned to Ethan, "I never answered you, Ethan. There is something I'm scared of."

Ethan focused solely on Doc as he waited for his answer. Nothing else mattered—his nerves were gone. His focus was broken by a sudden deep thunderous rhythm of pounding emerging from around the arena. The portcullis gate slowly opened.

Everyone who was seated suddenly exploded to their feet with hands raised high. The drumbeat continued to press through the roaring crowd. Ethan and Doc were pushed from behind into the arena. Ethan made his first few steps with his bare feet touching the lifeless cold sand.

The walls that covered both sides had men leaning over, shouting obscene comments and gesturing as their fingers sliced across their throats. Ethan felt their spit hit the top of his head. He and Doc placed their shields above their heads to block them from receiving any more human saliva.

Ethan didn't care too much about what anyone thought of him. However, this type of cruelty was painful even for him. So much animosity from the faces of people who didn't even know anything about him or Doc. Was this game so amusing and entertaining to these people?

Ethan looked toward the crowd to discern their faces. Each one yelled with hatred and scorn as they kept their pointed fingers on the two men. They were as wild as a pack of wolves ready to feast upon both of their deaths. Ethan's hands shook as he attempted to tear his eyes away from the evil that sprouted from the stands.

Drums turned to a more rapid pace, and the crowd only grew more agitated. He couldn't hear anything, not even his own mind. His breath was shallow, and he felt a heightened sense forming in his eyes. His body was adapting to his surroundings, checking to see where there could be a possible threat. He smelled the brew of the crowd's sweat, food, and just a tad of the mountain's musty aroma. It was as if Ethan's sense of awareness started to create an armor all its own.

His nerves moved with the beat and pounding from the crowd's feet. As he circled in place around the center, he couldn't help but have the impression that he was an ant in a box. It was bigger than any sports stadium he had ever seen. Despite the packed crowd, he felt intense loneliness at knowing there was no one there to stop this from happening.

The drums hammered faster with no pause. Ethan guessed that if the drums continued at this speed, someone would lose their balance and fall off the edge, onto the arena. He had never seen such chaos. The drums climaxed before they came to a halt.

It took a moment before the crowd realized the music had stopped. They looked around for any new activity. Soon, all the faces landed on the pulvinus, where the men in different colored robes were.

Ethan and Doc turned their heads to see the Shadow coming out of the door from behind the chairs. He wore a gigantic robe that filled out his broad shoulders and barreled chest. The color was black with a red belt, which slithered around his waist. His face was covered as usual.

Ethan hadn't seen the Shadow since he was put into the cell.

He must have gone on more trips to bring more prisoners in from the ship, or he could be Eubulus's bodyguard, thought Ethan.

The Shadow sat down in an empty seat next to what Ethan only assumed was Eubulus's chair.

Akhilesh had also joined the group, sitting back and toward the left side. He rubbed his hands back and forth like he was rolling a ball of dough. He seemed more nervous than Ethan.

Finally, the man everyone waited for revealed himself. He entered, wearing a bright white suit with a red tie the color of blood. There was a red handkerchief tucked in his left breast pocket that gave an accent to his tie.

How appropriate for him to wear those colors, Ethan sarcastically thought to himself.

The crowd cheered for their provider and creator. Ethan watched as Eubulus made his way to the front, waving at all the cheers and roars of happiness. The Shadow, Akhilesh, and the rest of the men stood and clapped as well. He nodded and smiled, appreciating all of the praise. He had waited so long for this day, and Ethan knew that he wanted everything to be perfect. He had done the impossible, and he was getting a standing ovation for it.

Eubulus stood in front of his chair looking over his masterpiece, watching it come alive for the first time. He paid no attention to Ethan and Doc, who were only pieces of the game to him. He spread out his arms like a peacock spreading its wings to show off. This caused the crowd to react with a rumble more chaotic than the first time the drums had played, and Ethan trembled with the atmosphere of this madness.

Eubulus kept a smile on his face, putting his arms in front of him, palms facing down. He moved them up and down, controlling the crowd to sit down and to bring their volume to complete silence.

Ethan glanced around at the tamed crowd, then back at Eubulus, amazed with how he was able to govern the entire arena with just his hands. He held ultimate power with them begging at his feet. It became all too surreal to Ethan and Doc, and they slouched with their shields and swords dropped to their sides.

"Gentleman, you have worked so hard and for so long to make this day a possibility. The road was harsh, and I asked for every ounce of your time." Eubulus's voice rang throughout the entire arena. There was not another sound that dared to defy taking the podium. "You gave me your complete trust that I would put breath back into ISIS. When the world was against you, I vowed to build the state into what it should have been long ago. I did not fail you. And today...today is the beginning of not a new but an old tradition where our descendants can come to be entertained, to bond with their brethren, and where they can thrive on the blood spilled in the arena. The world will finally see the fruits of our labor, and they will break the chains that have held their primitive side since the destruction of the gladiator."

The crowd shifted and moved as Eubulus's voice raised. It had the same effect on the crowd as the drums did.

"The cameras will soon be turned on for the world to see. Let them see you and let them see we are not afraid! Let them see we are a state to be reckoned with! We will gain their respect with the blood of their loved ones. How can they be protected when those sworn to protect them are bound here to die? Fear will once again rule them, and they will respect us."

Cheers and clapping began to pop in different sections around Ethan. This was more of a nightmare than he had ever imagined. Eubulus gave them what they wanted to hear. He had them eating out of his hands.

"All of you have made the travel to be here for the first round of the games. It shall not be the last. These men and women like the ones you see down there..." Eubulus pointed to Ethan and Doc, and it was the first time he had looked in Ethan's direction. "They are traitors and have no desire to join our ranks. There will be more who will be against us. We will show no mercy to them. They are your enemies who have sent many of your brothers and sisters, mothers and fathers to Allah far too early."

The crowd booed and snarled at the helpless men down below.

"Be merry and cheer for the blood that will be spilled in sacrifice for Allah! The cameras are on! The world is watching! Scream to the heavens and let them know that Hades' Colosseum breathes life!"

There was an outburst of men roaring, and it created a rumbling sound throughout the mountain.

Eubulus once again took a moment to bask in the glory. He posed as if he were Allah himself, just like the painting he had in the office. Ethan thought that Eubulus truly believed it.

Ethan felt the vibrations in the sand from their screeching screams. Doc moved with instinct near Ethan, putting his back up against his. Both of their swords were raised.

Ethan looked around and saw cameras mounted into the walls. Many of them blended in with the stone carvings and some were on the trim. One by one, the red lights revealed themselves. Suddenly, Ethan realized that this would be the first time many of his family and friends would see him. If only he was able to explain what was going on.

Ethan hadn't thought that they would have to see him die. He didn't wish that on anyone, not even his own family. He pictured his parents in the living room being interrupted from watching their favorite TV show. The screen turning to him in the arena, fighting until death. His mother holding onto his dad as she buried her head into his chest, crying in pain. This wasn't the way he wanted it to go. He wanted to go to a camera and apologize to them.

He had the urge to tell them more than an apology for seeing him die, but an apology for being a distant son. It wasn't that he didn't want their love. He wanted forgiveness, but he knew that was impossible to receive.

Eubulus spoke above the noises coming from the crowd. "Before the first match, I give to you two nameless men who have provoked the name of Allah. They are given no honor but are to die shamefully. I give to you a Prolusio!"

Again, the crowd waved with no pattern, and the noises did not die down.

Ethan could only stare at Eubulus, waiting for him to make contact once more. Finally, Eubulus looked down on Ethan, like a slave. A smirk formed from him telling Ethan he had won on all four corners of the Earth. Ethan's frustration built inside of him. He didn't want Eubulus to win.

Ethan smirked back at Eubulus before he threw his sword to the sand. An audible gasp sounded across the stands.

Eubulus continued to stand, his smirk twisting into a scowl. His eyes blazed with anger as his nose twitched.

Ethan had found a flaw in Eubulus. He wanted things to be perfect, but he had overestimated Ethan's ability to piss people off. Hundreds of boos reverberated from the mouths of upset terrorists.

Doc chuckled. "That's a bold move, my friend."

Ethan had never told him or anyone what he was planning. He'd denied Eubulus the chance to have a perfect opening. He would not kill anyone for the sake of this man and his immoral ideas.

Ethan only could watch as the man in the booth stared in horror. His breathing turned from shallow to a heavy bob, like a boat in waves. He overflowed with uneasiness as sweat protruded from each of his pores.

For a split moment, Eubulus had lost his control of the crowd, and his face showed it as he tried to calm them down. Ethan just stood, waiting for his next move.

"Looks like you have to play the game!" Ethan taunted Eubulus. He kept his feet together and spread his arms wide, like a confident eagle ready to catch a fish out of water. Men along the edges of the wall slapped their hands against it in violence.

Eubulus slammed his solid fist against the stone rail. He'd had enough of the shenanigans. He raised his hand and snapped his fingers, sending a queue to activate the next step of his entertainment.

Two heavy metal doors on each side lifted. Each one had a pair of men step into the arena from the darkness. On one side, there was a Secutor and a Thraex. They came out and spun themselves around as they continued advancing forward, taking in their surroundings, as though it was their very first time seeing the colosseum. And it could have very well been true. They did not walk with very much confidence and seemed timid as they continued to move closer to the center.

On the other side was a Murmillo and a Retiarius. These men came out almost the same way, except the Murmillo had a stronger presence than the rest of the group. The man was almost as big as Daniel, and he held a heavier sword than the rest.

Four against two seems a bit harsh, thought Ethan.

To add to the insult, Eubulus had given each individual brand-new armor and gear.

The Retiarius held a fine knotted rope with solid steel balls connecting to the ends. His trident was gold, displaying a sharp three-pronged spear at the end. He was even given a helmet, which was unusual for a Retiarius. Eubulus wasn't playing by traditional rules.

The Murmillo held a massive green shield with gold trim around the edges. In the center was a circle with a Persian pattern richly embedded in it. His helmet was pure silver with a bear printed on the side. He had a visor that wrapped around his entire head, and on the tip was a silver mohawk. He wore a greave made of cloth on his right arm, which held his sword.

The Secutor and Thraex held the same as Ethan and Doc apart from the leather greaves and helmets they had been given. They mirrored each other with the same rectangular shield, their round edges preventing the fighter from having a net latch on. Their helmets were similar, with a common look of a knight's round silver helmet. Each held a gladius sword with edges sharp enough to cut the wind.

As the crowd cheered for blood to be spilled, Doc kept his eyes outboard to the other fighters yelling above them. "Ethan, I never finished telling you my fear."

Ethan heard this and laughed. "You seem to be good at not finishing things, but uh, is this the right time?"

Doc didn't skip a beat. "That man who was saved that day changed my life forever."

Ethan humored him in this last-minute conversation.

"You were the one that had treated him?" Ethan yelled out the question to Doc, who shook his head.

"No, that man was me."

Ethan took hold of those words, and a warm fuzzy feeling came over him.

"That gentleman who had saved me was my brother. He was the reason I joined. I was foolish and wanted to prove to him and others that I could make a difference just like him. And he understood that more than anyone else. He sacrificed himself so that I would go on to live a full life."

Ethan's ears clung to each of Doc's words amid the chaos. He knew his time was almost up, and his clock was on his last few ticks.

"In honor, I came home later and married my childhood sweetheart, Margret. I vowed to my brother that I would grow old with my wife and die happily with her, because that's what he would have wanted."

Ethan didn't say a word but just listened.

"My fear is not fulfilling my vow to my brother."

Ethan resonated more with him than he had thought. He felt so guilty for not taking the time talking to Doc more when he'd had the chance. He had so many questions to ask him, and it wasn't going to happen.

He looked around his shoulder at Doc, who had his shield high and his sword ready to attack. Ethan had misjudged his friend. He wasn't ready to die.

Looking at the cameras, Ethan thought of Margret and whether she was watching her husband fight for his life. That vow didn't stop at his brother, but it stopped with his wish to die peacefully somewhere other than some sand in hell.

Ethan was conflicted by what Doc had told him. He understood that the other man must have been speaking his last words and confiding in someone before he died, but he didn't know how much this affected him.

All of the images and scenes he had played in his mind of dying in this arena were now gone. At the moment, he couldn't muster up a single one. He was again at war with himself.

He looked toward the four men who had merged close together. He couldn't see their faces, but he had to remember they were not his enemy; they were innocent men captured just like Doc and him. Would they listen if he shouted to not follow through with this? It was exactly what Eubulus wanted.

How far into the depths had he brainwashed these men? For all he knew, Eubulus could have lied to them, promising freedom if they would just do this one fight. There were so many variables and no time at all.

His fear of life had been molded by his own hands, and it was what made him the way he was, but no one had explained his purpose in life. To Ethan, Doc had been told his purpose.

Was he lost on accident? Did his heart harden by mistake?

His eyes went to Eubulus, who had taken control of the crowd. He stared at Ethan with repugnance as he raised his arm to the sky.

Ethan struggled to control his breathing. His heart felt like a bombshell exploding every time it hit his chest. His clammy hands grasped the shield's strap as tightly has he could. He played with his fingers in the other hand before balling it into a fist.

He looked at his gladius, placed a couple feet in front of him. What was he doing looking at it? He was finished with it. He'd made up his mind long ago. Ethan could hear Doc behind him, grunting as he attempted to control his body as well. The crowd's roars pushed them as close together as they could be.

The four fighters moved closer until they were fifteen feet in front of them. They turned around and watched as Eubulus shot his arm down, his fist hitting the rail with rage. The sound of an electronic foghorn—the same one used in the smaller arena in the yard—rang. The game had started.

Ethan wanted to puke. He was fighting with himself at the worst possible time. The four enemies surrounded them like predators. He needed to make a choice.

He closed his eyes and focused on his breathing. Time seemed to stop. The crowd's cry for death halted and faded from Ethan's ears. A ticking noise in his head grew louder, but the ticks became slower and slower. He focused past the ticking and on his breath. He planted his feet further into the sand without acknowledging it, and his breathing became controlled. He held in a large breath.

"Tick tock...tick ...tock."

All had stopped. There was complete silence.

An old rugged voice spoke. It was faint, and Ethan heard the begging in the tone. "Forgive me, brother."

He let out his breath and opened his eyes to hear a sharp yell from behind him. He grabbed Doc's shoulder and pulled him father away from the four men. He raised his shield before the sword from the Murmillo met with him, sending him on one knee. He placed his free hand underneath for more support.

The sound struck the crowd, which motivated them to their feet.

Ethan felt the vibrations from the hit sweep through his body. He pressed the sword off of him, sending the Murmillo back a few feet. Immediately, Ethan spun around to his right as he was engaged with the Secutor, who swiped toward his hip. Ethan blocked it with his shield, opening up his body and sending a punch to the other man's neck. Ethan heard him choke, and the Secutor dropped back to tend to his pain.

Ethan heard a clash behind him as the Thraex and Doc fought near the wall. It was impressive to see that Doc was holding his own. But for how long?

Ethan had one objective in mind, to protect Doc.

He began to run toward them before he heard the wisp of a net, and he felt a weird sensation wrap around his feet.

The weights of the net had tied together around his ankles. As he observed what had happened, the Murmillo came with an attack to his face. Ethan didn't have enough time to react, but he was saved from the pull by the Retiarius, who slammed Ethan to the ground and caused him to accidentally dodge the attack.

Eubulus slammed his fist on the armrest and shifted his body within the bisellium, not finding a comfortable position. Those around him could tell he was upset thinking that Ethan's final moment was thwarted by amateur fighters who couldn't work as a team.

One of the men dragged Ethan toward the one with the trident, and Ethan had a difficult time unwrapping himself from the net. His shield kept getting in the way, which resulted in his only using one hand. He looked above his head to see the Murmillo chasing him down as he got closer to the Retiarius. He was running out of ideas of how to get out of this pickle.

It didn't take any time at all for the Murmillo to catch up. He slammed the sword on Ethan, who forgot about untangling the net in favor of keeping his shield above his body.

Ethan had a few more feet before he was in range of the trident, so he had to think fast. He felt the rhythm of the sword clashing on his shield. He took a moment of patient waiting for the sword to lift back up. As the Murmillo lifted his sword to fire back down, Ethan sat up as the tip of the blade missed his back by a few inches. In doing so, Ethan dropped his shield from his hand, which left him completely vulnerable.

He sat up, grabbed the net with both of his hands, and pulled it with all his strength. As a result, the Retiarius unexpectedly fell forward on his face. Without looking, Ethan rolled backward, knowing the Murmillo would throw his sword once more on top of him. It was a guessing game to Ethan, but as he rolled past the giant, the sword missed Ethan and cut the line, freeing Ethan of the net.

Ethan didn't hesitate to jump on the Murmillo's back, wrapping his arm around him and putting him into a blood choke. The Murmillo panicked and dropped his shield as the strength of Ethan's bicep quickly cut off the flow of blood to his brain. He flailed his arms, trying to throw Ethan off of him. When he couldn't get ahold of him with his hands, he spun Ethan around like a cowboy on a bull. All Ethan could do was hold on for dear life, hoping that he would pass out soon.

He was bigger than the rest and would take more than a few seconds. Luckily, with all the spinning, the net that tied around his ankle managed to loosen up, freeing him.

As the Murmillo spun him around, Ethan managed to spot the Secutor, who was back in the fight after struggling to recover from the blow to his jugular. He took his sword and raised it parallel to the deck, ready to spear it into Ethan's back.

Waiting until the Secutor brought his arm back to plunge the sword into him, Ethan let go of the Murmillo. He dropped and placed his hands on the man's shoulders, forcing him around to face the attack.

The sword pierced into the giant's chest, breaking his bones, and liquid exploded through his back. The crowd had fallen silent, and the fighters stopped in place. Doc and the Thraex had stopped their fighting to watch this unfamiliar scene.

Eubulus and the group around him were in awe as they attempted to comprehend what had just happened.

The Murmillo looked down at his fatal wound then back at the Secutor. He dropped to his knees as the sword remained in place through his chest. Ethan watched as blood poured down his body and into the sand, which soaked it up like a sponge.

Ethan's eyes filled with remorse as the giant fell to his side. One last breath was taken from him before he left the world forever.

The crowd jumped with joy, praising the kill. The Secutor, realizing what he had done, moved backward with a shameful stance, his eyes lowered. Death entered into Ethan's nose as a coppery metal smell.

"It's okay, we don't have to fight anymore. Let this be the only death." Ethan pleaded with him, but that only stopped him from retreating.

The Secutor looked down at what he had done then back at Ethan, as if he were the reason he'd died.

He walked past Ethan nonchalantly, stood over the lifeless body, and grabbed his sword. Ethan just shook his head, asking him not to do it. He didn't want any more bloodshed.

The sound of the sword being drawn from his chest made Ethan turn away. The disrespect toward the dead was heartbreaking.

The Secutor took one look at the sword and swiped it down, throwing off the blood which saturated it. The blood splattered, imprinting craters into the sand, as he walked past them with thirst toward Ethan.

The Retiarius had dropped the rope that had been connected to his net and followed behind, trident in hand.

Ethan turned around to see that Doc was back in battle. His

energy was wearing thin, and Ethan knew that it wouldn't be long before he had no more strength to defend himself.

Between Ethan and Doc was his gladius sword, which he had so willingly thrown to the ground in rebellion. When Ethan planted his eyes on the weapon, the three immediately charged forward in a race of speed. Ethan dug his feet into the ground, pushing off the sand as fast as he could. Sand sprayed behind him with every step. His arms pumped as he picked up speed. When he came in range of the gladius sword, he drove his foot to the ground and sprang toward it, diving headfirst with his left hand stretched out.

He grabbed the pommel with ease while clutching a fist full of sand as he barrel-rolled forward. He turned toward the Retiarius, throwing sand into his eyes since he was the closest. Grains of sand hit the warrior's face, forcing him back and giving Ethan time to exchange two passes with the Secutor. Every strike Ethan defended from him was stronger than the last. There was no reasoning with whoever this man was. He was out for revenge.

The Secutor went for Ethan's left leg followed by his right shoulder, both blocked by Ethan. He avoided the next throw, giving Ethan time to impale down on the sturdy shield. It didn't seem to have much of an effect on his opponent, so Ethan went back to defense. His stamina dropped. He needed to make moves fast, but he had no idea how he was going to get around the shield with just his sword.

Ethan saw the Secutor move like the man did the night before when Aeliana had demonstrated her manipulation technique. A lightbulb went off inside his head, but he wasn't sure if he could pull it off.

It's worth a shot, he thought. *I have nothing else to lose.*

He waited for the right attack before he raised his left arm, just as Aeliana had done. Ethan turned his hips the opposite direction of where he wanted to go, causing the Secutor to move his shield across his body, taking the bait.

He reached underneath, kissing the blade between the wrist and the Secutor's leather greave. It wasn't what Ethan had hoped for, but he pulled back fiercely, causing a huge laceration in the Secutor's hand and forcing him to drop his sword. Without hesitation, Ethan picked it up as the other man backed away.

The Retiarius—who had cleaned his eyes—and the Secutor were now side by side, moving toward Ethan. Even though he had taken away the gladius sword, the Retiarius was always given an auxiliary weapon known as a pugio dagger. It was one of the most menacing daggers Ethan had ever seen. The Retiarius handed the Secutor his pugio, creating two opponents with weapons.

Looking over his shoulder, he noticed Doc on a knee, helplessly defending himself from the heavy hits raining down. He didn't have much time. He cast off his moral inhibitions and transformed into the monster he knew he had to be.

Ethan gained control of his breath and composure before flourishing both the weight and balance of his gladius swords, feeling complete with the extension of his hands.

He grinned ear to ear, as he was finally whole.

He ran forward, blocking the trident from piercing his chest with one sword before spinning away and pushing it off using the second one. Ethan spotted the next attack from the Secutor, and he blocked it with a perfectly fluid movement.

As Ethan defended and attacked the two different classes, he couldn't help but feel liberated. His nerves had gone away as he felt in control. His awareness of both men was transparent. He maneuvered about, missing a strike by only a few inches, which gave him maximum efficiency through minimal effort. He stumbled a few times, only to jump out of that dangerous space to reset his fighting position.

His confidence rose as the Secutor pushed forward, swiping the pugio at Ethan's head. He was able to stop it without thinking, but he didn't see the trident along the ground near his leg. The smaller of the three prongs went into the side of Ethan's leg like a knife scraping butter. The Retiarius retracted it as Ethan jerked himself backward, crying out in pain and stumbling on his back.

There was no time to tend to the wound, as the trident came back down toward Ethan's face. He raised both his swords, placing them vertically between the three-prong trident at a matching forty-five-degree angle. He used only the strength from his arms to prevent the tips from piercing his eyes. His power was depleting fast, and his focus shifted to the Secutor, who rushed forward to give the final blow. Ethan was helpless.

As Akhilesh and the Shadow watched intently, their stare was broken by the sudden movement of Eubulus rising from his chair, unable to contain his excitement.

Ethan grunted, struggling to keep the strength from leaving him. The trident moved within inches of his pupils. He cried out in his head for God to give him strength if it was in His will.

The pugio rushed down to enter into Ethan's chest. At the last moment, Ethan used the two swords and pushed the trident off center and underneath the oncoming Secutor's arm, deflecting the attack. This caused the Secutor's arm to extend forward, resulting in a loss of balance as he fell on Ethan. The crowd's gasp echoed throughout the stadium.

Ethan had removed one of his swords and ran it through the man's neck, the same spot he had punched him in the beginning.

The man's body lay frozen like a mannequin, and blood flowed like running bath water over Ethan's face and body. Ethan screamed with horror as the weight of the Secutor slowly descended on him. A cold wave of shock hit him, and he quickly pushed the man off and to the side, anxious to get away from the frothing blood.

The trident had plummeted to the ground near Ethan, but it was soon pulled out by the Retiarius, who struck at Ethan. He rolled out of the way, and sand glued to him, making him like a sugar cookie. He used the arm that wasn't covered in blood to wipe his eyes so he could see.

There was no time to mourn or realize what he had done. His adrenaline was higher than it ever had been in his life. The crowd cheered heavily as Ethan lunged toward the Retiarius with fierce aggression.

The man had backed up, scared that Ethan would do to him what he had done to the Secutor.

Ethan had fire in his eyes, and he was not backing down.

The Retiarius took off his helmet so that he could see better. His eyes were full of hopelessness when he realized that he was beat. His body could be seen trembling from a distance.

Ethan could not see any of it. He found himself in another world, hungry for the last little bit of fresh meat. Even as he limped, he didn't feel any pain or remorse for his enemy. He had been challenged, and he would win.

Ethan teased him by touching his trident over and over again, watching the Retiarius cringe, scared that the next move would be his last. Ethan laughed, realizing he had control of the other man.

The Retiarius class was known for long-distance fighting, yet struggled with close combat. Ethan had the upper hand.

Ethan was finished toying with his opponent. He stepped outward, trying to provoke the man to spear a spot where he suspected Ethan would be, but he was nowhere in that direction. He had been tricked. Ethan had already knocked the trident out of his hands and went to one knee, plunging his sword into the Retiarius's chest.

Ethan's face was inches away from the man he had just defeated. Their eyes met, and Ethan saw the life in his eyes leave like a gust of wind. Ethan awoke from his monster trance and realized where he was. His own eyes ran out of fire as he backed away slowly, seeing the man dead on his knees.

Ethan's breathing began to run out of control, and he looked up to see Eubulus with a gruesome smile, clapping for him. He had not failed.

Suddenly, Ethan heard a cry of pain.

He turned around to see the sword of the Thraex pierced down into Doc's shoulder, who had been brought to his knees. Ethan felt as if a ton of bricks dropped on him as he saw his friend suffer.

With the one sword Ethan held, he creeped behind the Thraex, who had completely forgotten about the other fight.

As he basked in his own small victory, a sword blasted through his chest toward the sky, and blood oozed out almost immediately. Ethan, who felt anger more at himself, quickly pulled the sword out and pushed the Thraex to the side. Seeing that he was finished with that one blow, he breathed a sigh of relief and dropped his sword. He looked at Doc, who was on his side and still breathing.

Ethan rushed to his side, cradling Doc in his arms. He looked at the wound where the Thraex had driven his sword into the top of Doc's shoulder. It was a method used to finish off warriors quickly but by no means an immediate death. Ethan tried to hold back his tears, knowing what was going to happen.

"It's going to be all right, Doc. We did it." Ethan gurgled the words as his emotions showed through his voice and eyes.

Doc looked at Ethan like a father does to a son. He spoke faintly as he fought to breathe. "Ethan, the only way to truly know someone is through their eyes. And I look into your eyes…" Doc took a moment to catch his breath. "Oh, how lost you are, son. You are here for a reason, and you don't understand why." Doc winced in pain.

Ethan held Doc tighter, and tears fell onto his friend's skin. "We need to get you out of here, they have to have someone look at you. We won. We deserve that. Someone help us!" he screamed at the crowd, who only cheered for such a dramatic outcome of victory. He felt helpless pleading at the men who had no sympathy. This made him feel even more desperate.

"Time is time, and mine is done. But yours is not. I hope you find your way."

Ethan looked at Doc before glancing around again for anyone to help him.

Doc grabbed Ethan's hand, which rested on his chest. "Ethan, I did...live a good life. I fulfilled my brother's promise. And I'm not afraid. I'm ready." He looked up at Ethan, his face full of love and sincerity.

Ethan understood, nodding and laying him down as his breath rippled through his lips. He continued to watch as Doc lay there, looking up through the hole of the mountain at the beautiful blue sky. He smiled as his face seemed to transform, as though he was meeting someone from long ago.

With one final breath, Doc spoke his last words, "Hello, old friend."

Ethan wept. As he kneeled over Doc, he slowly pulled his hand down his friend's forehead to his chin, closing his eyes and letting him rest in peace.

There were so many emotions running through Ethan's veins, he couldn't pin on one of them to feel. Crying made it difficult to breathe, and he choked on his own tears and spit. He reviewed the entire fight and what he could have done to change this outcome. Flashes of one image kept coming to his mind. The emotions that ran around like flies suddenly stopped.

Ethan wiped away the tears, smudging more blood across his face. He moved to his feet, turning around to stand in a heroic pose. He pressed his chest firmly out and raised his chin high.

The blood that had covered his body mixed with the dried sand. The sunrays beaming in from above made his skin look as though he had a plate of armor covering half the side of his body and face. Its color was dark black and crystalized like obsidian rock.

His chiseled face glowed with fire as he made a vow with himself.

The image in his mind was the one man who would plead guilty for all the deaths that had and would come until this mountain collapsed.

Eubulus, who had been watching this transformation, saw the rebellious stand. He stood and leaned over the edge with a devilish smile on his face. "The game has started, indeed."

CPSIA information can be obtained
at www.ICGtesting.com
Printed in the USA
LVHW090552240321
682294LV00042B/1701/J

9 781736 018903